Blood of Tomorrow

The Second Cycle: Book 1

Robert W. Riley

To my loving wife and daughter.
The Second Cycle exists because of your support and love.

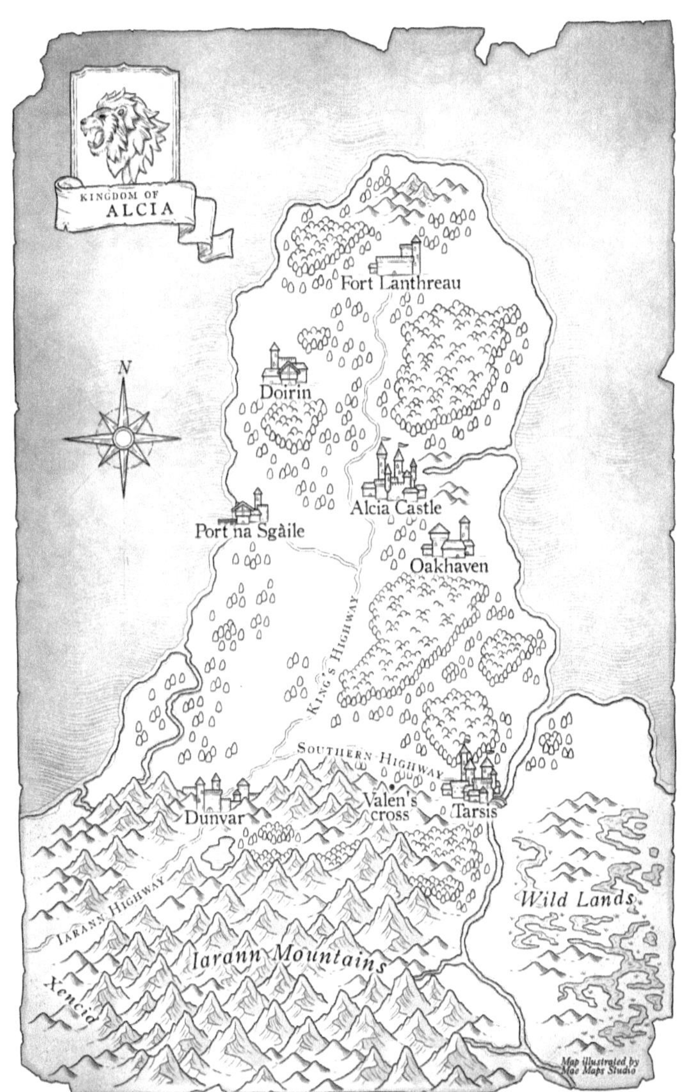

KINGDOM OF
ALCIA
N
Fort Lanthreau
Doirin
Alcia Castle
Oakhaven
Port na Sgàile
KING's HIGHWAY
SOUTHERN HIGHWAY
Dunvar
Valen's cross
Tarsis
Wild Lands
IARANN HIGHWAY
Iarann Mountains
Xencia
Map Illustrated by
Mae Maps Studio

The equation is simple.
The price must be paid in blood.
One life emptied. One life returned.

The Scrolls of King Alaric Lorindan

CHAPTER 1

THE CAPITAL SMELLED OF woodsmoke, wet limestone, and the heavy odor of horse sweat. Above, the flags on the battlements hung limp like damp shrouds against a gray, featureless sky.

Cedrik Theramond, Knight Commander and member of the Royal Guard, rubbed the neck of his mahogany warhorse, Bastion. He stamped a heavy hoof, the sound echoing in the evening quiet.

The markets were quiet these days. Too quiet.

Rumors of a phantom army on the horizon that had hit a stronghold in the North were spreading quickly. The people talked in hushed voices, converging on street corners when not staying within the protection of their homes.

Cedrik focused on his command. As Knight Commander, he made sure the gates to the Capital were manned and prepared at all times.

North Gate: Double rotation. East Gate: Standard watch.

The King's itinerary: Clear.

"Easy," he murmured, touching Bastion's muzzle.

The stable doors groaned open, as a runner entered. Cedrik didn't turn. He heard the weight of the gait. It was a stiff, heavy step. The walk of someone carrying a burden they didn't understand.

"You're an hour past the shift change, soldier," Cedrik said, his voice flat as he focused on Bastion. "Captain Fionn doesn't tolerate laggards on the East Gate."

"I'm not on rotation, sir." The boy's voice cracked.

Cedrik looked to the voice. A small runner stood before him. He wore the King's livery, blue and gold, but it was ill fitting.

The boy's eyes were darting toward the shadows of the stalls as if something in the dark was hunting him.

"Direct orders. From the High Marshal."

He held out a scroll. It was sealed with crimson wax in the shape of a roaring lion on a shield. Cedrik took it. The seal was still warm. He broke it with a snap of his thumb. As he read the script, heat rose within his chest.

City Command passed to Captain Fionn.
Fortify the Inner Ward.
Recall the Guard.
The Central Militias have been summoned.
Theramond - Report to Fort Lanthreau, immediately.

"This is madness," Cedrik whispered.

To pull the Guard back now would leave the lower city—the bakers' quarter, the smithies, the farming quarters—all naked without protection. To abandon the lower city was to abandon Alcia itself.

"The High Marshal has already sent a copy to Captain Fionn," the boy said, his voice wavering under the stress. "I was to make sure you saw the orders... all of them."

Cedrik looked at the boy for a long moment. His eyes were now quivering, trying to focus on anything but the Knight Commander's face.

"Go."

The boy fled. Cedrik crushed the parchment in his gauntlet, as the sound of groaning leather cut through the stable.

He needed Pasin.

***

The Royal Archives were cold. They always were.

Pasin was sitting at a long table, surrounded by maps of ancient Alcia. He wasn't reading them. He was staring at a candle flame, watching it flicker in the draft.

"You have a letter," the old man said. He didn't look up.

Cedrik threw the crumpled scroll onto the table. It rolled to a stop against a map of the northern mountains.

"He's ordering a complete lockdown," Cedrik said. "And he is stripping me of command. We are to go to Fort Lanthreau. To chase rumors."

Pasin finally looked up. His green eyes shone bright with curiosity but his hands, thin and spotted with ink, were trembling.

"So, the rumors are more than nonsense?"

"If there is going to be a battle, I need to be here. It is my duty to protect the Realm, and the Realm is the King."

"If the whispers are true, one man," Pasin paused, "not even you will change the tide of battle." The silence stretched between them, heavy and thick. "What I have heard is all in the Songs. They don't warn of simple violence—"

Cedrik slammed his hand on the table. The candle jumped. "Speak plainly, old man. I am a soldier. I deal in steel, not riddles. What whispers are you talking about? It's just bandits."

Pasin stood up and walked to the window. The glass was thick, distorting the view of the city that surrounded Alcia Castle.

"Cedrik, if Neelin is sending you away, it is because he needs to know exactly what happened. Alcia cannot survive a war on two fronts."

"We are not at war with Xencid."

"Not yet, but if there is any truth to what I have heard, Xencid won't ever have to declare war."

"You speak like we have already been beaten."

"I am speaking about things you do not understand yet. There are wars steel alone cannot win." Pasin turned back to Cedrik, the glimmer in his eyes now an intense darkness. "The First Cycle."

"Don't. I have my orders. Get your things. We are to leave immediately."

Cedrik turned on his heel. He couldn't listen to another story about The First Cycle. Stories were for children. Nothing more. This was real. *Duty.*

"Cedrik, just... be prepared." Pasin started rolling his maps up. "I will meet you at the stables."

Echoing through the stone corridors, each strike of Cedrik's boots signaled a finality to his stay. In the courtyard, banners hung limp under the weight of a fading sun. He paused just long enough to taste the stillness, then turned back to the stables to ready Bastion for the long ride to Fort Lanthreau.

Duty was to follow orders. Understanding was optional.

CHAPTER 2

BOOM. BOOM. BOOM.

Neelin Arran, Captain of Alcia's Royal Guard and High Marshal of the entire military, took a deep breath as he gazed out from his post atop the city walls. His lungs filled with crisp spring air that was charged with anticipation. It was the same air he had breathed his entire life, but today it tasted cold and bitter.

His shoulders carried thirty years of command. He rolled them once, feeling the familiar ache of mail and duty. He remembered standing on this very stone two decades ago, during the Unification, when the King had dubbed him High Marshal. The stone had been warm then, the city below a sea of cheering voices. Today, the streets were barren and hushed, save for the faint sound of marching in the distance.

The only hint of age came from pronounced streaks of gray around his temples, set forward by jet black hair that reached his shoulders when not tied for battle. He stroked a thick, neat beard that covered his square jaw as he scanned the ranks of his men with sharp, dark blue eyes.

Boom. Boom. Boom.

Clad in steel plated mail, the Royal Guards were ready for the calling of war. Comprised of seventy-five soldiers, their heavy armor was adorned with deep purple crests that spoke of their identity. Neelin knew every man by name. He knew whose wife was expecting, and whose father had served beside him at the Border. He could hear their breathing; a steady rhythm that felt like seventy-five pairs of lungs working as one, the living wall of Alcian pride.

Most wielded finely crafted shields and long swords, while others brandished halberds, crossbows, and elegantly deadly longbows. The light of midday caught on their steel, reflecting a legacy of three centuries of defense.

Neelin glanced down toward the front of the city gates and surveyed the hundreds upon hundreds of militiamen from the various lords that donned the Alcian Crest on their assorted armor. Steel breastplates and light chainmail glimmered in the sunlight. The militia were a patchwork of the realm; farmers in boiled leather and shopkeepers in rusted mail, their hands, white-knuckled, on spears that had likely been used for boar hunting only weeks ago. Spring dragonflies danced and swirled through the air, weaving playfully through the silent forest of spears and swords.

Behind the main force stood rows of solemn archers with bows at the ready, while two units of cavalry were positioned at the flanks.

Boom. Boom. Boom.

The Alcian troops stood their ground in dignified silence, their weapons held high. An anxious stir emanated from below, as if a thousand men were trying not to tremble but failing.

The low, repetitious beat of an oncoming assault could be heard clearly in the distance. Individual men shook with anticipation; the subtle clanging of metal on metal rang out, as the armored soldiers held their position in line.

The reports from the north had been terrifying. Fort Lanthreau had been leveled in hours, its defenders slaughtered by an unknown force. He had sent two men to investigate, but they had not yet returned.

Boom. Boom. Boom.

Now, hearing the perfect, metronomic boom of rhythmic marching in the distance, Neelin realized the reports had not been exaggerated. They were warnings he had not fully understood until this moment. There was no shouting from the enemy line. No war-horns. Just the sound of a machine moving across the earth.

"Everything is ready, sir," Lieutenant Tiernan said, stepping into Neelin's peripheral vision. The young man was barely twenty, his face still held the soft edges of youth. He was fidgeting with the signet ring on his finger, his father's ring.

"The men, they say the enemy... the enemy seems unnatural. Without fear. Have you seen anything like this?"

"Fear is natural, Tiernan. Let it sharpen your senses, not dull your blade. We are not here to feel safe; we are here to stand firm. And we will," responded Neelin. He placed a heavy gauntlet on the boy's shoulder, feeling the fine vibration of terror beneath the plate.

"Aye, Marshal. I just... I've never heard of anything like this."

"Neither have I. But I've seen men win battles they should have lost... Because they believed in something greater than fear."

The sound of enemy approaching echoed on in the distance, their steps rising and falling in complete unison.

Boom. Boom. Boom.

Like thunder before a raging storm.

Tension hung heavily in the air, almost thick enough to drink. Horses could be heard grunting and stomping as their riders struggled to keep them in check.

"Man your post, Lieutenant. Think of your sister in the Lower Ward. Think of the city at your back. The battle is about to begin."

As if on cue, a line stretching for what seemed like an eternity came over the top of the first hill. A murmur grew around him, but the High Marshal did not flinch. He looked onward, trying to get an idea of what was coming.

The mysterious soldiers marched ahead, not breaking their rhythm for an instant. Formations two deep, now three. They didn't look like men; they appeared as a dark tide of shadow-gray steel.

Neelin's lip twitched a little under his faceplate.

This is no barbarian army.

Rows of cavalry formed on the far side of the enemy front. The middle was a massive line of men that wore simple, dark gray steel, with unfamiliar red and purple markings etched on their armor. Each man wielded a sword and a small circular shield slightly larger than a buckler. The top of the hill was now fully covered; an ominous warning to the oncoming swarm.

The first enemy line strut forward, then abruptly stopped. The men shifted apart slightly to make way for a hulking figure to stride through from the back. Neelin snapped to attention as the figure stepped into view. He glared toward the High Marshal, as if seeking him out. Neelin could not make out the man's face. Too far to extract much detail, but he caught the strange purple markings etched into the man's polished silver plate and his heavy, blood-red cloak.

Yes, no doubt. He is the commander.

As the two gazed upon each other with a soundless, burning hatred, nervous noises from the Alcians grew louder. Even the Royal Guard shifted uneasily. Steel rattled against steel as shields trembled in their grips.

"There must be *thousands* of them! What're doin' against that?" someone blurted out.

Neelin Arran whipped his head in the direction the voice came from. When he spoke, his voice was ice cold. "You're right, they have numbers! But... BUT WE are the guardians of the King, protectors of the realm! They march as if they have already won, but they don't know us... They do not know Alcia!

"We are not just soldiers. We are sons, we are daughters, fathers, and friends. We fight not for glory, but for the people behind these walls. For the lives we've built. For the future we refuse to surrender.

"So... Stand tall. Stand proud. And let them learn what it means to challenge the heart of Alcia!"

At this, the men on top of the wall straightened up, ready for orders.

"*Ignite!*" Neelin boomed.

Arrows were lit by torches that ran across the wall in front of them.

Neelin brought his sword high into the air, calling for the attention of all troops in one swift motion. "Today, we will break this trap of fear and confusion set by the enemy! We will make them regret the moment they set foot upon our land, and they will pay for their insolence with their blood."

The archers on the ground readied their weapons as the enemy troops began to march forward down the hill, still a few hundred yards away. Neelin slammed his helmet back on and snatched up his shield.

He swung his blade into the stone castle wall with a sharp, crisp *clang*. The ancient sword, passed from one High Marshal to the next, left a deep rivet in the stone wall without returning a single scratch to the blade.

Flaming arrows blasted out from the archers standing in position, but the marching troops didn't flinch at the sight of the fiery projectiles. Men fell from the attack as the arrows pierced holes in their armor, but the soldiers kept coming. Relentlessly, they moved forward, trampling a path from the green hills directly toward the castle walls.

The enemy cavalry charged, coming around to meet the Alcian troops in direct melee combat, barely giving the Alcian archers enough time to reload and fire again. More men fell as Alcia's cavalry advanced, engaging in the very first hand-to-hand fighting of the battle with the enemy.

Neelin leaned forward, scanning the field intently to evaluate his enemy. The two forces clashed on the far side of the battlefield. The enemy soldiers rode their steeds swiftly and more skillfully than he had seen in a long time. They weaved artfully through the Alcian ranks, taking down their opponents with ease.

Neelin's heart tightened as he studied the raiders, noticing that they wielded a weapon he had never seen. It had a long, spear-like handle with a large crescent blade at one end that unfolded into an extended double blade with a single shake. The raiders wielded their weapons with grace and efficiency, as if they were far lighter than they appeared. Many Alcian soldiers fell victim to the weapon's deadly reach.

Signaling more men to descend the city wall to support the ground troops, Neelin looked towards the center of the battle just as the Alcian infantry began their march towards the dark horde. Archers had not stopped raining fire upon the moving enemy, but the men kept advancing.

Troops continued to appear at the crest of the hill, one line after another. An endless sea of death about to swallow the Capital of the Kingdom in its torrents. Neelin watched as the last of the Royal Guard descended from the wall.

He wasn't prepared for the horrific scene which followed.

The infantry lines clashed at the center of the battlefield with a deafening clap. Alcian soldiers were swiftly and mercilessly mowed down. As the purple-clad raiders slaughtered them with their strange, extended blades, screams of fear and agony ripped through the air like piercing daggers. Neelin's heart sank at the devastation and death.

The only thing left to do is fight.

The High Marshal dodged an incoming arrow and slid down the ladder, joining the Royal Guard behind the main portcullis. His face was concealed by a protective steel helmet, but his face was tight with dread.

"Men, the battle does not fare well," Neelin stated. "Fortify the castle; the lines are breaking. Protect the King. Make sure that the escape passage for the Royal Family is clear." He looked around at his elite guard, awaiting his final words. "I, for one, will fight with my last ounce of strength to protect and honor our great kingdom! I will die as a warrior, a warrior for Alcia...Honor guide you, brothers!"

A surge of cheers came from his men, momentarily drowning out the sounds of death and fighting behind them.

Tiernan stepped forward, his sandy hair matted with sweat, and bowed with esteem and confidence. "For your honor, Captain, and for the Glory of Alcia!" This line brought about another full blast of cheers.

Neelin surveyed his men as if it were the first time he had seen them. He saw in their faces not only respect and loyalty, but a burning faith. He felt a rush of pride at the honor of fighting alongside these men he called his brothers. He nodded, strength and hope filling his body with a fresh vitality.

The men turned towards the castle and marched with haste to fortify the defenses. Neelin turned back to the city gates to take one last survey of the battlefield.

Alcia's lines had broken quickly, snapping like a fishing line snagging a shark instead of a fish. The hills were strewn with bodies, of which only a small few were clad in dark gray armor. In this light, the odd armor shimmered in a way he had never seen. His men had fought valiantly, without reservation, but nothing could change the facts.

Where did this force come from? I've never seen its like...

Almost the entire company of the Alcian cavalry had been slain, and he could see men already retreating back to the walls. The fight would come into the city at any moment, and finally to the castle.

Neelin Arran signaled the retreat to the militiamen standing at the walls, hoping to muster as many men as he could to form the last line of defense at the castle.

***

The cacophony of battle drove on, just the other side of the door. The Alcians had now been pushed all the way back into the main castle, just a few feet away from the throne room, from where the King had hopefully made his safe escape. Neelin held his weapon firmly, awaiting his chance to strike the enemy. The Royal Guard manned the Grand Hallway, the last line of defense for the man who ruled them.

A low rumbling filled the air, then the gate bent inward with a dull, heavy crack.

"Battering ram!" someone yelled. "Barricades!"

Men moved forward to push the gate back, but a second impact splintered the gate, as the black head of a lion pushed through wood and steel. The men staggered back and the lion's head withdrew.

Neelin could see the fog of fear rise in several younger faces, and yelled with all his strength over the clatter, "Royal Guards of Alcia! This is our moment to give these bastards a real fight!"

The remaining hundred Alcians leapt forward into the fray, as the third blow blew the gate open with violent force and a deafening crash. Men in dark armor, their faces concealed by jagged faceplates, surged into the hall with weapons brandished high. Neelin was suddenly reminded of a swarm of hornets pouring into a defenseless hive, a scene he had witnessed when he was still young.

His entire body tensed in anticipation. He threw himself onto his first target, closing in as fast as his legs could take him. He roared as he brought his sword slashing down at the other man's chest, but the soldier brought his shield up just in time to deflect the blow. An inexplicable explosion of rage coursed through his veins.

Pulling his sword back, he thrust his shield at the enemy, connecting and momentarily disrupting their balance. Neelin reacted quickly at the opportunity and swung the blade of steel at his opponent's torso, neatly tearing the dark armor and flesh underneath. The victim barely let out a scream before he slumped lifelessly to the floor.

Neelin spun and saw one of the Royal Guard evade an attack, but the next caught him on the arm. The Alcian man dropped to one knee and tried to keep his focus, but the attacker was relentless and finished the job with a deadly blow to the head. They gray-clad soldier tried to withdraw his odd weapon from the Alcian's flesh, but Neelin, taking his opening, ran him through.

The High Marshal pulled his sword out of the lifeless body, leaving it covered in thick, dark blood. Just as he did so, another enemy sliced down at him. Neelin brought his shield up in the nick of time, feeling the impact on his arm as a loud clang resounded through his ears. His sword snapped to an attacking position, but it was quickly knocked away by another soldier, giving his opponents a two-to-one advantage. Neelin quickly withdrew, knocking attacks away however he could, hoping to find some sort of opening.

The initial attacker tried for an arching overhead strike as his partner went for a thrust, making it impossible to come away unscathed. Impossible for any normal man. Neelin nimbly hopped to the side and let the attackers' swords make contact. Then, in a feat of pure combat instinct, the Captain of the Royal Guard quickly stepped down on the blades, incapacitating them, and slashed one of the enemy's throats wide open. Blood spurted out as Neelin swung around and hacked the other man right above his knee, then pulled his weapon up across the torso. Both soldiers fell limply to either side, as Neelin turned back toward the battle.

Slowly, the legendary Royal Guardsmen of Alcia were being overwhelmed by sheer numbers. They fought valiantly and were more than a match for the aggressors, but there were simply too many men to hold.

Neelin glanced over and saw another enemy soldier charging, giving himself more than enough time to ready a defense. The inevitable attack came and was easily blocked by Neelin's large steel shield. He spun left, bringing his sword around in a wide attack. The enemy parried the move but had no time to counter Neelin's next blow. The Marshal changed his stance and circled his sword the opposite way, tearing his blade through the soldier's gut. Air hissed as his smoking entrails spilled onto the blood-soaked stone floor.

"Fall back," Neelin ordered, as some of his men had already begun opening the large doors to the throne room. As soon as the doors opened, the Alcians rushed in, closely followed by their inexorable pursuers. For a moment, the Royal Guard seemed to have an edge before the unending stream of foes turned the tide once more.

Neelin scanned the room. The escape passage door swung idly. *Move fast, King and Queen Lorindan.*

"Triangle formation, keep together. They want to isolate and conquer," Neelin bellowed.

His men did as best they could but were soon overwhelmed.

Two of the dark armored men charged. A figure leapt to action, Lieutenant Tiernan. He managed to surprise one and land a blow, tearing the attacker's back from shoulder to shoulder. Three new foes entered the fray, scoring hits on each of his arms and left leg. The lieutenant fell to his knees, not yet mortally wounded.

Neelin rushed forward to help. A lone fighter moved to intercept, but the Captain evaded. The enemy's sword fell to the ground, an arm still attached, as Neelin leapt past him and brought his sword to bear, desperate to save his trusted officer. He plunged his weapon deep into the heart of another adversary, leaving two men surrounding the lieutenant.

One moved in for the attack but aimed too high, and the young lieutenant leaned forward to evade, bringing his sword up across the midsection of the aggressor, killing him instantly.

"Alcia will never fall!" Tiernan screamed, but was cut short as the final enemy ran him through. A small spurt of blood escaped his lips, and he fell face down into the dust and stone.

Fury rose again from deep inside, spreading through his limbs, a scarlet hatred that almost blinded him. He reacted with lightning speed and moved in before the killer could withdraw his weapon, decapitating him in one swift motion. He was just about to kick the head to one side, when a sudden chilling presence made him stop and turn.

Around him, the battle raged on, but all Neelin Arran could see was the figure now standing before him. He immediately recognized the man who had stared him down at the gates, the silent hulking figure clad in silver and red who wielded a huge crescent scimitar. There was no sign of wear on the plates of his armor; he had not even used his shield, which was still strapped to his back beneath his dark red cloak. Unlike his men, he wore no helmet or protective gauntlets. Instead, his hands were bare, and his lower arms clad tightly in wraps that reached the bottom of his palms. His thick tangle of raven hair was tied and tucked into his protective steel gorget.

His face was deeply tanned, with shallow lines etched across his forehead. Neelin thought the man could not be past his middle years. His eyes, striking and enigmatic, were the color of desert sand. They burned with an intense determination and focus Neelin had never seen. Focused on Neelin.

The man threw back his cloak and spoke, his eyes never leaving Neelin's.

"Yes... I have been waiting for this," he said, with a strange thick accent. The voice was dark and deep, but somehow mesmerizing all at once.

Neelin wasted no time in accepting. He brought his sword and shield to ready position, as space opened around the two fighters. "I don't know who the hell you are, where you came from, or why you are bent on destruction. But you will pay for all of the lives you have ended. Here. *Now!*" Neelin shouted, shoving the fatigue, the aching muscles, the throbbing head behind a wall of hatred. He forced his arm to lift a sword that suddenly felt twice as heavy as it had just hours ago. He propelled forward on legs that burned with every step.

As he closed in, the mysterious man raised his arm and ball of flame exploded forth from his bare hand. Caught off guard, Neelin pulled his shield up, barely able to defend himself. Engulfed in a wave of pain and heat, the sharp impact threw him back, ripping his shield from his grip and sending it flying across the throne room.

Magic? Very rarely have I seen one who possesses the Gift...

"I had read... hoped for more than *this*," said the other man, a trace of annoyance in his voice, as he brandished his scimitar.

Neelin shook his head and tried to clear the grogginess, but before he could even stand, his opponent was upon him. The man wielded the large, jeweled scimitar like a toy. The crescent steel fell with the force of a guillotine, missing Neelin's head by a hair's breadth as the Captain rolled out of its path. Leaping up, Neelin darted in and feinted a high swing then brought his sword down to slash the man's legs, but his opponent was ready and blocked the attack with such force that Neelin could barely keep grip of his own sword.

A punch of enormous power struck Neelin in the chest, causing him to gasp for air. Another blow to the head knocked Neelin to his back, sending his helmet flying, as the black haze of unconsciousness hovered in his sight. For the first time in his life, the High Marshal saw the dark wings of death fluttering before his eyes, and knew hope was gone.

"Exactly as you have been described, Marshal..."

Expressionless, the figure brought his hand up again. Another orb of fire formed and headed directly toward the felled man. Neelin's body jerked violently upon its fiery impact, before the blackness overtook him.

CHAPTER 3

AROUND MIDDAY, TWO MEN on horseback came to the edge of a cliff overlooking a horrifying sight. The wind here was different, it didn't carry the scent of pine or the clean aroma of the grasslands. It carried the heavy, greasy odor of cold ash.

Fort Lanthreau, once the iron guardian of the North, was a charred scar upon the dusty, scenic landscape. Where the gray stone fort proudly stood, a pillar of black smoke, thick enough to choke the spring sun, rose into dark clouds.

Cedrik Theramond patted his horse, Bastion, on the neck. The Knight Commander's face was a mask of professional detachment, but his fingers twitched against the familiar, hard leather reins. The large mahogany charger, bred for war, gave a satisfied snicker under his master's gloved hand. Bastion had been his only constant for a decade; a partner that didn't ask questions about where a stray orphan from the Highlands learned to hold a sword.

"Your thoughts?" Cedrik asked the elderly man beside him. His voice was a deep resonant rumble that easily cut through the wind that whipped through the valley.

The older man, seated on a smaller black steed, stroked his white beard. Pasin looked at the ruins, but his eyes kept drifting back to Cedrik, specifically to the hard, unyielding line of his protégé's jaw. He remembered that jaw when it was smaller, covered in dirt and trembling as the boy clutched a stolen loaf of bread in a Tarsis alleyway.

"I do not think an attack from outcasts living in the mountain could do this. Fort Lanthreau was designed to be an early warning post. It should have withstood any simple force."

"Agreed." Cedrik nodded, his mind already cataloging the structural failure. He saw no signs of a long siege, no debris from catapults, no ladder fragments. "There is no way those vagabonds could have organized an assault of this magnitude."

"Another thought," Pasin added, his tone dropping into the scholarly hum that usually preceded an unwanted lecture. "If the attackers wanted riches, they would have taken their time plundering the city. It is odd that they moved on so... quickly."

"They didn't come for gold, Pasin. Of this I'm sure now," Cedrik said, tugging his reins. He felt a cold, familiar chasm open in his chest. It was the same feeling he'd had more than thirty years ago, when he watched his village burn. He had survived only because a passing scholar with a staff and a sharp mind had seen potential in a boy who refused to stop fighting.

***

It was already early evening when the two men closed in on the outskirts of the fort. The dusk sun cast a deep red stain across the carnage. The quiet was the worst part. These people had endured in this wreckage for days.

Cedrik scanned the field with cold precision. He straightened suddenly, gesturing to his companion. "It's strange... I only see Alcians. Where are the dead of the raiders?"

"Ah yes. I have noticed this," Pasin murmured, pulling his dark green robe tight around his shoulders.

They passed a woman squatting by the side of the road, weeping into her ash covered dress beside what looked like a burnt human torso. Cedrik looked away instantly. He hated the weeping, the sobbing. It reminded him of the sounds he used to make in the dark, before Pasin taught him that tears were not a shield, only a distraction.

He turned to look for Pasin and saw the old man had veered off the path toward a small, lanky figure a hundred feet away. Cedrik sighed deeply. The old man was still a collector of strays.

"Hey, you there, boy!" Pasin's voice boomed.

The figure was oblivious, fully invested in furious digging. As Cedrik closed in, he saw the boy was alone. The other survivors were avoiding him, casting weary glances as if grief were a contagion.

The two riders stopped their horses beside the shallow hole forming beneath the young man's spade.

Pasin dismounted. "Son, do you need some help?"

"Answer him, boy," Cedrik said, from his horse. He had meant to sound commanding, but the sight of the boy's spade hitting the hard earth made his own hands ache, as long suppressed memories of burial pits he himself had labored over gnawed at his fingers like phantoms, longing to be recognized.

"No. No one understands," the youth spat, his voice hoarse. "They just now let us out."

Cedrik glanced at the bodies beside the hole. A man in blood-soaked mail from a deadly cut across his chest. A woman, her hair clumped in blood from what was presumably a fatal blow to her head, wearing a healer's dress.

"It was for your own good, for your protection—" Pasin began.

Without warning, the boy jerked his head up. Cedrik saw his face for the first time; smooth, with soft edges under a mop of curly brown hair. Fresh tears began to flow from the boy's eyes as they flashed with anger.

"If they had only let me fight!" he yelled. His fists closed around the shovel so tightly that his knuckles shone a bright white. "I have nothing left, no one!"

Ah, tears. Cedrik grimaced.

He had no desire to assuage a child when there was work to be done. But beneath the irritation, a dark memory surfaced; his screams echoed at a burning barn, while an old man in a green robe stood behind him, waiting for the fire to go out.

Cedrik dismounted and pulled an extra pair of riding gloves from his saddlebag. He walked over, without so much as a smile, and handed them to the boy.

"If you are going to finish this, you may as well do it without losing your hands," Pasin said gently. "What's your name, child?"

"I am not a child," the youth said, his hands already grabbing the soft leather gloves. "My name is Fromme. Fromme Gorin."

Just like Pasin to get sidetracked, he thought. *There is time for this later.*

Cedrik turned away, his boots crunching on the hard dirt.

Behind him, Pasin knelt. He didn't reach for the boy, but for the earth near the lip of the grave. He pressed his bare palm against the cold, soot-stained stones.

Thump.

It hit Pasin instantly. Not a sound, but a vibration that rushed up his arm and rattled his teeth. The world behind his green eyes exploded with color.

He didn't see the darkness of Lanthreau. He saw the *veins.*

Beneath the soil, glowing with a sick, pulsating violet light, a network of roots was slithering through the bedrock. They weren't plant roots. They were jagged, geometric lines of raw energy, throbbing like an infection in the blood of the world. They were feeding.

And they were drowning it out. The deep, resonant hum of the land—the Song of the Stones that the texts claimed held the world together—was being choked. There was no harmony here. Only a screeching, hungry static.

This isn't just an attack, Pasin realized, a scream building in his throat. *The Gift... All over...*

The sensory overload brought on a migraine, as the hum turned into a shriek in his skull. Pasin gasped, jerking his hand back as if the ground had burned him. He staggered, his vision swimming with afterimages of purple lightning. A sharp, hot pressure burst behind his nose.

"Old man?" Cedrik's voice cut through the noise, sharp with suspicion and worry. "What is it?"

Pasin turned away quickly, wiping the back of his hand across his upper lip. It came away wet, warm and sticky. He shoved his hand into the folds of his cloak before the Knight could see the blood.

"Nothing," Pasin wheezed, forcing his voice to remain steady. "Just... death. Too much of it."

As he scanned the area, two figures were approaching at a trot. One seemed to be dressed as a civilian in a simple leather coat, while the other wore a silver steel breastplate of Alcia. The steel was dented and covered with dirt, blood, and who knows what else, but the man walked with purpose, though he seemed to sag under a heavy weight.

Pasin and Fromme both became silent, as Cedrik strode towards the newcomers. He met them with the traditional Alcian greeting, crossing his forearms in front of his chest with a slight bow. "Honor guide you, brother."

The soldier returned the greeting, with a noticeably deeper bow. "Knight Commander! I am Lieutenant Aiken. Thank the King you're here."

Cedrik nodded. "What happened here."

"The enemy was... ruthless," Aiken responded, his eyes darting to the ruined gate as if expecting the shadows to move. "They fought in a style that seemed almost familiar, but also very different. They didn't shout. They didn't even breathe heavily. It was like fighting a clock that just kept ticking. Their weapons... lances that unfolded into crescent hooks, swords that were longer but lighter. Once the real fighting began, we were outmatched and outnumbered." The lieutenant lowered his eyes, softening his voice. "It was almost as if they were here to... to purge. They weren't interested in gold, or the grain stores. We were planning to wait them out, see if help would come. Look there, they breached the walls to force a fight. The did not wait."

Cedrik quickly examined the area where the lieutenant was pointing. The main walls were in ruin, however the civilian quarters were relatively unharmed. The destruction was surgical, designed to expose the soldiers, not level the town.

"What of losses? Did we take any prisoners?"

The lieutenant shook his head, still trying to gather himself. "We're still doing the tally, but my best estimate is that we lost well over half our men. They drew us out beyond the walls." The man's face was overcome with sudden confusion. "Then, when we signaled the retreat, they simply left. They didn't even enter the fort. It was senseless."

The man in civilian garb stepped forward, his presence as sharp and cold as a winter morning. "Knight Commander, I am Ivanis Bryant, the magistrate here. Lieutenant Aiken is struggling with the 'senselessness' of it all. He is looking for the humanity, a logical reason. I can try to provide any more details needed." Cedrik dismissed the lieutenant and offered a formal greeting to the magistrate. "I'll be blunt with you commander. We stood no chance here. The only reason we are still alive is due to the mercy of whoever came to fight, forcing our men from the walls, butchering them and leaving."

"The force, were there any distinguishing features? Could it have been a Xencid assault?"

The magistrate shook his head. "Their banner was a design that I had never seen; a red disk, perhaps a sun, struck through its center by a streak of lightning. And there is another key thing, a great oddity." His brow furrowed deeply as a glaze came over his eyes. "There are no prisoners, no remains. Any men who were about to be captured, died immediately with blood pouring from their ears and mouths. And all of the bodies and their belongings—armor, weaponry—just... disappeared."

"Disappeared?" Pasin leaned forward, his scholar's curiosity warring with a visible dread. "It was an army, Magistrate. How would they have simply disappeared? Do you mean to say that their arms and shields, their dead... could just *vanish*?"

The magistrate gave a high, embarrassed laugh. The corners of his eyes creased with deep crow's feet when he did so. Cedrik noticed that those blue eyes were severely bloodshot from lack of sleep.

And there is a great confusion, justified if what he tells is true.

Cedrik had read hundreds of men during his time. A man who could not read the face of his opponent could not find the opportunity to deliver a sure-handed blow. What he saw now in the magistrate's face was fear, muddled with confusion. And he was trying to suppress it with all his might. Beneath his calm exterior, the magistrate and the lieutenant were not so different after all.

What could have happened here to instill such fear in these men?

He noticed that Pasin's voice was beginning to sound impatient. "Magistrate, this is not a time for humor. You are reporting to men who will be delivering your observations to the King."

The magistrate shook his head. In a flash he had regained his composure, his face again a calm pool of ice. "Pardon me, sir, but I swear upon the holy light of honor that I speak naught but truth. Witnesses say that after the enemy soldiers were captured. Within minutes... They began to bleed profusely. They fell to the ground, writhing in great agony until they died."

Ivanis cleared his throat. "And the dead, their bodies, all of their possessions, became blurred as if... as if we were looking at them from behind frosted glass. The air around them tasted of ozone and hot metal. Like... like the air after a lightning storm."

Pasin stared, transfixed at the magistrate and began to stroke his beard. Fromme's eyes grew wide with disbelief.

"This strange blurring seemed slow at first. Within mere seconds, Knight Commander, I swear to the Gods, the armor was gone. I could see through their flesh and bones to their organs, their hearts and frozen vessels of blood. In another moment, all that could be seen was a shadowy shape, a ghost. Then..." Ivanis took a deep breath to steady himself. "Then they were gone without a trace. And that is why I could not allow anyone to leave the fort until now. I know it disrespects our fallen comrades, but the risk was too great."

Cedrik let his own breath out slowly, and for a moment, no one spoke. The only time he had heard of anything like this came from the old tales that Pasin recited to him. Children's stories, nothing more.

Pasin broke the silence. "Complete your report, magistrate. Be sure to leave no details unwritten. We need to take this report back to the High Marshal with the utmost urgency, though I am afraid that you were correct. You have given us few answers, and created a great many more questions."

Ivanis Bryant nodded and let out a breath.

He looks to have found a great sense of relief, most likely that this is no longer his problem, Cedrik mused to himself, as the magistrate bowed and took his leave.

"Pasin, I suggest we—" Cedrik's arm was grabbed by fervent hands. The young boy had planted himself beside him, and looked up at him with eager, pleading eyes.

"Please, sire, let me come with you!" Fromme begged. His body shook with anticipation, his grip around Cedrik's arm tightening.

Instinctively, Cedrik shook his head. Fromme turned to Pasin, pleading.

"We can't have a child along, Pasin," Cedrik snapped. But as soon as the word left his mouth, he felt the tug of regret in his gut. The boy's face had collapsed with disappointment, cheeks turning ashen. He fell to his hands and knees, stirring up a cloud of dust.

"Father always said, 'Family is the greatest bond,'" the boy murmured, his hope draining. "Bond is broken, I can't do nothing alone, by myself."

Powerless. The word echoed in Cedrik's head like a church bell. He looked at the boy's mud-stained face and saw the ghost of a child who had stolen bread in Tarsis, just to see the next morning. He looked at the shallow grave, the desperate attempt to maintain a connection to a world that had been forcefully taken from him.

Powerless. Not now, not ever... Never again.

"You have a duty to your family, Fromme," Cedrik said at last, as he closed his eyes. "And as your new companion, I am obligated to help you finish your duty."

The Knight Commander strode to the shallow grave and took the spade from the boy's blistered, quivering hands. He didn't look at Pasin, but he could feel the old man's silent, fatherly approval.

Cedrik drove the spade into the earth. Each thrust of the shovel was a solemn vow. He had spent his life becoming the Steel Guardian to forget his beginnings, as an orphan. But as he dug the grave for

Fromme's parents, he realized that you can never truly bury your past. You can only build a fortress over it.

CHAPTER 4

THE SOUND OF ALCIA dying was a low, rhythmic thrumming that reverberated through the stone floor of the Royal Apartments.

Brighid Lorindan, Queen of Alcia, didn't need to look out the window to know the outer wall had been breached. She had spent years married to a man who treated her more like a structural necessity than a wife. She had learned to read the palace's moods through her feet, eyes and ears. The vibration wasn't the chaotic clash of a violent breach. It was the steady, surgical pulse of an army that wasn't just winning; but harvesting.

She stood in the center of her solarium, her hands steady. She had been trained since birth to lead. Her ancestors had held these lands for a thousand years. She would not provide the invaders with the satisfaction of a panicked queen.

The door to the solarium creaked open. King Alaric Lorindan entered.

He wasn't in his armor. He wore his familiar maroon, heavy velvet robes; the ones he usually donned for late-night sessions in the archives. Brighid had always taken comfort in those robes. They represented a king dedicated to knowledge and history rather than spears and gold.

Alaric held tightly to the traditions of his ancestors, the most sacred of which was the Sovereign's Pulse. Every decade, the people gathered to witness the King touch the Foundation Stone, in a ritual meant to symbolize the King's life-force sustaining the land. Just a month before, the Capital had been full of thousands of cheering

Alcians, sharing joy in the name of the King, who had ruled for over fifty prosperous years.

As Alaric walked to the window, Brighid noticed an odd scent clinging to the velvet. Not the dry, musty smell of old parchment, but a sharp, metallic tang, like a cooling forge or lightning storm.

"The defense has failed, Alaric," she said, her voice calm and level. "Neelin is losing the courtyards."

"Neelin is doing exactly what he was born to do," Alaric replied, watching the smoke rise. He looked less like a king watching his world end, and more like a gardener looking out over an unruly hedge in need of a good prune.

"You must hold the border. If Dunvar falls, if the Xencids cross the line, there will be nothing left of us." Brighid stepped toward him, her voice tight with a sudden, sharp desperation. "You know their way. They don't just occupy, they erase. They will burn our songs, rename our cities, and breed the Alcian out of our children until we are just another province of their empire. We cannot let them cull us from existence."

Alaric turned. For a moment, a flicker of something, pity perhaps, crossed his face. "Yes. The culling is... a heavy price. I agree, Brighid. We must ensure Alcia survives."

He said the words, but they were hollow. He spoke with the bored tone of a man agreeing with the weather. He wasn't taking the cultural death of his kingdom seriously because he wasn't looking at the fire outside; he was looking through it.

"Go, now," Alaric said, his voice dropping to a dismissive whisper. "The southern passage. An escort awaits to ensure safe passage to Tarsis."

"You're sending me away while our kingdom burns?"

"I am sending you to where you can survive long enough to see the new world," Alaric said. He turned his back on her, moving toward the door that led to the Throne Room. "Take what you need. The years to come will be difficult for most."

He left without a final word. No apology. No goodbye.

Brighid stared at the empty doorway. He had agreed with her, but the lack of fear in his eyes was more terrifying than the army at the gates. She didn't go for her jewelry box. She bypassed the gold necklaces and the crown she had worn like a yoke.

She went to Alaric's private desk. A letter, sealed in crimson wax with the crest of Xencids' Consul, was sitting at the top of the desk. The golden threads, a signature of their wealthy southern neighbors, shone brightly against the dark oak of the King's bureau. Her hand reached out for it, but she stopped before grabbing it.

Maybe Alaric reached out for help. Or peace... Please let it be so.

She pulled her hand back. If she opened it, she would know. If she knew, she could never pretend again.

It needed to stay. He would answer, after he made his escape.

She pulled open the bottom drawer and began shoving parchments into a heavy leather satchel: maps of various sections of Alcia, supply routes between the major cities. She picked up a small notebook, wrapped in battered leather casing. Loose pages threatened to fall from the bindings, yellow with age.

And then, there. The Royal Seal. A massive gold ring engraved with the Lion of Alcia.

She snatched it up, the weight of it grounding her.

Jewels were for victims. Information was for survivors.

Brighid adjusted the weight of the leather satchel against her hip. She took one last look at the empty solarium, the gilded cage that had defined her adulthood, and slipped into the service corridor behind the beautiful tapestry depicting the Lion of Alcia standing free over the foothills.

The tunnels were a jagged contrast to the silence of the solarium. Here, the palace was screaming. Servants collided in the dark, and the air was thick with the smell of wet stone and ozone. She moved against the tide, toward the southern passage, until a flash of gray light ahead forced her into the shadows of a grain chute.

Three invaders moved past. They didn't run; they glided with a synchronized, remarkable precision.

"Primary anchor secured," one said.

The voice stopped Brighid's heart. He spoke in Alcian, but the syntax was mangled. The hard, martial consonants of Regat fused with the melodic, elongated vowels of the Xencid south. She had never heard anything of its like.

"And the High Marshal?" the second asked.

"The General's orders are absolute," the leader replied, his voice devoid of any excitement or bloodlust. "Isolate him. Wear him down. But Neelin Arran must survive the night. He is the shepherd for the next phase."

They moved on, their footsteps carrying a faint, metallic vibration. Brighid remained in the dark, clutching the maps of a kingdom that her husband seemed to no longer care for.

The Queen held her breath until the sound of their movement had faded to a slight echo in the distance. The invaders weren't just killing; they were selecting. They were sparing the one man who could lead a resistance, and her husband was waiting in his robes to hand over the keys to his own kingdom.

Why, Alaric? Damn you, Why!

She quickly slipped through the castle to the southern passage. There, a small escort of three Royal Guards met her at the entrance with relief pouring over their faces at her appearance. She led them through the passage out into the cold air of the evening without any words.

Boom.

The doors to the main castle crashed onto the stone steps and splintered. She clutched the precious leather satchel to her chest. Contained within it were the keys to saving her country.

She turned her eyes toward Tarsis, not yet ready for his new world.

CHAPTER 5

Spending barely a night to rest the horses and replenish with a hot meal, the Knight Commander left Fort Lanthreau with great haste. The information contained in the magistrate's report, coupled with his own observations, had to be delivered to the High Marshal immediately.

Their return route was completely different from the initial journey. Foregoing all of his instincts, Cedrik made camp in wide open areas close to the main road. Time was not their ally. The Great Northern Highway was the main artery between the Capital and the North. It was normally well travelled, but now it was barren.

Little time for conversation was available given the pace that Cedrik set. Salted pork and hard bread was served for each meal. They rotated watches during the shortening spring nights and left at dawn each morning, hoping the horses had gotten enough rest for another hard day's ride.

Fromme was frequently on the verge of falling too far behind, but Pasin always seemed to need rest before the boy could ask for respite. Cedrik noted that Fromme did not complain at the harsh conditions, keeping quiet and mostly to himself.

"Pasin?" Fromme asked, his voice barely carrying over the wind. "The magistrate, he said the bodies disappeared. He said they blurred... like ghosts."

"The magistrate was frightened," Pasin said, his eyes fixed on the horizon. "But fear often sharpens the sight as much as it clouds it."

Fromme tightened the grip on his reins, anxiously. "My father, he told me stories of the First Cycle. He said the Highlands were forged by men who could shape stone with a whisper. He said the blood of Alcia used to course with fire, and ice, and lightning."

Cedrik, riding ahead, let out a scoff. "Fathers tell stories to help their sons sleep, Fromme. Stone is shaped by chisels. Blood is just blood."

Pasin didn't look at Cedrik. He shifted his grip on his staff, the wood polished smooth over decades of use and guided his horse closer to the boy.

"The world is older than steel, Fromme," Pasin said, his voice dropping to a low, resonant hum. Cedrik's chest vibrated with the words. "And memories are long. The First Cycle didn't end because the power vanished. It ended because the price became too high to pay." He looked at the boy then, his green eyes losing their playful twinkle, replaced by a deep, penetrating intensity. "Magic, the Gift...," Pasin whispered. "The stories do not talk of the terrible burden that comes with such power. And if what we saw at the fort was to become one of those stories, we should heed any warnings that went along with your bedtime tales."

Fromme stared at the old man, his jaw dropping. The awe in his eyes showed wonder and appreciation.

"Save your breath," Cedrik called back, oblivious to the expressions shared by the pair. "We have miles to cover before sunset."

Pasin winked at Fromme, a quick, conspiratorial flash, then tapped his staff against his boot. A subtle spark, no larger than a firefly, jumped from the wood and vanished.

Fromme blinked, wondering if he had imagined it.

"Did you... did you do that?" Fromme whispered, leaning in so Cedrik wouldn't hear. "From... from nothing?"

Pasin's face grew solemn. He slowed his horse slightly, shaking his head.

"No, boy. Never from nothing. That is the first lie of the stories." Pasin rubbed his thumb against the polished wood of his staff. "The Gift does not create. It trades."

Fromme frowned, confused. "Trades?"

"Our world is a miser, Fromme. It counts every copper," Pasin explained, his voice taking on the cadence of an old teacher. "To create that spark—that tiny speck of light—I had to give up heat. I had to draw warmth, from my own blood, trade it for the flash."

Pasin pulled off his glove. His hand was trembling slightly, the fingertips red and blue, as if he had plunged them into snow.

"If a man wants to lift a boulder with the Gift," Pasin continued, "he must pay the price of the weight on his own spine. If he wants to burn a city, he must be willing to turn his own veins, his soul, to ash."

Fromme looked at the old man's shivering hand with wide eyes. "So... it's just a transfer?"

"Precisely." Pasin nodded. "A transaction. And the exchange rate is generally terrible. Even if you know exactly how to access the Gift within you, the toll is steep. That is why the First Cycle ended, Fromme. The Gift didn't just disappear. Those who could use it spent themselves. They hollowed themselves out until there was nothing left to trade. And then, they started to trade what was not theirs to give."

"That's enough." Cedrik's voice cut through the air like a whip crack.

The Knight Commander had circled Bastion back. He looked at Pasin's trembling hand, then at the wide-eyed squire with a hardened glare.

"Stop filling his head with nonsense, Pasin," Cedrik growled. "The boy needs to learn how to hold a sword, not how to barter with demons."

"It is history, Cedrik," Pasin replied calmly, pulling his glove back on. "Ignorance is not a shield."

"It is when the knowledge gets you killed." Cedrik turned his gaze to Fromme. "Listen to me. Steel is honest. You swing it, it cuts. If it breaks, you get a new one. But that," he gestured vaguely at Pasin's staff, "it is nothing but a legend passed from one generation to the next. I have seen men try to be gods, Fromme. They died screaming for their mothers because they thought they had found a way to cheat the arithmetic."

Cedrik wheeled his horse around, kicking up a cloud of dust.

"We ride," Cedrik commanded. "And no more parlor tricks, Pasin. We need your strength for the road, not for filling his head with dreams and distractions."

Pasin gave a small weary shrug. But as Cedrik rode ahead, the scholar caught Fromme's eye one last time.

"He is right, you know," Pasin murmured. "Steel is honest, but sometimes... the truth requires a lie to be told."

Fromme gulped but Pasin was already looking forward, his lighthearted, albeit weary, face had returned.

Cedrik pushed forward, tightening their pace. *He shouldn't be encouraging the boy*, he thought, grimly. *He has no idea what he will see in the coming days.*

The miles dragged on. Cedrik knew there was little hope in returning in time to participate in the battle, but he had to try. Hope dwindled as they raced to their home. A force the size described by Ivanis should not have been able to move this quickly, especially without a significant supply train trailing behind, but the evidence was unmistakable.

"Very odd," mused Pasin idly, as they rode down the heavily traveled road. "Very odd indeed."

Cedrik grunted in acknowledgement and looked over at his old friend. Bastion continued forward at a steady pace, puffing deep breaths every so often.

"What do you mean? I don't understand," asked Fromme, as he increased his pace to ride alongside the elder. "Are we in trouble?"

"On the contrary. I'm more worried at how little trouble we seem to be in. Have you noticed that we have seen no travelers on this path for days?"

Fromme thought for a few moments as the group pushed forward. The young man peered in all directions but did not say a word. The bright sun, warm breeze, and spring foliage bathed the landscape surrounding the normally busy path in a bluish green tint.

"Whatever lies ahead, I fear we will be too late to affect any outcome," Pasin declared into the silence.

***

At dusk on the fourth day, a familiar stench wafted in with the otherwise pleasant breeze. Cedrik shared a grim look with Pasin, who only acknowledged the yet unseen. He picked up their pace silently. This nightmare was one he had experienced many times.

A few hours into their ride, Alcia Castle and the surrounding city appeared on the horizon, almost blending in with the long bluish grass that covered the landscape. As they topped the final hill of their journey, Fromme got a clear view of their destination. The boy gasped at the devastation. The sound of thousands of flies buzzing around the fallen remains filled their ears.

Too much for the boy. This is worse than the fort...

Dull gray tents surrounded all sides of the city walls. A flurry of activity flitted around the tents closest to the castle. Signs of battle littered the hills beyond the makeshift encampments. Arrow shafts, bodies, both animal and man, and wreckage still laid all across the apparent field of battle. The detritus of war lay in smoldering piles, forming a clear path directly to the main gates.

Impossible, how did this happen so quickly?

"Stay close, follow me," ordered Cedrik, quietly. "It looks like the battle ended days ago, but remnants could still be here."

The trio rode single file, with Bastion leading the way. Their descent was unpleasant; the air was thick with the foul, sweet smell of blood mixed with burning flesh on the brink of decay. It was a slow pace that Cedrik kept, looking for survivors.

"Cedrik, it is the same as Fort Lanthreau. No evidence of the enemy, not even their armaments," Pasin stated, looking for any clues.

The fields towards the castle were torn to shreds; the grass had been flattened and mud kicked up everywhere in divots from slashes gone awry. Smoke billowed slowly but continuously from the heaps of disordered remnants, which grew more common as they approached the outermost tents. Curiously, only the remains of Alcian soldiers littered the field. Too numerous and too fresh for the medic corps to attend.

"Commander...," a weak voice called out from beneath the smoke. "Is that really you?"

Cedrik raised his hand for the group to hold position and scanned the area. He patted Bastion on the neck, who snorted uneasily.

"Wait here," muttered Cedrik, as he dismounted and grabbed a waterskin.

He spotted the soldier, barely alive. His right leg had been severed at the knee, a haphazard tourniquet attempted valiantly to stem the blood loss. His whitish features were almost a ghostly white, and most of his body was covered by a shredded standard, unmistakably Alcian.

"You're safe now." A lie. The Knight Commander moved over to the soldier slowly and lowered his waterskin.

The man let out a slow, hacking, wet cough as he tried to sip the water. "They broke through... so easily... we were—" He coughed again, this time with blood in each labored breath. "I held the... the banner... for as long as I could..." He spat.

"You did well," Cedrik replied, softly. "Murphy, Specialist Murphy? We served together at Verona, in Xencid?"

Life came back to Murphy's face, only if for an instant. His brown eyes shone bright in the dim light of dusk. He smiled, toothlessly, as blood continued to seep from his nose and mouth.

"Yes... you remembered the banner, sir. At Verona. You said... you said if I held it high enough... the men would follow the cloth... even if they couldn't see you."

Cedrik's throat tightened. "And they did. They followed you all the way here, Murphy. All the way home."

Fromme had dismounted too. As he stood just behind Cedrik, the color drained from his face. Pasin said nothing, he just turned away.

"The fever, infection... you know... commander," pleaded Murphy. "Let me go... with honor and dignity..."

Cedrik closed his eyes, then gave a slow and deliberate solemn nod. "You saved lives, you held the line."

Murphy smiled faintly, as tears streamed down his bloody, dirt-streaked face. "Tell them... I... didn't run..."

"You didn't. Honor guide you, brother."

Cedrik slowly drew his greatsword, the familiar ringing of steel filling the air.

Fromme stepped forward to grab Cedrik's shoulder. "Sir, there must be something—"

"There isn't," Pasin replied in a low stern voice, final.

I'm sorry, Murphy. I swear you will be avenged. All of you here that fell, will be avenged.

For a split second, he wasn't looking at Murphy. He was looking at the burning grain wagons on the road to Fort Darrow. He was twenty years younger, kneeling in the mud while Captain Lachlan spat at his boots. *You didn't save anyone, Sergeant. You just chose who screamed where.*

Murphy took one more labored breath.

Cedrik stood and slowly raised his massive sword, tip down, then drove the blade through the soldier's heart.

Silence.

He withdrew it slowly and wiped the steel on the tattered Alcian banner. "May you find the peace you have earned."

Fromme had backed away, hand over his mouth and tears welling once again. His eyes brimmed with questions he did not yet know how to ask, or even if he should.

Cedrik sheathed his sword into his shoulder casing. Slow and deliberate.

"Mount up," Cedrik said quietly to Fromme, as he turned to remount Bastion.

"You bastard," uttered a loud, strong voice dripping with acid. "How dare you!"

Cedrik turned to the sound and saw a familiar figure in the smoke. He locked with her gaze. Her eyes were bright blue and burning with fire. Rage covered her sharp features. She was beautiful even when rippling with the ugliest of emotions.

"Taillte…" Cedrik began.

"You absolute bastard," she spat, as she turned away.

CHAPTER 6

THE WOMAN STORMED OFF without hesitation, her boots kicking up mud and debris. The accusation in her eyes stung Cedrik deeper than the smoke and misery lingering in the air.

Pasin shared a glance with Fromme, the young boy's face pale with dread.

"Taillte, hold on, listen to me," bellowed Cedrik, starting after her. "You don't understand."

She spun around. "He was not an animal to be put down!" Her voice was trembling with a rage that looked dangerously close to tears. She buried her face in her hands for a moment, then looked up, fierce again. "He was a man."

Cedrik slowed his approach, keeping his voice low and steady. "I gave him the honor he deserved. He asked a superior officer to end his suffering. Would you have preferred I let him drown in his own blood and rot? Would that have been duty?"

"I would have tried to save him!" she shot back, gesturing violently to the bloodstained medic's cross stitched to her leather tunic. "You weren't even here! You didn't see what they did. How dare you try to hide behind 'honor' and duty now!"

Why is she being so impossible?

Cedrik took a step forward, rage building inside. Pasin intervened, placing a gentle hand on the knight's chest to hold him back, then stepped into Taillte's space.

He lowered his voice, cutting under the noise of the wind. "Captain Cleirigh."

Taillte glared at him, her chest heaving, hands clenched into fists at her sides. Pasin looked down at those fists. They were trembling, vibrating, as if they were about to explode.

"I know where you trained, Taillte," Pasin whispered. "And I know the heat you feel in your hands right now. The itch to fix what is broken."

Taillte froze. Her eyes widened slightly, the anger momentarily stunned out of her. "You... you know?"

"I have studied the Gift for many years. I know the burden it places upon those who wield it," Pasin said, his eyes filled with a sad, ancient empathy. "But even the greatest Healers of the First Cycle could not knit a severed soul. Cedrik did not take a life that could be saved; he released one that was already gone." He reached out and gently touched her clenched fist. "Do not burn yourself out on a ghost, Captain," Pasin warned, softly. "Save your strength. The living have more need of it."

Her eyes, red with exhaustion and sorrow, held Pasin's gaze. The shaking in her hands stopped. The fight seemed to drain out of her, replaced by a crushing fatigue.

"It is all so confusing," she whispered, turning toward the smoldering city gate. "So much death... But... it could have been so much worse."

As if summoned by her words, a figure emerged from the smoke-shrouded path leading into the city proper. He was a Royal Guardsman. His purple crest was scorched and his helmet gone, revealing a bloody gash across his forehead. Limping badly toward them, he stopped and gave a weary salute.

"Knight Commander Theramond? Pasin?" the guard said, his voice hoarse. "The High Marshal requested your presence as soon you returned. I must be the first one who has seen you."

Cedrik's brow furrowed. "The High Marshal?" he asked, the question sharp. "We had heard Neelin Arran fell in the throne room."

The guard shook his head, a flicker of awe in his exhausted eyes. "They left him for dead, sir. But he's alive. He's in command," he finished, with a harsh cough.

"Lead the way," Cedrik ordered.

He glanced back at the trio. Fromme looked to Taillte, who hesitated only for a moment before offering the boy a reassuring, if strained smile. She fell in line, and together they walked into the ruins of the Capital.

***

"I have never been to the Capital," Fromme whispered quietly to Pasin, as the group strode through the inner gates.

The old man nodded, placing his cowl overhead to protect against the drifting ash. "I wish you were able to come under better circumstances, Fromme. This is no way to experience Alcia Castle for the first time."

The ruined roads were barren and unnaturally quiet within the Capital. People were trying to clean the paths, their weary figures bent double over piles of stone and debris. Occasional sobs were heard in the distance, echoing off the high walls of the noble district.

Cedrik surveyed the destruction. Smoke, burning parchment, and blood wafted through the air, as dust clouds shifted in the wind.

We took the boy from wreckage only to bring him into a larger disaster, Cedrik thought, grimly.

"Halt," Cedrik commanded the guard. He glanced back, finding the boy, the old man and the Healer paused in the street.

Fromme stopped suddenly, his boots crunching on something brittle. He looked down. It was a stained-glass window, shattered into a thousand glittering shards lying in the mud. He looked up at the building from which it had fallen; a chapel, its roof caved in like a cracked egg.

"My father said the Capital was invincible," Fromme said, his voice quaking as he kicked a shard of blue glass. "He said... its walls were created by magic."

Taillte knelt beside him, studying him for a moment. Her hands were gentle now, the earlier rage replaced by a focused, calm. She brushed a smudge of soot from his cheek. "Stone is just stone, Fromme. It breaks if you hit it hard enough."

"But the King..." Fromme looked at Pasin, then Cedrik, his eyes wide. "The King is supposed to stop this."

Pasin looked away, staring at the ruins of the Royal Library in the distance. Smoke was rising from the archives; the history of Alcia, burning.

"Kings are just men, Fromme," Pasin said, his voice heavy and distant. "And sometimes, men break before the stones do."

Taillte placed a hand on the boy's shoulder, steering him away from a dead cart horse that blocked the gutter. "Don't look at the ground," she directed him, gently. "Keep your eyes on Cedrik's back. We keep moving forward. That is how we survive."

Fromme nodded, wiping his nose on his sleeve, and hurried to catch up with the Knight Commander.

As they came upon the gates of the main keep, Fromme noticed the gates were twisted and turned, ripped apart by force. Arrows still littered the streets, though some effort had been put forth to clean the area.

Once inside the outer walls, the path to the main castle was closed off. The huge, stone steps that led to the interior of the keep were covered in rubble, blocking the main entrance inside the castle. The giant wooden doors had been pulled from their hinges, laying broken in pieces upon both sides of the steps.

"The castle bore the brunt of the attack," stated the guard, as the group turned eastward and strode past a set of stables. "The enemy went straight for the throne room. It was like they wanted to end the battle as quickly as possible. The High Marshal is using the Royal Guard Keep barracks as the war room."

The face of Sergeant Murphy flashed into Cedrik's focus. *Your death will matter. I swear it. Whoever did this will pay.*

Cedrik nodded at the guard and signaled for the group to advance.

CHAPTER 7

THE GUARD PUSHED OPEN the heavy door to the barracks. They were instantly hit by the smell; stale sweat, lamp oil, and the copper tang of drying blood.

The room had been hastily cleared. A large, oak table dominated the center, covered in a chaotic layer of maps and parchment. Around it stood the remains of Alcia's leadership: merchant lords looking pale and nervous, surviving officers with bandaged limbs, and Chancellor Eamon.

The Chancellor, usually a man of pristine velvet and manicured hair, looked like he had been dragged through a gutter. His bright blue robes were stained with grease and mud, and his hair a disheveled mess.

Pasin gestured for Fromme to move to the far corner of the room, as he moved to the foot of the table with Cedrik and Taillte. Cedrik placed his hand on the table as the room fell silent.

At the head of the table stood Neelin Arran, High Marshal of the Alcian Military.

If Cedrik hadn't known the man for twenty years, he wouldn't have recognized him. Bloodied bandages were wrapped haphazardly around the entire left side of his face and throat, and what remained uncovered of his face was covered in burns. His left arm was held tightly to his chest in a leather sling. He wore a navy glove on his right hand, flexing the fingers regularly as if testing they were still there.

He raised his one good eye—steel blue and sharp as a hawk's—to meet Cedrik's.

"Cedrik, Pasin," he said, painfully and slow. "I wish you were returning to a victory. But I'm glad you returned at all."

"We heard about the throne room," Cedrik said, inclining his head. "We feared the worst."

"The worst has happened, my friend," Neelin replied. He looked past Cedrik to the scholar. "And you, Pasin. I asked for siege engineers to reinforce the walls. Instead, the gods spared... a librarian."

The room went quiet. It wasn't an insult; it was delivered with no edge.

Pasin stepped forward, his robes dusty and torn. "You're right, I am not much for swinging a sword, High Marshal."

"Then why are you here?" Chancellor Eamon asked, stepping forward to the table. "This is a war room, not an archive."

Pasin straightened, a hint of a smile touching his lips. "I am here because I know how the King's mind works better than he knows it himself."

Chancellor Eamon scoffed, a painful sound. "You cataloged his tax records."

"I was his shadow, Chancellor," Pasin corrected, firmly. "For three years, Alaric and I didn't see the sun. We were in the Deep Vaults, in the archives. We weren't studying history; we were dissecting it. I know what he fears. And more importantly, I know what he was looking for in the dark."

"What are you implying?" Eamon shot back. "We don't need another history lesson; we need a solution."

Neelin paused, sensing the sudden weight in Pasin's words. "And what was he looking for?"

Pasin looked away, staring at the oil lamp flickering on the table. "A way to never lose. He told me once that a king who relies on luck is just a gambler with a crown. He wanted a guarantee."

"Preposterous," the Chancellor spat. "Alaric is... was a man of honor. He cared too much for the Kingdom to gamble it away, and certainly too much to confide in the likes of you."

Pasin shrugged his shoulders.

Neelin took a deep breath, wincing, and pointed to the map. "King Alaric has been declared missing. The escape tunnel from the throne room was collapsed from the outside. No bodies. No sign of capture. He simply vanished, along with the enemy." A low rumble of panic moved through the merchant lords. Neelin silenced them with a single glare from his good eye. "However, there is some good news in all of this," Neelin said, his voice growing stronger. "Queen Brighid and her personal escort were evacuated successfully. They were seen riding hard due south, towards Tarsis."

"The Queen lives," Taillte whispered. "That gives us a rallying point."

"She is the heart of Alcia now," Neelin confirmed. He turned his full attention to Cedrik. "Knight Commander, I have a task that requires absolute trust. I can spare no legions. Select a small team. Ride South. Find Queen Brighid in Tarsis. Protect her with your life. If the enemy finds her, or if Xencid hears of our fall, she is dead."

Cedrik nodded, solemnly. "It will be done. I leave within the hour."

"Good." Neelin traced his finger across the map, from the Capital to the Southwest. Dunvar. "As for me, I cannot stay here. I need to take command of our main forces. I will ride for Dunvar at first light. If our border garrisons fall, Alcia is nothing but land waiting to be conquered."

"You are going to the Xencid border?" Pasin asked, stepping closer to the map. "With the militia shattered? Neelin, we may need to look beyond our own lands for help."

Neelin shook his head. "If you are speaking of Xencid, stop. If we show weakness now, they will invade."

"And Regat?" Pasin pressed.

"Imperator Valerius has been clear," Neelin growled. "He does not involve himself in the problems of others. He commands a kingdom, not a charity."

"This invasion may involve him whether he likes it or not," Pasin noted, dryly.

"And who are you to know of diplomacy, old man?" Chancellor Eamon added, with acerbic derision. "Your suggestions. It's like you want to leave us to the wolves around us. We must show strength."

Pasin didn't retreat. His fingers curled around the polished ironwood staff, tightening their grip until the old man's knuckles turned white.

The wood groaned under the pressure, a sound like a ship's hull under deep water. For a split second, Cedrik thought a vein of violet light pulse through the grain of the timber, illuminating the dust motes in the air. Only for a split second.

The smell of ozone filled the small space between them, sharp as a whetstone.

Eamon blinked, stepping back. The air around the scholar suddenly tasted of a thunderstorm. The Chancellor opened his mouth to speak, but the retort died in his throat as he stared at the long staff.

"Yeah," echoed one of the merchant lords. "The Guilds will lose everything if we bargain for their help. They'll take our—"

"There may be nothing left to lose," Cedrik cut him off. "If you want to negotiate, then find a horse. I'm sure their army will be easy to find."

The merchant stared at Cedrik and closed his mouth.

"We'll fight with what we have. I'll send a letter to both." Neelin straightened up, addressing Chancellor Eamon and Captain Taillte Cleirigh. "The rest of you have the hardest task. Hold this city. Bury the dead. Salvage every scrap of food. When you are ready, you will march south to join the main force." Neelin surveyed the room, his gaze burning with intensity. "Alcia is wounded," he said. "But she is not dead. Dismissed."

The room emptied slowly, like a wound bleeding out. Merchant lords shuffled away whispering, officers limped toward their posts, and Chancellor Eamon left in a huff of silk indignation. Pasin lingered only long enough to give Cedrik a knowing look, before slipping out with Taillte and Fromme.

Soon, only two men remained.

Cedrik stood at the table, staring at the map without seeing it. Neelin leaned heavily on the edge opposite him, breath shallow, his good eye half-lidded with exhaustion.

For a long moment, neither spoke.

"You should be lying down," Cedrik said, quietly.

Neelin huffed, a laugh that turned into a wince. "If I lie down, I may not get back up."

Cedrik's jaw tightened. He had seen Neelin wounded before—cuts, bruises, broken ribs—but never like this. Never burned. Never half-destroyed. The man had always seemed cast from iron. Now, he looked like iron left too long in the forge.

"You shouldn't be riding to Dunvar," Cedrik said. "Not like this."

Neelin lifted his head, meeting Cedrik's gaze. "If I don't go, the border collapses. And if the border collapses, the kingdom follows."

"You have other commanders."

"Brogan? The man navigates the courts better than he can our supply lines. I am sure he is already trying to surrender to the Xencid Commanders by now. Dunvar doesn't need negotiators or strategists. It needs to be led by a fighter."

Cedrik swallowed hard. The truth of it sat between them like an enormous rock.

Neelin shifted, his injured arm trembling in its sling. "You think I don't know what this will cost me? I can barely hold a sword. I can barely hold myself upright. But if I stay here, I die useless. Alcia falls. If I ride... maybe I buy Alcia another week. Maybe I can hold Dunvar again, give you the time you need to find the Queen."

Cedrik looked down at the map, at the ink-thin line marking the Xencid border. "You've already given everything."

Neelin's voice softened. "So have you."

Cedrik didn't answer. He couldn't. The weight of the greatsword on his back felt heavier than armor.

Neelin watched him for a moment, then spoke more gently. "We all have great responsibility thrust upon us. If you had been here, you would not have made a difference, Cedrik."

Cedrik's hands curled into fists. "I am not a courier. I am the Steel Guardian, Neelin. I should have been here, to fight. To die with my brothers protecting the Crown."

"You can't always be the one in the fight. You will have to make tough choices. Some will save people. Some will damn them."

Silence again. Heavy. Raw.

Neelin exhaled slowly. "Listen to me. You are the only man I trust to reach Brighid. Not because you follow orders. Because you know when not to."

Cedrik blinked, taken aback.

Neelin pushed off the table, swaying slightly. Cedrik moved to steady him, but the High Marshal waved him off. "Go south. Find her. Keep her alive. That is your duty. The rest... the rest we will carry together when you get to Dunvar."

Cedrik bowed his head. "Yes, Marshal." He looked up, startled, but Neelin was already turning away. His silhouette framed by the flickering lamplight; a broken man still trying to stand tall.

CHAPTER 8

CEDRIK APPROACHED THE ROYAL Guard's stables which they had passed on the way to the war room. Though the castle was surrounded by rubble and ruin, these stables had been spared the brunt of the devastation. The acrid scent of smoke still lay heavy in the air and clung to the leather tack that adorned the majestic steeds within the stables.

A smile appeared on Cedrik's face as he saw his old friend, Bastion. "Sir, I had your horses brought here directly when we learned that you were summoned," the guard explained.

Cedrik nodded his thanks to the guard, then turned his attention to the large, mahogany charger who had gone through so many years with him. The stallion let out a small welcome whinny and shuffled his hooves as Cedrik approached. Bastion nudged his velvet nose hard into Cedrik's shoulder, appearing relieved to be reunited with his master.

"Easy, old boy," assured Cedrik, as he checked the leather stirrups. "We are going on another long ride, save your strength."

"The boy, you're taking him," came a familiar voice from the entrance of the stables behind him.

Cedrik slowly shook his head, recognizing the calm voice. It was confident, unbothered by the chaos and destruction around them. He had heard this voice many times.

"Am I?" Cedrik did not turn toward the voice as he moved to inspect the saddle bags.

"There is nothing for him here, you know this," replied Pasin. Fromme stood behind the elder man, hovering anxiously like a nervous shadow. "You saw Fort Lanthreau, you have seen it here..."

"I am," finished Cedrik. "To be more precise, we are. You know I need you. And anyways, the lad can always carry the water skins."

Pasin let out a chuckle that was reflected in his glimmering green eyes. "A squire it is then, boy."

Fromme gulped hard. "I... I... will do my best, I... swe... swear it!"

Cedrik nodded his head, suppressing another smile from appearing on his face, as he turned to face the pair. "Lots to learn. Go to the quartermaster on the other side of the keep and tell them Cedrik Theramond's new squire needs travel gear."

The boy eagerly looked to Pasin, nervous energy spilling out of him. Pasin gave him an approving nod. Fromme leapt to action, almost running out of the stables.

"Pasin, when the Chancellor pushed you on diplomacy. Did you notice anything?"

"What do you mean?"

"I swear, it smelled like the air after a thunderstorm. Just briefly, a hint of it. I've never experienced it, inside."

"Nothing to worry about, boy. I'm sure you were just concentrating on the High Marshal, perhaps a bit too intently... I am proud of you, Cedrik. Showing a lot of compassion lately. You must have a wonderful mentor..." Pasin trailed off, making no attempt to hide a wide grin.

"You know how dangerous this is going to be, Pasin." Cedrik threw a woolen cloak over his saddle and gave Bastion a rub on the neck. "Being kind to this boy may kill him, are you prepared for that?"

"If I wasn't, would I have started training you all of those years ago?" The old man rubbed his chin as he stared at his friend. "So, is your plan to take an old man, a grieving boy, and a knight to Tarsis and save the Queen?"

"She will have her escort. The fewer we have, the easier it will be to stay hidden. My goal is to avoid attention, not raise it," replied the Knight.

"Care for a bit of advice?"

"No, I have had my fill from you already today," Cedrik murmured, as Bastion stomped a hoof on the hard dirt. "But, there is no sto—"

"Captain Cleirigh," Pasin interrupted flatly.

"You can't be serious?" Cedrik asked incredulously, as he turned to face Pasin. "Did you not see her welcome?"

Pasin's tone turned very low and serious. "She is the best field medic in the kingdom. She can fight. Well. And she has more bravery than most of the soldiers I have ever met. Her skills will be invaluable."

"You know," Cedrik started.

"She doesn't have to like you, or any of us for that matter. She is loyal to the Kingdom, to the Crown. She will perform her duty and try to keep us alive. I think that should be clear enough to you by now... She is who we need," Pasin finished, calm but stern.

Cedrik stood quietly for a moment, weighing the words and their implications. He gave Bastion another pat on the neck. "I'll go get her."

"This should be interesting," mused Pasin, as Cedrik strode past him out of the stables into the darkening courtyard.

***

Cedrik had to maneuver around debris and rubble, as he made his way to the eastern door of the castle. He was informed that the great hall had been converted to a temporary triage center, but the only path in was through the side entrances, since the steps to main doors of the castle were blocked off by the wreckage.

He was greeted with a flurry of activity when he opened the familiar set of heavy oaken doors. Attendants were scrambling across the large, polished stone hallway in all directions. He took a moment, inhaling deeply, and then carefully navigated to one of the side entrances to the great hall.

Upon walking into the makeshift infirmary, he could feel the heat, and smell the sickness, the unwashed bodies and medicinal herbs. Tables, chairs, cots, pallets, all available space was occupied by the injured or the medical staff attending to them. Groans, murmurs and labored breathing borne from pain were intermixed with urgent whispers and commands from medical staff making quick decisions. The stream of sound echoed off the tall, vaulted stone ceilings, creating an almost overwhelming sense of dread.

Cedrik could stare down a charging phalanx without blinking, but the sound of weeping men—men who would never hold a sword again—made his skin crawl inside his armor.

He spotted her near the center of the room.

Captain Taillte Cleirigh was kneeling beside a low cot. With her sleeves rolled back past her elbows, she was swiftly but methodically changing the bandages of an injured soldier with practiced, efficient movements. Blood had already crusted on her hands and wrists; she had wasted no time in getting back to work after hearing the terrible news of the King.

Cedrik slowly made his way over to her, but paused for a moment to allow her to finish her work. His anxiety continued to rise. He felt out of place as a beacon of violence, dressed in his heavy armor and carrying weaponry intended for battle, contrasting starkly to the healers adorned with signs of mercy in a house of healing.

Taillte tied off the final bandage. "There you go, fresh and clean." She smiled faintly at the young soldier's resting face, fast asleep. She wiped the sweat from her brow with the back of her hand as she rose to her feet, leaving a trail of grime across her forehead and cheeks. She started to turn towards her next patient, but stopped abruptly when she saw Cedrik looking at her. Her smile was immediately replaced with a cold expression of fury, harder than the stone upon which they stood.

"Knight Commander," she greeted him, flatly. "If you're expecting a salute, my hands are a bit dirty."

"I'm not here for formalities, Captain," Cedrik responded, a bit harsher than he had planned. He glanced down at who he assumed was her next patient.

"Then what do you want, Commander? As you can see, there is a lot to do, and I think we've had enough time to catch up for today. That is, unless you plan to offer 'mercy' for another of my patients?" Her words oozed with venom, bitter and sharp.

Cedrik tried to ignore the barb, but his jaw tightened. "The Queen needs help. I have orders to ride south to Tarsis. Secure her safety."

"Yes, I heard the High Marshal, Commander. For her sake, you had better leave quickly. I'm not quite sure..." she responded, trailing off as she started to turn away towards the next patient.

Cedrik stepped forward, locking into her piercing blue eyes. "I need a second-in-command. Someone who knows the terrain, someone who can fight, someone who can keep us all alive if things deteriorate. Pasin suggested you."

Taillte let out a sharp, incredulous laugh. "You can't be serious?"

"This mission is of the utmost importance, Captain. We must secure the safety of the Queen," Cedrik pressed.

"Oh, my... you are serious," she said slowly, taking a moment to think. "Pasin? You agreed? You really believe, after what happened at the gate...?" She gestured broadly around the room and continued. "Look around you, Cedrik. My place is here. These men need me."

"The rest of the Healer Corps can handle this without you, they must," Cedrik countered. "If we don't save the Queen, Alcia falls. These men will have nothing left to return to. It won't matter how many wounds you stitch or bandages you replace if the enemy succeeds and wipes us off the map. The Queen is the heart of the realm now, and if that heart stops, the body will die."

Taillte's chest heaved, as she took a deep breath and glared at Cedrik. She shifted her gaze down to the young man she had just treated. He was in a state of deep sleep, seemingly serene, but she knew that deep within his body he was fighting for his life. A life that had barely begun; he was probably barely older than Fromme.

"I hate you for asking me to do this," she finally whispered. The fight had left her voice, replaced with exhaustion.

"I know. But you are expected to do your duty," Cedrik said. "We... I need you to make a difference."

She closed her eyes, taking a long moment to collect herself. After a deep breath, she opened them, the exhaustion replaced with steel. Gone was the cold fury from before; she now emanated the determination and resolve of a soldier.

"I will need twenty minutes to hand over my patients to the senior chirurgeon," she said, wiping her hands upon a rag that hung from her belt. "And, I will need a horse."

"Meet us at the stables." Cedrik nodded once, formal and distant. "We leave within the hour."

He turned and walked away, feeling her eyes burning into the back of his armor until the heavy oak doors swung shut behind him.

***

The hour passed quickly, dissolving into a deep, moonless night.

By the time Cedrik had returned to the stables, the air had cooled and created a stark contrast with the heat of the infirmary. The chill felt good and soothed his sweat-covered skin. His anxiety immediately quietened, disappearing completely when he saw Bastion standing tall in the courtyard. The charger let out a welcoming nick when Cedrik approached, greeting his master.

Pasin and Fromme were flanking the mahogany stallion, waiting to depart. The boy was mounted on a docile roan mare, enveloped by a thick, hunter green traveler's cloak. His hands gripped the reins with white-knuckled intensity, eyes darting at the slightest movement. Pasin sat atop his black steed with a casual comfort, his staff strapped to the saddle.

The old man shifted in his saddle as Cedrik approached. "She is coming," he said softly, nodding towards the keep.

Cedrik turned to see Taillte approaching. She had scrubbed the blood and grime from her arms and face, though the exhaustion was evident from the shadows beneath her hollow eyes, so dark they appeared as bruises. Her dark red hair was tied into a tight bun, prepared for travel. The healer's tunic was gone. In its place, she wore a worn but meticulously maintained leather armor set of a Royal Guard Captain, dyed in the deep blue of Alcia. A short sword hung at her hip, and a longbow was slung across her back. She moved with a lethal grace that made it hard to reconcile her with the woman who had been weeping over a dying soldier barely more than an hour ago.

She briskly walked past Cedrik and mounted her horse—a spirited gray gelding—without a word. She nodded intently at Pasin and offered a tight but reassuring smile to a terrified Fromme.

Cedrik looked to each of his companions, nodding approvingly. "To the South Gate."

The small company rode through the eerily empty city streets. Normally bustling with nightlife, everything was dark except for the soft shafts of light escaping through various windows that were not fully shuttered. Doors were barred and the silence was only broken by the familiar beat of hooves upon pavement.

As they approached the massive southern portcullis, a solitary figure stepped out from the guardhouse.

Neelin Arran struck an otherworldly figure as the torchlight flickered around him. His bandages were stark white against the darkness, and he leaned heavily on a spear he was using as a crutch. As the riders approached, he stood tall, trying to conceal the significant toll it placed upon him to do so.

Cedrik pulled Bastion to a halt. For a moment, neither man spoke. There was no need. They had served together for decades; they each knew what was being asked of one other.

"The main highways towards the border will be dangerous. It is the most likely path," Neelin rasped, struggling to be heard over the wind. "Once you get past the valley, split off southeast, then it should be fine." Another moment passed. "And Cedrik?"

"Marshal?"

"Do not let the heart stop beating." Neelin handed the knight a small pouch.

Leather groaned as Cedrik tightened the grip on his reins. "I will find her, Neelin. I swear it." He placed the pouch in his saddlebag, deliberate and careful.

"And... I will hold the line at Dunvar," Neelin replied, with a nod. He looked at Taillte, offering her an almost warm smile, which she returned with a crisp salute. He stiffened and gave Pasin a sharp salute. Finally, his gaze landed on Fromme. "Be brave, lad. Alcia needs brave men now."

The boy gulped hard, as Neelin stepped back and signaled the gatekeeper. "Open the gate!"

Heavy chains rattled, and the grating of metal against stone rang out in a heavy industrial groan that echoed through the night, as the steel portcullis rose slowly. There was no protection, no structure standing between them and the vast, empty darkness of the plains beyond. The wind howled through the opening, as if it had been waiting for an opportunity to burst through.

"Ride," Cedrik commanded.

He spurred Bastion forward. One by one, they passed under the stone archway and out into the night. It smelled of damp earth and coming rain, a downpour to cleanse the countryside anew.

Behind them, the gate slammed shut with a final, resonant boom.

CHAPTER 9

THE SUN ROSE INTO a beautiful orange sky, casting long, pale shadows over the meadows. Normally a sight to behold in reverence, the beauty of a new day felt shallow next to the echoes of a broken kingdom.

They had ridden through the night, putting miles between themselves and the capital. As dawn approached, Cedrik led the small company off the main highway and onto the less travelled path. The silence of the countryside was heavy, broken only by the rhythmic thud of hooves and the creak of leather.

Cedrik rode at the front, his eyes scanning the horizon. He removed his helm, wiping sweat from his shaved head with a rough gauntlet. The landscape here was untouched by the strange, surgical destruction they had seen at the capital and Fort Lanthreau. The fields were green, and the farmhouses intact. It further confirmed the chilling reports; the invaders had ignored everything that was not a military threat. They had marched through these lands like ghosts, focused only on dismantling the heart of the realm.

But where the lions had passed, vultures were now beginning to circle.

"We should rest the horses." Taillte's voice cut through the silence. It was the first time she had spoken to Cedrik since he had left the infirmary. She didn't look at him, keeping her gaze fixed on Fromme, who was swaying dangerously in the saddle, his face gray with fatigue.

Cedrik glanced at the sun. They had veered off the Kingsroad hours ago and the boy looked ready to fall from his horse.

"There is a ridge about a mile ahead. We'll water the horses in the stream and rest for an hour. No fires."

Taillte gave a stiff, perfunctory nod.

Pasin rode up beside Cedrik as they slowed their pace. "She hates you, you know."

"She has that right," Cedrik replied, shifting the weight of his massive greatsword strapped on his back. The leather bindings creaked under the familiar strain.

"Perhaps. Hate can be useful fuel. It can keep you warm when the nights are cold, but it can also burn so hot that everything around it is engulfed." Pasin took a sip from his waterskin, his eyes sharp and birdlike. "This quiet, this close to the capital... It is not normal. The wolves know the shepherd is gone."

As if in answer to the old man's words, a plume of black smoke rose into the sky just over the ridge line. It was thick, dark, oily smoke; not the clean burning of a hearth, but the uncontrolled blaze of a building on fire.

Cedrik signaled for a halt, raising a fist. "That is not the invaders. Too messy."

"Bandits," Taillte hissed, her hand instinctively going to the longbow slung across her back. "Taking advantage, feeding on the weak."

"We go around," Cedrik stated. "Our mission is the Queen."

Taillte wheeled her horse around to face him, the blue of her captain's armor flashing in brightening sunlight. "The Queen is safe in Tarsis with her escort. These people are here, *now*! We are guardians of the people, first and foremost."

"We are four riders on tired horses," Cedrik countered, his voice stern. "If we engage, if one of us falls, our mission will fail before it even begins. She could be defenseless. If she falls, the whole Kingdom falls."

"Then go," she snapped, her eyes blazing with blue fire. "I'll catch up."

Before Cedrik could respond with an order, the wind shifted, carrying the sound of a scream over the ridge. It was high and terrified. A child.

Fromme's head snapped up, his exhaustion melted away. He looked at Cedrik with wide, anxious eyes.

"We have to help them," Fromme pleaded, his voice small but steady.

Cedrik pulled in a deliberate breath, the air hissing through his teeth. "Fromme, listen to me. You are a squire now. Our duty is first to the Crown. The first rule is that the mission comes before the man. We cannot save everyone, no matter how much—"

"You saved me," Fromme interrupted.

Cedrik subtly reared back in his saddle, the words striking him like a physical blow. The boy pushed his advantage, pointing a shaking finger toward the smoke.

"At Fort Lanthreau... everyone... just walked past me. They left me to dig. My hands bled because... because they were afraid... or because they did not care. You were the only one who stopped." Fromme's eyes welled with tears, but he maintained Cedrik's gaze. "If we ride past them...," Fromme scrubbed at the wetness on his face, but the stream continued, "we are just like the people who watched my parents die, watched me lose everything..."

Silence stretched into the wind, heavier than even the greatsword on Cedrik's back.

Cedrik looked at Taillte. The fire in her eyes had shifted to penetrating curiosity. She watched him intently but did not speak. She had abdicated this decision to him, testing to see what kind of man he truly was outside of the safety of duty and structure. Her horse whinnied in anticipation as she pulled her reins, ready to act.

Then, he looked to Pasin. The old man, normally always willing to chime in on a discussion, was uncharacteristically quiet. He sat casually upon his steed, offering no advice, albeit a slight expectant raising of his weathered, white eyebrows.

Damn it all.

Cedrik closed his eyes for a split second, then tightened his grip on Bastion's reins.

"We hit them hard and fast," he ordered, his voice dropping into the command tone that welcomed no further discourse. "Taillte, take the ridge and provide cover fire. Pasin, keep the boy back and watch our flank."

Relief, instantly followed by terror rushed over Fromme's face, as the reality of the situation set in. Taillte nodded, a grim satisfaction and determination settling on her features.

"And you?" she asked, as the company turned towards the ridge.

Cedrik reached over his shoulder and gripped the white leather handle of his trusted sword.

A weight crushed down on his chest. *The mission could wait, just this once. But not for long. The Queen could not be left defenseless for long.*

"I'm going to remind the wolves what happens when the shepherd returns."

He kicked Bastion into a full gallop, the thunderous sound of hooves from a born-and-bred battle charger igniting the air as they crested the ridge.

Below, the farmstead was a portrait of chaos against the backdrop of a picturesque green meadow. A barn was fully engulfed in red and orange flames, spitting glimmering sparks and coughing thick smoke into the air.

A dozen men in mismatched furs and leathers—common brigands—were terrorizing a family in the yard. Two men were holding a farmer down while a third kicked him; another group was dragging a farmer toward the burning barn.

Cedrik let out a deep guttural roar that froze the bandits in their tracks. His greatsword was drawn in one fluid, practiced motion. Nearly two meters in length, this forged blade could have been made for killing giants. It caught the morning sun like a signal fire. A glinting beacon of raw power.

"Royal Guard!" Cedrik bellowed, wheeling Bastion around as he charged down the slope like an avalanche of steel and fury. "Throw down your arms or die!"

The bandits froze, their eyes widening, as the massive warhorse thundered toward them. For just a single heartbeat, survival instinct warred with greed.

"There is only one! Kill the horse!" the bandit leader screamed, raising a jagged spear.

It was the last order he ever gave.

A black-fletched arrow hissed through the air, striking the leader in the throat with a wet thud. He crumpled backward, gurgling, as his spear clattered to the dirt.

She did not miss.

The sudden death stunned the bandits. Their formation broke, but it was too late to run. Cedrik was upon them.

He didn't slow down. He didn't flourish his blade. He simply rode through them.

Bastion slammed into two of the men with the force of a battering ram, the sound of cracking bone and screams of pain sickeningly loud in the crisp morning air. Cedrik swung the greatsword, a single powerful backhand blow enhanced by the horse's momentum. The blade easily sheared through the leather armor of a bandit attempting to flank him, cleaving the man from shoulder to sternum.

Blood sprayed across the dry earth, like threads permeating through a tapestry.

"Flank him! Get behind him!" shrieked another bandit, scrambling over a fence. An arrow struck him in the thigh on his descent, pinning him to the wood. His hands immediately pulled at the arrow, as he cried out in pain.

Cedrik hauled on the reins, spinning Bastion in a tight circle to face the next wave. The horse's hooves kicked up clouds of dust and ash, blowing loudly with flared nostrils. Three men rushed him at once, too terrified to think.

Cedrik dropped the reins, guiding the charger with his knees. The white leather handle creaked as both hands now tightened on it. He parried a clumsy axe swing with the flat of his immense blade, the impact ringing like a church bell. As the axe retreated from the impact, Cedrik thrust the tip of his sword through the attacker's chest.

The man fell limp on the blade. Cedrik ripped his sword free and swung it in a horizontal arc. The other two aggressors dove to the dirt rather than lose their heads.

"Yield, now!" Cedrik roared, his voice booming over the screeching injured bandits and crackling barn behind them. "I will not ask again!"

The remaining bandits looked at the scene around them. Their leader, his eyes blank, an arrow still quivered in his throat. The towering knight upon his mighty steed, wielding an implausibly large sword streaked with the blood of their fallen comrades. Half of their numbers had been taken down in seconds.

Finally, they looked atop the ridge, from where an unseen archer had launched arrows with expert accuracy. From this distance, only a silhouette was visible, outlined in a faint tint of blue.

They dropped their weapons. Metal clattered onto the hard, compacted dirt.

Cedrik held his position, his chest heaving with exertion. The tip of his greatsword hovered inches from a bandit's face. "On the ground. Hands behind your heads."

As the dust settled, the silence returned, heavier than before.

From the ridge, Pasin and Fromme rode down slowly, leading Taillte's horse. She stayed mounted, arrow nocked, eyes scanning the horizon for stragglers.

Cedrik dismounted, his heavy boots crunching loudly in the dirt. He held his sword at the ready and walked over to the farmer. The man was huddled on the ground, shielding his wife, the other farmer, and his daughter.

The farmer looked up. His face was streaked with soot, tears and blood from his nose. He slumped forward, grabbing Cedrik's armored gauntlet with both hands, and pressed his forehead against the cold metal.

"Royal Guards...," the farmer sobbed, his voice cracking. "We thought... we thought you were gone. We heard the Capital had fallen... alone..." His words slowly became incoherent, overtaken by shock and relief.

A familiar weight settled in Cedrik's chest. Not of his armor, but the crushing burden of expectation.

"The Capital stands," Cedrik said, his voice softening. A small metallic clang rang out as he sheathed his sword. He reached down and gripped the farmer's shoulder, pulling him to his feet. "And you are not alone. The King still watches over us all."

The farmer's wife rushed forward, clutching her daughter. She fell to her knees before Fromme and Pasin, mistaking the squire for a young lord.

"Bless you," she cried, reaching up to touch the hem of Fromme's cloak. "Bless the King! We knew it... we would not be abandoned to these wolves."

Fromme looked terrified by the gratitude, never before being on this end of the exchange. He glanced at Cedrik, unsure what to do.

"Stand," Cedrik told the family gently. "Taillte, check their wounds. Fromme, tie these men to that fence."

Pasin steered his horse beside Cedrik, taking in the scene. No longer a playful observer, his face was covered by a strange, melancholic expression.

"They love him," Pasin murmured, watching the farmer weep with relief. "Even when their sky is falling, only saved by pure circumstance, they still look upon the throne as if it were the sun itself."

"That is why we fight," Cedrik replied, watching Taillte bandage the little girl's arm. "Because they cannot."

"It is a heavy thing, to be loved so blindly," said Pasin, quietly. "It gives a King, anyone, terrible power. I truly hope he is worthy."

Cedrik looked at the old man sharply. "King Alaric has held this realm together for forty years. He is the father of Alcia."

"Fathers are not the only members that can hold a family together, Cedrik," Pasin said, cryptically. He turned his horse away before the knight could respond.

Cedrik stared at the old man's back, irritated, but pushed the thought away. He turned to Fromme and the bandits tied to the fence.

"The magistrate in Oakhaven is a loyal man," Cedrik told the farmer. "Tell him these men must be brought to justice. Tell him the Royal Guard passed this way, that we go to secure the King's peace."

"Cedrik, no," Taillte cut in. "We can't leave this problem here with the family."

What is she doing?

She turned to the farmer. "We will take them to Oakhaven. If you need anything, we will let the magistrate know what happened. He will help you."

"We will, my Lords," the farmer said, standing straighter now. His fear replaced by renewed purpose. "Long live King Alaric! Long Live Alcia!"

Cedrik looked to the Captain, an immovable force. She had already motioned for Fromme to prepare the bandits to move and Pasin was anchoring the rear of the formation to take guard of their new responsibilities.

Cedrik growled, frustrated that this detour would delay the mission. But when he looked at the smiling faces of the family they had just saved, he realized the truth of it. The politics, vanishing armies, magic--it all complicated the simple reality. The people believed in the Kingdom and the Crown. Cedrik would die before he let that belief be broken. He was the shield that protected the Realm.

"We ride," Cedrik ordered as he vaulted back onto Bastion.

As they galloped away, leaving the farmhouse behind, Cedrik glanced back at the black smoke rising from the barn.

The smell of it—woodsmoke and burning hay—clogged his throat. It tasted familiar.

Suddenly, the green fields of the present blurred into gray mud.

He was standing in the mud of the central Highlands after a harsh rain. He was eighteen. The air smelled of wet thatch and victory.

Cedrik wiped his sword on the grass, his chest heaving. Around him, the hamlet of Doire Beag was safe. The bodies of twenty bandits lay scattered in the dirt—vicious men who had been torching the cottages when Cedrik and his squad rode in.

"Thank you," a woman wept, clutching Cedrik's greave. She held a small child against her chest, both of them covered in soot and mud, but alive. "The Gods sent you. The Gods sent you."

Cedrik felt a swell of pride in his chest that had nothing to do with war. This was why he had joined. To be the shield. To stand between the wolves and the flock.

"Get them water," Cedrik ordered his men. He felt tall. He felt righteous.

The sound of hoofbeats thundered down the main road, a cloud of muck kicked up around them.

Cedrik turned, expecting reinforcements. It was Captain Lachlan. The old officer rode into the village square, his horse lathered in foam and smelling musky. His face was a mask of purple rage.

Cedrik stepped forward, sheathing his sword. He smiled. "Report, Captain. Bandits neutralized. The village is secure. Casualties are—"

Crack.

The riding crop struck Cedrik across the face before he saw it moving. The force of it knocked him to one knee, splitting his lip.

The woman and child scrambled away in terror.

"You fool," Lachlan spat, his voice trembling with fury. "You arrogant, insubordinate fool. I knew it was a mistake to let you lead this mission."

Cedrik touched his lip, confused. "Sir? They were slaughtering them. We heard screams. We had to—"

"Your orders," Lachlan hissed, leaning down from his saddle, "were to escort the grain wagons to Fort Darrow. Where are the wagons, Sergeant?"

"I left Corporal Hines with them. It was only a small detour. I thought—"

"You thought?" Lachlan pointed back toward the road. A thick plume of black smoke was rising into the gray sky.

Shivers ran through him. Cedrik's chest squeezed, like a vice.

"Hines is dead." The words landed like stones. "The bandits you fought here? They were the distraction. While you were playing hero in the mud, their main force circled back. They took what they wanted, then burned the wagons, Cedrik. All of them."

Cedrik could not stop staring at the smoke. Then he looked at the woman he had just saved. She was alive. Her child was alive.

"I... I saved these people, Captain," Cedrik whispered. He had to make it balance, make sense. "There are thirty lives here... I saved them."

"Thirty lives," Lachlan mocked. "Do you know the numbers of war, boy? Or did you skip that during your training?"

The Captain gestured to the smoke.

"That grain was for the winter garrison at the Northern Pass. Without it, the rations are cut in half. Two hundred men will starve before the snow melts. Two. Hundred."

Lachlan pulled his horse around, looking down at Cedrik with disgust.

"You didn't save anyone, Sergeant. You just traded two hundred soldiers for thirty peasants who won't live through the winter. Just because the screams were close enough to hurt your ears."

Lachlan spat on the ground next to Cedrik's boot.

"Strip your rank. You're a man-at-arms again. And if I ever catch you trying to be a hero instead of a soldier, I'll kill you myself."

The Captain rode off toward the burning wagons.

Cedrik remained on his knees in the mud. The woman he had saved was still watching him, but he couldn't look at her. He looked at the smoke rising in the distance, from the wagons.

The image faded, the green hills of the present filling his view.

Cedrik gripped the reins until his knuckles popped. The farmer's family was safe behind them. Fromme was smiling, proud of what they had done. Taillte looked at him with respect.

But the math rattled in Cedrik's head like a loose coin. His hand came to his face. He licked his lips. He could taste fresh blood.

The Queen is the mission, he reminded himself, spurring Bastion faster. *We were lucky today. But luck runs out. And next time, the cost will be higher.*

CHAPTER 10

THE BANDITS WERE A pathetic sight, bound in a line by Fromme's practice rope. They stumbled along the dirt path, the soot from the burning barn turning their sweat into thick, black streaks across their faces.

Cedrik rode at the front of the column, Bastion's heavy gait setting a grueling pace. His greatsword sheathed but his presence casting a long, intimidating shadow over the prisoners.

"We should have left them," he stated, his voice grinding like two stones rubbed together. "We've wasted enough time playing judge. The Queen is moving, and we are standing still."

"If we left them, they would have been back at that family's throat before we reached the tree line," Taillte countered. She rode gracefully despite the exertion, wiping a smear of blood from her bowstring with a scrap of silk. "In the Highlands, if a wolf is caught in the fold, you don't just kick it. You bring it to the Túath—the community. You make the crime a matter of the stone."

"The Túath is a myth, Taillte," Cedrik snapped, staring straight ahead. "A fireside story. Invaders have turned the heart of the realm into an ash heap. You think a village magistrate cares about three sheep-stealers when the King has vanished?"

Pasin, riding near the rear of the column, chimed in. "Oakhaven is but three miles west, Cedrik. It sits on the main trade vein. If the outer towns see the Royal Guard delivering justice, the 'Shared Breath' will give hope. Right now, our people are frightened. They think the world has ended. Let's show them we are still here."

Cedrik looked back at Fromme. The young squire was staring at the bandits with a mixture of revulsion and a strange, desperate hope. The boy wanted to believe in the system Cedrik represented.

"Fine," Cedrik spat, a bitter taste rising in his throat. "We take them to Oakhaven. But if a single horse goes lame because of this detour, I'm executing them where they stand and leaving the bodies for the crows."

The ride to Oakhaven forced Cedrik to witness a side of Alcia that he had almost forgotten. As they moved deeper into the rolling hills of the Highlands, memories of simpler times flooded his mind. The squared, imposing limestone of the Capital gave way to *Raths,* circular settlements protected by high earthen ramparts and sharpened timber palisades.

They passed ancient "Standing Stones" draped in faded blue ribbons, markers of ancient boundaries and family pacts that predated King Alaric by centuries. But the atmosphere was heavy. They rode past a *Biolan,* traditional houses of hospitality meant to help weary travelers, but no fire burned in its hearth. The door was cracked open, revealing a family huddled inside in the dark, watching the riders pass with wide, frightened eyes..

"They're reverting," Taillte whispered as the wooden gates of Oakhaven came into view. "When the center doesn't hold, the Túath pulls inward. They're preparing for the end."

Oakhaven was a modest town of river stone and thick oak beams. As Cedrik's company approached the gates, men standing on thatched roofs instinctively raised rusted spears and hunting bows.

Then, one of the archers squinted against the fading sun. He saw the massive warhorse, the white leather of the greatsword, and the blood-stained royal crest on Cedrik's surcoat.

"The Guard!" the man shouted, his voice cracking. "Lower your weapons! It's the King's Guard!"

The tension broke like a fever. The heavy wooden gates were hauled open. As Cedrik rode into the town square, the silence of the countryside was replaced by a desperate, palpable relief. Women rushed out from doorways. An old man with a limp hurried forward to offer Bastion a wooden bucket of clean well-water before Cedrik could even ask.

They reached the center of town. A man emerged from a communal storehouse, dusting flour from his heavy wool mantle. A polished silver brooch—the mark of a *Flaith,* a local lord, gleamed on his chest. He was portly but weathered, his reddish blonde hair turning white at the temples. His face was lined with the exhaustion of a man trying to hold his world together with bare hands.

"Commander," the Magistrate breathed. He didn't bow; instead, he stepped forward and offered his forearm in the traditional Highland greeting. Cedrik gripped it. The man's grip was surprisingly strong. "By the Gods. We heard the Capital had fallen. We thought we were abandoned."

"The Capital stands," Cedrik lied, the words feeling like acid. He jerked the rope, pulling the weary bandits forward. "These men were found violating the King's peace at a local farm. They are for your cells, Magistrate. Under the Law of Restitution."

The Magistrate looked at the bandits. There was no malice in his eyes, only a profound sadness.

"The grain tax collectors haven't come in weeks, Commander, and the judges have fled," the Magistrate said softly. He motioned for two brawny men in leather vests to take the ropes. "But the law of the stone holds in Oakhaven. We will lock them in the root cellar. They'll get half-rations, same as the rest of us, until a proper trial can be held."

He turned back to Cedrik, his eyes sweeping over the battered, bloodied state of the four riders.

"My hearth is yours," the Magistrate offered, gesturing toward his longhouse. The smell of peat and a rich, savory stew drifted from the open door. "My wife has food on the fire. We have little to spare, but the Royal Guard will never go hungry in Oakhaven. Please. Rest your horses. Let us tend to your armor."

Fromme looked at the longhouse, his mouth watering, his shoulders slumping at the prospect of a warm fire.

Cedrik felt his chest tighten. The hospitality was genuine. These people were terrified and starving, yet they were offering him their own meager survival rations simply because of the crest on his chest.

"Your hospitality honors the Crown, Magistrate," Cedrik replied stiffly, forcing himself to sit perfectly straight in the saddle. "But our mission is the Crown's business. We cannot linger."

The Magistrate's face fell, but he nodded understandingly. He stepped closer to Bastion, rubbing the horse's neck, lowering his voice so the gathering townsfolk couldn't hear the fear underneath his words.

"Commander," the Magistrate whispered, the smell of peat and sweat clinging to him. "We heard the dark army drank the blood of the Guard. We heard... we heard the king was dead. Tell me... it's a lie."

"The King lives," Cedrik said, trying to believe his own words.

The Magistrate closed his eyes, letting out a breath that seemed to carry ten years of stress with it. He reached up and touched Cedrik's armored knee.

"Tell the King," the Magistrate said, his voice firm with loyalty, "that the outer towns are holding the line. The grain is short, and the stone is getting cold, but Oakhaven has not forgotten the First Song. Tell him to come back to us."

As they rode out of Oakhaven, the sun was lower, casting the town into a bruised purple twilight. A young woman ran up alongside Fromme's horse, pressing a small bundle of wrapped, barmbrack into the squire's hands before fading back into the crowd.

Cedrik stared straight ahead, the chatter of the townsfolk echoing at their backs. The "Shared Breath" Taillte spoke of felt less like a myth today. It felt like a chain pulling at his throat.

"You see it now, don't you?" Pasin asked softly as they cleared the town ramparts.

The Queen.

Cedrik didn't answer. He looked down at the scars on his gauntlets. He had saved a farm, and he had delivered three bandits to a loyal, desperate Magistrate. In the cold arithmetic of war, it was a negligible sum. As they galloped toward the darkening horizon, the weight of it all sunk into his chest.

The mission is the Queen. The mission is all that matters.

CHAPTER 11

THE ACHE IN CEDRIK's back throbbed, as Bastion continued the familiar travelling gait. They had ridden for countless hours without stopping after Oakhaven. The pace was fast, the relentless push trying to make up for time lost.

The Knight Commander scanned the horizon. They had been on the move too long. The sun dipped below the skyline, bleeding the last of the day's warmth into the west. The rich greenery in the meadows, so common during this time of year, began to cast long shadows as dusk quickly approached.

"Over there," Cedrik signaled at a dense thicket of oaks bordering a rocky stream. "We camp there. Cold camp, no fires."

The small company dismounted and led their horses to the clearing. The steeds blew out hard, their coats stiff with dried sweat. Fromme slid from his saddle, almost abruptly. He could barely maintain his footing; his legs were rubbery. He caught himself with the stirrup leather, his face was pale and waxy in the last rays of sunlight.

The boy didn't speak, he just walked stiffly toward the stream. He fell to his knees at the water's edge and plunged his hands into the babbling creek. No sound was made as he scrubbed his now red hands against the river stones, unable to control the shivering.

Cedrik watched from afar, pausing his own preparations for a moment.

The bandits. Death...

He took a step forward, but Pasin cleared his throat softly. The old man leaned against a tree, taking in the setting. The pair locked eyes. Pasin shook his head slightly, his gaze shifting to the Royal Guard Captain.

Let her handle it...

Cedrik's jaw tightened and his face was overcome with a passing wave of heat. He turned back to Bastion and began the familiar ritual of untacking the warhorse.

Taillte walked over to the stream. She watched the squire scrub the invisible blood from his skin. She did not crouch, just watched intently.

"Your hands, they're clean Fromme," she said, quietly.

Fromme froze. He stared at his hands beneath the water, pain pulsing through him. They were raw, blistered. He was not used to such endless physical exertion, digging, holding reins for days, and now the harsh scrubbing.

"Dad... he told me about this," Fromme whispered, his voice trembling. "The songs, the stories, everyone makes it sound so glorious. The knights charge. The wicked fall. Victory..." He looked up at her, eyes wide and haunted. "It was just... butchery, slaughter. And that man, the one you shot. He... he... he died slowly, painfully."

Taillte unslung her waterskin and knelt beside him. "Bards wrote those songs. Bards who have never held a sword. And they are sung in warm halls by drunk people with full bellies." She reached out. "Give me your hands."

Fromme hesitated, then offered his palms. Red and cold, a mess of weeping blisters and torn skin.

Taillte didn't reach to her pack for a bandage. She peeled off her left glove. Her hand appeared delicate and pale, her fingers long and slender. She placed her bare palm against his raw skin. Warm to the touch, hard yet smooth.

"This will sting," she murmured.

"What will—"

Fromme took in a sharp breath, as his back arched violently. A sudden, feverish heat surged from her hand into his. It wasn't the gentle warmth of a hearth; it was the aggressive, throbbing heat of a fever spiking.

From the trees, Cedrik paused, hands resting on his saddle. He watched Taillte's face. Her eyes rolled back, the blue irises dulling to a stormy gray. The veins in her neck bulged, abnormally dark against her pale skin, as if she were straining under immense weight.

Under her grip, the weeping blisters and angry flesh began to seethe. The skin knitted itself together, stitching over the raw flesh with unnatural speed. The wounds were gone within seconds, replaced by fresh, pink skin.

Taillte pulled her hand away abruptly as if burned. She slumped back against a rock, sweat beading on her forehead. Her breath came in shallow, ragged gasps.

The boy stared at his hands, then at her. His brown eyes sparkled, shifting from terror to awe. "What... you healed me... was that magic?"

"Don't get used to it." Taillte wheezed. She dug a strip of dried venison from her pouch and tore into it with shaking hands, chewing methodically. "My Gift has a cost."

"But... why?" Fromme asked, softly. "You look... it hurt you."

"Broken hands can't hold reins, can't make camp," she said flatly, between chews. She swallowed hard, trying to force color back into her cheeks. "And I'm not carrying you to Tarsis."

"Thank you...," stammered the boy.

She stood up, brushing the dirt from her knees. The moment of vulnerability was over, now locked behind an unseen suit of armor. "Drink water, eat something. Don't forget to check your horse's hooves. If she throws a shoe because you were too busy staring at your hands, you'll be walking."

Fromme eagerly nodded, the awe still controlling his features. "Yes, Captain." He said, respect holding fast in his gaze.

The squire scrambled off to his mare, leaving Taillte alone by the water's edge. She remained there for a long moment, breathing deeply, one hand bracing against a large rock for support. She looked down to her bare hand, flexing it to regain feeling. She glanced back over at the young squire, then looked back to the stream and wiped her cheek quickly. She slid the leather riding glove back onto her hand and then rejoined the others.

Cedrik watched Taillte as she emerged from the shadows of the creek bed. She didn't walk so much as scuffle, her movements stiff and careful. She leaned back against a moss-covered oak, thudding her head against the bark with a hollow sound that made Cedrik's own neck ache.

He noticed the way she flexed her hand; the one she'd used on the boy. It was still shaking noticeably, even though she tried to mask the tremor.

"You think it's just about walls and formations, don't you, Commander?" Taillte said. Her voice was thin, stripped of its usual acidic bite.

Cedrik adjusted his position as he continued to groom Bastion for the night. "The walls are what keep the people inside safe, Taillte. Without the stone, there is no Alcia."

"No," she countered, her blue eyes tracking a moth fluttering near the stream. "The walls are just the shell. My grandmother used to say Alcia wasn't built by masons, but by *Chead-Amhran*, the First Song. She believed the limestone of these hills remembers the rhythm of every person who ever walked them. That's why the stone stays warm in the summer, Cedrik. It isn't just the sun. It's the memory of us, our people."

Pasin stopped his whittling, the small knife hovering over a piece of driftwood. He looked at her with a quiet, sharp intensity that Cedrik rarely saw in the old man.

"The First Song," Pasin repeated. "I haven't heard a Highlander mention the Song in twenty years."

"Because songs don't stop arrows," Cedrik grunted, though he found himself looking down at the ground beneath his boots.

"It wasn't about conquest," Taillte continued, ignoring him. Her eyes were closed now, her face a pale mask in the dimming light of dusk. "It was the 'Shared Breath.' The idea that every Alcian—from the High Marshal to the smallest weaver—is part of one, single, slow heartbeat. When one of us is cut, we all bleed. When the enemy takes a village, they aren't just killing people; they're stealing a verse from the song. They're making the world quieter." She opened her eyes, pinning Cedrik with a gaze that felt heavier than his armor. "I didn't heal that boy because he's your squire," she said. "I healed him because if he loses his hands, Alcia loses a piece of its future. We aren't just protecting a lineage, Cedrik. Kings are just men. We're protecting the only place in the world where the stone still has a heartbeat."

Cedrik remained silent, the rushing of the stream filling the gap between them. He thought of the farmer at the ridge, weeping into his gauntlet. He'd thought the man was crying for his life. Now, hearing Taillte, he wondered if the man had been crying because the song of his home had almost been cut short.

"The stone has a heartbeat," Cedrik finally repeated, his voice low. He looked at the massive white leather handle of his sword. "The Shepherd and the Flock. It's a fine sentiment, Taillte. But a heartbeat can be stopped by an inch of steel."

"And a song can't be killed by a blade," she snapped back, though the effort made her wince and pull her cloak tighter. "That's why you're so afraid, Cedrik. You're afraid that when you finally find the Queen, you'll realize the song has already ended, and you'll just be the guardian of a very expensive tomb."

The camp settled quickly as darkness overtook the landscape. There was no fire to gather around, no warmth to chase away the chill. Only, the dry snap of hardtack and the heavy silence of exhaustion pulling at consciousness.

By the time the moon rose, the camp was quiet.

Fromme was already asleep, curled up near the tree roots. His breathing was shallow and rhythmic. Fatigue had claimed him the moment his rations were finished.

"The Magistrate at Oakhaven will send word to the Capital," Pasin said, breaking the silence. His voice was soft, barely a whisper, but it cut through the noise of the stream. He idly cut at a small piece of wood, the sound of whittling a constant. "He will report that the Royal Guard saved a farm. Fought against great odds. Probably fifty to one by the time it gets back to him."

"It will remind them we are still here," Cedrik said, staring into the dark where a fire should have been. "That the Crown still exists."

"Will it?" Pasin countered gently, peeling a long strip of bark free. "Or will it tell every bandit, warlord and petty noble between here and the coast that the Crown is now making ballads about simple guard duties?"

Cedrik looked at the old man. He caught Pasin's eyes in a glint of moonlight, sharp and unblinking. "What are you saying, Pasin?"

"I am saying that a pack of wolves will only fear the idea of the shepherd for so long. At some point they need to actually watch the flock," Pasin murmured. "If word spreads that the Inner militia, the Royal Guards, have been cut down—that they have to fight impossible odds in the countryside—what we saw today will happen all across Alcia unchecked."

"You are making too much of this," Cedrik replied. "The report will be like any other report from a magistrate."

"You underestimate what people see, Cedrik. The town guardhouses have been emptied. The patrols have stopped. The militia is decimated. The Guilds will realize that their protection is gone. They will hoard grain. The lesser lords will realize that for the first time in forty years, no one is watching them."

"Neelin is alive," Cedrik said, though the defense sounded hollow. "The garrison remains."

"Neelin is one man," Taillte interjected. Her voice was thin and tired. She was leaning back against her saddle, eyes closed, conserving every ounce of energy she had spent on the boy. "And the garrison is terrified. You saw the Castle. The Capital. If people believe the King cannot protect them, if they can't even see the King... They will find someone else who can. Or they will turn on each other."

Cedrik shifted uncomfortably, armor digging into his ribs. He knew they were right. He had felt it at the farm, the desperation of the farmer. The man hadn't just been afraid of the bandits; he had been afraid of the silence from the throne.

"Our mission is the Queen," Cedrik stated. The words came out rigid, rehearsed. "If the lineage is secured, the Kingdom endures. We cannot fight chaos across the country. We must provide the people with a symbol of Alcia's endurance. This was Neelin's strategy."

Pasin made one final cut to the short stick he was shaping. He gently placed his carving down onto the soft grass. "The Queen, yes. I do agree, she is the best chance, for all of us. I just hope you can convince her of that as well," Pasin noted.

"We will," Cedrik said.

"You sound like you are trying to convince yourself."

"I am commanding you to sleep," Cedrik snapped, lying back and pulling his cloak around him to use as a blanket.

Pasin chuckled softly to himself. "As you wish. Sleep is a command I am always happy to obey, though it rarely obeys me."

"I'll take first watch," Taillte said.

Cedrik lay still for a long time, listening to the sounds of the camp intermingling with nature. Fromme's breathing was heavy and even. Pasin's was a soft, rattling wheeze; the sound of lungs that had inhaled too much library dust and not enough fresh air.

But there was a third sound; a faint, repetitive *scratch-scratch-scratch,* coming from the base of the oak tree.

Cedrik sat up slowly, shedding his cloak. He moved silently to the edge of the clearing.

Taillte was looking into the darkness, her back to the tree. One hand continued to shake, resting on her knee. In the other, she held a small whetstone, running it along the edge of her dagger.

Scratch. Scratch. Scratch.

She didn't look up as he approached. "You walk loudly for a soldier, Commander."

"And you sharpen loudly for a healer," Cedrik replied, keeping his voice low.

He sat down on a mossy rock a few feet away. He looked at her left hand, the one she had used to knit Fromme's flesh. It was trembling, the fingers curled into a rigid claw.

"The spasms. How long do they last?"

Taillte paused her sharpening. She looked at her hand with a mixture of disgust and resignation. "An hour. Maybe two. Depends on how much I gave."

"You gave a lot. For a blister."

"He's a boy, Cedrik. He isn't built for this. If his hands rot, his spirit rots." She resumed the familiar grinding of the stone. "You wouldn't understand. You treat pain like information. Most people treat it like… pain."

Cedrik looked down at his own hands. They were scarred, callous layered over callous until the skin felt like boiled leather.

"I understand cost." He reached into his belt pouch and pulled out a small tin. It was battered, the brass dented from a dozen battles. He tossed it to her.

Taillte caught it with her good hand. She frowned, popping the lid. A pungent, minty smell wafted out.

"Winter-salve?"

"It helps with the tremors," Cedrik said. "Neelin used it after… after the fire at the Northern Border."

She looked at the tin, then at him. Her eyes were still guarded, but the sharp edge of her anger had started to dull, if only slightly.

"You carry salve for the High Marshal?"

"I carry it for anyone who needs to hold a sword in the morning," Cedrik said, standing up. "Rub it into the knuckles. It burns, but it works."

He turned to go back to his bedroll.

"Commander," she called out after him. He stopped. "When you killed Specialist Murphy… you didn't just end his pain, Cedrik. You silenced a verse of the First Song."

"Murphy was dying," Cedrik said, not wanting to revisit the memory. "He was in agony. He asked for peace."

"He asked because he was afraid," Taillte whispered. "And you gave him death because it was efficient. Because a dying man slows down the retreat."

"I gave him death because it was the only mercy left!" Cedrik snapped, the control cracking for a fraction of a second. "I have held the hands of my men while they screamed for hours. I have watched infection turn brave men into whimpering children. I spared him that."

"You spared yourself."

The accusation hung in the air between them, heavier than the smoke from the ruined capital.

"You treat war like arithmetic," Taillte said, closing her eyes. "Subtract the weak, carry the strong. But you can't subtract grief, Commander. Eventually, the numbers don't add up."

Cedrik turned back and looked at her; exhausted and pale, her hand trembling as she applied the winter-salve. She poured part of herself into a boy she barely knew. Then he looked at his own hands. Gloved. Armored. Stained.

"Keep it," he said, pointing to the tin. "Get some sleep, Captain. I'll take watch from here. We ride at dawn."

Silence reclaimed the campsite.

Cedrik turned away and returned to his spot, resting against a small oak. He studied the canopy of leaves blocking the stars.

He replayed the fight in his mind. The exertion of swinging his blade, meeting the resistance of armor and bone. The way the farmer had wept into his gauntlet.

The wolves know the shepherd is gone.

Cedrik closed his eyes, but he didn't see sleep. He saw the map of Alcia. He saw the fires starting to burn across the landscape. Each one a verse of the First Song being snuffed out.

CHAPTER 12

THE SWEEPING, BONE-WHITE LIMESTONE cliffs of Tarsis did not offer a welcome; they offered warning.

As the royal carriage creaked down the final switchback of the Southern Highway, Brighid Lorindan pressed her forehead against the cool, glass window. The vibration of the wheels traveled through her skull, rattling teeth that felt too loose in her gums.

Behind her lay the smoldering ruins of the Capital. Before her sat the "Jewel of the South," though today it looked less like a gem and more like a fortress bracing for war. She remembered visiting this city as a girl, when the air smelled of roasted spices and the harbor was a forest of vibrant masts. Now, the masts were gone, stripped away like dead timber. The docks were empty, save for the dark, churning water.

I am running, the thought whispered in her mind, bitter like raw dandelion greens. *While Neelin dies to defend the Capital, the Queen is sitting on velvet cushions, running away.*

"Your Majesty, we are being met at the gatehouse," Captain Cathal whispered, from his horse beside the carriage. He was the leader of the small escort assigned to her protection, a man who had not slept in four days. His Royal Guardian armor was worn from the difficult journey, the purple crest of Alcia unrecognizable under a thick layer of tan dust.

At the main portcullis, a mass of people was building. They were being funneled into the Lower Ward by the Tarsis Militia, recognizable by their bright blue tunics over chainmail. Brighid watched as families were torn apart at the rope lines; men sent one way and women another. It wasn't a chaotic rush; it was orderly segregation and selection.

"Stop," Brighid commanded, her hand reaching for the latch.

"Your Majesty?"

"They are separating them. Look, Cathal. They are treating them like livestock."

"We cannot stop, Majesty. If we stop in this crowd, we will be swarmed. My duty is to get you behind the inner walls."

Brighid froze. Her fingers hovered over the brass handle. She wanted to throw the door open. She wanted to stand on the step and command them to stop, to be the Queen the Songs promised. But fear, cold and paralysis, gripped her chest. She saw the desperation in the eyes of the refugees outside. If she opened the door, they wouldn't wait. They would tear her apart to get into the carriage.

Coward, she hissed at herself. She pulled her hand back. *You are just a coward in a royal box.*

The Queen looked carefully around her, at the commotion rising as people in the crowd began to recognize the royal crest on her carriage. A few hands reached out, slapping against the glass, begging for a word, a coin, or a miracle.

Captain Cathal rode ahead to clear a path into the city, his horse's hooves sparking against the stone. The Tarsis Militia manning the path to the Lower Ward paid her no attention, however. Their focus was tight, their eyes fixed not on her company, but on the crowds they were filtering.

Just beyond the glass, the brutality became specific.

A militia guard grabbed a man by the shoulder; a father, judging by the way he tried to shield the girl beside him. When he refused to move to the separation line, a crossbow stock slammed into his gut, folding him instantly. Two guards dragged him away, his boots scraping uselessly against the cobbles.

The girl didn't scream. She didn't chase them. She just stood, frozen in the surging current of the crowd, clutching a small, stuffed doll to her chest, watching the space where her father had been with wide, dry eyes. The guard didn't even look back at the shattered family. He simply pointed to another person in line.

"Next."

They are not looking for enemies... They are sorting these poor people. But for what?

But then, the militia saw the Royal Carriage.

For the Queen, the heavy iron gates swung wide open.

The carriage lurched forward, the iron-shod wheels echoing against the stone archway, unceremoniously announcing her arrival. The noise of the crowd, the weeping and the desperate bargaining for entry, was cut off as the heavy portcullis dropped behind them with a loud crash.

Inside the inner walls leading to the Upper Ward, the transition was immediate and unsettling. While the Lower Ward below was a choked holding pen of salt-stained sails and misery, the path leading to the Upper Ward was unnaturally pristine. The smell of travelling humanity was replaced by the cloying scent of jasmine and sea salt. The scent was so strong, it felt artificial.

Governor Gaughan was waiting in the courtyard of the Upper Ward Palace. He was a man of soft curves and damp palms, sweeping in a bow so low his nose nearly brushed the polished, white stone. He looked exactly as he had at the Midsummer Festival three years ago, but the smile didn't reach his eyes. They remained darting, calculating, examining her uncomfortably.

"Your Majesty!" Gaughan's voice was a practiced trill of oily exuberance. "The tragedy of the Capital... the King... my heart weeps for the Crown. But you are safe now. Tarsis will be your sanctuary."

Brighid stepped from the carriage. Her soft leather travel boots clicked sharply on the stone; a sound far too loud in the abnormal quiet. Her legs shook, threatening to buckle under her own weight. She forced them to lock. She gritted her teeth, masking the grimace of pain as a look of royal disdain.

Don't let them see you bleed. If you look weak, they will eat you.

She did not look at the Governor; she looked at his men. They wore the blue and gold livery of Tarsis, but they did not stand like soldiers. Their posture was fluid, hands resting on batons that looked more like branding irons than weapons. They stood like predators, waiting to be unleashed.

"Is there any word from the Capital, Lord Gaughan?" Brighid asked, her voice the level, cold steel of the North.

"My Queen, you have travelled—"

"I am aware of my journey, Governor," she cut him off. "I asked you a question. Is there any word from the Capital? You mentioned the King." Brighid took a step forward, her dark amber eyes daring the Governor openly. She felt the fatigue deep in her aching muscles, dragging at her shoulders and neck, but pushed it aside, relying on the iron discipline forged by countless days in a treacherous court.

"Well…" Gaughan stammered, his oily smile faltering for a fraction of a second. "The King… he… he has been declared missing." He paused for a moment, audibly swallowing his anxiety. "The High Marshal has taken command, but the central forces are shattered."

The High Marshal lives… so all is not lost. The thought was the first spark of heat she had felt in days. *Shepherd… why did they call him that…?*

She stepped forward, but the relief made her lightheaded. Her boot caught on the uneven cobblestone, and the wave of exhaustion she had been outrunning for hundreds of miles slammed into her like a tidal wave. She had hardly slept for days on end during their journey. Her escort took shifts, not allowing the pace to slow. But even if they had stopped, her mind raced with possibilities and options far too much to ever reach the comfort of slumber.

Captain Cathal rushed forward to catch her, his gauntleted hand gripping her elbow. "My Queen, the Governor is right. We kept a very fast pace for days on end. You need to rest."

"I am fine," she gasped, though the pounding in her skull said otherwise. "I must get a message to Neelin."

"All in good time, Your Grace," Gaughan replied, gesturing toward the looming white towers of the Palace. His voice had lost its trill; it was firmer now, more authoritative. "First, you must rest. The city is… uneasy. For your safety, we have prepared a suite in the West Wing. Secure. Private."

He snapped his fingers. Before Brighid could protest, the Tarsis militia moved. They didn't draw weapons, but they flowed between her and Captain Cathal; a wall of blue tunics isolating the Queen from her guard.

"My men will see to your escort's needs," Gaughan said, smoothly. "They look tired. We will take them to the barracks."

Brighid turned, panic flaring in her chest. "Captain Cathal stays with me."

"Protocol, Your Majesty," Gaughan said, his eyes hard and shiny as wet stones. "Trust me, the Palace is secure. We cannot have armed men in the Royal Wing who have not been vetted. It is for your own protection, and for the protection of all that are here with us."

Cathal looked at her. He saw the trap closing. He opened his mouth to shout an order, to draw his sword, but Brighid caught his eye. There were fifty militia men scattered in the courtyard. If he drew steel, he would die before he cleared the scabbard.

Don't throw your life away, she pleaded silently. *Not for me.*

She gave a nearly imperceptible shake of her head. Cathal's shoulders sagged, the fight draining out of him.

"I will see you in the morning, Captain," Brighid said, her voice trembly slightly.

"Your Majesty." Cathal bowed, but his eyes were filled with fear.

As she was led toward the great doors, stripped of her protection, she glanced up. High on a balcony of shimmering marble, a figure watched her. He did not wear the livery of Tarsis, or of anywhere she had seen before. He wore robes of shimmering red silk that moved, flowing like liquid fire; a fabric unique even in Alcia's Central trading city.

Even from this distance, she could feel his gaze. It wasn't the lecherous look of the court nobles, or the fearful look of the peasants. His eyes were violet. They locked onto hers with the cold, scholarly focus of a man examining an artifact he had just purchased. He tilted his head slightly, a gesture of curiosity devoid of empathy.

As the palace doors swung shut, the sound of the bolt sliding home was louder than the waves below. Brighid stood in the silent, perfumed hall. She hadn't found a sanctuary.

The Jewel of the South was no longer a safe haven; it was a golden cell.

CHAPTER 13

THE LANDSCAPE CHANGED ON the third day of their journey south.

The green meadows, farms and oak groves of the heartland gave way to the rocky foothills that bordered the Great Southern Highway. The small company had ridden hard, pushing their steeds to the limit. Focused on concealment, they navigated on goat paths and deer trails under the cover of night. The terrain fought them as they tried to avoid main roads, and the shortcuts Pasin recalled from his travels were washed out or blocked by rockfalls, funneling them to the very roads they worked so hard to avoid.

The air here was drier, tasting of dust and bitterness. The sun shone brighter during the peak hours, reflecting off the warm tones from the rock and dirt. Cedrik signaled a halt at the crest of a limestone ridge. He pulled Bastion up, the warhorse blowing hard, his mahogany coat matted with sweat and grit.

"We need the road," Cedrik said, his voice raspy from the dust. He didn't look back; his eyes were fixed on the road in the valley below. "The horses are failing. If we stay in the rocks, we'll lose them before we reach Tarsis."

Taillte pulled her horse to the edge of the ridge. She looked exhausted, the shadows under her eyes a dark purple contrasting with her pale skin. Her posture remained a rigid line of steel; proper form no matter the circumstance. She peered down to the road.

Below them, the Great Southern Highway stretched out as if it were a gray scar cutting through the foothills. Wide enough for ten men to march abreast, the highway was paved with flat cobbles to support siege engines, supply wagons, or any other form of transportation.

"The road is too exposed," Taillte mused. It was completely empty. There were no refugees, no merchants, and no sign of the enemy forces. Just miles of empty stone baking in the sun. "If you rush this, all of the hiding will have been for nothing."

"It's so... quiet," Fromme whispered. The squire rode up on Cedrik's left, sitting deeper in his saddle than just a few days ago. His untrained eyes scanned the horizon, not quite sure yet of what to expect.

"Too much so," Pasin agreed, his green eyes searching. "Impossible... a force that size should leave chaos in its wake. Stragglers, looters, bodies."

"They have locked the road down, Neelin was right," Cedrik said, his gut tightening. "Tarsis and Dunvar are cut off."

Cedrik raised his spyglass, sweeping the lens along the road until he reached a small crossing roughly a mile to the east. He stopped. "There."

At the junction, three soldiers stood in a triangle formation, facing outward to cover the compass points. They were motionless, statues of dark gray clad in purple tunics.

"A patrol," Cedrik murmured. "Holding that intersection. They know this is the main path through towards Tarsis."

"Should... we go around?" Fromme asked, hesitantly, his knuckles whitening on the reins.

"There is no around," Cedrik replied, checking the straps of his gauntlets. "Not without adding three days to the ride and risking the horses. We don't have three days. Nor does the Queen." He turned Bastion to face his small, exhausted company. "We have to break them."

"Four against three," Pasin considered, tapping his staff against his boot. Dust scattered from the impact. "Normally, those are odds I would take."

Taillte shot an angry glance at the old man. "You didn't see what they did, Pasin... how they did it—"

"We have the high ground," Cedrik interjected. "This is no different than the farm. We hit them before they can set. Standard heavy cavalry charge."

"This is *not* the Farm, Cedrik. Don't be such an arrogant—" Taillte warned.

"*Enough!*" Cedrik commanded. He locked eyes with the Royal Guard Captain, her exhaustion replaced with fury. "Taillte. I need you on the ridge for suppression fire. If they move to flank us, put them down."

A long moment passed as the order hung in the air. She gave a very slight nod, acknowledging the order but providing no other response.

"Fromme, Pasin... stay on my flank," Cedrik ordered, drawing his greatsword. The steel sang its familiar song as it left the shoulder casing, leather grip creaking under his grip. "Full speed, do not slow."

He kicked Bastion into a gallop. The warhorse let out a loud snort as the thunder from his hooves echoed off the limestone walls of the foothills. As they descended, the three dark figures did not scramble. They did not shout. As one, they turned to meet the noise. The lead soldier stepped forward, his crescent blade snapping into its full length with a heavy mechanical *clack*.

He didn't panic. He didn't brace for the horse. He crouched to lower his center of gravity, feet shifting into the High Guard.

Cedrik's breath caught. It was an Alcian Royal Guard defense, executed straight out of the textbook.

They know our maneuvers.

"Taillte, now!" Cedrik bellowed.

An arrow hissed from the ridge. It was aimed for the leader's throat, but the soldier didn't look up. He simply tilted his head a fraction of an inch, a minimal, efficient movement. The arrow sparked off his dark gray pauldron and skittered away. He hadn't guessed the shot; he had timed the snap of the bowstring.

Bastion burst into the crossroads. Cedrik expected to incapacitate one, maybe two soldiers, but instead they flowed like water around a stone, stepping aside with a synchronized precision that let the heavy horse thunder through empty space.

Cedrik swung his great blade in a sweeping low arc at the leader. The soldier raised his crescent glaive and parried the blow with a loud crash. He then twisted his grip and snagged the large blade, pulling it hard to the ground.

Pain shot through Cedrik's arm on impact. Bastion stumbled, opposing momentum battling balance. Cedrik hauled on the reins with his free hand, spinning the horse as the three soldiers reformed position around him instantly.

"Alcian, that charge is obsolete," the leader said.

The voice was thick with a strange guttural accent, muffled by the faceplate. It wasn't a taunt; it was a flat critique from a Master-at-Arms. "You overextended on that pass. Your center of gravity is too high."

Cedrik glared at him. The purple markings on the man's armor seemed familiar, but different. He could recognize certain features, but the design integrated other exotic details.

"Who are you?" Cedrik snarled.

"We are here to save you," the soldier replied. He signaled to his men. "Sanitize this area."

One soldier broke off, springing towards Pasin and Fromme with impressive speed in his light armor. The others advanced on Cedrik. Cedrik vaulted from his saddle, landing heavily with a loud thud, both hands now gripping the handle of his sword tightly. On a horse, he was a target; on the ground, he was a wall.

The leader lunged. The crescent blade moved with the force of a guillotine. Cedrik parried with the flat of his blade, entering the *Verona riposte*. He blocked quickly and thrust immediately for the gap in the man's armpit.

The strike was too slow. The leader had anticipated the riposte before Cedrik finished the block. He side-stepped, his glaive spinning to strike Cedrik squarely in the ribs.

Clang.

The impact dented Cedrik's breastplate, driving the air from his lungs. His ears rang from the sound as he stumbled back, gasping.

The enemy attacked again, a low sweeping strike aimed for the knee. A Xencid maneuver. Cedrik hopped over it, only to face a high, heavy Northern chop. They were using everything. Alcian strength, Xencid agility. Blended into a single, seamless style.

"You fight like a statue," the soldier said, circling. "Better than what we have faced so far, but still insufficient."

Cedrik gritted his teeth. He saw Taillte launching arrows at the soldier engaging Pasin and Fromme. The old man and the boy were retreating methodically towards the Royal Guard Captain as she provided cover fire.

No help. If I fight predictably, I die.

Cedrik lowered his sword. He relaxed his shoulders, letting his guard drop. The leader paused, sensing a trap, and motioned for his subordinate to step in. The second soldier, dressed in gray leather armor rushed forward, raising his short swords, one in each hand.

Cedrik spun hard, gathering momentum as the enemy approached. He pulled at his mighty blade with all of his strength, focusing only on the attack. Two short blades struck home, one glancing off the thick Alcian steel while the other cut through. Blood coursed out from Cedrik's left arm, as sharp pain jolted to his shoulder.

The Alcian armor did its job, blocking the worst of it. The foreigner's armor was too light, however. Cedrik continued his spin, slashing through and tearing an arm and shoulder from his opposition. No more than a gasp was released as the remaining body collapsed to the ground.

The leader did not hesitate. He sprang forward with a precise thrust of his blade to the heart. Cedrik did not parry. He stepped into the blade.

The dark gray steel scraped along the side of Cedrik's ribs, sending sparks flying as it gouged a furrow in his plate. White-hot spikes of pain coursed through him. Cedrik dropped his greatsword, reached out and grabbed the soldier's gorget. He roared, slamming his armored forehead into the man's faceplate with a sickening crunch. The impact stunned them both. Cedrik didn't use technique. He used raw strength and gravity. He lifted the man and drove him onto the cobblestones with his entire weight. The Knight Commander ripped the dagger from his belt and jammed it into the eye-slit of the helmet. Once. Twice.

The soldier convulsed.

"Taillte... Pasin..." Cedrik wheezed.

He heard the air split as an arrow sped through it, catching the attacker in the knee. In an instant, Taillte was at a full run, not bothering to nock another arrow. She leapt with her sword drawn and screamed as the attacker turned to face her, leaving his back open to the boy.

Fromme drove his spear into the back of the distracted soldier, pushing with all of his might at the resistance. She met the surprised soldier with the tip of her sword, piercing his neck as she landed. Taillte kneeled, her head down as the lifeless body crumbled beside her. Fromme had released the spear, looking from hand to hand in terror.

Silence returned to the crossroads.

Cedrik lay in the dust, clutching his injured ribs. He looked at the leader he had killed. Blood was leaking from the helmet; deep, dark red.

"Don't touch them!" Pasin warned, pulling Fromme back.

Cedrik drank in deep breaths as the bodies began to blur, edges of the silver armor losing focus as if viewed through frosted glass. The armor, the weapons, and the flesh faded into shadows; a ghost of what had been there seconds before. Then, with a final, silent ripple... They were gone.

Only a damp, dark stain remained on the stones.

Cedrik pulled himself to his feet. He bent to retrieve his greatsword, a slow painful process. His hands were shaking and his legs felt weak.

"He knew my attacks," he whispered. "Verona Riposte... obsolete... save..."

Pasin walked over, inspecting the wet stone at their feet. "War is a circle, Commander. Eventually, all secrets are exposed."

"That wasn't just simply learned," Cedrik spat, wiping blood from his forehead. "It's as if he was a Royal Guard, but more..."

Cedrik looked at Fromme. The boy was pale, staring at the empty air where a man had just been.

"Mount up," Cedrik ordered, his voice ragged and hollow. "We take the Southern Highway from here. And we don't stop until we see the walls of Tarsis."

They didn't make it to Tarsis. Not that night.

Two miles down the road, Bastion stumbled. The great warhorse caught himself, but his breathing was a ragged whistle. Cedrik patted the animal's sweat-soaked neck, feeling tremors in the muscle.

"Halt," Cedrik ordered.

They pulled off the road into a small grove of olive trees, their twisted branches offering scant cover from the dying sun.

Cedrik slid from the saddle. His boots hit the dirt, and his knees buckled. He didn't fall, but he had to grab the stirrup to stay upright. His side felt like it was on fire. The gouge in his breastplate from the glaive was deep, the metal folded inward, pressing against his already broken ribs.

"Sit down before you fall down," Taillte ordered, appearing at his side. Her voice was sharp, but her hands were gentle as she guided him to a flat rock.

She began unbuckling his armor. Her movements were efficient, practiced. She stripped the dented breastplate off him with a clang.

Cedrik hissed as the cool air hit his bruised skin. A fresh line of blood was seeping from the cut on his arm, soaking his tunic.

"You're a mess, Commander," the healer muttered, pouring water from her skin onto a rag. She dabbed at the wound. "Hold still."

"He was faster than me," Cedrik admitted, staring at his hands. They were quaking with uncertainty. "He knew the riposte. He stepped into it before I even moved."

"They certainly are efficient," Pasin said, from the other side of their makeshift camp. The old scholar was sitting with Fromme, who was staring blankly at his hands. "They fight without fear. Without hesitation."

"It wasn't just efficiency," Cedrik insisted.

Taillte tightened the bandage around his arm, pulling it hard enough to make him wince.

"You stepped into the blade," she said, quietly. Not a question.

Cedrik looked up at her. Her blue eyes were dark in the twilight, searching his face.

"It was the only way to close the distance."

"You traded a rib for a kill. Is that the plan, Cedrik? You just keep trading pieces of yourself until there's nothing left?"

"If it keeps the Queen safe. Yes."

Taillte sat back on her heels. She looked tired. The anger drained from her face, leaving only a profound exhaustion.

"You can't spend yourself like a coin," she said, softly. "Eventually, the purse runs empty. And then who protects her?" She stood up, brushing the dirt from her knees. "Rest, I'll take the first watch."

Cedrik watched her walk to the edge of the grove, her silhouette stark against the purple sky. He looked over at Fromme. The boy hadn't moved. He was still staring at his hands, as if he could still feel the soft pressure of steel ripping into flesh.

"It doesn't go away," Cedrik said.

Fromme jumped slightly, then looked at him. His eyes were wide, but his pupils were focused on nothing.

"He... he didn't even scream. He just... stopped."

"Yes."

"I killed him. I stuck a spear in him... and I killed him."

"You saved Taillte and Pasin," Cedrik corrected.

Fromme looked down at the dirt. "It felt... easy. That's the worst part. It was just pushing. It shouldn't be that easy... to kill."

Cedrik reached out and placed a heavy hand on the boy's shoulder. "It isn't easy, Fromme. The killing is the easy part. Now, you have to move forward with the hard part."

Fromme leaned into the touch, a small sob escaping his throat. "I don't... I don't want to be strong. I just want to go home."

"I know," the Knight Commander said, looking out at the darkening road where the ghosts of their enemies had vanished. "So do I."

The grove fell silent, save for the wind rustling the olive leaves. It was a peaceful sound, at odds with the violence of the day.

Cedrik leaned his head back against the tree bark and closed his eyes. The pain was still there, a dull throb in his side. But for a moment, in the quiet, the shield was not deflecting blows or bashing enemies.

Just for a moment.

CHAPTER 14

PAIN WAS A CONSTANT companion now. It throbbed in Neelin's jaw, radiated down his left arm and burned beneath the bandages wrapping his ribs. He'd tied his left arm to his chest with a strip of leather cut from his saddlebags, but the makeshift sling did little to dampen the agony.

He lay flat on his stomach atop a rocky crag overlooking the Southern Highway, the grit of stone pressing into his leather travel tunic. Below him, the world had turned to steel and dust.

"Have you ever seen anything like it," whispered the Lieutenant, lying prone beside him. The young officer's voice trembled, just a fraction. "Three days, Marshal. No stopping, only just barely to eat and sleep. They move like a small company, not an army of thousands..."

Neelin adjusted the focus of his trusted spyglass. The lens was scratched, a casualty of frequent use and many trips.

The Southern Highway was the main artery connecting the capital to the southern states. It should have been clogged with merchant wagons, refugees and panic. Instead, it was filled with the unyielding, terrifying march of the enemy.

Thousands of them.

They marched with great discipline, in perfect synchronization. A dark gray ring flowing through the valley at this juncture. There were no camp followers. No supply wagons. No stragglers. Just endless ranks of soldiers in that strange, shifting gray armor, interspersed with many sleek wagon-like constructs pulled by various beasts of burden.

"Look. Look at the farmsteads," Neelin rasped. His throat was still raw from the injuries sustained and smoke inhaled at the Capital..

Kael shifted his gaze. "They... they ignored them?"

Neelin moved the spyglass to the hamlet of River's Bend, just a mile off the road. Smoke drifted from a chimney. Farmers were standing in their fields, leaning on hoes, watching the army pass. They weren't running. They weren't being slaughtered or pillaged.

The enemy did not care about them.

In almost forty years of warfare, Neelin had never seen or heard of an invading force ignoring soft targets. Armies needed food, supplies, and they needed to instill terror to break the populace. But these soldiers treated the civilians like rocks in a stream, obstacles to be ignored. Not enemies to be crushed.

Surgical, Neelin thought. *What is the purpose of only attacking the army?*

"Sir, movement at the front," Kael hissed.

Neelin shifted his scope to the vanguard. A cluster of riders moved at the head of the column. "Command unit."

His breath caught in his chest.

The central figure rode a massive black stallion, larger than any breed he had seen. But it was the rider that made Neelin's blood run cold.

He wore no helmet. His face was tanned, lines of age and wisdom etched around eyes the color of desert sand. He wore the dark silver plate, but his cloak was a deep, blood red.

This was the man who had walked into the throne room and dismantled the Royal Guard with his bare hands. The man who had broken Neelin with a wave of fire. Left him for dead.

Why did you leave me? You checked the bodies. You knew I was still breathing...

The hulking figure was speaking to man beside him. Neelin shifted the glass slightly.

No...

Neelin tightened the grip on his spyglass until his knuckles cracked. He blinked, not believing what his eyes clearly saw.

The second rider was younger, perhaps late twenties. He sat tall in the saddle, his posture a mirror image of the statues that lined the Hall of Kings in Alcia Castle.

It cannot be...

Neelin searched for a difference, a flaw in the illusion. He wore armor of gold and white, intricately detailed with a lion crest, very similar to that of Alcia. But it was different. It was rampant, roaring, surrounded by a halo of lightning. It had script around it, sharp and angular, not Alcian.

But the face. It was undeniable. The sharp jaw, the brooding brow, the way he held the reins with a casual, regal arrogance.

It was King Alaric Lorindan.

Not the old King who had ruled for decades, heavy with the weight of the crown. This was Alaric as he had looked twenty years ago, during the War of Unification. As if he had ridden straight out of the history books.

The memory burst through his throbbing headache, to a simpler time.

The courtyard stones were still wet with dawn when Captain Neelin Arran was summoned to the inner keep. He had expected a reprimand. The border skirmish at Dunvar had cost him thirty men, and though they had held the line, the price gnawed at him like a dull blade.

He entered the keep alone. No guards. No heralds. Just the echo of his boots and the faint scent of parchment and cold iron.

The King was waiting.

Alaric Lorindan stood beside the great map table, his maroon cloak draped over one shoulder, his hands clasped behind his back. He looked much as the man in gold and white did now. Except for the hair. Blonde in his memory, black on the horse.

"Captain Arran," Alaric said, without turning. "You held Dunvar."

Neelin bowed. "At cost, Majesty."

"All victories have cost." Alaric finally faced him. "The question is whether the cost was worth paying."

Neelin said nothing. He had learned long ago that kings preferred silence to excuses.

Alaric studied him for a long moment. "You have served Alcia for twenty years."

"Twenty-one, Majesty."

"Twenty-one." Alaric's lips twitched. "And in that time, you have refused every promotion offered to you."

"I am a soldier," Neelin replied. "I serve best where the fighting is."

"Do you?" Alaric stepped closer. "Or do you simply fear the weight of command?"

Neelin stiffened. "I fear failing the men who follow me."

"Good." Alaric's voice softened, but the cold calculation remained in his eyes. "A man who fears failure is less likely to invite it."

He reached under the table and retrieved an ancient longsword, sheathed in white leather with brilliant blue crests representing the Kingdom and Crown. Neelin instantly recognized it. Every officer did.

It was the High Marshal's sword, passed from generation to generation. Yet, it had been sitting with Alaric for nearly a decade, since the last High Marshal had died.

The pommel, a golden lion's head with obsidian eyes that gleamed like midnight stars.

Neelin's breath caught.

"No," he said, before he could stop himself. "Majesty, I am not—"

"You are exactly what Alcia needs," Alaric interrupted. "A shepherd. A man who knows the land. A man who knows the people. A man who will not bend."

Neelin felt the weight of the words settle on his shoulders like fresh armor. *Shepherd.* The title tasted wrong. He was a soldier, not a herdsman.

Alaric held the sword out.

"Take it."

Neelin didn't move. "Majesty, there are others more suited. Men of noble birth. Men with political ties. Men who—"

"Men who would negotiate. Men who debate the cost of blood. I do not need a diplomat, Neelin. I need a lion." His eyes sharpened. "The world is growing wild, Captain. There are weeds in the garden. I need someone to hold the gate shut while I do the pruning."

Neelin felt something cold coil in his gut. He had always believed loyalty was a virtue. But in that moment, he wondered if it was a leash.

Still, he went to one knee.

"I will serve," he said, the words heavy as stone. "Until my last breath."

Alaric placed the sword in Neelin's hands.

"Rise, High Marshal."

Neelin rose. The lion's head gleamed in the morning light, its obsidian eyes catching the sun like drops of frozen night.

Alaric leaned in, his voice barely above a whisper. "Do not fail me, Neelin. Our future depends on you. Even if you do not understand the path I choose."

"Marshal," Kael asked, sensing the tension. "Do you recognize them?"

The question rattled Neelin from his daze. He lowered the glass slowly and reached to his hip. The sword was there, as magnificent as it had been on the day he received it. His heart hammered against his ribs, a frantic drumbeat against the dull ache of his injuries.

A son? A bastard? Neelin's mind raced. *Alaric never had a son... no offspring. It had always weighed heavily on the Queen...*

"No," Neelin lied. The words tasted like ash. "Just... demons."

He looked back at the column. They were moving south. Towards the border.

Directly towards Dunvar.

The realization hit him with the force of a physical blow. Neelin looked at the map in his mind. The Capital had fallen. The norther fort at Lanthreau was gone. The central garrisons and militia had been shattered.

He had spent the last three days rallying every surviving battalion, every straggler unit he could find. He had sent runners with a single word: Dunvar.

It was one of the strongest defensive positions in all of Alcia. High walls, narrow approaches. The bulk of Alcian forces were already stationed there. Their cold war with Xencid had been escalating for years. This was the main stronghold and access point between the two countries.

And the enemy was marching right towards it.

They weren't chasing him, or conquering land. They were *herding* him.

But why? Why had he been spared? They had to know that he would gather their forces, create the strongest front in all of Alcia. And they were marching right into it.

Even with the forces he saw here, the enemy may not be able to take Dunvar. The Alcian forces would outnumber them two to one. These would not be the militias of the central Lords. These would be the battle-ready Alcians sent to protect the southern border from invasion.

You wanted me to gather at Dunvar... The horror of realization was colder than the wind biting at his face. *You want us all on the border. A pincer?*

"Marshal, if we move now, we can cut through the woods," Kael suggested, pulling a map from his tunic. "They won't see us. We can beat them by maybe a day, perhaps more with good fortune."

Neelin looked at the young lieutenant. Hope shone brightly in the boy's eyes. The belief that if they just got to the big fortification, if they just built the walls high enough, they could win.

The truth settled in his gut like a lump of coal. Going to Dunvar was suicide. It was exactly what the enemy wanted.

But what choice did he have?

He had never wanted command. It was forced upon him. And now it was his burden, whether he chose to accept it or not.

If he did not go to Dunvar, the four thousand men gathered there would be leaderless. They would be slaughtered in confusion and Alcia would fade into history without so much as a whimper. If he went, he walked into a trap. But maybe... just maybe, if he knew it was a trap, he could spring it before it was in place.

"Put the map away, Lieutenant," Neelin said, pushing himself up. His body screamed in protest, but he forced himself to his knees.

"Sir?"

"We aren't going to cut through the woods. We're going to ride hard for the pass." Neelin grabbed his spear, using it to haul himself upright. He looked down at the dark silver river of death one last time. "We need more time to prepare Dunvar. Drive straight through the pass, take the highway direct from there."

He watched the young man who wore Alaric's face laughing at something the monster of a man had said.

I don't know what you are, Neelin thought, staring at the pair. *But I will not let you have my army for free.*

"We ride for Dunvar," Neelin commanded, his voice finding the steel that had made him a legend. "And we dig in. If they want a fight, Kael... we are going to give them a war."

Neelin turned his back on the valley. He knew he was marching toward his own grave. He just hoped he could make it deep enough to bury the enemy with him.

CHAPTER 15

THE AIR IN THE Governor's Palace of Tarsis tasted of jasmine, sea salt and betrayal.

Queen Brighid Lorindan sat before a vanity mirror of polished silver, her hands resting idly in her lap. The reflection staring back was composed, a porcelain mask that hid the dread coiling in her being.

At thirty-two, she was in the prime of her life, yet she was being dressed for a funeral. Her hair, a cascade of reddish blonde, was being pinned back by a servant girl whose hands trembled violently.

"Easy, Mara," Brighid said softly, her eyes tracking the girl's reflection. "I am not made of glass. You cannot break me."

"Forgive me... Your Grace," the girl stammered, dropping a pearl hairpin. "It's just... the rumors. They say the Capital is ash. They say the King..."

"The King is missing," Brighid corrected. Her voice was level, the refined dignity of the Court she had perfected over twelve years of marriage. "And until we see a body, Mara, we do not mourn. We prepare."

She stood tall, the black silk of her mourning gown rustling like dry leaves. It was an exquisite dress, cut to accentuate a waist that had never thickened with a royal heir.

A pang of familiar, cold iron twisted in her stomach.

The Barren Queen.

That is what the court called her behind closed doors. They whispered that Alaric had married a flower with no seeds.

Brighid walked to the balcony doors. She tried the handle, the brass cold against her palm. They were locked. Locked from the outside.

She didn't rattle it. She didn't scream. She simply noted the condition of the metal, newly installed and reinforced, and turned back to the room.

"Mara," Brighid said, her tone pleasant but sharp as a razor. "Why are these doors bolted?"

The servant girl flinched, retreating toward a heavy oak door. "Lord Gaughan... he insisted, Your Grace. The city is full of refugees. He said... for your safety. A stray arrow, a rock from the street. He worries about many things..."

"Lord Gaughan also believes I am made of glass, it seems."

Brighid scanned the room. It was a suite fit for royalty. Lush tapestries, bowls of exotic fruit from the coast, a bed large enough for five people. And huge, reinforced doors. A cell. A golden, velvet-lined cell.

For three days, she had been the 'Guest of Honor' of Governor Gaughan. For three days, she had been gently refused every request to leave this wing. For her safety. For her health. The Queen must rest.

With the King missing, we must protect you at any cost.

"Open the main door, Mara. I wish to visit the Temple. If my husband is indeed lost, I will pray for his return."

"I... I cannot, Your Grace. The guards—"

"I am the Queen of Alcia," Brighid said, stepping forward. The kind mistress vanished; the Monarch appeared. "Open the door."

Mara scrambled to obey, pulling the heavy latch on the large oak door. She swung it open, revealing the corridor.

Two guards stood upon either side. They were not Royal Guards that had traveled with her. They wore the blue and gold livery of Tarsis, but their stance was wrong. Their feet were too wide apart, the grip on their halberds too casual. Mercenaries in borrowed clothes.

"Your Grace," the soldier on the left said. His tone was polite, but his eyes were anything but. "Governor Gaughan sends his regrets. The streets are in chaos. He can't allow you to risk yourself."

"I am commanding you to move," Brighid stated, keeping her chin high.

"I take my orders from the Governor, Ma'am."

Ma'am. Not Majesty.

Brighid studied the man. He wasn't nervous. He wasn't awed by royalty. He looked at her with indifference, as if she were a piece of furniture that had been put into storage.

"I see," the Queen said coolly. "Then inform Governor Gaughan that if he does not come to see me within the hour, I will start throwing his priceless pottery off the Balcony. Alcian, Xencid, Regat. All of it. I imagine that will attract quite the crowd."

She slammed the door in their faces before they could respond.

***

Lord Gaughan arrived in twenty minutes.

The Governor of Tarsis swept into the room, the familiar scent of his syrupy perfume preceding him. He performed once again his signature bow, his face so low his nose nearly brushed the carpet.

"Your Majesty!" Gaughan exclaimed, wringing his hands. "My deepest apologies. The guards are brutes. They lack nuance! I explicitly told them to ensure your comfort, not to imprison you!"

"And yet, the door was locked, My Lord. All of them." Brighid sat in a high-backed chair, refusing to offer him a seat.

"A misunderstanding, I assure you. The city is on edge. We only wish to protect... the Kingdom's most precious asset."

Brighid watched him. Gaughan was sweating, but not from fear. He was excited. There was a manic energy to him. A man whose capital had just burned should be terrified. Gaughan looked like a merchant who had just closed the deal of a lifetime.

"Asset," Brighid repeated. "Is this what I am? Tell me, Lord Gaughan. Have you had word from Neelin? Has the army regrouped? Where does the enemy march to now?"

Gaughan waved a dismissive hand. "Marshal Neelin is... handling the border. He is a soldier. He fights. That is his nature."

"And what is your nature, Gaughan? To hide in your palace while the North burns?"

Gaughan smiled. It was a greasy, patronizing expression. "My nature is diplomacy, Your Grace. While Neelin fights the battles, I must secure a future for Tarsis. For all of us. In fact," he turned to the door, "I have someone who is dying to meet you. He has traveled a very, very long way."

Gaughan clapped his hands. "Ambassador, if you please."

A man stepped into the room.

Brighid's breath caught in her throat. He was tall, slender, and strikingly beautiful. He wore robes of shimmering red silk that seemed to catch the light in impossible ways, the fabric looked more like flowing water than thread. His skin was flawless, tanned and smooth, and his eyes were a startling, almost unnatural violet.

He looked Xencid; the features were undeniable.

He did not bow. He walked toward her with a fluid grace that made Gaughan look like a stumbling toddler. He stopped three paces away and looked her up and down.

It was not a lecherous look. It was the look of a scholar examining an artifact.

"So, this is she," the man said. His voice was melodic, with the deep, dramatic cadence from Xencid. "Brighid of High Vales. The Lioness."

"I am Queen Brighid Lorindan," she corrected, standing up. "And you are entering my chambers without leave."

The man smiled, no merriment in his eyes. "Forgive me. I have not properly introduced myself. I am Ambassador Xarion. I represent interests... from the South. And beyond."

"Xencid." Brighid spat the word. "Have you come to pick from our bones when you might be next?"

"Never." Xarion glanced at Gaughan.

Gaughan chuckled nervously. "The conflict between us is a misunderstanding, Your Grace! A relic best left in the past. Ambassador Xarion brings terms of lasting peace and harmony. Generous terms. King Alaric... King Alaric understood this."

Brighid froze. She noticed the slight hesitation in Gaughan's voice at the mention of the King.

"You sound as if you have spoken to my husband."

Xarion's violet eyes locked onto hers. "I know Alaric well. Better than most, I suspect." He took a step closer. "He spoke of you fondly, in his way. He said you were... dutiful."

The insult was delivered so softly it took a moment to sting.

"Dutiful," Brighid whispered.

"He regretted the burden he placed on you," Xarion continued, walking around her chair, inspecting the fine fabric of her dress. "He knew the court was cruel. They blamed you for the empty nursery, didn't they?"

Brighid stiffened. "I will not discuss my marriage with a foreign spy."

"It wasn't your fault, Brighid," Xarion said gently. "Alaric did not refuse you an heir because of his age, or out of spite."

Xarion stopped in front of her. He smelled of ozone and something sharp, like sterilized metal.

"He refused you because he already had one."

The words didn't land. They hung in the air, her mind refusing to accept the gravity of what they meant.

An heir. A son.

She thought of the nights she'd waited for him in their chambers, and then he never came. The careful, dutiful way he'd touched her in those early years. Before even that courtesy had stopped. The pitying looks from the court ladies when her belly refused to swell.

"No." The word came out small, a child's desperate denial. "He would have... I would have known." Her throat seized up, blocking airflow for a moment. "That is a lie," Brighid let out, her voice rising, cracking the porcelain mask she had worn for almost a decade.

"THAT IS A LIE! I would have known! There were no bastards! He was faithful, I am sure of it."

"Oh, he was faithful," Xarion said, softly. "Just not to this bloodline. His legacy was already written, Queen Brighid. His son is already grown. A strong man. Half-Alcian. Half... my people."

Brighid stared at him. The puzzle pieces she had ignored for years slammed together. Alaric's distant gaze. The way he would look at her not with love, but with apology. The long nights he spent locked in the archives with his 'researchers.'

He hadn't been protecting her from childbirth.

She hadn't been a wife. She had been a placeholder. A warm body to occupy the throne until the real family arrived.

"You are lying," she said again, though her voice lacked conviction. The fight was draining out of her, replaced by a cold, hollow shock.

"It does not matter what you believe," Xarion said, straightening his robes. "What matters is that the transition has begun. Tarsis will become the new Capital of Alcia. You will be comfortable here. You will be cared for. You will remain the Queen in title, and you will live a long, quiet life of luxury. As long as you comply."

He smiled again. "It is more than you deserve, frankly. In most versions of history, you simply... disappear."

Xarion turned to Gaughan. "We are done here. Ensure she stays inside. She is vital to keep the populace calm."

"Of course, Ambassador," Gaughan bowed.

They turned to leave.

"Gaughan!" Brighid called out.

The Governor paused at the door.

"If you think Alcia will accept a Xencid peace," she said, her voice low and dangerous. "If you think Neelin will stand for this—"

"Neelin is dead, my dear," Gaughan said, with a sad, oily smile. "He just doesn't know it yet."

The door slammed shut. The bolt slid home with a heavy, final clank.

Brighid stood alone in the center of the room. The scent of jasmine was overpowering now, choking her. But beneath the perfume, the air in the room felt suddenly stale. Dead.

The memory rose unbidden, sharp as a blade.

Brighid stood in the Great Hall of the Capital, the air thick with incense and the cloying sweetness of summer wine. It was the Feast of Renewal, the night the court celebrated the Sovereign's pulse. A night meant for joy.

She remembered the heat of the torches. The glitter of jewels. The way the nobles' laughter echoed like breaking glass.

She remembered the dress she wore; pale gold silk, chosen by Alaric himself. "You look radiant," he assured her. "The people will adore you."

She had believed him.

A cluster of noblewomen drifted past her, their fans fluttering like the wings of trapped birds. Lady Mereth, the Chancellor's wife, leaned in too close, her breath warm against Brighid's ear.

"Such a lovely gown, Your Majesty," she cooed. "Gold is a bold choice for a woman in mourning."

The Queen blinked. "Mourning?"

Mereth's smile sharpened. "For the heir you have not given us, of course. The Kingdom grieves with you."

A ripple of soft, sympathetic laughter followed. Not cruel on the surface, but polished, practiced, honed to a razor's edge.

Brighid felt the heat rising in her cheeks. She opened her mouth to respond, but another voice cut in.

"Lady Mereth," Alaric said, appearing at Brighid's side. Relief flooded her, until she saw his expression.

He wasn't angry. He wasn't offended. He wasn't even surprised.

He looked... tired. As if this conversation were inevitable.

"As you know," Alaric said, mildly, "the matters of succession are delicate. The Queen has my full confidence."

Mereth bowed, the smile never leaving. "Of course, Your Majesty. We only worry for the future of Alcia."

The future. Always the future.

Brighid waited for Alaric to take her hand. To reassure her. To tell the court to hold their tongues.

It never happened. He didn't even look at her.

His gaze drifted past her, toward the far end of the hall. Toward the sealed doors of the archives. The place he had been disappearing to more and more often.

"Alaric," she whispered, her voice barely audible over the music. "Say something."

He blinked, as if waking from a dream. "About what?"

About me, she wanted to say. *About us. About the child we do not have. About the way they look at me.*

But he was already turning away, murmuring something about "matters of state."

She watched him walk toward the archives, the gold of his cloak catching the torchlight. He didn't look back.

Lady Mereth's voice drifted behind her.

"Poor thing. She tries so hard."

Brighid stood alone in the center of the hall, surrounded by silk and jewels and the soft, poisonous pity of the court.

She had never felt colder.

The cold from that memory snapped her back into the present, freezing the tears in her eyes before they could fall. She wasn't a 'poor thing.' She wasn't a failure. She was a distraction. While Lady Mereth had mocked her, Alaric had been in the archives, planning for a son that wasn't hers.

Emotions erupted into the empty room. Anger... Confusion... Sadness... Pity...

She looked at the fruit knife on the table. It was small, silver, and sharp.

She walked over and picked it up.

They thought she was a decoration. A trophy wife who had failed to do the one thing Queens were supposed to do.

He already had a son. How is that possible?

She would not let these emotions control her. Instead, she focused on something else. Something hot and bright and purifying.

She walked to the ornate tapestry hanging on the west wall; a depiction of Alaric's coronation. She raised the knife and slashed it diagonally, tearing the fabric from corner to corner.

Brighid moved to the balcony door. She didn't scream. She didn't cry. She placed the tip of the knife against the glass pane, searching for the weak point in the seal.

Nothing.

She had to wait. She had to watch.

There were too many unanswered questions. How could he have a successor, from Xencid. In her time with him, she had never known him to travel there. No visitors to the Castle.

Brighid scanned the room, her chest tightening with dread. The heavy silk of the tapestry lay in ribbons on the floor, the painted face of King Alaric severed from the neck down.

It wasn't enough. Destroying his image didn't stop the supposed truth Xarion had just planted in her brain like a poisoned seed.

An heir. A son. A future.

"He didn't just find a new wife," Brighid whispered to the empty room, the silence pressing against her ears. "He found a new bloodline."

She threw the knife onto the bed. Her hands, still shaking with rage, went to the battered leather satchel she had guarded since the Capital. She had carried it for hundreds of miles, using it as a pillow in the carriage, but she hadn't yet truly opened it. She had been too afraid of what Alaric's private mind would reveal.

Now, fear was a luxury she couldn't afford.

Brighid dumped the contents onto the duvet. Scrolls of star charts, loose pages covered in geometry that looked like jagged teeth, and a small, black notebook bound in cracked vellum.

She picked up the notebook. It was Alaric's handwriting on the cover, but also someone else's. It was that strange old scholar who had spent so much time in the archives. The one with the green eyes.

She would never forget the green.

She opened the notebook to a marked page near the middle. The date was from three years ago; the summer Alaric had stopped coming to bed, claiming that "matters of state" kept him in the archives.

Day 40 of the Deep Vaults Excavation, 9th Level

The air down here is wrong. It does not smell of rot or earth. It smells of ozone and dead iron. The torches burn blue, starved of oxygen, yet Alaric does not seem to need to breathe. He stands by the obsidian gate for hours, just listening.

Brighid traced the ink. The handwriting, neat on other pages, was jagged here. Rushed. Panicked.

We broke the seal on the First Cycle chamber today. I begged him to stop. I told him the texts warned of a hunger that eats the soul to feed the Gift. But he wouldn't listen. When the doors opened, the room didn't stay silent. It exhaled.

A low, violet thrumming. The walls are veined with it. The Graft. It is not the Gift as we know it. It is a mix of biology and the Gift, from the First Cycle. A parasitic magic that promises power in exchange for humanity.

Alaric touched the central pillar. I saw the violet light flash as it contacted his flesh. I thought he would scream, I thought it would burn him.

He laughed.

He looked at me, his eyes reflecting unnatural colors and said, "The world is messy, Pasin. People are chaotic variables. But this... this is efficient. I can fix the equation. I can prune the dead branches and make the tree grow straight."

She flipped the page, her thumb catching on a sheet that felt like dried skin. It was a loose page, not part of the binding. It was covered in frantic, circular geometry that she could not understand. There were calculations next to the shapes.

The Iron Fleets, she read, though the word fleet seemed to refer to ghosts rather than the equations. Beneath the diagrams, the script became a panicked scrawl:

The arithmetic is clear... The Graft... bridging life. The price must be paid in blood. The equation is simple. Equal...

Brighid stared at the numbers, her mind refusing to resolve the shapes. Nothing made sense. She had never heard of Iron Fleets or the Graft. He had hidden so much from her.

Brighid slammed the book shut. The room felt suddenly freezing, as if the cold air from that underground vault had bled through the pages and into her chambers in Tarsis.

"Three years," she whispered, her voice cracking.

She had slept beside him. She had poured his wine. She had worried about his cold moods and his distance, thinking he was stressed by taxes or the Xencid border disputes.

All the while, he had known. He had been researching. Planning. Preparing to rewrite the world. A world where I do not have a place.

She wasn't going to be a pawn. She wasn't going to be a forgotten victim.

If Alaric had written her out of history, she would pick up a pen—or a blade—and write herself back in.

CHAPTER 16

THE SOUTHERN HIGHWAY DID not end at the gates of Tarsis; it was swallowed by them.

Cedrik pulled Bastion to a halt on the limestone ridge overlooking the coast. Around the city, the gray expanse of the channel churned against the cliffs, sending sprays of cold mist drifting inland. Tarsis sat perched on that precipice, the last major city of Alcia, before opening to the wildlands and the border with Regat.

Usually, the city was a jewel of white stone and blue tile, gleaming under the southern sun. Today, it looked like a bruised eye.

"No sign of the enemy," Taillte whispered, her hand resting instinctively on the pommel of her sword. She sat rigid in her saddle, scanning the dark plumes of smoke rising from inside the walls. "But it's burning."

"Fires of chaos, unease," Pasin murmured. He pulled his weathered cloak tighter against the salt wind. "When the people don't trust the lamps to stay lit, they burn whatever can be found. It's the smoke of a city holding its breath."

Below them, the approach to the main gate was oppressed from all angles.

"Look at the carts," Pasin noted, pointing to the line. "That's not farm equipment or simple belongings. Its furniture, silks."

There were the merchants, the minor nobles, and families of officers stationed in the North and West. Not simple peasants fleeing because of devastation to the hamlets and farmland, but people whose worlds had been ravaged by the collapse of the military and trade routes.

"They aren't refugees," Cedrik realized, grimly. "They're the surplus. The people who have no place without the King and Queen to keep order."

As they rode down the switchbacks, the smell hit them. It wasn't the stench of unwashed poor; it was the smell of panic masked by stale perfume and the sweat of people who had never walked a mile in their lives, until now.

The reception was not what Fromme had expected. He had spent his life hearing stories of the Royal Guard. How the populace cheered when the Silver Lion rode past. But as Bastion pushed through the thick crowd of carts outside the gatehouse, there were no cheers.

There was only resentment.

"Look at his armor," a man in a dusty velvet doublet hissed, clutching a ledger to his chest. His eyes were wide with a mixture of terror and entitlement. "Silver and gold. Such excess. Paid for by the people! And for what?!"

"Where were you at the wall, Commander?" a woman shouted from a carriage blocked by the mass of humanity. "My husband. The militia called him to the Castle... Why are you here? Why *him*?"

Cedrik didn't flinch. He kept his eyes forward, fixed on the portcullis. Beside him, Taillte's fingers were clenched on her reins.

"Don't," Cedrik commanded, softly. "They aren't the enemy."

"How can...," Fromme started. "Why do they blame you?"

"They think we failed them," Taillte answered, calmly.

"We did," Cedrik said.

The small company reached the shadow of the gatehouse. The standard Tarsis militia, usually seen in polished ceremonial armor, were gone. In their place were hard-faced men in boiled leather, armed with heavy crossbows. They looked tired, their patience worn thin by days of arguing and complaints from wealthy refugees with ridiculous demands.

"Halt" the Sergeant of the Gate barked.

Cedrik recognized him. Harlen. A man he had shared ale with during the spring festivals three years ago.

"Sergeant Harlen," Cedrik said, his voice a low rumble. "I have wounded. And I carry word for the Queen. Open the gate."

Harlen didn't look him in the eye. He looked at the dented Royal Guard sigil on Cedrik's chest, then gestured vaguely at the angry crowd behind him.

"The Governor has issued a decree, Commander," Harlen said, making the title sound like an accusation. "Tarsis is under martial law now. No military personnel from the northern or western theaters are to enter the city with their arms. You're to surrender your steel at the gatehouse. Then report to the triage camps in the Lower Ward."

"Surrender our steel?" Taillte's voice cracked like a whip. "You'd dare try to disarm the Royal Guard of the Crown?!"

"The Crown does not rule in Tarsis today, Captain," Harlen snapped, finally looking up. "The Governor has kept Tarsis safe where the Crown could not. Look around you. Listen to them. He won't be letting you walk his streets with swords and crests while the city is on the edge of a riot."

A heavy ledger book whistled through the air, striking Fromme's shoulder. As the boy cried out, the crowd surged forward, emboldened by the guard's disrespect. They were shouting now, demanding entry, demanding answers, demanding to know why their status meant nothing.

"You see?" Harlen shouted over the noise. "To them, you're just the reason they have lost their homes. If I let you in like that, you'll be lynched before you reach the market square.

"Commander Cedrik," Harlen's face softened as he leaned into the Knight Commander. "Give them in. It's the only way you're getting to her."

Cedrik looked at the dark tunnel of the gate. He looked at the faces of the people crowding him... the 'surplus' of a dying kingdom. Then he looked at his greatsword. It had never left his side in twenty years.

To give it up was to admit that the order he served was truly gone.

Slowly, painfully, Cedrik unbuckled his shoulder strap. The heavy mountain of steel slammed into the dirt with the sound of a coffin lid closing.

"Take them," Cedrik whispered.

***

The iron portcullis dropped behind them with a booming crash. Cedrik flinched, not at the familiar sound but at the smell. The animals, the mass of people, the unwashed streets. It triggered a memory, he had tried to hold down deep, unwelcome.

He was six again, barefoot on the Lower Ward cobblestones, the winter wind cutting through the holes in his tunic. His stomach cramped with hunger. He'd been searching for scraps behind the bakeries, hoping for a crust of burnt bread or handful of flour someone had spilled.

He found nothing.

But the older boys found him.

Three of them; bigger, stronger, wrapped in patched cloaks that made them look like wolves circling a stray pup. One kicked the small cloth sack from Cedrik's hands, scattering the few wilted greens he'd scavenged. Another shoved him hard enough that he slipped on the frost and hit the ground.

"Got nothin' again, rat?"

"Maybe he eats dirt."

"Maybe he eats fists."

Cedrik scrambled for the greens, but a boot came down hard on his hand, grinding his fingers into the stone. He cried out, but the sound was swallowed by the alley walls.

He tried to fight back. He always tried. But he was too small. Too hungry. Too slow. One boy grabbed him by the collar and lifted him off the ground with ease.

"No'un's comin' for ya," the boy sneered. "No'un 'ver does!"

Cedrik remembered the helplessness most of all. The certainty that he could scream until his throat bled and no one would hear him. Or care. No one would help him. He was just a child in the Lower Ward, unseen, unprotected, forgettable.

The memory dissolved as quickly as it came, leaving a cold ache in his chest.

He glanced back and saw their horses being led away, presumably to the militia stables as Harlen had promised.

Cedrik forced his shoulders square and marched forward, his back free from the weight of his greatsword. His hand drifted back out of instinct, only to close on empty air. The absence of it felt like a missing limb, a phantom weight that threw his balance off with every step. Behind him, Taillte and Pasin led the horses through the narrow gauntlet of the Inner gatehouse, their faces tight with the same indignity. They were no longer the King and Queen's Guard; they were four more refugees in a city that was already full.

Pasin walked over, his head close. "You with me?"

"I'm fine."

"Stay sharp. We will get out of here."

"I know." Cedrik took a step forward, not wanting to dwell on his thoughts.

"Keep your eyes down," Pasin muttered, his voice barely audible over the din of the streets. "The Governor's men aren't looking for soldiers. They're looking for examples."

The Lower Ward of Tarsis had once been a vibrant sprawl of tanneries and weaver shops. Now, it was a holding pen. The narrow cobblestone streets were choked with pallets of straw and makeshift lean-tos made of salt-stained sails. The smell was the first thing that hit them, a thick, cloying mixture of unwashed bodies, gangrene, and the acrid smoke of medicinal herbs being burned in iron braziers.

"Medic!" a voice screamed from a nearby alley. "We need a medic!"

Taillte paused, her eyes darting toward the sound. A woman was huddled over a man whose legs were wrapped in blood-soaked linen bandages, looking as if they had been scavenged from a dirty tunic.

"Taillte, no...," Cedrik said, his voice low.

"I still have my kit, Cedrik. I can't just—"

"If you stop here, a hundred more will swarm you. Look around," Cedrik interrupted, grabbing her arm. He hated the words, but he looked at the shadows beneath the eaves. Hard-faced men in blue-and-gold livery of the Tarsis militia were watching them from the rooftops, their hands resting on the pommels of their short-swords. They weren't helping; they were patrolling. They were keeping the mass of the North contained in the slums.

Taillte roughly pulled her arm from his grasp. She scanned the area for a moment and fell back into pace with the others.

They were herded toward a cordoned-off section of the old wool market, hemmed in by hastily erected barricades of torn-up paving stones and sharpened timber.

"Here," Taillte whispered, guiding Fromme to sit on a discarded crate near the eastern wall. She immediately began checking his eyes, her movements sharp and professional despite the filth around them. "Cedrik. He's in shock. He needs clean water. Now."

Cedrik looked around, his ribs burning. There was a trough in the center of the pen, but the water was gray, with a coating of slick oil on top. Men were fighting over a ladle, their faces twisted with the desperate, animal panic of survival.

"I'll get it," Cedrik said, stepping forward.

"Wait," Pasin interrupted. The old man was leaning against the wall, his green eyes scanning the crowd too sharply for a man of his age. "Look at the gates, Commander. Watch the rotation."

Cedrik followed his gaze. At the far end of the pen, near the exit leading to the Inner city, a squad of the Governor's militia was pulling people from the crowd. But they weren't random.

"They're taking the strong," Pasin noted, coolly. "Anyone who can hold a spear or swing a hammer."

"Conscription?" Taillte asked, looking up from Fromme.

"Filtration," Pasin corrected. "They aren't arming them, girl. They're removing them. If you want to control a herd, you cull the bulls first."

A chill went down Cedrik's spine. He watched as a burly blacksmith was forcibly dragged away from his weeping wife. The man shouted, tried to resist. He reached out for her but was immediately silenced by the butt of a crossbow to the stomach.

Suddenly, the crowd near the main gate parted. The murmurs of complaint died out, replaced by startling silence.

A group of officers walked through the mud. They wore the blue of Tarsis, but the man walking in the center did not. He wore high-collared gray leather, unadorned by any sigil, but the cut was precise, well beyond normal armor. He moved with a fluidity that bordered on unnatural, his steps were silent despite the heavy boots.

He wasn't looking at the refugees. He was scanning.

"Don't look at him," Cedrik hissed, instinctively stepping in front of Fromme and Taillte. "Eyes down."

The officer paused ten feet away. He turned his head slowly. Even from this distance, Cedrik could see the strength and vigor in his eyes. They were incredibly focused. On his hip, there was no sword. He carried a curved, serrated baton.

"That's not Alcian," Taillte whispered, her breath hitching.

"No," Cedrik replied, his muscles coiling tight. "It's not."

The officer's gaze swept over them, lingering for a heartbeat on Cedrik's size. On the military sigils that dirt couldn't hide. Then he moved on.

As the squad passed, Pasin let out a deep breath he had held for what felt like minutes.

"We need to get out of here," the old man said. "Tonight."

"How?" Taillte asked, looking at the barricades. "We have no weapons, and the gates are barred. I see no one willing to help us contact the Queen either."

Cedrik looked up toward the looming white towers of the Palace, just visible over the tops of the slum roofs. It gleamed in twilight, pristine and untouched by the squalor below.

"We don't go out," Cedrik said, grimly. "We go up. Harlen said the Queen is in the Palace. If we can't talk our way in, we will need to break in."

"You want to break into the Governor's fortress?" Pasin asked, a dry smile touching his lips. "Without our weapons?"

"We don't need weapons to get in," Cedrik said, watching the Grey Officer disappear into the crowd. "We just need to look like we belong in a cage."

CHAPTER 17

THE DANK SMELL OF wet wool, unbathed bodies and the sulfuric odor of fear nearly overwhelmed Cedrik, as he pushed through the crowds in the Lower Ward. Mixing with the ripe sting of manure, his senses were reminded that this district had been a place for livestock and was now a pasture for those displaced from the North. Under Governor Gaughan's leadership, the distinction between cattle and brethren from the afflicted areas had vanished.

He found a spot near a rotting wooden piling and sank down, pulling his knees to his chest. It was a calculated posture. For twenty years, Cedrik had stood at full height, his spine a rigid line of Alcian steel. The counterweight of his prized greatsword that constantly pulled at his shoulders was gone, an undeniable emptiness. Now, he had to unlearn a lifetime of discipline. He had to learn to slump, that much harder with his injured ribs.

"You still look like a statue trying to fold itself," Pasin mumbled. The old scholar was sitting in the mud beside him whittling a piece of driftwood with a small, rusted knife he had hidden in his boot. "A laborer's back is curved by the load, Cedrik. Yours looks like it's waiting for armor."

"I feel naked," Cedrik grunted, staring at his hands. They were broad, scarred, and calloused. The hands of a man who broke things for a living. He shoved them deep into the armpits of his threadbare tunic to hide the knuckles. "Without the weight on my back, I feel like a strong wind could blow me into the channel."

"Let the wind take you, then," Taillte whispered. She was crouched near them, rubbing ash and grease into the vibrant red of her hair until it was a muddy, forgettable brown. She had discarded the authority of a Captain like a used cloak, shrinking into the role of a camp follower. "If we stay in these pens, we starve. If we want to find the Queen, we have to get out of this ward."

She nodded toward the far end of the market.

Beyond the makeshift fences, the muddy expanse had been transformed into a geometric grid of ropes and barricades. At the bottleneck, beneath the gray, overcast sky, stood a large gate.

It wasn't a chaotic mob; it was strangely organized given the mess surrounding it. A line of prisoners stretched from the pens to the gate, moving with a steady, shuffling silence. Flanking the line were the Tarsis militia in their dirty blue surcoats, but they were merely the dogs. The handlers were the gray officers, finishing their rounds for the moment.

They walked up and down the line with a fluid, predatory grace, their high-collared leather absorbing the dim light. They didn't shout. They didn't push. They simply tapped their serrated batons against their thighs—*click, click, click*—a metronome counting down the utility of the people in line.

Harlen, the thick-necked militia sergeant who had been manning the gates, climbed onto a crate near the Inner gate. He banged the hilt of his sword against the wood, the sound cracking like a whip over the murmuring crowd.

"Volunteer detail!" Harlen bellowed, his voice straining against the salted wind. "Palace labor. Structural repair and sanitation. Hot meal and a roof for those who pass the check. The rest of you stay here with the surplus."

Cedrik looked at Taillte. She gave a single, imperceptible nod.

Cedrik stood up. He did not rise like a Knight Commander. He forced his knees to wobble, rounded his shoulders until his spine bowed, and he let his head hang low. He stepped into the mud, not marching, but trudging. He coughed; it rattled his insides and burnt with fresh pain.

Fromme was the hardest to disguise. The boy kept shaking.

He stood in the shadow of Cedrik's bulk, clutching a bundle of dirty rags to his chest like a shield. He had rubbed mud on his face, but his eyes were wide, darting frantically between the gray officers and the archers positioned on the wool warehouse rooftops.

"Stop scanning the high ground," Cedrik ordered, without moving his lips, his voice a low rumble. "Squires check the perimeter. Laborers look at their boots."

Fromme flinched, his gaze snapping down to the muck. "Sir, I... I can't help it. The way they move... it's not right. They... they don't blink enough."

"Then don't look at them." Cedrik reached out, his heavy hand clamping onto the boy's shoulder. He squeezed with a mix of reassurance and warning. "You are my apprentice today. You mix the mortar. You carry the water. You are invisible. If they ask you a question, you are too stupid to answer. Do you understand?"

"Invisible," Fromme whispered, the word trembling on his lip. "Stupid..."

"Good." Cedrik released him but kept his body angled to shield the boy from the direct line of sight of the gate. "Stay glued to Pasin's left flank. If he stumbles, you catch him. But make it look like you're tired, not trained."

Fromme nodded, shrinking into himself. He adjusted the bundle in his arms, hunching his shoulders until he looked less like a soldier in training and more like a frightened child. He looked like he had when they first met.

Taillte laid a gentle hand on the boy's arm, trying to stop the nervous shuddering. "Breathe Fromme," she instructed, her voice soft but stern. "This nerve controls the shake." She pressed her thumb hard into the soft spot between his neck and shoulder. "Do it now, or you'll get us all killed." Fromme gasped, the tremor in his hands instantly dulling as his biology reacted to her command.

"Let's go, old man," Cedrik muttered, offering a hand to Pasin. "Try not to look too wise."

"And you," Pasin whispered back, accepting the grip with a feigned, trembling frailty. "Try not to look like you're storming the gates."

They stepped out of the shadows and into the line funneling towards the large stone gate; Cedrik the broken mason, Pasin the senile elder, Taillte the camp follower, and Fromme, the terrified shadow binding them all together.

The transition was immediate. Inside the crowd, there had been the low constant hum of weeping and prayer. But once they crossed the rope line, they were encased in silence. The air here felt pressurized, heavy with an ozone static that made the hair on Cedrik's arms stand up.

They joined the rear of the column, four insignificant figures in a river of muted gray misery. Ahead of them, the line snaked toward a desk. To their left, the towering limestone cliffs of Tarsis rose up, topped by the pristine white walls of the palace. To their right, the wide torrent channel separating Alcia and Regat churned viciously.

And everywhere, weaving through the mud like sharks in shallow water, the gray officers watched. They weren't looking for weapons. They were scanning for posture, muscle density... utility.

The shuffling progress of the line stuttered to a halt.

Ten paces ahead, an older man—a tanner by the stains on his apron—had stopped. A militia guard shoved him backward, toward the pens.

"Quota is full for the elderly. Move along, surplus."

The tanner didn't move. He lunged forward, grabbing the sleeve of the young man ahead of him. "He is my son! He doesn't know the trade, I have to show him!"

The son turned, eyes wide with panic, reaching back. "Father, no—"

A gray officer stepped in. There were no words. No warnings. The serrated baton blurred through the air.

CRACK.

The sound of the baton striking the old man's knee was sickeningly loud in the quiet. The tanner collapsed into the mud, howling, clutching his shattered leg.

Cedrik's muscles locked. The instinct was instantaneous; a flare of heat in his chest, a shift of weight to his forward foot. The phantom weight of the greatsword screamed to be drawn. He took a half-step out of line, his jaw set.

A hand gripped his wrist. Hard. It was Taillte.

She didn't look at him; she looked straight ahead at the mud.

"He is already gone," she whispered, her voice a razor wire of restraint. "Don't spend the Queen's life on a ghost."

Cedrik watched the militia drag the sobbing, broken man away by his collar, leaving a furrow in the slime. The son stood frozen, tears streaming down his face, until the Grey Officer simply pointed forward. The boy turned and walked.

Cedrik swallowed the rage, tasting like iron, and forced his foot back into the mud.

He shuffled forward, his boots squelching in the muck. He kept his eyes on the heels of the man in front of him, breathing through his mouth to filter out the smell. He forced himself to cough, a wet, rattling sound deep in his chest.

Head down, he told himself. *Strength won't win this.*

But as they drew closer to the front, the silence was broken by a sound. Pasin stiffened beside him. It wasn't a scream. It was a voice. Melodic, structured, and unlike anything he had heard before. It came from the throat of a Grey Officer standing no more than ten paces away.

"Kratas-io vulta."

Pasin stopped his act for a split second. His head snapped up, his green eyes wide as they strained against the wind to catch the impossible syllables drifting through the Tarsis fog.

"Eyes down," Cedrik urged, nudging the old man's shin with his boot. "You're a senile grandfather, remember? Stop looking like you're reading a map."

Pasin blinked, the old man's sharp focus dissolving back into the clouded gaze of the infirm, but his hand gripped Cedrik's sleeve with a strength that belied the act.

"Did you hear that, Cedrik?" Pasin whispered, his voice unsteady. It sounded as if he was thinking too fast to speak. "Kratas... -Io... Those are... they don't belong together."

"It's just gibberish," Cedrik grunted, shuffling forward as the line moved.

"No," Pasin breathed. "It's a graft. Alcian sentence structure. The words are a mixture of languages. Regat, Xencid. This isn't a random dialect, Cedrik. It's as if they are speaking all of our languages at once, but also, none of them at the same time."

Cedrik didn't have time to process the implication. The line stopped abruptly.

Just ahead, the Grey Officer who had spoken raised his serrated baton. He didn't point it at the gate. He pointed it at a young weaver standing three spots ahead.

"Selection," the Officer commanded.

Two militia guards grabbed the weaver. The boy didn't fight; he looked too exhausted to understand what was happening. But they didn't drag him toward the palace gate. They dragged him toward a heavy, frosted glass pillar standing near the cliff's edge.

A man in a blood-red cloak, stepped out from behind the pillar. He placed one palm on the weaver's chest and the other on the pillar, completing a bridge.

There was no chant. No ritual. Just a sudden, violent intake of air that sounded like the crack of a whip.

A violet spark leaped from the weaver to the pillar.

The weaver collapsed. He didn't just fall; he crumbled like an empty sack. His skin turned the color of old parchment instantly, his eyes rolling back as if every ounce of his being had been savagely pulled out through his pores.

The pillar then glimmered, bright enough that Cedrik had to shield his eyes. As his eyes regained their focus, a soldier, encased in familiar dark gray armor with that strange red crest, strode through the column as if it was a portal. His heavy boots crunched hard on the packed dirt as he bowed to the cloaked figure.

Impossible... One life emptied. One life returned.

"It's a tithe," Taillte whispered, her face pale beneath the mud and ash. She wasn't looking at the soldier; she was staring at the husk of the weaver. "They didn't kill him. They drained him. That wasn't an execution... it was a transfusion."

Cedrik felt a cold sweat break out beneath his tunic. He had seen the Healer Corps perform miracles only explained by the Gift. But never anything like this.

Before he could signal to exit, the Grey Officer turned. His light brown eyes locked onto Cedrik. He didn't see a mason. He saw a man with the physical Gifts that would serve nicely as the next offering.

The serrated baton rose, pointing at Cedrik's chest.

"Tu... valer-us?" the Officer asked. The language sounded familiar yet alien, completely at odds with anything Cedrik had heard before.

Cedrik forced his knees to buckle slightly. He coughed into a rag, hiding the sharp line of his jaw. He held out his hands: scarred, broad, and shaking.

"Mason, master," Cedrik rasped, pitching his voice into a gravelly whine. "From the North. I know the stone. I know the mortar... But my lungs... the ash took my lungs."

The Officer stepped closer; ozone and metal. He circled Cedrik, the serrated baton hovering inches from his ribs. The Officer's gaze examined Cedrik intensely, moving from his shoulders to his chest, finally to the blood-stained rag. Calculating. A butcher appraising meat.

"The Upper Ward requires your skills," the Officer said, switching to a mangled, mechanical Alcian. "This palace is... inefficient. We require those who understand the stone to prepare for new... adjustments."

He turned to the scribe at the desk.

"Selection," the Officer directed. "Palace detail. Move the mason. Move the shadows with him." He motioned toward Pasin, Taillte, and Fromme. "The placeholder," he gestured vaguely at the palace, "requires servants who won't break on the first day."

The militia sergeant shoved Cedrik toward the large gate. "Move it, Northman. Governor Gaughan doesn't pay for loitering."

As they were herded through the great stone archway to the Upper Ward, leaving the desiccated husk of the weaver behind them in the mud, Pasin leaned in close to Cedrik's ear.

"We have to get the Queen out, Cedrik," the old man whispered. "If they realize what she really is, what she means to the people, they won't just kill her. They'll break her in the most horrific way possible, and break the spirit of Alcia with her."

CHAPTER 18

The transition was instant, violent. Silent.

As the heavy oak gates of the Upper Ward swung shut behind them, the roar of the surplus crowds was cut off, as if by a guillotine. The unforgettable stench of uncleansed, grimy bodies, the sour sweetness of rotting straw, the tang of ripe manure and fear that choked the senses in the Lower Ward vanished. Immediately replaced by a cleansing wall of air that tasted of jasmine, sea salt and cold, sterilized ozone.

Cedrik forced his boot to catch on a perfectly level paving stone, stumbling slightly. He pitched his shoulders forward, rounding his spine to hide the width of his chest, fighting twenty years of disciplined muscle memory.

"Easy, grandfather," he rasped, gripping Pasin's arm with a hand that was deliberately shaking.

Pasin leaned into him, playing the part of the senile elder. But as the old scholar looked around the pristine courtyard, his grip on Cedrik's forearm tightened until it was painful.

"Too clean," Pasin whispered, the words barely escaping his lips. "Cedrik, look at the shadows."

Cedrik kept his head down, staring at the white limestone beneath his feet. It was spotless. There was no horse dung, no dust, no boot marks. Just pure white, polished limestone. The Upper Ward didn't look like a fortress preparing for a siege; it looked like a mausoleum prepared for a viewing.

He risked a glance upward, wiping away some dirt and ash from his disguise to mask his intent.

They were being led through the Avenue of Kings, a wide thoroughfare lined with ancient statues of Alcia's past monarchs. But the avenue had been sanitized. The stone heads of the kings had been sheared off. Not smashed, but sliced cleanly, leaving smooth, flat surfaces where the faces of history used to be.

Atop each flat neck sat a small, frosted glass pyramid, pulsing with a faint, violet rhythm.

Fromme let out a small, high-pitched whimper. The boy was walking behind them, clutching his bucket of tools like a shield. He was staring at the glass pyramids, his eyes wide and wet.

"Eyes on your boots, boy," Cedrik grumbled, the vibration low in his chest. "Remember, you're a laborer. You don't look at the art."

"It's... it's humming," Fromme stammered, shrinking into Taillte's shadow. "Can't you hear it? Like... like bees inside the stone."

"I hear it," Taillte confirmed. She walked with a slump that disguised her height, but her energy was coiled tight, a viper waiting to strike. "Keep moving. Focus on the mission, nothing else. If you stop, they'll notice the shake."

A Grey Officer walked ten paces ahead of them. He moved without sound, his high-collared leather armor absorbing the bright southern sun rather than reflecting it. He didn't look back to see if they were following. He knew they were. He moved with the arrogance of a creature that had no natural predators.

They reached the central plaza of the Upper Ward. To the left, the Governor's Palace loomed, a sprawling complex of white towers and gold-leafed balconies. It was beautiful, breathtaking. A grand departure from the more utilitarian architecture of the Capital. The mark of a city defined by its traders and negotiators.

Servants in the blue and gold livery of Tarsis scurried along the edges of the plaza, their heads bowed so low they were practically doubled over. They gave the Grey Officer a wide berth, pressing themselves against the walls as he passed.

The Officer stopped at the base of the West Wing, the structure that housed the Royal Apartments. He turned slowly, the movement fluid and oily.

"Halt," he commanded. The word was Alcian, but the intonation was wrong; metallic, clipped, stripped of any regional accent.

Cedrik dropped to one knee, feigning a coughing fit to hide his face. He spat onto the pristine white stone.

The Officer stared at the spittle, an ugly stain on an otherwise sterile landscape. His eyes, light brown and unblinking, moved to Cedrik. He hesitated for a moment, studying the supposedly pitiful mason.

"The structural integrity of the West Corridor is… compromised," the Officer said, pointing his serrated baton toward a heavy service door. "The anchors require reinforcement. The mortar must be mixed to exact specifications." He looked at Pasin. "You understand the old mixtures?"

Pasin blinked, letting his mouth hang open slightly. "Aye… aye, master. Lime and ash. Strong as the cliffs themselves. I built the… uh… the wells in Oakhaven, I did."

The Officer stared at him for a long moment filled with uncomfortable silence. He was scanning. Searching for a pulse rate that didn't match the senility, a muscle density that betrayed the act.

Cedrik felt the phantom weight of his greatsword pulling on his back. His hand twitched toward a hilt that wasn't there. *Don't do it… Don't tense.*

"Inefficient," the Officer finally decided, turning away. "But sufficient for labor."

He gestured to the door. Two Tarsis militia guards, looking pale and sweaty in their ill-fitting armor, struggled to pull it open.

"Inside," the Officer ordered. "Do not wander. The interior is… active."

As Cedrik hauled himself up, grabbing his tools, the humming Fromme had noticed earlier grew louder. It wasn't just a beehive anymore. It was a deep, barely audible thrumming that vibrated in Cedrik's teeth.

He looked at the open door. It didn't look like a service entrance. It looked like the mouth of a beast, with an insatiable appetite.

"Let's go, apprentice," Cedrik muttered to Fromme, shoving the boy gently forward. "And remember, you're invisible."

The heavy service door slammed shut behind them, sealing out the blinding sun of the courtyard.

They were instantly plunged into a suffocating twilight. The air in the service corridor was hot, unnaturally so, and thick with the smell of ozone and singed dust. But it was the sound that dominated their senses.

The barely perceptible hum they had heard outside was no longer a suggestion; it was a physical weight pressing against their eardrums and squeezing their chests. It throbbed in the floorboards, a pulsing, mechanical heartbeat that seemed to be shaking the very foundation of the Palace.

"Down," Cedrik ordered, shoving Fromme toward a patch of exposed brickwork near the entrance. "If that Officer comes back, he needs to smell work."

Fromme fumbled with the bucket, his hands shaking so hard the metal handle rattled like a dinner bell. He poured the water from his skin into the dry powder the Grey Officer had provided.

"Quiet, boy," Cedrik said, dropping to his knees beside him. He grabbed a trowel, forcing his movements to be rough and clumsy, masking his lethal dexterity.

Fromme stirred the mixture. It didn't look like lime and ash. As the water hit the gray dust, the slurry hissed. Bubbles of dark, iridescent violet rose to the surface, popping with the smell of copper and old blood.

"Don't get it on your skin," Pasin whispered, leaning over Fromme's shoulder. The scholar's eyes were wide, reflecting the faint, sick glow of the bucket. "Look at it. Like it's moving."

The mortar wasn't just settling; it was knitting itself together. The sludge pulled toward the center of the bucket like a living organism trying to form a spine.

"It's conductive," Pasin murmured, reaching out but stopping inches from the sludge. "It isn't meant to hold stone together, Cedrik. It's meant to carry power, energy. They're connecting the walls."

A shadow passed over the frosted glass of the door they had just entered. A heavy boot scraped against the stone outside.

Cedrik didn't hesitate. He scooped a glob of the hissing violet sludge onto his trowel and slapped it onto the wall. It sizzled against the cold limestone, bonding instantly with a grip that looked less like masonry and more like a scab forming over a wound.

"Work," Cedrik breathed.

Cedrik smoothed the repulsive sludge, Fromme stirred the bubbling bucket, and Pasin inspected the wall. The shadow lingered on the glass for three heartbeats. Then, the boots receded.

Cedrik exhaled, the sound harsh in the humid air. He looked at the wall. The mortar he had applied was already hard, pulsing with the same faint rhythm as the corridor.

"We're helping them," Fromme whispered, staring at the bucket. "We're helping them... build it."

"We're buying time," Cedrik corrected, wiping the trowel on his pants. The violet stain didn't come off. "Leave the bucket. We move," Cedrik whispered, gripping his hammer until his hands ached. "Look busy. If anyone passes, we're checking the mortar."

They moved single file down the narrow stone hallway. This passage was meant for servants, unseen arteries designed to keep the lifeblood of the palace hidden from the royals. Now, it felt clogged and degenerative.

"Look at the walls," Pasin breathed, pausing to run a trembling hand along the stone.

The ancient Alcian limestone was no longer pristine. Veins of a dark, metallic substance had been injected into the mortar, pulsing with a faint violet light. It looked as if the castle itself was being infected.

"It's a graft," Pasin murmured, his eyes wide with a horrific fascination. "They aren't repairing damage, Cedrik. They're... rewriting the architecture. Just like their language."

"Don't touch it," Taillte warned, slapping the old man's hand away. "It feels... hungry."

They turned a sharp corner and nearly collided with a figure standing in the shadows.

Fromme gasped, dropping his bucket. The clang echoed like a hammer cracking stone in the confined space.

Cedrik spun, stepping in front of the boy, his body poised to strike. But the figure didn't attack.

It was a young woman, dressed in a servant's uniform that hung loosely on her small frame. She was leaning against a wall, her head lolling back, eyes fixed to the ceiling. Her skin was the color of gray parchment, drained of any other hue.

She didn't blink. She didn't breathe. She just stared up at a glass node embedded in the ceiling that was pulsing in time with the hum.

"One life emptied," Taillte whispered, the clinical coldness of observation apparent in her voice. She stepped forward, reaching for the woman's wrist. "She's alive... barely. Her pulse is threading."

"Taillte, no," Cedrik hissed, grabbing the back of her tunic.

"She's dying, Cedrik! I can save her! They're draining her to power the—"

"If you heal her, the hum stops," Pasin cut in, his voice sharp. "If the hum stops, the Grey Officers come. Is she worth the Queen? Is she worth all of Alcia?"

Taillte froze. She looked at the desiccated woman, then at Cedrik. The fire in her bright blue eyes warred with the ice of her duty.

Finally, she pulled her hand back, shaking. "Focus on the mission," she said, the words sounded rehearsed. "We keep moving."

They left the woman in the dark and pushed deeper into the tower. The corridor opened up into a maintenance alcove that overlooked the main hallway of the Royal Apartments.

Cedrik peered through the heavy iron grate.

Ten feet below, the hallway was guarded. But not by the Grey Officers.

Two men stood outside a set of heavy, oak double doors; the only doors in the corridor that had been reinforced with fresh iron bands. They wore the blue livery of Tarsis, but they leaned on their halberds with the sloppy, dissociated posture of prolonged boredom.

"Mercenaries," Cedrik noted.

"That's her door," Pasin whispered, pointing to the fresh welding marks on the hinges. "Locked from the outside."

"And guarded by men who look like they'd trade their mothers for a wineskin," Cedrik added. A plan began to form behind his eyes; brutal and efficient.

"We need to clear that hall," Cedrik said, turning to the others. "I'm going to need a distraction. A loud one. Pasin... you said this was a graft?" Cedrik asked, as the old man nodded his head. "Taillte, what happens if the body rejects the transplant?'

She studied the walls for a moment. "A fever, Commander. A very violent fever."

"Can you induce it?" Cedrik asked, eyeing the pulsing violet veins in the limestone.

"The architecture is trying to accept a foreign agent," Pasin interjected, his voice low and hurried. "I assume its biological. It must be stable because the flow is controlled. But... if she introduces a sudden, chaotic surge of raw life energy... the host will try to expel the parasite."

Taillte was already rolling up the tattered sleeve of her disguise, revealing the pale skin of her forearm. "My Gift was meant to knit flesh, not... whatever this is."

"Life is life, my dear." Pasin's eyes lit up with a dangerous spark. "And right now, this building needs to get very sick, very quickly."

Taillte took a deep breath, centering herself. She hovered her hand inches above the largest vein of the violet material. The thrum in the corridor seemed to pitch up, reacting to her presence like a snake sensing a mouse.

"Fromme, cover your ears," Cedrik ordered, pulling the grate loose from its hinges. It came away with a silent, heavy shift of iron.

Taillte slammed her palm against the stone.

She didn't gasp this time; she snarled. The reaction was instantaneous.

The violet light in the veins turned a deep, angry crimson. The low hum spiked into a high-pitched shriek, sounding less like masonry and more like a kettle screaming on an open fire.

The wall convulsed.

Chunks of limestone cracked and were spat out from the mortar as the stone heated up. A cloud of acrid, burning steam erupted from the graft, filling the service tunnel with the stench of cooking meat and ozone.

Down in the main hallway, the two mercenary guards jumped as if whipped.

"What in the Hells?" one shouted, backing away as the ceiling above them began to vibrate.

"It's a breach!" the other yelled, raising his halberd uncertainly. "The pipes are bursting!"

The screaming noise in the walls intensified, echoing down the corridor like a banshee. The graft was rejecting the surge of life, violently overheating to burn it out.

"Go check the valve!" the first guard screamed over the noise, pointing down the hall away from the Queen's door. "Before the Governor skins us alive!"

"I'm not touching that! Look at it, it's glowing red!"

"Move, you idiot!"

Both guards scrambled away from the door, running toward the junction where the steam was billowing thickest from the vents.

"Now!" Cedrik commanded.

He dropped, landing on the plush carpet of the Royal Corridor with a heavy thud, absorbing the impact in his knees. He ignored the pain in his joints, his ribs, and the phantom itch for his greatsword, crossing the distance to the Queen's door in three long strides.

"Pasin, keep that noise going for ten more seconds!" Cedrik ordered up at the grate.

He reached the heavy oak doors. They were reinforced with iron bands, the lock mechanism new and complex. A Tarsis heavy lock. Without a key, it would take a battering ram to open.

Or a mason who knew exactly where the stone was weak.

Cedrik didn't go for the lock. He pulled his chisel from his belt; a heavy, flat-headed tool he had grabbed from the supply yard.

He jammed the chisel into the gap between the doorframe and the wall, right where the hinges were anchored into the stone.

Mason, master... I know the stone, he thought, echoing his lie to the Grey Officer.

He struck the end of the chisel with his heavy hammer. Once. Twice.

The stone around the top hinge cracked. It wasn't a move of finesse; it was brute force applied with the precision of trained combat. The integrity of the anchor failed.

Cedrik hooked his fingers into the gap, and pulled with everything he had. His arms and legs screamed with fire at the intensity of the resistance, a comfort to be active again. The heavy door groaned, the top hinge pulling free from the crumbling limestone with a screech of tearing metal.

The door sagged outward, leaving a gap just wide enough for a man to slip through.

Cedrik didn't wait. He shoved his way inside, gashing his shoulder against the iron banding, and stumbled into the room.

The noise of the fever outside was instantly muffled by the heavy tapestries lining the walls. The air here smelled of the signature jasmine of Tarsis; rich and sweet, wrapped in a cold, stale silence.

Cedrik scanned the room. It was empty. The bed was made. The vanity untouched.

Then he saw her.

Queen Brighid Lorindan was standing by the balcony doors, a small, silver fruit knife in her hand. She wasn't cowering. She was crouched in a fighting stance, her amber eyes glowing with the ferocity of a lioness on the hunt.

She looked at Cedrik, a dirty, hulking laborer with a hammer in his hand, blood pouring from his shoulder, who had just burst his way into her sanctuary like a beast.

"One step closer," Brighid warned, her voice smooth and as hard as steel, "and your blood will color this rug."

Cedrik straightened and dropped his hammer. He slowly moved his empty hands to his sides. He bowed, not as a servant, but as a Knight Commander.

"Your Majesty," Cedrik rasped, his voice rough with dust. Relief then flowed through. "Neelin sends his regards."

CHAPTER 19

Boom. Boom. Boom.

The heavy tapestries lining the walls could not contain the pulsing and screeching of the graft in the corridors. The sound of a mechanical heartbeat pulsed and pounded with rising intensity.

Cedrik Theramond looked less a savior, and more a creature dredged from the bottom of the Tarsis canals. He was covered in gray sludge, reeking of ozone and bleeding freely from the gash on his shoulder where the iron banding had bitten into his flesh.

He gasped for air, his lungs burning from the acrid steam filling the corridor behind him. The fever Taillte had induced in the palace walls was no longer just a noise; it was a physical assault. The floorboards beneath his boots vibrated with a high-pitched, mechanical shriek, like a thousand metal gears grinding against stone without oil.

Cedrik straightened, his hand instinctively reaching for the greatsword that wasn't there. Instead, he held his empty, scarred hands out, palms open.

"Your Majesty," he rasped, the words scraping against his dust-coated throat. "We really must—"

Queen Brighid Lorindan did not scream. She did not swoon. She did not step back. Instead, she held her ground by the balcony doors, her solid blue dress a juxtaposition against the pristine white curtains that fluttered behind her in the sea breeze. In her hand, the small, silver fruit knife gleamed in the light. Not held with a trembling grip, but with the steady, lethal intent of a cornered cat.

"I said, one step closer," Brighid warned. Her voice was terrifyingly calm, cutting through the industrial scream emanating from the walls. "And your blood will cover this rug."

Cedrik paused, blinking the sweat from his eyes. He saw the tension in her shoulders, the way she shifted her weight to the balls of her feet.

Boom. Boom. Boom.

She isn't waiting to be rescued, he realized with admiration. *She is waiting to take someone with her.*

"I have no desire to bleed more than I already am, my Queen," Cedrik said, slowly lowering himself to one knee. It was a clumsy, painful movement, his joints stiff from the unnatural posture he had adopted by way of a disguise. He bowed his head again, exposing the back of his neck; the ultimate sign of submission. "I am here by order of the High Marshal, Neelin Arran."

The knife did not move. "Neelin is at the border," Brighid said, her eyes narrowing. "Or he is dead. That is what *they* told me."

"Neelin is alive. Broken, burned, and currently digging a large grave for the enemy at Dunvar, Your Highness. But very much alive," Cedrik replied, looking up. He reached into the dirty folds of his laborer's tunic and pulled out a pouch he had refused to surrender at the gate. He slid it across the plush carpet.

Brighid's eyes stayed locked onto Cedrik as the small pouch stopped at the toe of her boot. She focused on him as she slowly bent down, grabbing the pouch with her free hand. Cedrik stayed calm, not moving. The Lioness hesitated but then opened the pouch. She softened, just for a heartbeat, surrendering to the exhaustion of a woman who had spent three days in solitary confinement.

"Cedrik?" she whispered. She looked at him then, really looked at him, piercing through the layers of mud and the laborer's disguise. "You look... ruined."

"I'm blending in," Cedrik grunted, hauling himself back to his feet. A tremor ran through the palace, shaking a vase off the mantle. It shattered; the sound lost in the rising cacophony of the walls. "We don't have time for pleasantries, Your Majesty. Captain Cleirigh is currently convincing the architecture that it's dying. I don't know how long it will last."

Boom. Boom. Boom.

Brighid stepped forward, finally lowering the knife. "The noise... the heat in the walls... that is your doing?"

"A distraction," Cedrik confirmed. He glanced at the ruins of the door. The steam billowing in from the corridor was turning pink as the violent veins in the limestone overheated. "The Grey Officers are confused. Their graft is rejecting the host. But once they realize what is causing it, they will be on us. We have to move, now."

Brighid didn't move toward the door. She turned back to her desk, her hand hovering over a stack of parchments.

"I know about the boy, Cedrik," she said, a pained whisper. "Ambassador Xarion... he told me. Alaric has a son. A successor." She looked up, her amber eyes searching Cedrik's face for a lie. "Tell me it's a trick. Tell me my husband didn't spend thirty years building a replacement family in Xencid, while I sat in his court."

Cedrik could not hide the disbelief on his face. The shock rumbled through his body, shaking his insides like thunder. "If this is true, I have not heard. Neelin said no such thing... I cannot believe—"

"Many things have happened that I cannot believe," Brighid cut in. "Their plan... I am just a pawn—"

"No," Cedrik stepped forward, his bulk blocking the light from the balcony. "You are the only thing left that matters. King Alaric is gone. You are the single heart of Alcia now." He gestured to the ruin of the door. "But hearts are fragile, Your Majesty. And right now, you can choose to be their pawn in this golden cage, or you come with me and live to make them regret their lies."

Boom. Boom. Boom.

Brighid looked at the fruit knife, then at the heavy, leather satchel sitting on the vanity; the one she had stuffed with maps and royal seals before fleeing the Capital. She sheathed the knife into the folds of her dress and grabbed the satchel. She moved toward him, the silk of her gown wisping against the floor. She smelled sweet, with the overbearing floral scents of Tarsis, but her jaw was set hard, highlighting the striking Northern features of her face.

"You have a plan to get us out of the Upper Ward?" she asked. "The gates are sealed."

"I have a squire, a scholar, and a very angry medic waiting in the service tunnels," Cedrik said, kicking a piece of the doorframe out of the way. "We aren't going out the front gate. We're going down."

"Down?" Brighid paused at the threshold, looking into the steam-filled corridor. The heat hit her like a physical blow.

"Into the guts of the palace," Cedrik said, offering a dirty, scarred hand. "It's going to be hot, loud, and filthy. You will ruin that dress."

Brighid took his hand. Her grip surprised him with its strength, and her skin felt cool against his feverish palm.

"Good," the Queen said. "I never liked this dress anyway."

Cedrik didn't wait like a courtier. He pulled the Queen's hand with a grip meant for hauling stone. "Stay low," he commanded, pulling her through the splintered gap in the doorframe.

They spilled out into the corridor and were hit by a wall of blistering heat, like walking through the opening of a furnace. The fever Taillte had induced was reaching its peak. The limestone walls were no longer just vibrating, they were sweating. Beak-sized chips of plaster popped off the ceiling, raining fine white dust onto the luxurious carpet.

Brighid gasped, shielding her face with her free hand. "The walls... they're bleeding. I've never seen it's like..."

Cedrik glanced at the masonry. The violet veins of the graft had turned a sickly, boiling crimson. The metallic substance pulsed violently, looking less like structural support and more like an infection trying to burst through the skin of the palace.

Boom. Boom. Boom.

"Don't touch them," Cedrik warned, steering her toward the maintenance grate where his team awaited. "If the graft touches bare skin, it drains you. Completely."

He stopped beneath the open vent in the ceiling. It was ten feet up; an impossible climb for a woman in a royal gown, but a trivial lift for a man who had spent his life in plate armor.

"Pasin!" Cedrik roared over the shrieking architecture. "Incoming!"

A weathered face framed by white hair appeared in the dark square above. Pasin looked down, his eyes wide as he spotted the woman standing in blue amidst the falling debris.

"By the First Cycle," Pasin shouted down, a grin breaking through his tight face. "You actually found her! And she's armed." He nodded at the satchel Brighid clutched to her chest.

"Pull her up," Cedrik ordered.

He turned to Brighid. There was no time for protocol. "Your Majesty, forgive the indignity."

Before she could protest, Cedrik grabbed her by the waist and hoisted her upward with ease, as if she were a sack of grain. Brighid didn't flinch. She tossed her satchel into the dark and grabbed the iron rim of the grate, hauling herself up with a surprising strength.

Cedrik jumped, catching the lip of the stone, and hauled his bulk up behind her.

The service tunnel was cramped, dark and sweltering.

Taillte was slumped against the far wall, her face pale beneath the grime. She was clutching her left arm, her chest heaving as she fought to recover from the strain of inducing the fever. But when she saw the Queen, the exhaustion vanished from her face.

The Royal Guard Captain scrambled to her feet, snapping into a rigid salute despite the low ceiling.

"Your Majesty," Taillte said, her voice cracking with emotion. "We thought... the reports said..."

Brighid stared at the woman dressed as a camp follower, the mud in her red hair and the fierce loyalty burning in her blue eyes. The Queen reached out, her hand trembling slightly, and touched Taillte's shoulder.

"At ease, Captain," Brighid said, softly. "You look like hell. And I have never been so happy to see anyone in my life."

Boom. Boom. Boom.

"We need to move," Cedrik interrupted, squeezing past them to take the lead. He didn't want to break the moment, but the tunnel floor was shaking hard enough to rattle his teeth. "We don't know how much longer it will take the Grey Officers to stabilize the graft. If we're still in the walls when the hum stops, they can focus on finding us."

"Fromme, take the rear," Pasin ordered, tapping the boy with his staff. "Watch the vents."

The boy nodded, his eyes huge as he stared at the Queen. He clutched the bucket of tools to his chest, looking terrified that he might accidentally brush against royalty.

"Go," Cedrik barked, as the Queen grabbed her satchel.

They ran.

It wasn't a graceful escape. It was a scramble through the intestines of a dying beast. The service tunnels twisted and turned, narrowing in places until Cedrik's broad shoulders scraped the stone on both sides.

Servants were scrambling through the tunnels with them, not knowing what to do. Cedrik had to push them aside forcefully, no time for manners.

A voice cut out from one of the tunnels. "Your Majesty!"

Cedrik snarled. The last thing they needed was a servant reporting the Queen running through the service tunnels. He turned toward the sound, but was restrained by a firm hand.

"Mara!" Brighid said. "Come. Now. We are leaving."

Cedrik looked at the Queen, ready to protest, but her face showed the resolve of finality. No protest was going to be heard.

The small girl joined the company, fitting in with the laborer's disguises with her tattered servant rags. She clutched the Queen's arm for comfort, her face covered by her oily brown hair and awash with fear.

The hum of the palace began to change pitch. The piercing shriek of the fever was dropping, deepening into a heavy, resonant thrum.

Boom... Boom... Boom...

Cedrik's blood went cold. The beats were getting farther apart, slowing and softening. It was the sound of the building's heart stabilizing.

"They're resetting the graft!" Pasin hissed from behind him. "Faster!"

They burst out of the narrow corridor into a wider junction used for water pipes. Cedrik skidded to a halt. Ahead, the path split. To the left, the tunnel sloped upward toward the kitchens and the Upper Ward. To the right, it dove deeper into the dark, sloping aggressively downward.

"We need to get off the Palace grounds," Pasin said, eyeing the downward slope. "The waste chutes dump directly into the harbor channels. It's a hundred-foot drop, but it clears the walls."

"No," Cedrik said, his voice hard. He turned away from the waste chutes.

"Cedrik, we cannot fight our way out of the main gate!" Taillte argued, wiping sweat from her eyes. "We have no weapons!"

"Exactly," Cedrik snapped. "And we aren't walking two hundred miles to the border in labor rags. We need steel... and we need horses."

He pointed into the darkness of the downward tunnel, but not toward the sea. He pointed toward the City.

"Harlen took them," Cedrik growled, the memory of surrendering his greatsword burning in his gut. "He took Bastion. He took the gear. And he took them to the Militia post in the Lower Ward."

"The Lower Ward?" Fromme squeaked. "That's... that's where the cages are. Where the Grey Officers are doing the... the transfusions."

"It's also where the confusion will be the highest," Cedrik countered. "This fever, was it just in the palace, Taillte?"

The Captain shook her head. "No, you're right. The graft is connected throughout the City. I felt it."

"Then the rest of the buildings in the Upper Ward screamed, and the pillars in the Lower Ward screamed too," Cedrik said. "The militia will be panicked; the Grey Officers will be draw here." He looked at Brighid. "Your Majesty, the drop into the ocean is safer. But without horses, the Grey Officers will run us down before we clear the foothills."

Brighid adjusted the heavy strap of her satchel. She looked at Cedrik, but he could not hide his desperation. It wasn't just strategy. A knight was nothing without his sword, just as a rider was nothing without his horse. His companion, his friend.

"I am done hiding in towers, Commander," Brighid said. "And I am certainly not walking to Dunvar. Get us our horses."

This Queen... She is the Alcia that we fight with our lives to protect.

Cedrik nodded, a genuine smile touching his lips. "Then we go down. Into the Lower Ward."

CHAPTER 20

THE TUNNEL SPAT THEM out behind a dyer's shop, into an alley ankle-deep in blue-stained mud.

The air here didn't smell of the jasmine or sterile ozone of the Upper Ward. It reeked of burning hair, the dirt of humanity, raw sewage, and the copper tang of blood.

Cedrik wiped the tunnel grime from his eyes and scanned the Lower Ward. It was no longer a holding pen; it was a pressure pot ready to burst.

The fever Taillte had induced in the palace grid had surged through the entire city's network. The Transfusion Pillars—those towering, frosted-glass monoliths that had stood silent over the refugees—were dark.

Without the humming pillars to keep them subdued, the terror of the surplus had turned into rage.

The mob suddenly parted around the center of the square, creating a bubble of silence in the chaos.

"Don't look," Cedrik warned, trying to shield the Queen with his body.

But Brighid stopped. She pushed his arms aside.

In the center of the mud stood one of the Transfusion Pillars. It was cracked down the middle, leaking thick, black smoke that crawled along the ground like blood pouring from a wound. Clustered around its base were a dozen bodies. They weren't trampled. They weren't bloody.

They were... hollow.

Cedrik saw a man lying face up in the muck. His skin was gray and papery, pulled tight against his skull like cured leather. His eyes were open, but they were milky white, devoid of moisture. It looked as if he had been left in the desert sun for a decade, yet his clothes were damp with the morning's rain.

Next to him lay a mother clutching a child. Both were in the same condition; withered husks, every last drop of vitality drained from them.

"What…" Brighid's voice shuddered, her hand flying to her mouth. "What is this? What happened to them?

"The Pillar," Taillte whispered from behind, her face pale. "When the surge hit, it didn't just stop. It must have absorbed… everything at once."

Brighid looked up at the towering glass monolith. "They didn't just lock them in. They were harvesting them." Her amber eyes hardened, the shock burned away by a cold, diamond-hard rage.

She looked at Cedrik. There were no tears. Only judgement.

"Get us out, Commander," she said, her voice dropping to a chilling register. "If we die here, these bastards win."

Thousands of refugees were pushing against the barricades. Wooden fences splintered under the weight of the mob. Tarsis Militia guards, usually arrogant in their blue and gold livery, were retreating toward the gatehouses, swinging their halberds blindly to keep the tide of humanity at bay.

"Stay close," Cedrik ordered, his voice was low but cut through the screams.

He shoved his way into the mob, using his bulk as a plow. He kept one hand near the dagger concealed in his waistband, the other gripping Mara's shoulder to keep the terrified servant from being swallowed by the hordes.

"If we get separated, head for the main gatehouse. Do not stop for anything."

Brighid moved beside him. Her dress was torn to ribbons, stained with grease and white dust, but she held her head high. She didn't look like a refugee. Even in the filth, she moved with a precise, regal focus. She wasn't looking at the ground; she was watching the people—her people—being crushed against the walls they couldn't climb.

"They locked them in," Brighid whispered, seeing the reinforced barricades blocking the side streets. "Gaughan trapped them in here with those... things."

"Focus, Your Majesty," Cedrik said, shouldering a path through a knot of screaming merchants. "We can't save the city. We have to survive it."

They reached the edge of the Militia Post near the main gatehouse. It was a sturdy stone building attached to the outer wall, flanked by the stables where they had surrendered their mounts many hours ago.

The chaos here was different. It was the organized panic of soldiers realizing they were losing control.

Guards were running back and forth, shouting orders that dissolved into the din. In the center of the yard, Sergeant Harlen stood atop a crate, his face flushed red as he tried to rally his men.

"Hold the line!" Harlen bellowed, pointing his sword at the approaching mob. "The Governor says the grid is stabilizing! Keep them back... If they breach the Inner gate, we—"

"Harlen!"

The roar cut through the noise like thunderclap.

Cedrik stepped into the torchlight of the yard. He dropped the laborer's slouch he had worn for hours. He rolled his shoulders back, expanding to his full height; a mountain of scarred muscle and determination.

Harlen froze. He looked at the dirty, bloodied giant bearing down on him, and recognition dawned in his eyes.

"Commander?" Harlen stammered, lowering his sword an inch. "You... I was told you were in the labor detail... They Grey Officers..."

"The Grey Officers are busy," Cedrik snarled, stalking forward.

Two militia guards leveled their crossbows at him, but their hands were shaking. They looked at Cedrik, then at the strange company behind him; an old man with a staff, a woman with the eyes of a wolf, a terrified boy next to a scrawny servant girl, and a

Queen covered in tattered silk and sludge who still carried the air of royal authority.

"You have something of mine, Sergeant," Cedrik said, stopping three paces from the crate. His voice was dangerously low, filled with the promise of violence.

Harlen looked at the crossbows, then back at Cedrik's empty hands. He saw the look in the Knight Commander's eyes. It wasn't the look of a prisoner. It was the look of a man who was done hiding.

"The lockdown is in effect," Harlen tried, though his voice wavered. "No one leaves the City. Governor's orders."

"I am taking my horse," Cedrik said, taking another step. "And I am taking my steel. You can either open the door, Harlen, or I can beat you to death with your own helmet and open it myself."

Silence stretched across the yard, heavy and thick.

From the street behind them, the sound of the mob breaking through the outer barricade echoed like a breaking wave.

Crack.

Harlen flinched. He looked at his terrified men, then at the unstoppable force in front of him.

"Stand down," Harlen ordered, lowering his sword completely.

"Sergeant?" one of the guards protested, his finger twitching on the trigger. "If the Grey Officers find out—"

"I said stand down!" Harlen snapped. He looked at Cedrik, a mixture of fear and relief washing over him. He tossed a ring of heavy iron keys to the Knight.

"The stables are unlocked," Harlen said, quietly. "Your gear is in the back room. Take it and go."

Cedrik caught the keys out of the air. He turned to his squad.

"Get the horses," Cedrik commanded. "I'm getting the steel."

"Commander," Harlen said. "There is a switchback you can take, the emergency route out of the stables. It's washed out now, but it's your best option."

Cedrik walked past the Sergeant as he went to grab their gear. "You did the right thing today, Sergeant. Honor guide you."

"Honor guide you, Commander."

Cedrik kicked open the door to the tack room. The familiar smell of oiled leather and cold iron hit him, a welcome change to the sewage of the Lower Ward.

His armor was piled in the corner, a heap of dented plates that had been tossed aside like scrap. He ignored the breastplate and greaves; there was no time to strap on his full suit.

Too much weight on a crumbling trail. The warning about the washed-out switchback echoed in his mind.

Instead, he grabbed his shoulder harness, buckling the thick leather over his stained laborer's tunic. He tightened the straps until they dug into his ribs; a familiar grounding, pressure.

Then, he turned to the wall.

The greatsword lay there, wrapped in white leather bindings that had turned gray with dust. It was nearly two meters of Alcian steel, forged for killing giants and breaking lines.

Cedrik gripped the handle. The leather creaked as his hand closed around it. The weight of it wasn't a burden, it was a blessing. For the first time since entering Tarsis, the phantom weight was replaced by physical mass. He swung the massive blade onto his back, the metal ringing softly as it settled into the harness.

He wasn't a mason anymore. He wasn't a refugee. He was a Knight Commander of the Alcian Army.

I am powerless no more.

He grabbed a sack with Taillte's gear and turned on his heel.

He burst into the stable block. The air inside was thick with the smell of panic. The horses were thrashing in their stalls, their eyes rolling white at the stench of ozone and the roaring mob outside.

A loud, aggressive whinny echoed from the end stall. Wood splintered as a massive mahogany hoof kicked the gate.

"Bastion," Cedrik breathed.

He ran to the stall. The warhorse was in a frenzy, lathered in sweat, ready to trample anyone who came near. But the moment Cedrik laid a hand on the animal's nose, the beast froze.

Bastion snorted, blowing hot air against Cedrik's chest. The horse pressed his velvet muzzle against the Knight's shoulder, shivering violently.

"I know, boy," Cedrik whispered, resting his forehead against the horse's neck. "I know. We're leaving."

Behind him, Pasin and Taillte were saddling their own mounts; the black mare and the spirited gray gelding. He tossed Taillte's gear to her, she nodded her thanks.

He moved with purpose and speed, trained by muscle memory, tacking up the charger in seconds. He reluctantly secured his greatsword to Bastion's side, recognizing the need to be flexible.

"Up you go," Taillte said, lifting Mara onto the back of Fromme's roan. "Hold onto his waist, girl. And don't close your eyes. If you fall, we cannot stop."

Mara nodded, burying her face into the squire's back. Fromme did not notice, fear and anxiety tugging at his face. He gripped the reins with quivering hands, but he sat deep in the saddle, remembering the lessons from the road.

Cedrik vaulted onto Bastion's back. The warhorse danced beneath him, sensing the shift in his rider. The hesitation was gone.

"Your Majesty," Cedrik said, reaching down.

Brighid took his forearm. She didn't scramble; she swung up behind him with the grace of someone raised in the Highlands, settling onto the croup of the horse. She wrapped one arm around his waist, the leather satchel sandwiched securely between them.

"The switchback is narrow," Pasin warned the group. "It has been a while... but I believe it drops straight into the ocean on the left."

"Don't look down, Your Majesty," Cedrik assured her. "I—"

"Just ride, Commander," Brighid said, her voice hard against his back.

Cedrik wheeled Bastion toward the rear exit Harlen had described. He kicked the doors open.

Instead of the riot of the main street, they faced a narrow, crumbling goat path cut into the side of the limestone cliff. The wide torrent separating Tarsis from the wildlands and Regat, roared a hundred feet below. Water crashed into the rocks in a spray of white foam. The path was slick with sea spray and mud, barely wide enough for a single rider.

"Single file!" Cedrik ordered over the crashing waves. "Pasin, take the rear. Don't let the boy lag."

He spurred Bastion forward. The warhorse hesitated for a fraction of a second, feeling the loose shale shift under his hooves, then surged onto the ledge.

Behind them, the sounds of the riot in the Lower Ward were already fading, replaced by the roar of the channel and the terrifying sound of hooves on slippery wet stone.

They were out of the cage, but they were walking a tightrope over the abyss.

CHAPTER 21

THE WORLD NARROWED DOWN to three things: the roar of the wind, the crash of the channel, and the nervous breathing of the horse beneath him.

The switchback Harlen had promised was barely a memory of the road it had once been. It was a jagged scar cut into the limestone cliff, slick with sea spray and eroding under the relentless assault of the tides. To their left, the white stone dropped away into a churning abyss of gray water a hundred feet below. To their right, the sheer wall of the Tarsis plateau rose up like a prison cell.

"Hug the stone!" Cedrik shouted over the gale, leaning his weight to the right.

Bastion scrambled, his steel-shod hooves sparking against the wet rock. The warhorse was built for charging lines of infantry on open fields, not tiptoeing along a goat path. Every muscle in the great beast's neck was corded tight, fighting the instinct to bolt.

Brighid pressed her face against Cedrik's back, her arms now locked around his waist like iron bands. She didn't make a sound, but he could feel her heart hammering against his spine through the thin laborer's tunic.

"Keep moving!" Cedrik roared, risking a glance back. "Don't let the line break!"

Behind them, the squad was a portrait of desperate concentration. Taillte was wrestling with her gray gelding, forcing the animal past a section where the path had crumbled away, leaving a gap no wider than a man's torso.

The squire was pale, his eyes fixed on the churning white water below. Mara was clinging to him, her eyes shut tight, burying her face in his cloak. The roan mare stumbled, a hind leg briefly slipping over the edge of the wet shale.

"Don't pull back!" Cedrik bellowed, seeing the boy yank the reins in panic. "Let her find her head! Give her rein!"

Fromme froze, paralyzed by the drop. The horse scrambled, its hooves scrabbling for purchase on the slick rock, sending a shower of pebbles tumbling into the abyss. The rear of the horse dipped, gravity claiming its due.

"Fromme!" Taillte screamed, reaching out from her saddle, but she was too far ahead to help.

For a heartbeat, time suspended. The roan tipped backward.

Suddenly, the boy moved. Driven by some instinct buried deep beneath the fear, or perhaps awakening to the tightening grip of the terrified girl clinging to his waist, Fromme loosened his grip. He kicked the horse forward, shouting a wordless cry into the unrelenting wind.

The roan surged. She found a sliver of solid rock and heaved herself forward, scrambling away from the edge with a spray of mud. They slammed into the cliff face, safe, shaking violently.

Cedrik let out a breath he didn't know he was holding.

"Please, don't make it too easy on an old man," Pasin yelled from the back, carefully guiding his black mare through the crumbling path.

They climbed for another agonizing ten minutes. The path wound upward, putting distance between them and the ocean, until finally the limestone leveled out. The slick rock gave way to scrub grass and the hard dirt of the Tarsis headlands.

Cedrik spurred Bastion up the final rise and broke onto the sandy, open plateau.

He immediately wheeled the horse around, reaching down to the leather scabbard lashed to Bastion's flank. He ripped the greatsword free in a smooth, fluid motion, the heavy steel humming as it cleared the leather bindings that had kept it from damaging the Queen's leg during the climb.

"Defensive formation!" Cedrik ordered.

Taillte and Pasin scrambled up behind him, fanning out to cover the flanks. They looked back at the city walls, expecting a barrage of crossbow bolts, or the pursuit of Grey Officers.

But there was nothing.

The walls of Tarsis stood tall and white against the darkening sky. The main gates remained closed. No alarm bells rang. No riders poured out to chase them.

The City was back to the unnerving silence, save for the distant rhythmic thrumming of the graft resetting itself deep within the stone.

Boom. Boom. Boom.

"They aren't following," Fromme said, sliding off his horse and falling to his knees in the dirt. He pulled Mara down with him, both shuddering as their nerves finally crashed.

"Why?" Brighid asked, her voice sharp. She sat up on Bastion's rump, smoothing her torn dress. Her amber eyes scanned the horizon, looking for a trap. "We just broke out of their prison. We stole horses. We shook the foundations of the Palace. Why aren't they hunting us?"

Pasin trotted his black mare forward, staring at the silent city with eyes that had seen too many wars. He leaned on his staff, his expression grim.

"Because they don't need to, Your Majesty," the old scholar said, softly. "A shepherd doesn't chase the sheep that run toward the pen. He lets them go."

"Neelin," Cedrik realized, lowering his sword until the tip rested on his boot. The cold feeling in his gut returned, heavier than the armor he had left behind. "They know we are going to Dunvar. To the High Marshal."

"Then we are walking into a trap," Brighid said.

"We are walking into a war," Cedrik corrected. He turned Bastion's head away from the City, looking south toward the distant mountains where the last of the Alcian army waited. "And we're bringing the only thing they fear." He looked at the Queen, and then to the satchel she clutched in her hands. "Ride," Cedrik said. "We don't stop until we hit the tree line."

They rode until the moon began its slow descent, turning the pockets of silver grass mixed with the dusty hills into a sea of obsidian shadows. Cedrik didn't call the halt until the horses were lathered in sweat and the ancient, gnarled oak line of the Old Forest offered a canopy thick enough to hide them from the sky.

"Dismount," Cedrik ordered.

His leg swung over Bastion, but as his boots hit the earth, a sharp, white-hot spike of pain flared in his side. He gasped, doubling over, his hand flying to the ribs he'd ignored for days. For a second, the forest blurred.

"Cedrik?" Brighid was beside him instantly, her hand on his arm.

"I'm fine," he grunted, though his face was the color of curdled milk. He pushed her hand away, too quickly, too harshly. He saw the flicker of hurt in her eyes and felt a different kind of ache in his chest. "Check the horses. Fromme, untack the roan. Now."

Cedrik leaned against the trunk of a twisted oak to catch his breath, his thumb tracing the worn leather that bound the hilt of his sword. He scanned the camp. Taillte was already a motionless lump beneath her cloak, exhausted from the ride. Brighid had moved next to Pasin, clutching her satchel, her gaze distant.

But near the horses, two figures still had energy. The energy of youth.

Fromme had laid his bedroll out next to Mara's. The servant girl was shivering, her knees pulled tight to her chest, staring into the dark with wide, glassy eyes.

Cedrik shifted his weight, the steel of his armor clinking softly. He considered telling them to sleep; rest was a weapon to be used all the time, not only when you felt the need for it. But something in the boy's posture stopped him. Fromme was leaning forward, handing Mara his own canteen. His movements were stiff, clumsy with fatigue, but gentle.

"It fades, you know," Fromme whispered. The wind carried his voice to Cedrik's ears. "After a while, the noise gets quieter."

Cedrik frowned. *That is a lie,* he thought. *The noise never gets quieter. You just learn to live with it.*

Mara took the canteen, her hands shaking. "I close my eyes and I see the pillars," she murmured. "I was just a laundry girl, Fromme. I worried about wine stains. And then I was told to attend to the Queen... Now..."

"I was a stable boy," Fromme interrupted, his voice trying to sound steady, trying to sound like a soldier. "I was worried about flies biting the mares. I hated those flies."

Cedrik watched as Fromme awkwardly patted the girl's shoulder. He looked like a child wearing a man's responsibility.

"We'll make it," Fromme said. I won't let them take you back to the pillars, Mara. I promise."

Cedrik looked away, a heaviness settling in his gut that had nothing to do with his physical pain. He recognized the tone. It was the same tone Cedrik used when he told his men they would hold the line. It was the necessary lie of the protector.

He is learning, Cedrik realized. The thought tasted like ash. *He is learning; to be the shield, you must let the hammer break you first.*

He turned away to hide the tremor in his hands. He was the Commander. He was the anchor. If he showed a crack, the whole squad would shatter.

He moved to a flat stone near the center of their cold camp, and watched as Brighid sat opposite him. She didn't reach for her jewelry or a mirror. She reached for the heavy leather satchel.

"You risked the cliff for paper, Your Majesty," Cedrik said, his voice level again, but his breathing remained shallow. "Maps and seals. Not even a change of clothes?"

"Jewels are for victims," Brighid said, her voice carrying a hardness that hadn't been there in their previous encounters. She undid the buckles, pulling out a sheaf of parchments covered in Alaric's precise scholarly script. "My husband didn't spend his nights in the archives studying history, Cedrik. He was studying the plumbing."

She carefully spread out a map on the mossy ground. The colors were faded, barely indistinguishable, and the paper looked as if it might turn to dust any instant. It wasn't a map of Alcia's borders. It was a map of its veins. Violet lines, identical to the ones glowing in the palace walls, converged at three distinct points: Tarsis, the Capital, and Dunvar.

"The Sovereign's Pulse," Brighid whispered, looking at Pasin. "You remember the ritual, old man? The King touching the Foundation Stone to 'renew the land?'"

Pasin didn't look at the map. He looked at the fire, illuminating his face pale. "A metaphor for the King's sacrifice."

"It wasn't a metaphor," Brighid said, her amber eyes catching the moonlight. "It was a test. Alaric was testing if the cities were still connected."

"How?" Taillte scanned the map, sitting up from her bedroll. "I could feel the Gift when I touched the graft. Only it was... twisted somehow. Extremely powerful. No one has carried the Gift with such power since the First Cycle."

The Queen nodded. "Alaric told me the First Cycle didn't end because the magic died; it ended because the kings were too timid to pay the price. I never knew what the price was... until I read your journal, Pasin." The camp went silent. Cedrik looked at Pasin, as the old scholar shrunk into his robes. "You were there," Brighid said, her voice cold. "Three years ago. In the Deep Vaults."

Pasin sighed, a long rattling sound. "I was."

"Tell them."

Pasin looked up, his green eyes reflecting the firelight. "We found a door. Alaric opened it. The energy down there... it wasn't dead. The graft isn't just magic, Taillte. It has an insatiable hunger; it wants to eat everything. Created in the First Cycle."

"And the King?" Cedrik asked, his hand tightening on his sword hilt.

"He let it back in," Pasin whispered. "He touched the pillar. I saw the violet light. It reacted to him. He didn't scream. He laughed."

Cedrik looked at the map, then at his own hands. "And the people? The ones we saw in the square?"

"The surplus," Brighid replied, the words sounding like a death sentence. "This is no invasion to destroy Alcia, Cedrik. It is being reformed, and we are being herded. He must have started all of it on that day. The Sovereign's Pulse."

"The Royal Line has always had the Gift. But no one knew how strong," Pasin said, as he tapped on his staff. "I never went to the vaults again after he touched the column three years ago. I was too afraid of what he had awakened. I never imagined... The harvest began a month ago with the Sovereign's Pulse. He must have figured it out."

"The amount of energy, the exertion required to do this," Taillte said, quietly. "He wouldn't just 'have the Gift.' He would have to be one of the most prolific users of our time. I thought only Faradeen—"

"No one has heard from the emissaries of Faradeen for a great many years," Brighid said. She continued to study the map. "These veins... they're old. Tarsis was infested with them."

"If the King lives, he was not there. How would they have built more?" Cedrik checked the bandage on his shoulder. The thin material of the laborer's tunic was saturating quickly.

"You saw the pillar, Cedrik," Taillte said, as she came over to help with the bandage. "The Grey Officers have soldiers with the Gift. Whatever the King started, they may not need him to finish it."

"They will need him," Pasin replied. "Neelin said Alaric vanished in the exit passage at the Capital. Just like the enemies vanish upon death, or on appearance."

Brighid dug through her satchel and pulled out a weathered leather book. The parchment was yellowed with age. She flipped through the book until she found a loose page and spread it out carefully by the fire.

"Look, here," she pointed to the document. Cedrik leaned in, along with the old scholar. "I can't make sense of these numbers or shapes." Her eyes rose to match to Pasin's. "But you were there. What does it mean?"

Cedrik's eyes scanned the document.

Iron Fleets.

The price must be paid in blood.

Equal...

One life emptied. One life returned.

Cedrik stood up, the pain in his side forgotten momentarily in the face of a much colder realization. He looked southwest, toward the distant, invisible peaks of the border mountains.

"Neelin," Cedrik said. "He's gathering the bulk of the army at Dunvar. Four thousand fighting men."

"In a box canyon," Pasin added, his voice uneasy. "The largest collection of Alcian fighting force in a century. All in one place."

Cedrik looked at the Queen, his heart aching worse than the broken ribs or gashed shoulder. The court had called her the Barren Queen because she did not provide an heir. If they did not stop this incursion, the whole world would know her by that name, because the lifeforce of Alcia would be bled dry.

One life emptied. One life returned.

"We aren't going to Dunvar to join a defense," Cedrik said, his voice low and dangerous. "They've made a bridge, bringing their people here. And we've gathered our people to pay the price of blood."

CHAPTER 22

THE SCENT OF A miracle always left an aftertaste.

Vane adjusted the brass dials on the apparatus fitted over his left eye. The Sighted Lens buzzed with a low, ionizing resonance, turning the world into a grayscale map of thermal signatures and decaying magic.

He stood at the very edge of the limestone switchback. The wind off the channel was strong enough to knock a normal man flat, but Vane's boots were attuned to the stone, anchoring him against the gale. Below, the white surf churned against the rocks. A hundred feet of vertical death should have claimed the Queen and her obsolete guardians.

They hadn't fallen. They had descended.

"Tell me they are dead," a voice snapped behind him.

Vane didn't turn. He recognized the heavy, nervous tread of Ambassador Xarion. The man smelled of stale wine and overpowering florals.

"Gravity did not claim them," Vane said, his voice flat. He tapped the side of his lens. "Look, here."

Xarion stepped up to the ledge, clutching his fur-lined cloak against the wind. He didn't have a lens; he had to squint. "I see nothing but wet rock."

"That is because you look without any tools," Vane said. He pointed a gloved finger at a jagged section of the cliff face, ten feet down. "There. That violet scorching. It is not heat; it is residue. The medic... she used the Gift to bind stone. She anchored a slide that should have killed them."

Xarion cursed, slamming his fist into his palm. "The General will strip the skin from my back. The City is in chaos. We lost the prisoners. And now the Queen is running for the border with the Royal Seals."

"The Seals are irrelevant," Vane corrected, calmly. "The Queen is the asset. If she reaches Dunvar, she could still rally the people. If she explains what is happening here, the herd will spread. It would greatly delay our plan."

"Alaric, why did he not just let us follow the natural course and eliminate her? Why did he take pity?" Xarion grumbled. "I will send three hundred riders. We will sweep the plateau. She is headed for Neelin."

"No," Vane said. The word was quiet, but it stopped the Ambassador cold.

"You do not give the orders here, Hunter," Xarion shot back.

"I fix problems," Vane replied. He turned, the violet light of his lens flaring in the darkness. "A garrison is loud. A garrison is slow. And that Commander, Cedrik, has proven his mastery against your men already. If you send soldiers, he will outmaneuver them in the forests. He will bleed your three hundred riders until you have nothing left." Vane reached into his belt pouch and pulled out a small glass vial. Inside lay a crushed mountain lily, preserved in oil. "You do not hunt a wolf with sheep, Ambassador," Vane said. "You hunt it with something hungrier."

He gestured to the shadows behind Xarion.

Out of the darkness, the Hounds shuffled forward.

Xarion took a step back, covering his mouth with his sleeve.

They were not dogs. They were men, once. But the graft had been cruel to them. Their arms had been broken and reset, lengthened to match their legs, forcing them onto all fours. Their skin was pale and stretched tight over distended spines. But it was their faces that made Xarion gag.

Their eyes were gone, the sockets sealed shut with scar tissue. In their place, the nasal cavities had been surgically widened, the nose dominating the face like a bat's. Pulsing violet veins mapped their necks, pumping a slurry of alchemical fluid that kept them awake, alert and perpetually hungry.

"The Hounds are ready," Vane said. He walked to the creature leading the pack. It didn't growl; it made a clicking sound in its throat, tasting the air.

"Despicable souls," Xarion muttered, looking away from the creatures. "I know we had to adapt when the invaders came but—"

"But nothing." Vane uncorked the vial. "If we did not test the limits of the Gift, in all ways, you and I would not be standing here today, Ambassador."

He poured a single drop of the oil onto the creature's snout.

"The medic's magic leaves a residue," Vane explained. "It is a heat signature in the ether. Every time she uses her Gift—to heal a cut, to warm a camp—she lights a fire that these things can see for miles."

"And if they don't use magic?" Xarion asked, watching the Hound with a mix of revulsion and curiosity.

"They are traveling with an injured man and a terrified boy," Vane said, looking out at the dark expanse of the Old Forest. "They are weak. They are sentimental. Eventually, the pain will become too much, and the medic will try to help. That is when we will take them."

The Hound threw its head back, its oversized nostrils flaring. It shuddered, the violet veins in its neck bulging as the scent hit its blood. It had the trail.

"Bring me the Queen," Vane commanded. "The rest... harvest them."

The Hounds didn't hesitate. They launched themselves off the switchback. There was no mechanical whir, only the wet snap of muscle and the slap of calloused flesh against stone as they scrambled down the vertical drop, moving like spiders made of meat.

Vane looked at Xarion. "Go back to your palace, Ambassador. Prepare your report for General Ruzzim. Tell him the timeline is being corrected."

"Just ensure the correction is clean, Hunter," Xarion warned, his voice low. "We have already had to deviate from the plan too many times. We cannot delay the evacuation."

The Ambassador and the Hunter bowed to each other. They turned in opposite directions, one towards the Palace to continue the transition. The other, to do what he was born to do.

CHAPTER 23

THE SILENCE WAS THE first thing Brighid noticed.

It wasn't the calm, serene quiet of the wilderness, where birds sang and wind rustled in the leaves. It was a dead, heavy silence, as if the world itself was refusing to exhale.

They had been riding for six hours since leaving the cliffside. The sun was high now, a pale disc behind a ceiling of gray clouds, casting a flat, shadowless light over the Southern Highway. This road should have been busy. It was the main artery between Tarsis and the mountain pass of Dunvar. There should have been merchant caravans, messengers, farmers moving grain.

There was nothing.

"Keep your eyes on the tree line," Cedrik rasped from the front.

Brighid looked at the Commander. He was slumped in the saddle, his posture rigid. Every time Bastion's hoof struck a stone, she saw the muscles in Cedrik's jaw clench. He was bleeding internally, she was sure of it, but he had refused to stop.

His mind is trying to outrun his own body, Brighid thought.

"We're coming up on Valen's Cross," Pasin said, pointing his staff forward. "It's a waystation. Fresh water. We can water the horses, pause for a short break."

They rounded a bend in the road, and the small village appeared.

It was a cluster of twenty or so structures; timber-framed inns, a blacksmith's open-air forge, and a row of merchant stalls.

"Something looks... wrong," Fromme whispered, pulling his roan mare closer to Cedrik.

The chimneys were cold. There was no smoke. But more disturbing was the lack of damage. There were no broken doors, no scorched thatch, no arrows stuck in the timber. The village hadn't been sacked.

It had been paused.

"We walk from here," Cedrik ordered, sliding painfully from his horse. "Weapons ready."

Brighid dismounted. Her legs were numb from the ride, but caution sharpened her senses. She kept her hand near the small fruit knife she had taken from Tarsis; a pitiful defense against an army, but it was all she had.

They walked into the main square. A cart was stopped in the middle of the road, laden with sacks of flour. The horse was gone, the harness unbuckled and lying in the dirt as if the animal had been led away calmly.

"Where are the bodies?" Fromme asked, his voice cracking. "If the Grey Soldiers came, where are the dead?"

Brighid stepped toward the open door of the mess hall. A tankard sat on a table outside, the ale it once contained having long since evaporated into a sticky brown residue. Beside the tankard, a pipe lay on the bench, still filled with unburnt tobacco.

And then she saw it.

On the ground, near the blacksmith's anvil, lay a set of clothes. A leather apron, a heavy woolen tunic, and trousers. They weren't scattered. They lay in a heap, the boots still standing inside the pant legs, the belt still buckled.

It looks as though the man wearing them had simply... evaporated.

"Here," Taillte called out. Her voice was tight, trembling with a rage Brighid had not yet heard from the medic.

The Queen turned. Taillte was standing near the well. She was looking down at a small pile of fabric on the cobbles. A yellow dress. A small pair of knitted socks.

"They didn't fight," Taillte said, kneeling down. She didn't touch the clothes. She hovered her hand over them, as if feeling for heat. "Nothing remains, not like the pillars. What could have done this?"

"The Pulse," Brighid said, the weight of realization slamming into her chest hard enough to stop a heartbeat. "The map showed Valen's Cross. It was a node between the main southern cities…"

"This is where it began," Pasin said.

Taillte looked up, her eyes wet. "This isn't war, Your Majesty. In war, you kill the enemy to stop them. This… this is a harvest. They took the people and left the wrappers."

Brighid looked around the silent square. Now that she knew what to look for, she saw them everywhere. Piles of tunics in doorways. A heap of armor where a guard had stood. It was a mass grave with no bones.

"It's efficient," Brighid whispered.

"Efficient?" Taillte snapped, standing up. "Is that what you call this?"

"That is what Alaric calls it," Brighid corrected, her voice hardening. She wasn't defending it; she was diagnosing it. "He hated waste. He used to complain that burials were a loss of resources. He said the First Cycle ended because we were too weak to pay the price, too timid to use every resource available." She looked at the empty yellow dress. "They're not here to just conquer us. They're here to optimize."

"We need to move," Cedrik interrupted. He was leaning heavily against the cart, his face the color of ash. A dark stain was spreading on the side of his tunic where the ribs had shifted.

Taillte was at his side in a second. "Cedrik, you're bleeding again. Let me set the bone. I can seal the wound with a—"

"No," Cedrik grunted, pushing her away.

"Don't be a stubborn fool," Taillte argued. "You can barely stand."

"Listen to her, Cedrik," Pasin urged.

"I said no," Cedrik barked. He looked at the sky, his eyes scanning the gray clouds as if he expected lightning. "You need to save your strength. We don't know what waits for us at Dunvar."

Brighid watched him. It wasn't just stubbornness. Cedrik was looking at the empty clothes, a haunting depth in his gaze.

"He's right," Brighid said, stepping between them. "We ride. If we stay here, we join the ghosts."

They mounted up in silence, save for Mara's muffled sobs. Leaving the village felt harder than entering it. The silence of Valen's Cross felt infectious, as if the emptiness was trying to pull them out of their saddles and leave their clothes in the dust.

***

They rode for hours, the terrain rising sharply as the foothills of the southern range began to swallow the horizon. The air grew colder and thinner as the sun crossed east to west in the cloudy sky.

Brighid pressed her face against the rough wool of Taillte's cloak, her arms wrapped tight around the healer's waist. They had switched positions hours ago, Cedrik had insisted. He needed his sword arm free to ride point, and he couldn't protect them if he was worrying about Brighid slipping from his saddle during a skirmish.

But now, Brighid could feel Taillte trembling. The Healer's posture slumped with every stride.

She must be exhausted.

"Cedrik is slowing," Taillte said over the wind, her voice thin.

Brighid lifted her head, squinting against the biting cold. Ten yards ahead, Cedrik was a dark silhouette against the bruising purple of the twilight sky. He wasn't just slowing; he was swaying. His eyes were fogged, closing.

"Cedrik!" Brighid called out.

He didn't answer. He didn't even try to catch himself.

One moment he was the vanguard, an unstoppable force leading them west. The next, he simply slumped sideways. He hit the ground with a heavy, sickening thud, rolling once before coming to a stop, face-down in the shale. Bastion, spooked by the sudden loss of weight, skittered to a halt a few feet away.

Not now! You can't, Cedrik! Brighid's breath hitched.

"Hold on," Taillte gasped. She hauled on the reins, bringing their own mount to a shuddering stop.

Brighid didn't wait for the horse to settle. She slid off the back, her legs nearly buckling as her boots hit the ground. Her muscles were stiff, locked from hours of clinging to Taillte, but panic drove her forward.

She reached Cedrik just as Taillte scrambled down beside her.

"Turn him over," Taillte commanded, her hands already free of the protective leather riding gloves.

Together, they heaved him onto his back. Cedrik's eyes were closed, his face gray and drawn, stripped of the grim determination he usually wore like armor. He looked... mortal.

"He should have let you help him," Brighid said, her voice trembling.

The others had rushed over, Fromme and Mara's breathing rising in pitch. Pasin stepped forward.

"*Don't crowd!*" Taillte pushed him back. "Get back, I need space!"

The old man stepped back, his face twisted and anxious.

Taillte ran her bare hands over his chest. "His ribs, they've caused internal bleeding. His heartbeat, it's erratic. Bad." The Captain looked back to the rest of their small company. "We need to rest. There, we'll make camp." She pointed at a small rocky outcrop that could shelter them from the wind. They dared not light a fire. The darkness was their only shield now.

An hour later, Brighid sat with her back against the cold stone, knees pulled to her chest. Beside her, Taillte was methodically breaking a piece of hardtack in half.

"Eat," Taillte whispered, handing a piece to Brighid.

The Queen took it, staring at Cedrik's unconscious form. "I'm just baggage," she murmured, bitterly. "I moved to your horse to be less of a burden to him, and he still broke himself trying to haul me to safety."

"He does it because that is who he is, Brighid. Just as ruling is who you are," Taillte said, softly. She leaned back, their shoulders touching. It was small contact, but it anchored Brighid to the moment. "Don't rob him of his purpose by feeling guilty for it."

"You don't seem to mind," Brighid said, carefully.

"I knew of Cedrik... stories of his bravery and skill in battle. The entire Royal Guard has heard them," she replied. "He is so stubborn. So focused on honor, duty, his own sense of self-righteousness. He has forgotten about the why, the people. If we cannot all agree on the why, then what else matters?"

Brighid looked at the healer. She was usually so guarded, an enigma of emotion and sharp wit. But here, huddled in the dirt, she looked just as tired as Brighid felt.

Taillte looked back at the Queen. She pulled out a short, bone-handled dagger, offering it pommel-first. The steel was dull with oil. A tool for killing, not for show.

"Take it," Taillte said.

Brighid stared at it. "I have Cedrik, Taillte. I have you."

"You had a wall, too," Taillte said, her voice hard as the stone around them. "Walls crumble. Guards die. Take it."

Brighid reached out. The weapon felt heavy; a dead weight in a hand used to holding quill and silk. She moved to slide it into the belt of her tattered dress, but Taillte's hand shot out, stopping her.

"No," the Captain corrected. She lifted the hem of her leggings to the hidden fold in her boot, strapped against the inner calf. "Men check the waist first. They check the boot last. But the best place?" Taillte tapped the inside of her thigh. "If a man gets close enough for you to need this, you aren't fighting for honor. You are fighting to live, and we won't be there to help you. You don't swing this like a sword, Majesty," she continued. "You wait until his breath is on your neck. Until he thinks he has already won."

Brighid looked into Taillte's eyes. She didn't see a healer or even a Royal Guard; she saw a teacher preparing a student for a test that only had one passing grade.

"The neck. The armpit. The groin," Taillte listed. "You push until you feel the resistance break, and then you twist."

Brighid gripped the handle. "Twist," she whispered.

"Good," Taillte said, stepping back. "Now forget you have it. Until the moment you have no other choice."

Brighid shifted the grip, balancing the blade in her fingertips. "And if I need to keep distance? Do I throw it?"

Taillte's hand shot out again, grabbing Brighid's wrist, hard. "Never."

"But if I have to?" Brighid pressed.

Taillte sighed, frustration tightening her jaw. She reached out and took the dagger, but instead of holding the handle, she pinched the tip of the cold steel blade between her thumb and forefinger.

"If the Gods have abandoned you and you have no choice," Taillte said, flipping the knife so the handle pointed away from her. "You don't hold the handle. You hold the tip. Let the heavy end do the work." She handed it back, blade first. "Hold the steel. Lock your wrist. Pray it lands point first."

Brighid mimicked the grip, her fingers gingerly touching the sharp edge. "Hold the steel."

"Good," Taillte said, stepping back and reclaiming the weapon to sheathe it. "Remember, you miss the heart by an inch, you die. You hit a bone, you die."

The Lioness nodded, imagining the blade flying end over end at Ambassador Xarion, striking his heart.

If only I had the courage, she thought, as the memory of his taunting dominated her ears.

She shifted her gaze past the rocks to the horizon. "Do you think he's really there?" Brighid asked. "Neelin?"

Taillte followed her gaze. "The Shepherd of the North. The stories say he held Dunvar against Xencid's assault for a winter without any resupply. That stopped the war. He is the anvil that breaks the hammer. If anyone can stop what is coming for us, it is him."

"We just have to reach the gates," Brighid whispered, clutching the hardtack like a talisman.

"We will," Taillte said, though she closed her eyes as she said it. "Rest now. When the sun hits the horizon, I will have to heal Cedrik whether he agrees or not. Once we are inside Dunvar's walls, we will have time to think about what is next."

Brighid nodded, letting her eyes drift shut. The wind howled through the pass, sounding like a thousand distant screams, but she pushed the fear down. The cold of the ground seeped through her cloak, settling into her bones. She pulled her knees to her chest, trying to preserve what little warmth remained, but the shivering wouldn't stop. It was a sharp, biting cold that made her long for the stifling heat of the Capital.

***

Three years ago.

The memory washed over her, replacing the smell of wet earth with the scent of lavender oil and roasted pheasant.

She was standing in Alcia Castle, the Great Hall, encased in a ceremonial gown of blue velvet so heavy it felt like armor. The air in the room was thick, heated by a thousand bodies and roaring hearths. It was a celebration of progress; the first time the Xencid Consul had stepped foot inside Alcia's walls in decades.

"Smile, my Queen," Alaric whispered, leaning close to her ear. His hand rested on the small of her back; confident, possessive, firm. "They are looking for weakness. Do not give it to them."

Brighid straightened her spine, ignoring the ache in her feet and the crushing pull of her corset. "I am not weak, Alaric. I am just... tired. The Court has been whispering all morning."

"Let them whisper," Alaric said, his thumb stroking the fabric of her dress. "Let them talk of heirs and bloodlines. We are building something greater than a dynasty. We are building a future for all."

He sounded so certain. So protective. Brighid leaned into his touch, grateful for his strength. She felt small in front of the massive chair, acutely aware of her flat stomach in a room full of nobles who measured a Queen's worth by the swell of her belly.

The heavy oak doors groaned open. The herald slammed his staff into the stone floor.

"Consul Riccardo Dominici of the Xencid Republic! And the Lady Isobel!"

The room went silent.

Dominici was a tall man, draped in shifting, iridescent silks of the south. He moved with a fluid grace that made the stiff Alcian nobles look like statues. But Brighid's eyes—and the eyes of every person in the hall—went to the girl beside him.

Isobel was young. Perhaps eighteen. She wore no jewelry, no heavy velvet. Her dress was a slip of sheer crimson fabric that clung to her frame, showcasing a vitality that Brighid felt she had lost years ago. Her skin was flawless, glowing with the olive warmth of the southern sun. She looked... alive. Abundantly, aggressively alive.

"Your Majesty," Dominici said, bowing low. His voice was smooth, like oil on water. "Alcia honors us with this welcome."

Alaric stood up. He didn't bow. He descended the dais, walking slowly toward the guests.

Brighid followed, a step behind, as protocol demanded.

"Consul," Alaric said, stopping a few feet away. "We welcome you to the heart of Alcia."

"And we welcome the partnership," Dominici replied. He stepped aside, presenting his daughter with a gesture that felt less like an introduction and more like a merchant unveiling a rare artifact. "My daughter, Isobel. She has heard much of the... strength... of the North."

Isobel curtsied. It was perfect, practiced, and utterly devoid of emotion. When she rose, her dark eyes locked onto Alaric. She didn't look at Brighid. Not even a glance.

Alaric stepped closer. He wasn't looking at Isobel's face. His gaze was clinical, sweeping down her frame; from the pulse beating in her throat to the width of her hips.

Heat flared in Brighid's gut, spiking through her chest. She expected to see lust in her husband's eyes. She expected the look of a man tempted by a younger, more beautiful woman.

But when Alaric looked up, his eyes were cold. Empty of desire. A look she to which she had grown accustomed.

"She is... robust," Alaric said, quietly, as if commenting on a horse from the Highlands.

"The Xencid blood is resilient," Dominici said, dropping his voice to a murmur meant only for the King's ears. "She heals quickly, tires rarely. She is the best of our line, Majesty. The raw material is... flawless."

"Raw material?" Brighid asked, stepping forward. "She is your daughter, Consul. Not a shipment of iron."

Dominici smiled at her, a smile that didn't reach his eyes. "Of course, Your Majesty. A figure of speech."

Alaric turned to Brighid. He took her hand, squeezing it. To the court, it looked like a gesture of reassurance. But Brighid felt the pressure, it was a warning.

"The Queen is protective of the dignity of all people," Alaric said to the Consul, his eyes never leaving Isobel. "But she understands value when she sees it."

Alaric turned back to the girl. He reached out, taking Isobel's chin in his hand, tilting her head to the side. He studied the line of her jaw, the clarity of her skin. It was an audit. He was checking for defects.

"Strong stock," Alaric whispered, barely audible.

Isobel didn't flinch. She stared back at him with a terrifying emptiness. No smile, no emotion, and certainly no desire.

"We will have much to discuss, Consul," Alaric said, finally releasing the girl. "About the... future of our two peoples."

"Indeed," Dominici said. "The graft requires strong roots, does it not?"

"It does," Alaric agreed. "All gardens do."

He turned back to the throne, pulling Brighid with him. As they walked up the dais, Brighid glanced back. Isobel was still watching them. Her hand was resting on her stomach, her fingers spread wide.

"She is lovely," Brighid lied, as they sat back down, trying to keep the tremor from her voice.

Alaric didn't answer immediately. He was watching the Xencid delegation merge into the crowd. He rubbed his thumb over his signet ring: the lion of Alcia.

"She is necessary," Alaric finally said. He looked at Brighid, and for a second, she saw a flicker of something like pity in his eyes. "Do not worry, my Queen. You are the Queen of the Present. No one can take that from you."

The Queen of the Present.

At the time, she thought it was an odd promise.

Brighid gasped, jerking awake on the cold ground. Her fingers were raw from digging into the dirt. The velvet and heat were gone. Above her, the full moon of the Whispering Valley pressed down like a lead weight.

He told me, she realized, the cold settling back into her heart. *He told me exactly what I was. And I thanked him for it.*

Never again.

Chapter 24

Boom. Boom. Boom.

The sound was haunting. He had heard it before, right before the Capital fell. The earth itself shuddered under the weight of what was coming.

High Marshal Neelin Arran stood atop the Northern battlements of Dunvar, his hands resting on the freezing granite of the parapet. The wind here was different than in the Capital. It was a living thing, howling down from the jagged peaks of the Iarann Mountains, biting at the burns that covered the left side of his face. The bandages were no longer needed, but the skin was still raw and sensitive. A further reminder of what was coming.

He closed his eyes for a moment, listening to the fortress breathe.

Dunvar was not merely a castle; it was a geological advantage. Carved centuries ago, from the towering rock of the pass, it acted as an impenetrable gate to the Southwest. To his left and right, the sheer, vertical cliffs rose thousands of feet high, their peaks lost in the swirling clouds. There was no going around Dunvar. If you wanted to move an army from the fertile heartlands of Alcia to the iron-rich borders of Xencid, you had to walk through this gate.

For over three hundred years, this stone had never fallen.

Neelin turned from the edge. The view from this height was strategic, but a leader needs to be seen, heard and felt. He needed to see the eyes of the men he was about to send to their deaths.

He descended the spiral stairs to the lower ramparts, his boots thumping loudly on the stone. The fortress was a hive of organized chaos, but up close, the cracks in the façade were visible.

Neelin walked the line of archers, stationed along the secondary wall. They snapped to attention as he passed, but he could see the tremors in their hands. They were staring at his face, at the ruin of his left side. To them, he wasn't just the High Marshal; he was a symbol of what was coming for them.

He stopped in front of a boy who couldn't have been more than sixteen. The lad's helmet was slightly too large, sliding down over his brow, and his hands were red with tension where he gripped his longbow.

"Name, soldier," Neelin said.

The boy jumped, nearly dropping his weapon. "T-Toren, sir! From the Lowland levies, sir!"

Neelin reached out with his gloved hand and adjusted the boy's pauldron, which had slipped loose. "You're gripping the bow too tight, Toren. You'll cramp before you fire a single arrow."

"Yes, sir. Sorry, sir." The boy swallowed hard, his eyes darting to the empty horizon. "Marshal, sir... is it... true? What they say about the Grey Army? That they... they don't bleed?"

A silence rippled through the line. Every ear was straining to hear the answer.

Neelin looked at the boy. He thought of the courtyard in the Capital. He thought of the cold, surgical way the enemy dismantled his forces.

"Everything bleeds, Toren," Neelin said, his voice steady as iron. "If you cut it deep enough."

"And... the walls?" the boy whispered. "Can they breach Dunvar?"

Neelin tapped his knuckles against the massive stone merlon in front of them. "This rock has held against Xencid's heavy cavalry for centuries. It lasted through the destruction of the First Cycle. It will hold against this."

The boy's shoulders dropped an inch. He breathed out heavily. "Thank you, sir."

Neelin nodded and moved on, his heart twisting in his chest. It was the burden of Command. The Shepherd of the North had to lie to the flock so they wouldn't scatter. The walls would hold, yes. But the enemy wasn't trying to knock walls down. They were hunting Alcia's soldiers.

He made his way back up the stairs to the high command tower, the boy's hopeful face burned into his mind.

Cedrik... where are you? Neelin scanned the empty eastern road, willing riders to appear. *The Queen must be safe. The heart cannot stop beating.*

"Report," Neelin said, his voice exuding strength and confidence he had to conjure.

Lieutenant Kael, his aide who had come with him from the Capital, stepped forward. The boy looked hollowed out, his tunic hanging loosely on a frame that had lost ten pounds in a week.

"The heavy infantry is rotated every four hours, High Marshal," Kael said, pointing to the lower barbican. "We have confirmed the oil and food reserves. We are prepared for a long stand. The civilians have been evacuated, dispersed to the nearby hamlets and villages."

Neelin nodded. "And the morale?"

Kael hesitated. "They are Alcian, sir. They will hold."

"That is not what I asked."

"They are scared, sir," the Lieutenant admitted. "The stories have spread."

Neelin turned his gaze back to the Northern Horizon. The valley floor stretched out for three miles before vanishing into the tree line. It was empty. Quiet.

Boom. Boom. Boom.

The rhythmic thudding was getting louder.

"High Marshal!"

The sharp bark of a command interrupted them. Neelin didn't turn immediately. He knew that voice. It was the voice of a man who believed wars were won with paperwork and polished boots.

Field Marshal Brogan stepped onto the battlements.

The Garrison Commander of the West was a stark contrast to Neelin's battered, ash-stained appearance. Brogan was a thick-necked man in polished plate armor adorned with the gold filigree of high office. His cloak was pristine velvet, completely unsuited for the grime of a siege. He was a creature of the court, sent here five years ago to manage supply lines, not to hold the line against an apocalypse.

He looked pale, with sweat beading on his forehead despite the unusually chilly wind of spring.

"High Marshal," Brogan said, offering a stiff, by-the-book salute. "The levies have been deployed to the ridge as you ordered. But... we have a situation at the rear gate."

Neelin turned slowly. "A situation?"

"The Southern Pass is blocked." Brogan wiped his brow with a silk handkerchief. "Xencid has mobilized."

Neelin's grip tightened on the stone parapet, his jaw clenching. "Mobilized to assist? Or to invade?"

"Neither." Brogan held out a scroll case. It was made of polished ebony, sealed with the deep red wax of Xencid High Command. "A rider approached under a white flag. He refused to speak to me, even though I have been the Commander here for years... He said this was for the *High Marshal* only."

Neelin took the case, ignoring the wounded vanity in Brogan's tone. The case felt heavy, the weight of a nation determined by its contents. He broke the seal and unfurled the parchment.

The wind snapped at the document, whipping its corners. As Neelin read, the hush on the wall grew heavy. Kael watched him with concern; Brogan watched him with anxiety.

"...*The Sovereign Nation of Xencid formally recognizes the transition of power... Treaty of the Lineage... borders closed...*"

Neelin lowered the letter. He looked South, past the rear towers of the fortress. Wind snatched at the parchment.

Through the narrow gap of the pass, he could see them. A glimmering wall of Xencid iron and steel. Thousands of pikemen stood in formation, blocking the pass to the South. They weren't advancing. They were waiting.

Boom. Boom. Boom.

We need the Lioness. Now, more than ever.

"The Treaty of the Lineage?" Brogan raised his eyebrows. "Sir, there were rumors. Dispatches from the Palace before communications went dark. They said the King was negotiating a peace with Xencid, to secure the Southern border."

Brogan looked at the Xencid pikes glimmering in the distance to the South, then back to Neelin.

"High Marshal, if we fight here," Brogan said, his voice dropping to a terrified whisper. "If we engage the Grey Army... Xencid will consider any mobilization an act of aggression. We are violating the King's peace."

"There is no peace, Brogan!" Neelin snapped, crumpling the letter. "Look to the North! Do you see peace marching toward us?"

"I see an army that hasn't attacked yet!" Brogan argued, desperation creeping in. "But if we fire the first shot, if we provoke them... The King signed this treaty. We are the ones breaking the law!"

Neelin stared at him.

This was the trap. It wasn't just physical; it was political.

What could the King have possibly gained from this? Neelin looked at his own damaged hands. *Is this why I was spared?*

Alaric had set it up so perfectly. He hadn't just fooled the soldiers; he had neutered his own generals. Men like Field Marshal Brogan were terrified of disobeying the Crown, even when the Crown had fed them to the wolves.

Boom. Boom. Boom.

"Sirs! Movement to the North!" a sentry shouted.

Neelin turned. The Northern Horizon was turning dark gray.

The enemy army was arriving. And as they began to drive translucent glass spires into the ground, fencing them in, Neelin felt the chilling cold of isolation.

He had the enemy in front of him. A hostile ally behind him. And beside him, his second in command was paralyzed by a piece of paper that signed their death warrants.

"I must insist, Neelin, we must find a way to talk to this army. Maybe this is all... a misunderstanding." Brogan's eyes never left the tidal wave slowly coming.

"Then ride out, Field Marshal," Neelin said, his voice flat. "Take a white flag. If you trust the treaty, put your life on it."

Brogan flinched. "That... that is not my place. I am a Garrison Commander. My duty is to the logistics and chain of command, not front-line diplomacy."

"Your duty is to the men," Neelin corrected, stepping closer. "And those men are about to die because of that piece of paper you are clutching."

"You have failed the Capital, and the North!" Brogan snapped, his fear turning into defensiveness. "You are *not* the King! You have no right to disobey his orders! I have heard the rumors, Neelin. I know what they say about you. That you let the City burn to save your own skin!"

Neelin didn't yell. He didn't bluster. He just looked at the polished, pristine armor of the man in front of him.

"I am preparing to defend the Kingdom of Alcia, Brogan. That is what I do," Neelin said quietly. "Now, are you going to ride out and talk to them? Or are you going to hide behind your rank?"

"I... I will not be bullied by a scarred cripple," Brogan stammered, backing away toward the stairs. "I will find Captain Finley. He is sensible. He will arrest you for this treason. I will ensure the King hears of—"

"You aren't going to find the Captain," Neelin said. "You are relieved. You're going to your quarters. Or you can evacuate, to hide with the refugees. Anywhere but in this command."

"How dare you!" Brogan roared, his voice cracking. "I am a Field Marshal! I am—"

"Field Marshal Brogan," Neelin cut him off, his voice deadly calm. "You are relieved of command."

Brogan blinked, his face flushing red. "Excuse me? I am the Commander of the Western Reach. You cannot simply—"

"I said you are relieved," Neelin barked. He turned to Kael. "Lieutenant, escort the Field Marshal to his quarters. If he speaks to the men about 'peace' or 'treaties,' put him in irons and take him to the brig."

"This is madness!" Brogan sputtered, as Kael stepped forward, hand on his sword. "This is treason, Neelin! You are dooming us all!"

"No, Brogan," Neelin whispered, looking at the violet pulse of the fence rising around them. "The King did that a long time ago."

CHAPTER 25

THE SUN DID NOT so much rise as bleed through the gray ceiling of clouds, casting a flat, sickly light over the shale. Normally, the skies would be clear in the spring, but things were different since the invasion. Even the weather was rejecting the invaders.

Brighid Lorindan had not slept since the nightmare. She sat with her back against the cold stone of the ridge, leather satchel secured firmly around her torso. But her eyes were fixed on the shallow, rattling rise and fall of Cedrik's chest.

Beside him, Taillte sat tall, a statue made of pure willpower. Her bare hands rested near the Knight Commander's blood-stained tunic. She looked brittle, as if a strong wind would scatter her into dust.

"The sun is up," Brighid whispered, her voice cracking from the cold. "We cannot wait any longer."

Taillte didn't answer with words. She simply reached out and placed her palms over Cedrik's ribs.

The reaction was immediate. Cedrik's body lurched, his back arching off the cold stone as if struck by lightning. Brighid watched, in horror and fascination, as Taillte's eyes rolled back, the veins in her neck turning a dark, bruised purple against her pale skin.

A low, feverish heat radiated from the pair, shimmering in the morning mist. Brighid could almost hear the wet, grinding sound of bone knitting and flesh sealing shut.

Taillte let out a ragged gasp and pulled away, her hands shaking so violently she had to tuck them into her armpits to stop the spasms.

She slumped forward, forehead resting on her knees, breathing in sharp, whistling inhales.

Cedrik's eyes snapped open. He didn't wake like a man returning from sleep; he woke like a soldier returning to a fight. He sat up, his hand reflexively reaching for a sword that wasn't there, his chest heaving.

"Easy, Commander," Brighid said, placing a reassuring hand on his shoulder. It was rock hard with tension. "Your song isn't over yet."

Cedrik looked at her, wild-eyed for a heartbeat, before recognition settled in. He looked at Taillte, who was fumbling with her belt pouch, methodically chewing a piece of hardtack to reclaim her spent energy. He looked down at his side. The dark stain on his tunic remained, but steam rose from his ribs. Brighid had never seen anything like it.

"You shouldn't have," Cedrik grunted, his voice rough. He rubbed his face with a calloused hand. "We needed her strength for the road, and when we arrive at Dunvar. Not for me."

"You are the road, Cedrik," Brighid said, standing up and brushing the dust from the remains of her tattered blue dress. "Without you, we don't reach Dunvar. Now, can you ride?"

Cedrik hauled himself up. He swayed for a second, then locked his knees. "I can ride."

Pasin approached and studied the Knight. "For some reason, I thought the boy would be my biggest worry, but you never cease to amaze me." His eyes twinkled with a mischievous spark.

"Don't push your luck, old man." Cedrik tried to suppress a smile as he stretched his newly repaired torso.

Good. He must be feeling a lot better. Remarkable, the Gift.

"M'lady." Mara slowly stepped over to the group. "Thank you, thank you. I... I don't know how to repay you. It was so awful. The Governor, those strange men, the sounds, the... the..." Tears were streaming down her face.

"Hush..." Brighid rushed over to embrace the diminutive girl. She couldn't have been more than fifteen years of age. The Queen could feel the eyes of the small company upon her as her heart wept. "It's alright... you're safe with us. We are going to be ok."

Through the edge of her vision, she could see Taillte, still shaking from the effort of the healing, but tears had also welled in her eyes. A rare smile was on the healer's face as she watched the Queen comfort the servant.

Fromme silently finished packing up their camp. He had brushed the horses and led them over to the group. When he brought the gray gelding to the Captain, he offered his hand to her.

"I know, what that... cost you," Fromme said. "You have my gratitude. All of our gratitude. What you can do... what you choose... it is like the stories I heard. From my father."

"Never forget the why, Fromme. Power is nothing without purpose." Taillte took his hand. She rose, slowly, her unsteady legs still tremoring from the exertion. She finished the last bite of her breakfast, then put on her riding gloves while flexing her hands.

Brighid looked around. *This, this is the Alcia that we must protect. This is the Alcia that my husband is throwing away. I just cannot understand...*

They mounted in a silence that felt heavier than the rocky foothills. The ascent was a slow, meandering torture, carving a path through the gray, slate-ribbed foothills that guarded the Iarann peaks. Here, the earth felt older, the air tasting of wet stone and ancient dust.

Cedrik was wavering in his saddle. Brighid watched him from behind, her heart tight. He looked less like a Knight commander and more like a suit of armor being held together by sheer, stubborn habit.

Taillte pulled her mare alongside Bastion. She looked at Cedrik with a clinical, icy scowl. Blood pooled beneath her nose, dark and thick.

"You're dripping sweat on the pommel, Cedrik," she said, her voice cutting through the wind. "You're pushing too hard. Don't waste our sacrifice."

Cedrik didn't look at her. His gaze remained fixed on the horizon. "The Marshal is waiting. The Queen is out in the open. I'll rest when the gates are behind us."

"There it is," Taillte snapped. "The Great Alcian Wall. You think if you just stand straight enough and keep your jaw shut, the world will stop breaking. You saw Valen's Cross. You saw those clothes. Steel didn't save them. Your 'oaths' didn't keep their marrow in their bones."

Cedrik finally turned his head. "I serve the Throne, Taillte. If the world is breaking, then I am the mortar that holds the stones in place. That is the way of the Highlands."

"No," Taillte said, leaning closer. "That is the way of the Capital. You've lived in the shadow of the Keep for so long you've forgotten the actual Highlands. My mother used to sing the Song of the Stones when the winter drifts were high enough to bury the chimneys. Do you remember the lyrics, Commander? Or did they beat them out of you in the barracks?"

Brighid knew the song. Every child born in the shadow of the Iarann knew it. *The stone does not serve the mason; the stone serves the mountain.*

"The song is about endurance," Cedrik shot back.

Brighid winced. The disagreement was predictable to her at this point.

"The song is about *belonging*," Taillte corrected. "The mountain doesn't care about crowns. It cares about the minerals that feed the roots. You love the King because he gives you a badge and a purpose. I hate him because he treats the people of this land like dry timber for his hearth. Everyone is a number. You're dying for a man who says '*efficient*' and '*optimize.*' And... you're too proud to admit you've been guarding a tomb."

"I guard the Queen. She is the Throne now," Cedrik growled. *His loyalty, so fierce.*

"Steel Guardian or not, Cedrik, you are still just a man," Taillte said, her voice dropping. "Look at us. Look at Brighid. If you want to save her, stop acting like a statue and start acting like a man who understands that the only Alcia left, its HEART, is in the saddle behind you. And we can't fight what is coming to stop us with only steel and honor."

Cedrik stared at her through the heavy silence between them. For a second, the mask flickered. Then, it slid back into place.

"Ride on, Captain," Cedrik said, his voice icy as the mountain air. "The wind is picking up."

She's right. Taillte is right. But she can't shatter him to make her point. Brighid rested her check on Cedrik's back, the warmth a small comfort.

As they rode higher into the Southern Vales, the Iarann Mountains started to appear in the distance. The cover of large oak trees gave way to a labyrinth of slate and twisted scrub brush. The wind here carried a new scent; not the florals and ozone of Tarsis' Upper Ward, or the clean air of the Highlands, but a damp, earthy musk that made Bastion's ears pin back in warning.

The quiet of the Vales was unnatural. There were no birds circling the thermals. No insects buzzing in the brush. Just the hollow clatter of hooves on stone.

Click. Click. Click.

Brighid frowned, tightening her grip on Cedrik's waist. The sound echoed off the limestone walls, sharp and dry. It wasn't the rhythmic *Boom* of the Palace heartbeat. It sounded like a thousand dry fingernails tapping on stone.

"Hold," Cedrik ordered, his voice low. He drew his greatsword, the steel ringing a warning note as it cleared the leather bindings.

"What is that?" Fromme whispered. The boy could feel Mara's tight grip around him, as he scanned the cliffs above with his pale face.

"Something... that doesn't belong here," Pasin murmured, raising his staff.

From the shadows of a jagged crag above them, a blur of mottled gray skin erupted.

It didn't move like a wolf or a bear. It moved on all fours, but its limbs splayed wide like a spider's, its spine distended and pulsing with violet veins.

Brighid's breath caught in her throat. It was a man, or it had been once. The eyes were gone, the sockets sealed shut with scar tissue. The nose had been altered too, into a bat-like snout that flared as it tasted the air.

"What are they!" Brighid shouted, the horror of Vane's work finally visible.

"Defensive circle!" Cedrik roared, as he reared on Bastion's reins.

But the creature didn't aim for the Knight. Ignoring the steel, it launched itself from the crag, aiming straight for the source of the magic residue.

It aimed for Taillte.

But Taillte was shielded by the bulk of Cedrik's warhorse. The Hound adjusted in midair, its claws scrabbling on the rock with a shower of sparks and lunged for the easiest prey: the roan mare carrying Fromme and Mara.

"Fromme!" Brighid screamed.

The beast slammed into the flank of the roan. The horse screamed, buckling under the weight of impact. Fromme didn't freeze. He didn't cower. In a split second of startling clarity, he shoved Mara off the back of the saddle, sending her tumbling into the safety of the scrub brush.

He twisted, drawing the short sword he had taken from the Capital.

"Get away!" Fromme yelled, slashing at the horrendous creature.

The Hound hissed, a sound like steam escaping a vent. It lashed out with a clawed hand, its fingers elongated and pulsing with violet light. The strike was surgical.

It tore through Fromme's leather tunic easily, deep into the flesh of his chest. A jagged arc was carved from shoulder to sternum.

Fromme let out a strangled cry, as his body arched backward. He didn't bleed red, immediately. For an instant, the wound seethed with a blinding violet flash. Then the blood came.

"NO!" Taillte shrieked, already exhausted from the exertion of healing Cedrik.

She drove her heels into her gelding, slamming the horse into the Hound with a loud crunch. As the beast stumbled, Cedrik was there. The greatsword whistled through the air, cleaving the creature's head from its shoulders in a spray of black ichor.

The body of the Hound convulsed and dissolved into gray ash before it hit the ground.

"Get him to the ridge!" Cedrik bellowed, pointing to a sheltered overhang fifty yards up the slope. "More are coming!"

They scrambled up the loose rock, dragging the sobbing Mara and the semi-conscious Fromme. They collapsed in the shadows of the overhang, chests heaving.

Taillte jumped from her horse and fell to her knee beside the boy. She ripped away the ruined fabric of his tunic and leather protection.

Brighid gasped. The wound was gruesome. It wasn't a clean cut. It was a seething, jagged trench of gray, papery skin that glowed with a faint, sick light. Blood seeped from the opening, like black ink instead of the thick dark red that normally pulsed through veins.

"Hold him," Taillte commanded. Her voice was weak, shaking.

"You can't," Cedrik warned, grabbing her wrist. "You just healed me. It will kill you."

"If I don't, *this* will kill him," Taillte snapped, ripping her arm free.

She tore her riding gloves off and placed her palms against the unnatural violet light. Brighid watched as the Healer's face went white, her eyes rolling back as she poured the last dregs of her strength into the boy.

The flesh bubbled, resisted, but eventually the trench closed. Not at all like what Brighid had seen with Cedrik. The exertion was evident, both from Cedrik and the Healer, but the wounds did not fight like this. Cedrik's obeyed. Fromme's battled.

Taillte pulled her hands away, collapsing into Pasin's arms.

A thick, raised scar remained across Fromme's chest. The violet light did not fade. It throbbed with a persistent, low-level glow.

"I... I can't mend the scar... the light..." Taillte wheezed, her voice a dry rattle. "It's... in the bone. It's anchored."

Fromme opened his eyes. He looked down at his chest, his hands shaking as he touched the glowing mark.

"Am... am I, one of them now?" the boy whispered, tears cutting tracks through the dust on his face.

Brighid stepped forward. She knelt in the dirt, ignoring the tatters of her dress. She reached out and placed her hand over the glowing scar. It was warm, uncomfortably so.

"No," Brighid said, her voice fierce. She looked at Cedrik, then at Pasin. "It means you survived them, Fromme. It means they tried to harvest you. And you refused."

She looked out at the valley below, where more clicking sounds were echoing off the stones.

"We are not victims," Brighid said, standing up. "We are the ones who are going to burn this infection out. Get the boy on a horse, Commander. We ride for Dunvar."

CHAPTER 26

THE RAIN HAD TURNED the slate beneath their hooves into black ice.

Cedrik held up a clenched fist. The signal was barely visible in the gloom of the ravine, but the squad halted instantly. There was no sound but the hiss of the freezing drizzle and the heavy, wet breathing of the horses.

They were huddled in a narrow fissure between two sheer cliffs, a chimney of rock that Pasin had sworn would hide their trail. They had been riding for sixteen hours straight thus far today, not to mention the hours of pushing after Fromme's injury. They had taken a couple of short rests over the past two days, no more than two hours at a time.

Cedrik knew their horses and the riders were meeting their limits. Even though they were pushing forward, the difficult conditions in the ravine forced a slower pace, giving the horses a brief reprieve, that was desperately needed.

"Don't dismount," Cedrik ordered quietly, trying to keep his voice from carrying. "If we have to run, we run."

Brighid shifted behind him, her cheek resting against his soaked tunic. She didn't complain. She hadn't complained since Tarsis. She just shivered, a constant, low-frequency vibration that traveled through Cedrik's own bones.

"Did we lose them?" Taillte asked, softly. She was rubbing the neck of her gray gelding, trying to keep the animal calm.

Cedrik listened. He strained his ears against the wind, looking back the way they had come. The ravine was a well of darkness.

"I don't hear the clicking," Pasin offered, wiping the rain from his face. "Maybe the stream masked the scent." Heavy bags had appeared under the old man's eyes. He looked strangely fatigued, even considering the conditions.

"It's not... the scent."

The voice came from the roan mare. Fromme was slumped forward, lashed to the saddle horn with leather strips to keep him from falling. He hadn't opened his eyes in hours.

"Fromme?" Brighid whispered.

The boy lifted his head. His face was a mask of gray pallor, sweat beading on his forehead despite the freezing cold. But it was his chest that drew their eyes. Beneath the soaked leather of his tunic, the violet scar was pulsing. It wasn't a steady dim glow anymore. It was throbbing.

Thump-thump. Thump-thump.

"They stopped clicking," Fromme said, his eyes squeezing shut as if in pain. "Because they are listening."

"Listening to what?" Cedrik asked, his hand drifting to his sword.

"To me," Fromme cried out, a small sob escaping his throat. "I'm... I'm loud. I'm so loud inside... my head. I think... they can hear me..."

Pasin moved his horse next to the boy, Mara clung to the old man with locked arms. He rested a hand on the boy's forehead and focused his green eyes, devoid of any playful mischief. Cedrik swore he saw a spark twirl off the old man's staff in the darkness, but he couldn't be sure.

"So LOUD... I can't... stop them..."

"An... Anchor." Pasin shook his head. "The boy is right. They can hear him."

As if on cue, a sound drifted down from the cliff edge, hundreds of feet above them.

It wasn't a click. It was a long, wet inhale. The sound of a predator sniffing the air, searching with all of its heightened senses.

Cedrik looked up. A silhouette appeared against the bruised purple of the night sky. It was quadrupedal, low to the ground, its spine protruding violently. It peered over the edge, defying gravity, its claws digging into the vertical rock face.

It didn't see them. The darkness of the fissure hid them.

But then, Fromme's chest flared. A bright, violet strobe light erupted from beneath his tunic, illuminating the wet rock, the horses, and the faces of the small company in a harsh beacon powered by the twisted infection.

The Hound on the ridge shrieked like an iron gate being torn apart.

"Go!" Cedrik roared.

He spurred Bastion on. The warhorse launched himself forward, hooves sparking on the slick stone.

The stealth was over. The hunt was on.

They scrambled up the steep slope at the end of the ravine, the horses slipping and thrashing. Behind them, the shriek was answered by others.

Click. Click. Click.

"They're coming down the walls!" Pasin yelled, pointing his staff upward. Another spark popped off, and Cedrik felt a small surge of energy. A dot of blood appeared on the old man's upper lip, but he wiped it away quickly.

Shadows were detaching themselves from the cliff face, dropping like spiders. They didn't fall; they slid, claws controlling their descent, ignoring the laws of nature that bound the horses to the earth.

"The pass!" Cedrik shouted, pointing to a notch in the horizon where the moonlight broke through. "We have to make the high ground!"

They hit the upper trail at a dead gallop. This wasn't travel anymore. This was a race, and if they lost, the consolation prize was execution.

"Cedrik!" Brighid screamed over the wind. "Behind us... there's a man!"

Cedrik risked a glance. The Hounds were fast, but they were erratic. They scrambled clumsily over rocks and scrub. But behind the creatures, moving with a fluid grace, as if it were a calm spring morning, was a rider.

He sat atop a pale, hairless beast that glided smoothly without bobbing, its legs working like pistons. The rider wore the dark, slate-gray armor of the invaders, but he carried no shield. He held a long, curved blade that rested easily across his saddle, and wore a dark billowing cape with traces of red visible in the moonlight.

"He wants us tired," Cedrik growled, facing forward again. He urged Bastion, forcing the exhausted animal to give more than he had. "He wants us to reach a dead end, so he doesn't have to chase."

"Fromme is burning up!" Taillte shouted from the flank. The boy was thrashing against his bindings, screaming at voices only he could hear.

"Keep him on his horse!" Cedrik ordered. "We don't stop! Not until we see Dunvar!"

***

The gallop lasted for an hour before the horses began to die.

It wasn't a sudden stop. It was a slow, agonizing disintegration of strength. Bastion's stride shortened. The roan mare stumbled on flat ground. The wet, rattling sound of their breathing grew louder than the wind.

"We have to slow down," Taillte shouted, her voice thin and forced. "Fromme is bleeding through the bindings! The movement is tearing the wound!"

Cedrik looked back. The ravine behind them was empty, but the feeling of being watched—the tingling at the base of his skull—had not faded. They were back there. Keeping pace. Managing their stamina, while draining ours.

"Walk them," Cedrik conceded, seeing the foam dripping from Bastion's bit. "But we keep moving. No stopping."

The night dragged on, a blur of misery and cold slate. They transitioned from the jagged ravines into the high foothills. The rain stopped, replaced by a biting frost that coated their cloaks in white rime.

Pasin slumped in his saddle, his head lolling. Cedrik noticed the old man's staff was dim now, the wood looking gray and brittle, mirroring its owner. He had never seen Pasin so drained before.

Did he... I have never seen him use the Gift. He only told stories, children's tales. Cedrik watched the old man carefully, trying to make sense of it.

"Why doesn't he attack?" Brighid whispered, hours later. The moon was setting, casting long, distorted shadows across the path. "He had us in the ravine. Why let us go?"

"Because he knows the terrain," Cedrik said, grimly. He was walking beside Bastion now, leading the horse to save its strength. "The Southern Vales are a maze. If he attacks now, we scatter. We hide in caves. We can delay him for days. He wants us where there is only one path."

"The Dunvar Pass," Pasin murmured, rubbing his milky green eyes.

"It's the only way through the mountains," Cedrik nodded. "It's narrow. No trees. No caves. Just a road and a drop. He's herding us, like cattle to a slaughterhouse."

Behind them, Fromme let out a low groan.

"They're... close," the boy mumbled. His fever had spiked. Heat radiated off him in waves, warping the cold air.

Taillte re-wetted a cloth from her waterskin and dabbed the boy's forehead. "Hold on, Fromme. Just a little longer."

"Their voices," Fromme whispered, tears leaking from his closed eyes. "So loud now... so... beautiful."

Cedrik stiffened. *Beautiful.* That was worse than pain, worse than fear. Pain they could fight. Fear they could overcome. Seduction was a different kind of weapon.

"Dawn," Brighid said, pointing east.

An orange hue was seeping in to push the dark away. As the light bled over the peaks, the landscape revealed itself. They had climbed high. The Vales fell away behind them, a labyrinth of gray stone and mist. Ahead, the path smoothed out, widening into a proper road paved with ancient, cracked flagstones.

And there, three miles ahead, blocking the rising sun, was the Iarann Range.

Split perfectly down the middle, as if a god had struck the mountain with an axe, was the Dunvar Pass. And nestled in the throat of the canyon, its black walls rising seamlessly from the rock, was the fortress.

Dunvar.

It was magnificent. Towers of black granite bristled with defensive positions. The banners of the Alcian Army—The Golden Lion on Blue—snapped in the wind on the battlements.

"We made it," Mara sobbed, clutching Pasin's cloak. "We made it."

Even Cedrik felt a surge of hope. It was right there. Safety. Walls. The army.

"Mount up," Cedrik ordered, swinging his aching leg over Bastion. "Last leg. We ride in with our heads up. Eyes open, if they are going to attack, it will be here."

They spurred the horses. The animals, smelling the stable or perhaps just sensing the relief of their riders, found a trot, then a canter. The distance closed. Two miles. One mile.

They could see soldiers on the walls now. Tiny figures in mail, patrolling the ramparts.

But to the North, visible only now that they had rounded the final bend, was a sea of dark gray. In the valley floor below, far below the elevated road, translucent violet spires adorned the landscape, surrounding the approach to the canyon.

"May the Gods... have mercy," Mara uttered, as they rounded the pass.

"Dunvar has held for centuries... it was built during the First Cycle, child," Pasin said, squinting. "But something is wrong. Dunvar should see us."

Cedrik looked closer. The main gates, massive slabs of ironwood bound in steel, were shut tight. That was standard for a siege alert.

But there was no traffic. No refugees camped outside. No patrols on the road.

On the wall, a horn blew. But it wasn't the welcoming dual note of the army. It was a single, low blast.

Warning.

"They're waving us off," Cedrik said, seeing the archers on the battlements draw their bows. "They must think we're the vanguard of the enemy."

"We have the Queen!" Taillte shouted, though they were too far to be heard.

"Keep riding!" Cedrik yelled. "Once we get closer to the gate, they'll recognize us!"

They galloped onto the final stretch of road. To their left, the mountain rose sheer. To their right, a steep drop-off into the valley below. Into the sea of dark gray.

If you are out there... this is the place.

Suddenly, Bastion screamed. The warhorse slammed to a halt, his hooves skidding on the stone, nearly throwing Cedrik over his neck.

The other horses reared in panic.

"What is it?" Brighid cried, clutching Cedrik's waist.

Cedrik looked back. The road looked empty. But Bastion refused to move. The horse was trembling, eyes rolling white, backing away from an invisible line in the dust.

"Gravity," Pasin whispered, looking at the floating pebbles near the ground.

Small stones were rising from the road, hovering an inch in the air, vibrating.

Fromme screamed. A high, piercing shriek of agony. The violet scar on his chest erupted with light, burning through his tunic like a flare.

"They're here," the Cedrik said, his voice sharp.

The Knight drew his greatsword. He looked back down the road.

Fifty yards behind them, standing alone in the middle of the path they had just traveled, was the rider. The Hunter.

He had dismounted. His massive, hairless, pale horse stood like a statue behind him. The Grey Officer held his curved blade loosely at his side. He wasn't running. He wasn't even out of breath.

He raised his free hand, palm open, free of gauntlet or glove. He pushed it gently toward the ground.

Bastion's knees buckled. The gravity around the company multiplied. The horses collapsed, pinned to the stones by an invisible, crushing weight.

"Get off the horses!" Cedrik roared, struggling to lift his own sword, which now felt like it weighed a hundred pounds.

The trap had sprung. They were in sight of the gates of Dunvar, in sight of salvation, and they couldn't move.

CHAPTER 27

THE STEEL PAULDRONS ON his shoulders were pressing down upon him, the weight unlike anything Cedrik had felt before. They weren't just heavy; it was like the world itself had been rewritten to crush him.

He was on his knees; hands braced against the flagstones of the road. The stone beneath his gauntlets was beginning to crack, spiderwebbing outward from the pressure. His greatsword lay inches from his fingers, but it might as well have still been in Tarsis.

Behind him, the horses were screaming. They had collapsed onto their bellies, legs splayed, unable to rise. Cedrik could hear the slow, wet creak of Bastion's ribs bowing under the invisible load.

"Stop fighting it, Commander," Vane said. His voice was calm, muffled slightly by the charged energy in the air. A strange lens over his left eye flared with the same violet hue that had infected Fromme. He walked toward them, his boots clicking softly on the stone. He moved effortlessly, a predator strolling through a cage, unaffected by the crushing pressure that was flattening them.

"The General will be very interested, albeit saddened that he could not be here. He is quite the historian, you know."

"Who... what are you?" Cedrik grunted. Blood began to drip from his nose, hitting the gray stone in heavy, dark droplets.

"I think your question should actually be more a matter of 'when.'" The man paused, licking his lips as he studied his prey. "But, to answer your question, my name is Vane el-Tariq. From Faradeen."

"Faradeen..." Pasin wheezed, his fatigue evident. "How—"

"You, old man. I do not remember reading about you in the books. But you," Vane pointed at Brighid. "The Lioness of Alcia. We have much to discuss on our ride back to Tarsis..."

"You'll never take her!" Cedrik grunted against the weight pressing down from his pauldrons. His vision was tunneling, black spots dancing at the edges of his sight.

The slow walk forward continued, as Vane's footsteps cut through the sounds of their desperate struggles.

"This hunt has been... exhilarating. General Ruzzim told me about his encounter with the Shepherd of the North. There are many stories about him in the books. Unfortunately, I was told it was quite the disappointment."

"But you." Vane pointed his curved blade at Cedrik. "They didn't mention the stubbornness."

A slight frown crossed the man's features, the first sign of emotion, however brief. Vane tilted his head, looking at Cedrik not with hatred, but with academic curiosity.

"You died three miles from here, Commander," Vane said, softly. "Fifty years ago. I'm just enforcing the timeline."

Pasin crawled forward, grabbing his staff. He gripped it with both hands. The wood, gray and brittle, creaked as he tightened his hold.

Vane stopped five paces away. He looked at the squad with the dispassionate gaze of a butcher eyeing cattle.

"The Queen," Vane said, moving the tip of his curved blade to Brighid. Pinned against Bastion's flank, she was gasping for air, her face white with strain. "She comes with me. The rest of you... are to be harvested."

He raised his free hand. The pressure increased.

Fromme cried out, a thin, high-pitched wail. The boy was curled in a ball, clutching his chest. The violet scar flared, reacting to Vane's use of the Gift. Mara hugged him, trying to soothe the inconsolable.

"Let... them... go," Pasin said.

The old scholar was slumped against a boulder on the roadside. His face was ashen, his lips blue. But his green eyes were burning with anger.

"Pasin, don't!" Cedrik choked out.

Pasin didn't listen. Suddenly, his staff ignited with emerald light. It wasn't the gentle spark that could be mistaken for an illusion; it was a blinding, desperate flare of the Gift.

"Not... here!" Pasin roared, his voice regaining the thunder of youth. "Not... now!"

He slammed his staff into the ground.

A shockwave of green energy rippled out. It didn't just push the air; it tore through it. The emerald wave collided with violet streaks of lightning around Vane. The air shrieked; the sound of two realities grinding together, tectonic plates of magic shifting violently.

For a heartbeat, the weight vanished.

"Go!" Pasin screamed.

But the effort was too much. The staff shattered, exploding into splinters of dead wood. Pasin crumbled to the ground, his eyes rolling up into his head. He didn't move. Cedrik couldn't even see the rise and fall of his chest.

The weight on his shoulders lifted, for just a moment, but it was enough. He could breathe. He could move. But the greatsword, still too heavy to lift, was not an option.

Cedrik lunged.

He launched his bodyweight forward, a human battering ram, tackling Vane around the waist.

They hit the dirt together. Vane grunted, surprised by the ferocity, but he didn't panic. He twisted, bringing the pommel of his sword down on Cedrik's injured shoulder.

Fresh blood began gushing from the reopened wound. Cedrik roared in pain, white-hot spikes driving into his nerves, but didn't let go. He drove his forehead into Vane's face, once, twice.

A sickening crunch upon the third strike. Vane's nose twisted sideways.

Vane snarled, his Sighting Lens cracking from the repeated impacts. He shoved his open palm into Cedrik's chest. "Anchor."

The gravity returned, but this time its net was not cast wide. It was a pillar, focused entirely on Cedrik.

Everything collapsed. It felt like a mountain had been dropped onto his sternum. Cedrik was flattened, pinned to the ground atop Vane. His armor groaned, the steel rivets popping under the strain. Now, he couldn't draw breath, he couldn't move his arms. His lungs burned for air that wouldn't come.

Vane lay beneath him, smiling, as blood poured from his nose across his cheeks and into his mouth. He raised his curved blade, shortening his grip to drive it into the gap at the neck of Cedrik's armor.

"You have heart, Commander," Vane whispered, spitting blood. "But you were never a match for me."

Cedrik strained, his vision swimming with black spots. He couldn't reach his dagger. He couldn't reach Vane's throat. He was going to die here, pinned by his own weight, staring into the eyes of a monster that spoke in riddles.

"Cedrik!"

He couldn't turn his head, but he saw the flash of blue silk in his peripheral vision.

Brighid had crawled forward. She wasn't running away. She was right there, amber eyes blazing with rage from deep within.

"Catch!" she screamed.

She threw something silver. It wasn't a weapon of war. It was a small, delicate fruit knife—the one she had taken from the palace in Tarsis.

It spun through the air, end over end.

Vane didn't flinch. He watched the small blade spin towards them with a look mixed of amusement and disappointment.

"Silverware," he noted, flatly. "Desperate."

He intensified the gravity field, lust overtaking reason as the hunt neared its end. The gravity field shifted, pulling everything toward the center of Cedrik's chest. His heart felt like it was about to explode.

And that was the mistake.

The knife entered the gravity well.

Normally, it would have fallen harmlessly, bouncing off Vane's armor. But Vane had increased the gravity in this specific spot to an unimaginable level.

The small silver blade didn't just fall; it accelerated.

The air around the knife warped. It ceased to be a piece of simple cutlery and became a gleaming silver arrow, pulled down by the crushing force Vane himself controlled. It moved faster than the eye could follow, a blur of motion breaking through the air with a sharp crack.

Cedrik saw it coming. He didn't try to catch it. With the last ounce of strength in his body, he shifted his shoulder, just an inch, exposing Vane's gorget.

The knife hit.

Thwack.

It didn't sound like metal on metal. It sounded like a hammer hitting meat.

Driven by the magical gravity, the small blade punched through the reinforced leather of Vane's neck guard. It sank deep, buried to the hilt in the soft flesh above his collarbone.

Vane's eyes went wide. The arrogance vanished, replaced by shock.

He gasped, a wet, gurgling sound.

The concentration broke. The gravity field shattered instantly.

Cedrik felt the weight vanish, but so had his strength. He sucked in a desperate breath, his lungs screaming as they finally expanded, and rolled off the Grey Officer, scrambling for his greatsword.

Vane staggered to his feet. He clutched his neck, as blood—dark and thick—seeped from between his fingers. He looked at the small silver handle protruding from his neck guard, then at Brighid.

"You..." Vane rasped, blood bubbling on his lips.

But then he stopped. He looked at the fortress of Dunvar in the distance. He looked at Cedrik, rising with his greatsword and getting stronger with every heartbeat. The Steel Guardian had risen.

Vane made a calculation.

He turned. He reached into his belt to grab a small glass vial. As he crushed it, a cloud of thick, violet smoke erupted around him. The familiar smell of burnt air and rot filled the passage.

Cedrik staggered forward. He swung his greatsword with everything he had left, a cleave meant to take the man's head off.

The blade hissed through the smoke. It hit nothing but air.

When the smoke cleared, Vane was gone. Only a trail of dark blood remained on the stones, leading toward the cliffs. His massive white steed had disappeared with him.

"He's gone." Cedrik grunted, dropping to one knee, leaning on his sword like a crutch. He looked at Brighid.

She was trembling, staring at the blood on the ground. Her hands were held out, as if she couldn't believe the knife had left them.

"You missed," Cedrik said, a breathless laugh escaping.

"No," Brighid whispered, her eyes still locked on the empty road. She slowly lowered her hands, her face hardening. "I didn't."

Cedrik looked at Pasin. The old man lay still as death against the rocks. Taillte was already over him, checking for a pulse.

"He's alive," Taillte called out, her voice tight with panic. "But barely. He's... he's gone deep, Cedrik. I can't wake him."

Cedrik looked at the gates of Dunvar, less than a mile away. The massive iron portcullis was visible now, a line of black teeth against the gray mountain. They had won the fight, but the cost was rising by the second.

"Get him on a horse," Cedrik ordered, forcing himself to stand. "We ride the last mile. And pray Neelin opens the gate."

Chapter 28

The wind atop the battlements of Dunvar did not smell of pine or clean mountain air. It smelled of sulfur and iron.

High Marshal Neelin Arran gripped the cold stone of the parapet, his hands aching. He stared south, down the winding ribbon of the Iarann Highway; the last stretch of Alcian land before it crossed the border to Xencid.

He was waiting for a ghost.

Boom. Boom. Boom.

The sound wasn't real. It was a memory echoing in his skull, as persistent as the ache in his bad knee. It was the rhythm of the march he had heard in the Capital just over a week ago. The rhythm of the end of Alcia.

Neelin touched the fresh burn scar on his face. The skin felt tight and shiny. He hadn't received it from a fire. He had received it from *him.*

The General.

The figure sat in his mind, staring deep into his heart. The leader of the Grey Army. The man—if he could still be called that—who had walked through the gates of the Capital without drawing a weapon, as if the stone walls had bowed to his will.

Neelin had fought him. Rage drove his attack, his defense. Neelin had been outmatched, his opponent did not even have a scratch on his silver armor. The red sigils flared, wrists in wraps rather than gauntlets.

Fire leapt from the General's fingertips.

Neelin shivered, pulling his blue cloak tightly around him to block the mountain chill. He had lost. He was spared. He had gathered the remnants of the legions here, at Dunvar. This was the correct defense, the right strategy. This fortress had not fallen in a century. Now, looking at the line of Xencid pikemen in the distance, holding the line, he realized he had just simply followed orders.

The orders of a King that had betrayed his own Kingdom.

"Marshal?"

Neelin didn't turn. "What is it, Kael?"

The young lieutenant shifted uncomfortably in his armor. He was a good lad, barely twenty, with the wide eyes of someone who had never contemplated loss.

"The scouts, sir. From the North. The Grey Army continues to set up those spires."

Neelin shifted his gaze to the northern ridges. He didn't need the spyglass to see them anymore. They were black slivers against the gray sky, like needles driven into the flesh of the valley. They hummed with a low, thrumming vibration that Neelin could feel in his teeth. They weren't siege engines, meant to break walls. They were something else, something that filled the air with the taste of copper.

"They are not approaching the gates," Neelin observed.

"No, sir. They continue to consolidate their forces. They must outnumber us by at least two-to-one now. We don't know where they keep coming from."

"Anvil and Hammer," Neelin murmured to the wind.

The Xencid army was the anvil. The Grey Army was the hammer. And Dunvar was the metal waiting to be forged. Beaten. Changed.

"Sir!" A shout came from the watchtower above, sharp with panic. "Riders! On the approach!"

Neelin's eyes snapped open. He leaned over the edge, squinting into the gloom of the high mountain pass.

At first, he saw nothing but the shifting gray mist that plagued the mountains. Then, movement. Shapes emerging from the fog like wraiths.

Four horses. Moving slowly. Stumbling.

Neelin raised his spyglass; a heavy brass tube he had carried since the Unification Wars. He focused the lens, feeling the cold glass against his eye.

The lead horse was a massive mahogany charger; its coat stained with mud and dried blood. It was limping, favoring its left foreleg, but its head was high.

"Bastion," Neelin breathed. The name caught in his throat.

On it was a battered man, the only armor left was on his shoulders. An immense sword was strapped to the side of the beast. He slumped forward, holding the reins with one hand. His face was a mask of dried blood. Dust and grime clung to it in crusty patches, as if it were tar. But the jawline... it was unmistakable.

Cedrik. Neelin blinked and looked again. It felt impossible. The Commander should have been here days ago.

Neelin swept the glass back. He saw a second rider, a woman in a tattered blue dress that had once been silk. Her hair was loose, wild, the hue of autumn leaves. Her face was devoid of all color, save for the dark purple shadows under her eyes. She rested her head on Cedrik's back, but her eyes were wide. Searching. Alert.

The glass slipped from Neelin's fingers, catching on its lanyard and clattering against his breastplate.

The Queen. The heart still beats!

"Open the gates!" Neelin roared, his voice cracking with a sudden, desperate hope. A hope that felt very dangerous. He spun around, grabbing Kael by the gorget. "Open the main gates! Now! Get the Medics! Get fresh horses!"

"But, sir," Kael stammered, his face pale. "Enemy riders were spotted in that direction, just minutes ago. Protocols—"

"Damn the protocols!" Neelin shoved him toward the stairs. "That is the Queen of Alcia! Move!"

***

The mountain pass entrance to Dunvar was much smaller than the main gates. It was extremely difficult to reach and attackers had no cover, nor was there a way for a large force to traverse the tight path through the mountains. Notwithstanding, a large iron portcullis protected the flank. It rose with a screech of protesting metal that echoed off the canyon walls.

To the soldiers on the wall, it sounded like a rusty machine. To the riders below, it must have sounded like the choir of the Gods.

Neelin didn't walk; he ran down the stone steps of the keep, ignoring the sharp stab in his injured knee with every impact. He burst into the courtyard just as the heavy timber doors groaned open, revealing the gray mist of the pass beyond.

The four horses limped into the cobbled yard. They looked like they had ridden straight from the nightmares of the First Cycle. The animals were trembling, covered in a freezing sheen of sweat that steamed in the frigid mountain air.

Bastion was the first through. The great warhorse took two steps onto the stones and stopped, his head lowering until his muzzle nearly touched the ground. The animal's labored breathing carried across the yard, a wet, rattling scraping.

Cedrik let the reins slip from his numb fingers. He tried to dismount, swinging his leg over the saddle, but his strength was gone. He didn't land; he fell. He slid sideways, catching himself on the stirrup before his black boots hit the cobbles with a heavy, clumsy thud.

"Commander!"

Hands were grabbing him. Soldiers in the Alcian livery—blue and gold—were swarming them. The courtyard, usually a place of discipline and order, had dissolved into controlled chaos. Men dropped their spears to rush forward. They weren't looking at Cedrik, though. They were looking at the woman sliding from the saddle. Their faces were a mixture of relief and fear at the state of the Knight Commander and Queen.

Silence rippled outward from the gate. It hit the soldiers like an invisible wall of force.

They had heard the stories passed down from the Capital. The Queen rode in a carriage, surrounded by banners. Pomp and circumstance. Instead, they saw a woman in rags, covered in road dust, streaks of blood and grime interlaced with her striking royal features.

But she stood tall.

Someone took Bastion's reins, but the horse did not want to leave its master's side. Bastion snorted hard and pulled its head back, but Cedrik put his hand on the long muscular neck and whispered to its muzzle.

A group of soldiers untied Pasin's comatose body from the saddle of his black stallion, lifting him gingerly to move him to the infirmary.

"Gentle with him!" Taillte's voice cut through the noise, gruff and thin. She slid from her gray gelding, stumbling toward the old man. "He's fragile! Support his head!" The blue leather armor of the Royal Guard Captain was battered and scratched, but she moved with urgency that reflected a doctor and patient.

"Bring the boy, too. *move!*" She pointed at the small roan mare as she rushed toward the inner sanctums of the keep with Pasin.

Cedrik swatted the helping hands away. He staggered, unbuckling the immense greatsword from the saddle and using the sheathed weapon as a crutch to stay upright. He looked up, his eyes bloodshot and hollow, scanning the perimeter like a wolf that refused to believe the hunt was over.

Neelin strode across the courtyard, pushing through the circle of awe-struck guards. He stopped three paces away.

Up close, the damage was worse. Cedrik wasn't just tired; he was ruined. His tunic was slashed to shreds, hanging by threads. His skin was the color of old ash. But it was the eyes that stopped Neelin cold. They were the eyes of a man who had seen horrors, who had killed too much.

Then Neelin looked at Brighid.

She had slid from behind Cedrik and was standing by Bastion's flank, holding a battered hand to her ribs. Her dress was torn, her boots worn through, but she stood straight. She looked small and delicate against the backdrop of the massive walls of the fortress. But she was not broken.

Neelin dropped to one knee. It wasn't only a ceremonial bow; it was the heavy collapse of a man surrendering his burden.

"Your Majesty," Neelin said, his voice on the verge of breaking. All of the soldiers in the courtyard went silent. It was like a wave rolling across sandy beaches. Every single man and woman kneeled just as Neelin had. The clatter of armor hitting stone echoed off the walls of the keep. They didn't kneel out of protocol. They knelt because they had thought she was dead, and seeing her alive was a miracle.

"Rise. Rise, Marshal," Brighid said, hurriedly.

Her voice was not loud, but every person in the courtyard heard it. It carried the authority of the throne. She stepped away from the horse, her hand leaving her ribs to gesture to the soldiers.

"Rise, all of you. We are not ghosts. And I do not plan to become one." She stepped forward and laid a hand on Neelin's shoulder, urging him to stand. Slowly, he stood.

The rest of the soldiers followed their commander, uncertainty warring with adoration in their eyes.

"Your Majesty... Commander," Neelin stammered. "I... I thought you were dead."

"We were," Cedrik croaked. He looked around the courtyard, at the high stone walls, at the archers manning the ramparts. He took a deep, shuddering breath, the first breath of safety in over a week. "I found her Neelin... and you held Dunvar."

The joy of seeing them alive was already fading, replaced by the cold reality of their situation.

"Get them inside, close the gates," Neelin ordered the guards, his voice flat. "Food. Wine. Get the old man and the boy to the infirmary. Then get back to your stations."

"Neelin?" Cedrik frowned. He hadn't missed the tone. "What is it?"

Neelin looked as the open gate started to close, then shook his head.

"You need to rest. If I am right, we have some time," Neelin said, softly. "Highness, you can have the Field Marshal's quarters." He looked at a sergeant, who left immediately to make preparations.

"I won't argue with you," Cedrik grunted. He tried to take a step, but his knee buckled. He caught himself on Neelin's shoulder. The contact was solid, real. Neelin gripped his arm, holding him up.

"I've got you, brother," Neelin whispered.

Brighid stepped forward. She reached out, placing a hand on Neelin's vambrace. The metal was strong, but he could feel the strength of her grip.

"Marshal," she said, her amber eyes locking onto his. "You have done well to bring the legions here. We now have a chance to fight back."

Neelin swallowed hard, the praise stinging more than the cold wind.

"We can speak of our tactical position later, Your Majesty. For now, you need to regain your strength."

"Resting can wait," Brighid said. Her face hardened, the fatigue momentarily pushed aside by a flash of steel that Neelin had not seen in her before. "I would prefer to be briefed on the situation as soon as possible. We saw the Grey Army approaching from the North. We need to discuss your defensive plan."

"The Grey Army isn't the only problem, Your Majesty," Neelin said. He gestured toward the south, their only escape route.

"The Iarann Highway is closed. Xencid has mobilized."

CHAPTER 29

CEDRIK STOOD AT THE narrow arrow-slit of the officers' quarters, watching the light catch the frost on the crenellations. His side ached, a deep, periodic throb that Taillte's magic hadn't quite cured. It wasn't the sharp bite of a fresh wound, but a dull, vibrating tension, as if his ribs had been stitched together with wire instead of bone.

Yet, for the first time in days, the ground beneath his feet felt truly solid. Sleeping inside walls again, even on a stiff officer's cot, felt like a luxury after the week he'd survived. The constant watch, the dodging, the running. It reminded him of being a child again. But stone? Stone he understood. The walls of Dunvar didn't judge him; they simply held him.

He could be the Steel Guardian.

A heavy knock at the door preceded Neelin's entry. The Marshal didn't wait for an invitation. He came into the room carrying a wooden tray with two steaming bowls and a loaf of bread that looked as dense as the granite walls.

"Eat," Neelin rumbled, kicking a three-legged stool toward Cedrik before settling himself on the edge of a spare cot. "A man who fights on an empty stomach is just a corpse that doesn't know it yet."

Cedrik sat, the smell of salted oats and goats milk hitting him with a sudden, sharp memory of the foothills. It was a peasant's breakfast. An honest breakfast.

"You know..." Cedrik said, stirring the thick gray mixture, feeling the steam warming his face. "There were times out there, I wasn't sure if we were going to make it."

"But you did," Neelin responded, blowing on his bowl to cool it. "You found the Queen. Kept the Heart of Alcia beating."

If only he knew how close it came to stopping, Cedrik thought to himself, as he took a bite of the oats. His mouth welcomed the rich, nutty taste, the heat spreading through his chest, chasing away the lingering chill of the Valen's Cross ruins.

"It's quiet," Cedrik commented between chews.

"The quiet before the storm," Neelin replied. He tore into the bread with his teeth, looking less like a Marshal and more like the shepherd his honorary title suggested. "I've spent my entire life guarding this pass, Cedrik. I've fought Xencid raiders, Highland rebels, and mountain cats big enough to drag a man from his saddle. But I've never fought a ghost."

Cedrik looked at him, another spoonful pausing halfway to his mouth. "The Grey Army?"

Neelin stopped chewing. His eyes, usually sharp as flint, looked haunted. "It isn't just the army. Cedrik, I saw a man in their ranks on the highway. It was *him*. Alaric. But not the man we served. It was Alaric as he looked twenty years ago. In his prime. Arrogant. Strong."

"A trick," Cedrik said, though his gut tightened. "An illusion. We have all seen things lately that shouldn't exist."

"Maybe." Neelin grunted. "But illusions don't cast shadows. And this thing... it cast a long one. And he wasn't alone. Their General was with him. The General that spared me. I shouldn't be here right now."

Cedrik set the spoon down. The hunger he'd felt moments ago had vanished. "And neither should I, Neelin. We saw their forces in the valley. The Spires. Thousands of troops. Whatever Alaric has done, this is not war. They aren't just conquering territory. They are rewriting the rules."

Neelin set his bowl down on the floor. The candlelight caught the scars on his knuckles. "Taillte told me what she said to you on the road," he said, shifting the subject. "About the steel and honor."

Cedrik stiffened. "She has a sharp tongue."

"She has a *Highland* tongue," Neelin countered. "She knows the *Song of the Stones*. Do you remember the old verses, boy? Or did the Royal Guard wash the mountain out of your blood when they gave you that blue cloak?"

Cedrik looked down at his hands. The hands of a Knight Commander, calloused by the hilt of a sword Alaric had forged for him. The lines came to him unbidden, whispered in a voice he hadn't heard since his mother died.

"*The stone does not serve the mason; the stone serves the mountain,*" Cedrik whispered. "*The root does not serve the gardener; the root serves the rain.*"

"Alaric acts like the Gardener," Neelin said, leaning forward. "He thinks he can prune this land. He thinks he can cut away the parts of Alcia he deems too wild or too weak to make room for whatever new fruit he's growing in Tarsis."

"He has the power to do it," Cedrik argued, the hopelessness rising in his throat. "We have walls. He has monsters. How do we fight a man who is willing to burn his own garden just to replant it?"

Neelin stood up. He walked to the window, blocking the gray light with his thick frame. "We be the things he can't prune," Neelin said, his voice a low growl. "If Alaric wants a manicured garden, if he wants symmetrical rows and silent compliance... then we become the weeds."

Cedrik looked up. "Weeds?"

"Aye." Neelin turned back, a jagged, wolfish grin spreading across his face. "You can pull a rose, Cedrik. You can cut down an oak. But you can't kill a weed. We grew in the cracks of the stone before he built his palace, and we'll be here long after it falls. We're the stubborn, jagged things that refuse to be pulled."

Neelin reached out and gripped Cedrik's shoulder. His hand was massive, heavy. It wasn't the touch of a commanding officer; it was the touch of a father sending a son into a storm.

"You aren't a Knight of the Royal Guard anymore, Cedrik. That man died on the Southern Highway. Today, you are a weed. And we're going to choke his garden until it dies."

I had always thought the Crown held the Kingdom together, Cedrik realized. *I thought the King was all that mattered.*

Maybe Taillte was right. Maybe the Crown is just a hat. The person that wears it must earn our devotion.

The Queen is that person now. He has seen it over and over, since Tarsis. He can't give up now.

"I can't be just a weed, Neelin. I can't fight from the cracks, run in the shadows. I am and always will be a shield that protects the Kingdom. The Queen."

"Look out there, Cedrik. Look at what is coming. Look at how quickly they have marched through our lands. We can't be so rigid. You can't be so rigid. Taillte was right, but you need to understand it."

"I became a Royal Guard, I wear this armor, to protect those who can't protect themselves. To show the people that honor, duty, and loyalty are what makes Alcia great. Without those, we are no different than animals in the wild."

The two men sat in the quiet, scanning wood planks for answers that only their hearts could give.

"The Queen will be in the war room soon," Neelin said, releasing his grip. "She has to be the one... to unite us here. She is Alcia now."

Cedrik stood up. He reached for his sword harness, cinching it across his chest. His knee buckled and his ribs ached, but nothing would stop him from doing his duty.

"She is worth it, Neelin," Cedrik said, with a confidence that surprised even himself as the words came out. "She is the Lioness, and I would give my life for her."

Neelin nodded. "Good. The men will need a Knight of the Royal Guard to tell them we have a chance. That will be easier now that we have a reason to fight."

"They won't see just a Knight," Cedrik replied.

"No?" Neelin asked.

"No," Cedrik answered. He picked up his cloak, clasping it with the golden lion of the Guard, then threw it over his shoulder. "They'll see the Steel Guardian."

Neelin nodded. "Good. Finish your bread, boy. Whatever happens out there, you're going to need all your strength."

***

Dunvar's courtyard was filled with soldiers preparing for a siege. As they stepped out into the crisp mountain air, Neelin cut a path through the mud, his stride devouring the ground.

Cedrik followed, his eyes scanning the garrison. The 'weeds' Neelin had spoken of were littered all over the keep, you just had to take notice.

To his left, a group of archers were fletching arrows with fingers wrapped in rags. To his right, a blacksmith hammered dents out of a breastplate that had seen generations of war. There was no symmetry here. No drills. No heraldry. Just a collection of Alcia's remaining battalions preparing for an assault.

Shoulders sagged beneath tight faces, and a lack of boisterous conversation was noticeable.

Neelin paused near the heavy oak door leading to the guest quarters. He glanced at the sun.

"You have five minutes," Neelin said. "Go check on your flock. I'll clear the guards at the tower."

Cedrik nodded and ducked inside.

The infirmary smelled of boiled sage and sickness. In the far corner, separated by a linen cloth, he found them.

Fromme was sitting on the edge of a pallet, his chest heavily bandaged. The boy looked pale, his breathing shallow but steady.

Beside him stood Taillte, wiping a mortar clean with a rag. She was dressed in her riding leathers, her Captain's insignia pinned to her collar.

She looked up as Cedrik approached. Her eyes went to his side—to his damaged ribs—before meeting his gaze.

"You're walking stiff," she observed, quietly.

"The cold," Cedrik lied. He looked down at Fromme. "Will you fight?"

"Yes, sir."

"Good, we need everyone who can fight."

"He asked for his sword the moment he woke up. I told him if he rips those stiches, I'll let him bleed." A flicker of sadness crossed Taillte's face.

Cedrik hesitated, his hand resting on his hip. "Taillte. On the road.... I understand why you said it. But, my steel, my honor, my duty. It is the only way I know how to fight back. We don't have to agree to fight together."

Taillte paused. She studied him. Like she was trying to find him from the inside, to find his soul.

"The walls are just stone, Cedrik," she said, softly. "It's the people standing behind them that matter. Just make sure you're standing when this is over."

"I plan to be," he promised.

A low, muttering voice drew his attention to the next cot. Pasin was curled in a ball, his old gray cloak pulled tight around him despite the heat of the braziers. He was shivering, his eyes darting back and forth under closed lids.

"The ships..." Pasin whimpered, his voice thin and quivering. "Black iron... smoke on the water... the hunger is eating the horizon..."

Cedrik stepped closer, alarmed. "Pasin?"

He reached out to touch the old man's shoulder, but Pasin flinched violently, his eyes snapping open. They weren't their usual bright green. For a second, they swirled with a deep violet, violent light. Familiar.

"They're coming!" Pasin gasped, grabbing Cedrik's wrist with a grip like a lion. "Not the Grey Soldiers. The graft... Too late... Can't change it..."

"Easy, Pasin," Taillte soothed, moving to place a cool cloth on the old man's forehead. "It's just the fever. He spent too much on the pass."

Pasin slumped back, the light fading. "Not sickness," he whispered, a tear leaking from the corner of his eye. "History. Repeats..."

Cedrik felt a chill that had nothing to do with the drafty room. Neelin had been right. This wasn't just a simple invasion.

Don't worry, old man. We will hold. And then we will find out what is wrong with you. I swear it.

"Rest, Pasin," Cedrik whispered. He stood up, looking at Taillte. "The war room. The command staff is assembling."

She nodded, securing a dagger to her belt. "I'm ready."

Fromme stood up, swaying slightly before locking his knees. He reached for his sword belt.

"You should stay, Fromme."

"Sir, I'm not staying," the boy said. He touched the bandage on his chest, where the violet scar lay hidden. "I carry the mark of what's coming. If they don't believe the threat, I'll show them."

Cedrik looked at Taillte. She gave a small shrug. "He's stubborn. He gets that from the Highlands."

"Many do. Let's go."

They left Pasin to his fever dreams and walked out into the courtyard. Neelin was waiting by the doors to the war room. They Marshal saw the group—the battered Knight, the defiant Captain, and the wounded Squire—and his expression softened, a small smile creasing his lips.

"Bringing reinforcements?" Neelin said.

"Witnesses," Taillte corrected.

Neelin nodded. He pushed open the heavy iron-bound doors.

Warm, stale air rushed out to meet them, thick with the smell of old maps and nervous sweat. A dozen faces turned toward the light.

The commanders looked at Neelin. Then Cedrik. Then the woman and the boy.

One of the adjutants frowned, opening his mouth to object to the boy, but Cedrik stepped forward. He didn't flinch. He walked into the room, not just as the Knight Commander, but as the tip of the spear.

CHAPTER 30

BRIGHID STARED AT HER hands, resting on a plush velvet duvet, pale against the deep crimson fabric. Someone—a servant, perhaps, or an extremely efficient adjutant—had scrubbed them while she slept. The road dirt, the horsehair, and the dried blood were gone. Her fingernails were clean.

But the tremors remained.

Brighid sat up, her body crying out in soreness that went from her toes to her forehead. She was in the Field Marshal's quarters, a room of dark oak and heavy tapestries illustrating the various crests and houses of Alcia. Lavender and beeswax permeated the room, filling the air with a warmth not found in the florals of her gilded cage in Tarsis. A fire crackled in the hearth, casting a warm, deceptive glow over the furniture. It was a room designed for comfort, for men who waged war from a distance.

Today, it was a tomb.

Reluctantly, she swung her legs out of the massive four-poster bed. She was wearing a clean nightshift, likely stolen from some noblewoman's luggage train. The tattered blue silk that had covered her since Tarsis had been thrown out. In its place, laid out at the foot of the bed, was a set of riding leathers. They were small, likely belonging to a squire, dyed a deep midnight blue. Underneath was her battered leather satchel, full of the documents taken from Alaric's personal desk.

Brighid dressed slowly. The leather was stiff and unyielding, not like the nightshift. It chafed her aching body as she buckled the straps, but she did not call for help. She would never call for help to get dressed again.

She caught her reflection in the standing mirror in the corner. The woman staring back was a stranger. Her face was gaunt, the cheekbones sharp enough to cut. The color had not yet returned to her skin, which was marred with small scrapes and bruises. Her hair, washed and brushed, fell around her shoulders like a copper curtain, but it couldn't hide her eyes. They were hard. Bright.

"You are not a ghost," she whispered to the reflection, remembering her words to the soldiers in the courtyard. "At least, not yet."

A knock came at the heavy oak door. It was polite, hesitant.

"Enter."

The door creaked open, and a man stepped inside. He was older, thick around the middle, wearing a soft, clean tunic. Golden lions on the neckline signaled a high-ranking officer. His white beard was trimmed to perfection, obscuring imperfections of his jawline. A velvet cape was untouched by mud or dirt.

Field Marshal Brogan. Garrison Commander of the West.

Brogan bowed low, a sweeping, theatrical gesture that felt obscenely out of place. "Your Majesty. The Gods be praised. When the sentries said you had arrived, I didn't dare believe it."

Brighid turned, fastening the final buckle on her vambrace. "Field Marshal. Thank you for allowing me to use your quarters. Neelin must be keeping you very busy."

Brogan straightened, his face flushing. He clasped his hands behind his back. "High Marshal Arran is... zealous. He relieved me of duty when we arrived with his sentry. He has been... unrestrained."

Brogan stepped closer. Brighid fought the urge to recoil and held her ground.

His voice dropped to a conspiratorial whisper. "Majesty, I must speak plainly. Arran is a fine soldier, but he has been broken. He lost the North. You had to flee the Capital. And he has now brought all of our forces into a trap with no chance of survival."

Brighid studied him. Two weeks ago, she would have listened. She would have deferred to his age, his rank, his confidence. Now, she just saw a man who smelled of rosewater while his men smelled of sweat and fear.

"And...? What is your strategy, Field Marshal?"

"Diplomacy," Brogan said, quickly, seizing the opening. "The Xencid forces to the south... they are aggressive, yes, but I think they can be rational. The King signed a treaty. If we offer terms—rather if *you* offer terms—we might secure passage. We cannot fight the Grey Army. We must negotiate a retreat."

Brighid looked at the man before her. Really looked at him. A man who cared more for the glory of the Courts and privileges of rank than those that secured the peace and prosperity of her people.

"The Grey Army does not negotiate, Marshal. They harvest."

Brighid walked past him toward the door. She moved differently now. Quieter, with the economy of motion she had learned from Taillte, Cedrik.

"But the Xencid—"

"The Xencid were invited!" Brighid cut him off, her voice cold. She stopped with her hand on the door latch. "Can't you see what is in front of you? This treaty. The King, my husband, has betrayed us. You. Neelin. The entire *Kingdom*! And me..."

Brogan's mouth opened, then closed. And for the first time in her memory, the pompous veneer cracked. His gaze dropped to the knife at her belt.

"Yes, Your Majesty," he murmured.

"Good. Now I am to meet Neelin in the war room. You may join, or not. I will leave that up to you."

***

The war room of Dunvar was located in the heart of the keep, a circular chamber dominated by a massive table carved from a single slab of local granite. Hanging torches lit the room, warmed by a large fireplace raging against the chill of the mountain air. Windowless, save for narrow arrow slits that looked out toward the northern valley.

It was crowded. Neelin stood at the head of the table, looking washed out and gray in the torchlight. He had shaved, but it only exposed the deep lines of fatigue etched into his features. Cedrik sat to his right, slumped in a high-backed chair, his leg propped up on a stool. Taillte was in the corner, grinding herbs in a stone mortar, while Fromme sat silently on the floor near the hearth, staring blankly into the flames.

When Brighid entered, the low murmur of conversation died.

Neelin straightened, snapping to attention. Cedrik tried to rise, gripping the arms of his chair and wincing as he reached for his ribs.

"Sit," Brighid commanded, her voice echoing off the stone walls. She moved to the empty chair at the foot of the table. Brogan lingered by the door, looking like a chastised schoolboy who wasn't sure if he was allowed in for the lesson.

"Report, High Marshal," Brighid said, placing her hands flat on the smooth granite. "What is our position?"

Neelin didn't waste time with pleasantries. He grabbed a long ebony pointer and tapped the center of the map. "We are here, Dunvar. The fortress seals the pass through the Iarann Mountains, effectively our border with Xencid." He slid the pointer north. "They Grey Army is here. They have established a perimeter three miles from our walls. They are not advancing. They are building."

"Building what?" Cedrik asked, his voice scratching.

"Spires," Neelin said. "Black columns. We've counted twelve so far. They don't look like siege towers. I have never seen anything like them."

"We have, Marshal." Taillte did not look up from her mortar. "We saw columns, very similar in Tarsis. They were much smaller, but I can only imagine what they are meant to do." She continued to grind.

"Captain, please explain." Neelin turned his head to her.

"They are here to..." Her voice trailed off. "They are using magic... the Gift... to trade. Our lives for theirs."

"Magic…" Neelin's voice wavered. "I fought their General, in the Capital. He used magic. But the scale…"

"Yes, sir. Even with the Gift, I would not have believed it unless I saw it with my own eyes," the Captain confirmed. "Not since the First Cycle… the old stories… has anything happened like this. This is blood magic, Marshal. It's the kind of power that breaks the world to save it. There's a reason the Gift is so rare now; because this is the cost."

A moment passed. Every person deep in their own thoughts.

"And the South?" Brighid asked, though the knot in her stomach told her she already knew the answer.

Neelin moved the pointer to the southern edge of the map, where the narrow Iarann Highway wound down toward the border. He placed a heavy iron marker there.

"Blocked. The Xencid Kingdom has deployed three phalanxes across the highway. Roughly ten thousand spears. They have fortified the chokepoint."

"We have a treaty with Xencid," Brogan interjected from the door, unable to help himself. "King Alaric—"

"King Alaric is the one that set us up!" Neelin snapped, not looking up. "You saw their response. Their treaty is meant to hold us here. To keep us in place… for the Grey Army. Our lives… for theirs." The room went cold. Even the fire seemed to dim. "We are between the Hammer and the Anvil," Neelin continued, looking directly at Brighid. "This has been their plan from the beginning. They have been using us—"

"Harvesting, Neelin," Brighid said, softly. "They are harvesting us, to feed their magic. This blood magic."

Brighid studied the map. It was a perfect trap. Alaric had engineered this beautifully. He had sold his own army to the Grey Army's process, and he had used the conflict with Xencid to ensure no one escaped the slaughter. To make sure the 'harvest' was plentiful. It was surgical. Absolute.

"What are our numbers?" Brighid asked.

"Four thousand combat-effective," Neelin said. "All army, not militia. Mostly infantry. A few hundred cavalry, but the horses are in good shape. Rations for two months, if we ration, maybe three."

"We can't hold this," Brogan muttered, stepping further into the room. "Not against *them*. We saw what happened at the Capital. Stone walls mean nothing to them."

"We hold as long as we can," Cedrik growled, his hand drifting to the pommel of his sword. "We make them pay for every inch of stone."

Neelin shifted his attention to the granite table. He didn't look like a man planning a battle.

"There is no victory here," Neelin said, delicately. "I will not lie to you. We cannot defeat the Grey Army in the field. They outnumber us by more than two to one. And we cannot break the Xencid line with our current numbers either. Our only strategic goal is... delay."

"Delay for what?" Brighid asked.

Neelin hesitated. He looked at Kael, the young lieutenant standing by the wall, then back to the Queen.

"To give us time to find a way to get *you* out, Majesty. There are goat paths. Smugglers' routes through the high peaks to the east. Dangerous, but narrow. If the legion holds the main gate and draws their attention, a small group might be able to slip through the blockade."

"No." The word hung in the air. Brighid leaned forward. "I am done running, Neelin. I ran from the Capital. I ran from Tarsis. I ran through the woods and mountains while Vane hunted us like deer. I will not run from Dunvar while my soldiers, my people, die, just to buy me another day of breath."

"Majesty, you are the last of the line," Neelin pleaded, his composure cracking. "If you fall, Alcia falls with you."

"Alcia has already fallen!" Brighid slammed her hand on the table, making the wine cups rattle. "Look at this map. There is no kingdom left. There is only us. This room. These men." She set her eyes on Cedrik, then Taillte. "We fight here. If we die, we die standing."

"We might not have a choice," a small voice said.

Everyone turned.

Fromme was standing up. The boy had abandoned the warmth and comfort of the fire. He was walking toward the table, but his eyes weren't focused on the people. He was staring at the map, specifically at the black markers representing the Grey Army.

"Fromme?" Taillte stepped forward, reaching for his shoulder. "What is it?"

The boy flinched away from her touch. He reached out, his small, scarred fingers hovering over the northern valley on the map.

"High Marshal, Taillte, you are right. These aren't siege towers," Fromme whispered. His voice sounded wrong. It was too deep, overlaid with a metallic rasp that made the hair on Brighid's arms stand up.

"What are they, lad?" Cedrik asked lightly.

Fromme looked up. His pupils were dilated, swallowing the irises until his eyes were entirely black.

"They are harvesters," Fromme answered. The word seemed to vibrate in the air. "The General isn't waiting for the walls to break. He is waiting to use... the graft. Like in Tarsis."

Neelin frowned. "The graft? What are you talking about?"

Fromme grabbed the edge of the granite table, the color draining from his face. Blood dripped onto the parchment map. The boy wiped his nose.

"The Spires," Fromme choked out, fighting for control of his own tongue. "They don't just trade blood for blood... They are going to send the graft through the stone, shatter the walls."

A deep, resonant *thrum* vibrated through the floor of the keep. Brighid could feel it through her feet, a subsonic pulse that ascended through her bones and rattled the teeth in her skull.

"It's starting," Fromme screamed, clapping his hands over his ears.

Neelin ran to the narrow window overlooking the north. He threw the wooden shutters open.

"Gods save us."

Brighid rushed to his side, ignoring the aches and pain that fought her every step.

In the valley below, the twelve black spires had ignited. They weren't burning with fire. They were glowing with a sick, violet light; the same light Brighid had seen in the veins of the graft in Tarsis. Purple lightning sparked from the Spires, the smell of ozone emanating throughout the valley.

The Grey Army did not advance. They did not react.

"We need to prepare, we don't know how long this is going to take," Cedrik said, limping up behind them.

"Agreed. Captain. Commander. Lieutenant. Please go, see to the rest of the keep. I don't think there is much left to do now but wait," Neelin said. "I will be up shortly."

"Honor Guide You, brother." Cedrik saluted and turned to leave. Lieutenant Kael followed suit, the formal greeting of the Alcian military signaling closure.

"Honor Guide You, Marshal," Taillte responded, and followed Cedrik out of the war room with Fromme.

Brighid was left alone in the room with Neelin. They stared out of the window, watching the lightning, hearing thunder now, crashing in the sky. If she did not know what it represented, it would have been beautiful. Mesmerizing. Otherworldly.

"Highness," Neelin began. "Before we go, I must tell you something. I do not know the words—"

"Marshal, just tell me."

The man inhaled sharply, hesitating just a moment. "I saw... him."

"Who did you see?"

"The King." Neelin's shoulders sagged, the air leaving his chest in a rush. "But... it wasn't the King of today. It was the Alaric of twenty years ago. In his prime. He was wearing... strange armor, not ours. With their General."

The Barren Queen. Could it be... Had Xarion been telling the truth? But... here? Now?

How?

"Ruzzim."

"Who?" Neelin asked.

Xarion's words echoed in her mind. 'An heir. A son.'

"He was with Ruzzim, the General of the Grey Army," Brighid said, her voice quivering. "And that was not Alaric. That was his son..."

Neelin lurched forward, his grip on the windowsill slipping. He turned to her, his blue eyes bouncing, searching for a sign from the Queen that she had misspoken. She stood fast, feeling the heat of the questioning eyes upon her.

"Alaric is out there, Marshal. With his son. I am sure of it. This will be the last stand of the true Alcia, the end of the Songs. If Alcia dies here, Marshal... it will be murdered by its own blood."

CHAPTER 31

THE HEAVY OAK DOOR of the Field Marshal's quarters slammed shut, severing the connection to the war room, but the stillness inside was worse than the shouting.

Brighid leaned against the wood, her breath coming in shallow, ragged gasps. The news about the son was a physical weight that pressed down upon her entire body. A cold shroud of betrayal that made her want to vomit.

He does have a son. The future, it's real. And I am just the past.

"Your Majesty?"

The voice was small, trembling like a leaf in a gale.

Brighid pushed off the door and turned. Mara was standing by the hearth. The girl had tried to make herself useful; she had laid out a basin of water and a fresh towel. Her hands were shaking so violently that water had sloshed over the rim, soaking the rug.

"I... I heard them," Mara whispered. "The soldiers in the hall. They say the Spires are glowing. The army is growing."

Brighid stared at her. In Tarsis, Mara had been the only source of comfort; a soft presence who brushed hair and poured tea. Who listened to her. But here, in the shadow of the apocalypse, Mara's terror was a mirror Brighid didn't want to look into.

"The soldiers talk too much," the Queen said, sharply. She walked to the bed and grabbed the leather satchel containing Alaric's notes.

"Are we going... going to die, Brighid?" Mara asked. She didn't use a title. Fear had stripped away the protocol. "Please... I don't want... I don't know how to die."

Brighid froze. Her hand tightened on the leather strap. She felt a surge of pity, but it was quickly drowned by a flash of blinding anger. She couldn't afford pity. Pity was heavy. Pity would get them killed.

She crossed the room in two strides and grabbed Mara by the shoulders. She didn't hug the girl. She gripped her, hard, digging her fingers into the soft wool of the servant's tunic.

"Listen to me." Brighid scowled, leaning in until their foreheads almost touched. "Stop shaking. Stop asking. Do you think I am not afraid? Do you think I do not want to curl up on this floor and weep for better times? For the life I had before all of this?"

The life before my husband had a son. A future that did not have me in it.

Mara flinched, a fresh tear tracking through the dust on her cheek. "But you... you are the Queen. You are strong."

"I am not strong!" The Royal mask slipped from her face, for a fraction of a second. "I am just as terrified as you are. But I cannot carry you, Mara. I have to carry a kingdom. I have to walk out there and convince four thousand men that we can win a fight against the Gods know what, and I cannot do that if I am worrying about you fainting in the corner."

She released the girl with a shove, harder than intended. Mara stumbled back, looking stung, as if Brighid had struck her physically.

Good, Brighid thought, the guilt tasting like sulfur on her tongue. *Let her be hurt. Hurt is better than hysterical. Hurt is a motivator.*

"Stay in this room," Brighid commanded, turning back to hide her own trembling hands. "Bar the door. If you hear fighting... hide under the bed and cover your ears. Do not come out until I come for you."

"You sound like him," Mara whispered.

"Who?"

"Counselor Gaughan. You sound cold. Selfish. Like him."

The words hit Brighid harder than an axe. She looked at her reflection in the dark windowpane; gaunt, pale, hard.

"Counselor Gaughan made his choice," Brighid said, softly. "He chose to sell Tarsis to the enemy in order to survive. I need to make sure our Kingdom survives."

She opened the satchel and dug through the loose parchments and books until she found it. Carefully, she pulled the old page from the satchel and studied it for a moment.

Brighid left her quarters, leaving the weeping girl behind.

Her boots clicked softly on the cold stone of the spiraling corridor. She needed air. The heat of the fires and weight of her thoughts had become too much to bear. She needed to see the sky, even if it was burning.

She stepped out into the main courtyard. Packed with bodies, yet there was almost no movement. The four thousand soldiers of the Alcian Army—the last breath of Alcia—were waiting, as an unnatural storm raged over their heads.

A group of pikemen huddled around a small fire. They weren't talking. One man was sharpening his spearhead with a whetstone, the repetitive *shhk-shhk-shhk* the only sound in the night. Another was writing on a scrap of paper, using his knee as a desk.

A letter home? Or a last will for a family?

The cloak tightened around her throat. She wanted to say something to them. Anything.

Stand fast. For the King... Honor Guide You.

But the words died in her throat. They felt like slag. These men didn't need platitudes from a Queen who had spent the entire invasion running... or in a gilded cage. They needed a miracle, and she only had a knife.

"Make way," a sergeant called out as she passed, nudging a young boy who sat dazed on a supply crate. The boy scrambled up, bowing clumsily.

He looked no older than Fromme. His pauldrons stuck out past his shoulders, sagging where there was no support.

Brighid stopped. She studied the boy, then the massive stone walls towering above them.

Dead branches, she repeated in her mind. *Pruning the tree.*

She felt a surge of bile rising in her throat. This wasn't a pruning. It was going to be a massacre.

She forced herself to nod to the boy, a stiff, regal acknowledgement that felt entirely inadequate, and hurried toward the stairs leading to the northern ramparts. She climbed until her legs burned, until the air grew thin and cold, until she was alone with the wind.

She found a quiet place between two crenellations to watch the horizon.

Beautiful, she thought. *Just like the stories.*

The sun had dipped behind the western peaks hours ago, but the valley remained bathed in a sick, pulsating luminescence. The violet glow from the twelve spires washed over the stone ramparts, flashes of lightning and the rumble of thunder droned on in the distance.

There was no sound of battle. No war horns. No clash of steel. No marching. Only the *hum* of the graft.

It was a low, resonant vibration that didn't just ring in the ears; it rattled the marrow. It was the sound of a magical machination, not seen since the First Cycle.

Brighid stood on the northern battlements. She had found a quiet place to watch the horizon. Sizzling streaks of violet tore through the night sky, each larger than the last. Three miles out, a sea of soldiers blanketed the valley. A blob in the dark, only discernable when the lightning struck to illuminate the Grey Army.

"It's quite magnificent, in a twisted sense." Brighid didn't turn. She knew the heavy, limping gait approaching her. "If Pasin were here, I'm sure he would have some old fable to tell," Cedrik said, coming to stand beside her. He leaned his weight against the stone, taking the pressure off his bad leg and ribs. He wasn't wearing his helmet. His face had aged ten years in a week. "I never really believed in those old tales. But after what we've seen—"

"Stories...," Brighid whispered. "If only that is all they were..."

She reached into her leather tunic and pulled out a folded, crumbling piece of parchment. It was one of the pages she had stolen from Alaric's desk in the Capital. The day the Song stopped...

Not yet, not as long as we still have blood in our veins. The Song must continue.

She smoothed the paper out on the stone wall. The violet light made the ink look like dried blood. It was covered in Alaric's handwriting; feverish, sharp angles of geometry and equations she could barely comprehend.

"He knew the stories were real," Brighid said, barely a whisper. "The Foundation Stone... the Sovereign's Pulse... Valen's Cross. I can see it all here, they're connected. Valen's Cross must have been first blood to fuel this invasion."

Cedrik looked at the paper. "So, they didn't invade from the mountains in the North. He replaced the entire townsfolk with soldiers... and the targets grew from there?"

Brighid nodded. "We saw in Tarsis, they needed our lives, to make their soldiers appear. Those Spires, this trade... He was referencing the First Cycle texts in his notes."

"But why?" Cedrik asked, confused. "Why are they only attacking the army if that is their plan. Why not just use the civilians?"

"I don't know... He wrote here"—she pointed to the old paper—"*'To save the tree, one must prune the dead branches.'*" She looked up at Cedrik, tears stinging her eyes. "We are the dead branches, Cedrik. Me. You. The people in this keep. He sold us; to save a future he deemed more worthy." She crumbled the old paper in her fist, parts of it disintegrating into dust. "I should have seen it. I slept beside him for years. I saw him staring at the stars, muttering numbers and talking about possibilities. If I had been smarter... if I had been a better wife, or a better Queen... maybe I could have stopped his hand... changed his mind..."

"You couldn't have stopped him."

"You don't know that."

"I do." Cedrik turned to face her. The violet light caught the sharp angles of a scar on his brow. "Because men like Alaric don't see people, Brighid. They see numbers, words about history. You were just a variable to him."

"And what am I to you?" The question slipped out before she could stop it.

Cedrik went still. His gaze was penetrating. Cold sweat tingled at the small of her back, as heat flowed to her face.

"Do you know where Pasin found me?" Cedrik asked, quietly.

Brighid blinked, surprised by the shift. "No. I assumed... a military academy. A minor noble house."

Cedrik let out a dry, sharp laugh. "I was starving in the gutters of the Lower Ward, in Tarsis. I was six years old. My father was a drunk who died in a tavern brawl, and my mother..." He trailed off, looking out at the light. "I didn't even have a name. Just another mouth to feed...

"Every day, I remember the smell. Living with the animals, in their pens. I was so hungry." He drew a breath. Something in Brighid's chest cinched tight. "Pasin caught me trying to steal a loaf of bread from his saddlebag. He didn't beat me. He gave me half the bread and told me that if I wanted to eat again, I had to work." He looked back at her. "I spent my life learning to be Steel. To be the Guardian. To protect the 'Sanctity of the Crown.' I thought if I wore the armor, I could forget the gutter."

He reached out, his rough calloused hand covering hers on the bitter stone. It was a breach of protocol so severe it would have been treason a month ago. Now, it was the only source of support she had left in her world.

"I have served King Lorindan for my entire life," Cedrik said, his voice quaking. "He always seemed to do the right thing for the people. He kept our traditions strong, held the peace. But you... watching you ready to die in Tarsis? Watching you throw that knife to save my life? You are the first Royal I have ever seen who actually possesses the strength the rest of us pretend to have." His hand closed on hers, a strong but gentle squeeze. "You are not a dead branch, Brighid. You are the heartbeat of this Kingdom... the only thing here worth dying for."

Brighid let out a breath she didn't know she was holding. The distance between them—the gap between Throne and

Gutter—vanished. She turned her hand over, interlacing her fingers with his.

"We aren't going to die tomorrow, Cedrik."

"The math says otherwise," he murmured, nodding toward the darkness to the north.

"Then damn the math," she said, fiercely. "Alaric plays with numbers. We play with steel. If his son wants this fortress, he's going to have to choke on it."

Below them, the *hum* changed pitch from a low vibration to a deafening clap of thunder. Violet light surged forward, lightning leaping from the pillars and carving the valley below. The graft slithered across the ground, racing toward the outer walls of Dunvar.

"They're coming," Cedrik said, drawing his blade. The massive greatsword sang its own song as it cleared the scabbard.

Boom. Boom. Boom.

Brighid didn't flinch. She drew the dagger at her belt; the small, simple blade Taillte had taught her to hold.

"Let them come," she whispered.

CHAPTER 32

NEELIN ARRAN, HIGH MARSHAL of Alcia, stood on the balcony of the Inner Keep and watched the sun rise, its rays cutting small holes through the cloudy skies.

It was a pale, watery dawn. The light spilled over the eastern peaks, painting the sky in shades of gray mixed with orange, but it brought no warmth to the valley. It only served to bring into focus the scale of the impending disaster.

Below him, the outer wall of Dunvar—a fortification that had stood since the First Cycle, had repelled the aggressive nation of Xencid, and stood firm against countless mountain storms— was dying.

The graft had struck it hours ago, during the night. Now, in the cold light of the morning, the damage was undeniable. The violet energy from the Spires hadn't exploded against the stone; it had integrated itself, infecting it. Thick, pulsing veins of deviant purple power had spread across the granite structures like black ivy. Pumping, beating like a heart, louder with each passing minute.

"Marshal," a grizzled sergeant said, joining him at the rail. "The men are asking. Will the Queen address them?"

He scanned the courtyard. Near the east tower, he saw a flash of copper hair. The Queen, rushing with Commander Theramond and Captain Cleirigh to the stables. They were moving horses to the Inner Keep.

Safe. For now.

Neelin returned his focus to the wall. "The Queen has other duties. She is securing the—"

A hush swept across the lower courtyard. It started at the Inner Keep doors and rippled outward, silencing the noise of four thousand men.

Neelin looked down.

Brighid Lorindan walked out of the heavy oak doors of the Keep. She wasn't wearing her travel cloak. She wore a fitted breastplate of hardened leather over a padded tunic, gear clearly scavenged from the armory. Perhaps fitted for a squire, but she wore it as if it were royal plate. Cedrik Theramond walked a step behind her, his greatsword drawn, resting on his shoulder.

She didn't stay on the safe, elevated walkways. She walked straight into the mud of the muster ground.

"She shouldn't be down there," Neelin grumbled, gripping the rail. "It's too exposed."

I see it, Cedrik. I understand now who she is.

Brighid climbed onto a stack of supply crates near the center of the yard. She didn't look like a statue or a painting. She looked tired. Her honey hair was pulled back in a severe braid, her face illuminated in the violet of the Spires.

She looked out at the sea of frightened faces. "Soldiers of Alcia!" Her voice wasn't a booming baritone, but it carried. It was sharp, clear, and stripped of all courtly affectation. "I know what you see," she said, pointing a gloved hand toward the glowing Spires on the horizon. "I see it too. They bring a storm that defies nature. They bring a magic that seeks to rewrite the very stones we stand on." She paused, looking directly at a group of young pikemen who were trembling near the main gate.

"They want you to believe that you are obsolete," Brighid called out. "They want you to believe that steel cannot fight the storm. They want you to believe that you are nothing but fuel for their machine."

She drew the small dagger from her belt. It the vastness of the courtyard, it looked pitifully small. But she held it high, the blade catching the dawn light.

"But they have forgotten why we built these walls!" she shouted, her voice rising, cracking with raw emotion. "Alcia was not built by magic. It was built by blood, by Songs! It was built by the stubborn refusal to kneel!"

Cedrik stepped up beside the crates, slamming the flat of his greatsword against the wood. *Thud.* A punctuation mark of violence.

"My husband looked at the stars, at our people, and saw equations." Brighid cried, tears of fury shining in her eyes. "He saw a future where he could trade your lives to save a Kingdom. But I look at you and I do not see numbers. I see the Shield! I see the Shepherd!" Her gaze caught Neelin's. "I see the very heartbeat of this stone!"

A low rumble started in the throats of the men. Not a cheer, but a growl of affirmation.

"Let them come with their lightning!" she screamed, driving her dagger into the air. "Let them come with their Spires! They are here to harvest us like wheat? Then let them find that this field is made of steel! If they want our lives, let's make them choke on the price!"

"*Steel!*" Cedrik roared.

"*Steel!*" Four thousand voices roared back.

The Lioness, not just in name. She is here.

He shifted his gaze back to his men, and for a heartbeat he saw resolve. The violet light of the Spires seemed to dim against the sudden, ferocious flare of human defiance. Neelin felt the hair on his arms stand up. She had done it. She hadn't promised them safety; she had promised them purpose.

Cedrik and the Queen left the courtyard and entered the outer stables followed by Taillte and Mara. Neelin's orders had been to prepare the wounded for transport, which included the boy. And Cedrik was not going to leave her side.

Then, the ground lurched.

Boom... Boom... Boom...

The roar of the crowd was cut short by a sound like the earth splitting open.

"Report!" Neelin barked, his voice raw from a night spent shouting orders.

"The wall... Marshall!" Lieutenant Kael shouted, running up the steps, his face pallid in the weak morning light. "The stone... it is crumbling. The men on the ramparts say the floor is breaking under their boots! We've pulled the archers back to the courtyard but—"

A groan cut him off.

It was a deep, tectonic grind that vibrated through the soles of Neelin's boots. The violet veins had converged in the center of the massive gatehouse. A gigantic plume of dust blasted out from the wall, filling the air with suffocating particles, hindering vision.

This magic... they are going to tear our walls down without any attack!

"Get back!" Neelin roared at the men in the courtyard below, leaning over the railing. "Clear the gate!"

With a sound like a cracking rib that echoed across the valley, the entire northern section of the wall slumped.

Highness... I am sorry... The Song...

It didn't fall outward. It collapsed in on itself, turning into a landslide of gravel, limestone and violet-charged dust. The massive iron gates twisted like wet parchment, the sickening grind of steel bending against its will thundering through the fort. It smelled as if lightning had struck after an intense rainfall, yet there were no water droplets to be seen.

The dust cloud billowed up, choking the dawn light in its gray thickness, highlighted by unmistakable violet specks of magic.

A sudden quiet shrouded the fortress.

The soldiers in the main courtyard froze. The First Battalion stood rigid before a gaping hole, like statues in a great hall. The wall was gone. The pass was open.

"Impossible... By the First Cycle..."

Neelin stared at the void where the gatehouse had been. His insides churned, his vision blurred. Not from fear. From helplessness. He had spent thirty years studying siege warfare, leading men to victory. He knew how to counter trebuchets, how to undermine sappers, how to starve a blockade.

But this? This wasn't war. War was a contest of will. Training. Discipline. Heart. The better soldier wins. This was just erasure.

We are fighting a storm with paper shields, he thought, the bitter, cold stone digging into his fingers. *Centuries of granite, gone in a night. What can any of us do? What can I do against this?*

"Steady!" Neelin roared, his voice amplified by the acoustics of the Keep. "Form the shield wall! Spears up! Hold the line!"

The dust began to settle, revealing the Vale.

And then the sound began.

Boom.

It wasn't thunder, or the slow heartbeat. It was the synchronized impact of iron boots on stone.

Boom.

His stomach turned to ice. All he could see was the wave of dark gray steel cresting the ridge outside of the Capital. The sound... it echoed through the burning streets of the Capital. It was the advance of the Grey Army.

Boom.

Out of the dusty haze and morning mist, they appeared.

They did not run. No screaming or war cries. Marching. In complete unison, an inexorable advance. A phalanx of dark gray steel, twenty men abreast, moving with mechanical precision. Their armor was dull and unpolished, except for those strange red markings, absorbing the dawn light. Faces hid behind visors, caged like unseen predators.

At the front of the column, riding a massive black warhorse that seemed unbothered by the magical destruction, was General Ruzzim.

I have been waiting for this... General. There will be no mercy today, for either of us...

And beside him, on a smaller white mount, a figure in royal armor of gold and white, contrasting against the dark tide that enveloped him. The same rampant, roaring, Lion Crest, surrounded by a halo of lightning.

Brighid must be correct... Alaric's son...

A spitting image of Alaric in his prime years, save for the jet-black hair, reminiscent of Xencidians. He wasn't leading the charge; he was observing it.

Copper and ash filled his mouth, bitter and molten, heated by rage. He knew that face. He remembered Alaric at that age, standing in the training yards of the Capital. Eager to learn... Eager to be good for his subjects. They had trained together. The King had taught him, instilled in him, nothing overrides the duty of a King, and Marshal, to protect the realm.

Is this your legacy, Alaric? Neelin thought, staring at the implausible heir casually riding towards them. *You can't even show yourself to me. You spared me, to watch... No, to command, the slaughter of what we held most dear, the realm.*

The betrayal cut where no blade could reach. Honor... Duty... Respect...

Neelin drew his sword, unable to contain his anticipation. A weight pressed down upon his shoulders, heavier than any armor, as he surveyed the scene. Heat simmered within his veins as fresh drips of sweat covered his back.

"Archers!" Neelin screamed, pointing his blade at the breach. "Loose!"

A volley of arrows whistled from the Inner walls, blotting out the light and smashing into the invading column like a dark rain.

Arrows shattered, most of them bouncing off the pauldrons and helmets like twigs. The Grey Army didn't even raise their shields. They just kept marching.

Boom. Boom. Boom.

"They aren't stopping," Kael whispered. Standing beside Neelin, his eyes were wide with panic. "Marshal, they aren't stopping."

"Then we make them stop," Neelin growled. He turned to the Lieutenant. "Go to the lower courtyard. Take the First Battalion. Plug that breach. If they get into the Keep, it's over."

Kael hesitated, looking at the gray tide approaching the gap. The young man took a deep breath. "Honor Guide You, Marshal!"

Neelin looked at him, knowing he could very well be sending this fine young officer to his death. "Honor Guide You, Kael."

The smell of a lamb, freshly butchered, the metallic tang of blood, the guts, overwhelmed the Marshal's senses. What use was honor here? He was feeding the boy to a grinder. Kael had a mother in the lowlands. He wrote her letters every week. Neelin had seen them on the desk in the barracks.

I am spending him, Neelin realized, the guilt crushing his chest like a vice. *I am spending a human life like a copper coin, just to buy twenty minutes of air.*

He hated himself. He hated the uniform. He hated King Alaric Lorindan. But... he kept his face like iron, because that was what the lie required.

The Lieutenant slammed his fist to his chest and ran down the stairs.

Neelin turned back to the enemy. Within minutes, they were stepping over the rubble of the wall. Brushing aside the remains of the gatehouse unceremoniously as they continued forward.

Kael had made it to the courtyard, rallying the First Battalion. The young Lieutenant raised his sword, screaming a challenge that Neelin couldn't hear over the din of the march.

"Shields!" Kael cried, his mouth shaping the word.

The Alcian soldiers locked shields, creating a wall of steel and oak across the rubble of the breach. It was a good formation, executed well. Strong. Traditional.

It didn't matter.

General Ruzzim casually waved a hand, covered in the wraps that had been burned into Neelin's memory. The dark steel immediately reformed into a wedge, a giant man wielding a war hammer at the forefront.

Clank... Clank...

The mechanical clanking resonated in the square, as thousands of crescent blades were clicked into place, their odd, double blades coming to bear. The extra reach, combined with the sudden shift to the wedge formation was the perfect counter.

The collision was nauseating. The Grey Army didn't charge; they simply walked into the Alcian line, no hesitation.

Neelin watched as the giant Grey Soldier wielding the war hammer stepped into Kael's path. The Lieutenant lunged, his sword striking the giant's breastplate. Sparks flew, but the blade deflected off harmlessly.

The goliath didn't even slow down. He swung the hammer in a flat, brutal arc.

Neelin flinched.

Kael raised his shield just in time. The hammer struck the oak with the sound of a thunderclap. The shield exploded into splinters. Kael was thrown backward ten feet, crashing into the mud. He didn't get up.

"Get him!" Neelin screamed from the balcony, knowing no one could hear him.

Three Alcian pikemen abandoned the line, one stepping into the path of the gargantuan man. The others ran to grab their fallen officer.

The pikeman thrusted his weapon forward. The tip and shaft of the spear was crushed by a parry of the war hammer. Air crackled and whistled as the Grey Soldier took a long stride forward. One twirl after the parry to build momentum, he brought the massive hammerhead down onto the Alcian with implausible force.

A disgusting thud reverberated through Neelin's chest as the Alcian exploded in a blast of gore from the impact.

The other pikemen grabbed Kael by his harness, dragging the unconscious Lieutenant backward through the muck. Retreating from the line, surrounded by chaos.

The Alcian line disintegrated.

Shields buckled. Spears snapped. Men were tossed aside like ragdolls, cut down in droves by the crescent blades. Alcians fought valiantly, shifting formation to try and plug the cracks in the line, but their foes countered every time. As if they knew their tactics before the battle had even begun.

"Fall back!" Neelin screamed. "Second Battalion! Flank Them! Use the oil!"

On the eastern side of the courtyard, a squad of Alcian engineers tipped cauldrons of boiling pitch from the ramparts. The black sludge cascaded down onto the Grey Army's left flank.

Steam hissed. Men should have screamed.

A ball of fire shot out from the center of the formation. It struck the ground, exploding and knocking men of both sides in all directions. A huge hole was formed, the oil now drawn to the path of least resistance and away from the main force.

I need to take down their General...

The courtyard was a slaughterhouse. The gray tide was pushing the blue defense force back, step by bloody step, compressing them against the doors of the Inner Keep.

A flash of blue movement near the chaos caught his attention. Cedrik.

The Knight Commander was fighting a rearguard action near the stables, his greatsword flashing in the sun. Unlike the other soldiers, Cedrik was making an impact. He ducked under a Grey Soldier's clumsy swing and drove his blade horizontally at the knees. The soldier lost both legs, crying out a very human scream of agony, before the Commander finished him with a brutal strike to the helmet.

But, for every one Cedrik felled, three more took its place.

And behind the army, the Spires were approaching.

Neelin checked the horizon. The black columns were no longer stationary. They were floating, just barely off the ground, drifting towards the Keep like monolithic ghosts. As they moved closer, the violet veins in the ground pulsed brighter.

Lifeless Alcian bodies started to convulse. Bile rose into the Marshal's throat, but he choked it down. The blood, the coloring of the skin, he watched the lifeforce being drained from their lifeless bodies, pulled upward and into the pulsating veins, toward the black stone.

Harvesting...

Brighid was right. They weren't just conquering a Kingdom or killing an army. They were reaping it.

"Marshal!" A sergeant burst onto the balcony. "They've breached the secondary barricade! The courtyard is lost! We're pulling the wounded inside!"

Neelin surveyed the battle, if you could call it that, one last time. He saw the two pikemen dragging Kael's limp body through the heavy oak doors of the Inner Keep, followed by a stream of retreating bloodied soldiers. Arrows continued to rain down upon the dark gray forces, but the oppressive surge sustained.

"Seal the doors," Neelin said, his voice dead.

"But, sir... the First Battalion... there are still men out there!"

"We can't save them," Neelin snapped, turning away from the railing so he wouldn't have to watch them dissolve. "Seal the doors. Barricade the Great Hall. We make our stand inside, where the numbers count for nothing."

He looked up at the pale sky, the sun struggling to burn through the smoke and debris.

"Sir!" A young soldier, his face slender with no scars, no wrinkles, grabbed his arm. "My brother... He's still out there!"

"Everyone out there is someone's brother," Neelin said, not unkindly. "And we can't save them. Get inside."

The boy's face collapsed. "You're just going to leave them?"

"No," the Marshal responded, quietly. "I'm going to remember them."

CHAPTER 33

THE GROUND BENEATH THE stables bucked violently, throwing Brighid against the wooden stall door. Cedrik had just taken Bastion to the Inner stables, but work remained here.

Inside, the horses screamed, high, terrified whinnies that cut through the morning air. A massive black stallion reared, its hooves flashing inches from Brighid's face, snapping its tether.

"Hold them!" Taillte shouted, wrestling with a bridle. "Get them to the Inner Keep! We need the mounts!"

Brighid scrambled to her feet, covered in straw and dust. She grabbed the large stallion's halter, pushing the animal's head down through force and sheer will.

Then came the sound.

Crack.

It wasn't wood, or steel. It was the sound of the stone walls themselves shrieking in pain.

Brighid looked toward the main gate. Through the gaps in the stable roof, she saw the impossible. The Great Wall of Dunvar, the shield of the north, wasn't falling. It was slumping. The stones shook, dust and chunks leaking from the violet veins.

And then it happened.

The walls fell into themselves, imploding in an eruption of debris and purple sparks.

"May the Gods...," Mara whispered, freezing with a saddle in her arms.

The dust cloud rolled over the courtyard, blinding them. And then, the rhythm began.

Boom.

Boom.

The distinctive thunder of the Grey Army approaching.

Brighid didn't freeze. While the soldiers around her stared in horror at the breach, her mind raced. She looked at the Inner Keep. Neelin would retreat there. He would seal the doors. It would be a tomb.

We cannot win with steel, she realized. *Not against that.*

She looked south, toward the rear of the fortress. Toward the Xencid blockade.

The Hammer and Anvil. The hammer was crashing down. But the anvil... the anvil was silent.

"Taillte!" Brighid dropped the stallion's lead rope. The horse bolted into the smoke.

The healer was kneeling beside a fallen groom, checking for a pulse. She looked up, her face smeared with soot. "Highness? We must get to the Keep! You have to get to safety!"

"No," Brighid said, her voice hard. "Leave the horses."

"What?"

"Get Fromme. Now."

"The boy?" Taillte blinked, confused by the chaos. "He is in the wagon, but—"

"Get him... And Mara. We are leaving."

Brighid grabbed Mara by the arm, spinning the girl around. "Forget the saddle. We are heading to the Iarann Highway."

"The rear gate?" A sergeant in blue and gold livery stepped forward, his sword drawn, eyes wild. "Your Highness, that leads to the Xencid lines! You'll be captured!"

"That is the point, Sergeant."

"I cannot allow—"

"You have a wall to defend, Sergeant!" Brighid screamed, pointing at the breach where the first of the Grey Soldiers were emerging from the dust. "Go! Do your duty! I intend to save us!"

The sergeant hesitated. He looked at the oncoming slaughter, then at his Queen. He slammed a fist to his chest and ran into the chaos.

"Come," Brighid urged. "Before it's too late."

***

They moved through the shadows of the Inner Keep while the battle raged behind them. The stone walls vibrated with the collision of the two armies, dust trickling down from the ceiling.

When they emerged from the rear gate onto the Iarann Highway, the quiet was shocking.

The wind howled, biting and cold, blocking the screams of the dying soldiers in the courtyard. Here, on the south face, there was no dust. Only the stark, freezing clarity of the mountains.

"Stay close," Brighid said, her breath pluming in the air. "Mara, I need you."

Between them, Taillte and Mara supported Fromme, with arms around his waist. The boy was conscious, but delirious, his teeth chattering. The graft infection on his chest was reacting to the attack; it pulsed with an eerie, violet luminescence that shone through his tunic.

Mara carefully shifted Fromme's weight entirely to Taillte and scurried over to Brighid. "Yes, M'lady?"

"Take this," Brighid handed her a small leather pouch. It was the only thing that still mattered from the leather satchel laying in her quarters. "Guard it with your life."

The girl nodded, burying the pouch into her dress as if she were a squirrel preparing for winter. She did not ask why the package was given to her or what it was. Only eager obedience. Loyalty.

She deserved better than Tarsis, Brighid thought, watching the girl's shivering frame. *Better than this.*

Brighid nodded and gestured back to Taillte. The Captain was following slowly, supporting the fragile boy who was deteriorating before their very eyes.

"There...," Mara whispered, her voice trembling.

Below them, on the flat expanse of the pass, lay the Xencid lines.

Brighid had expected a siege line. She had expected fortifications, trenches, archers ready to fire. But the lines of pikemen had stood down.

Instead, she saw a festival.

Pavilions of dyed velvet—crimson, silver and deep azure—were arranged in neat boulevards. Banners snapped in the wind, displaying the complex sigils of the Merchant Families: The Silver Coin, The Silk Loom, The Iron Ship.

The Red Sun.

The Xencid. The Southern Realm. The bankers of the continent.

The soldiers patrolling the perimeter wore burnished black plate armor, engraved with intricate silver filigree, their cloaks trimmed in fine wool. They stood around braziers, warming their hands, watching the smoke rise from Dunvar with casual interest.

"Walk," Brighid ordered, brushing her blue leather tunic. "Heads high. We are not refugees."

They descended the highway, striding directly into the hands of what had been the biggest threat to Alcia just weeks ago.

"Brighid...," Taillte said, her tone wary. "Are you sure this is what you should be doing?"

"I have no choice..."

A sentry spotted them. He did not scream. He did not charge. He simply raised a gloved hand, and a squad of crossbowmen emerged from the shelter of a rock formation, their weapons leveled with professional calm.

"Haaalt," the man said. The word was drawn out, the vowels elongated and melodic. He removed his helmet, revealing olive skin and thick, dark hair oiled back from his forehead. "You are faaar from home, *Signora.*"

"I am Brighid Lorindan. Queen of Alcia," she stated, her voice steady despite the hammering of her heart against her ribs. "Take me to Consul Kassar."

His eyes flicked over her ill-fitting leather armor, the soot on her face, and the hay in her hair. Then he saw the boy.

He smiled, a flash of white teeth. "The Queen? We heard the Queen was... caged?"

"I am here to negotiate terms."

"Terms?" The soldier chuckled softly. "We do not make terms with the dead, *Bella Regina*. But... the Consul is a man of hospitality. Follow."

***

The Consul's pavilion was deep within the encampment, a world away from the freezing wind.

It was warm, scented with lavender, roasted garlic, and expensive tobacco. The floor was covered in thick, crimson woven rugs that muffled their footsteps.

Consul Riccardo Dominici. He sat behind a heavy desk of carved mahogany, studying a ledger.

We fight for our lives, for our existence, and he brings this desk... all the way to the border. Brighid fought to bury the rage welling up in her gut. The waste, the casual arrogance...

He was not a warrior; he was a shark in silk. He wore a doublet of crushed crimson velvet, and his fingers were heavy with rings of ruby and sapphire. He had the dark, heavy-lidded eyes of a man who bought and sold kingdoms for sport.

He did not look up immediately. He let the silence stretch, a power play Brighid knew well from her time in the Court.

Outside, a muffled *boom* echoed from the fortress. The walls were falling.

"So," Dominici said, finally. His voice was smooth like polished marble. "The Alcians have finally descended from their stone nest." He looked up. His gaze was sharp, intelligent, and utterly devoid of mercy. "You look... tired, *Signora.*"

"And you look comfortable, Consul," Brighid countered, refusing to bow. "For a man about to lose his investment."

Dominici smiled, a wolfish smile, and leaned back in his chair. He picked up a goblet of wine, swirling the dark red liquid. "Lose?

On the contrary. My actuaries assure me the returns on this venture will be... quite magnificent."

"Alaric lied to you," Brighid said. She beckoned Taillte forward. "Show him."

Fromme was carefully brought into the light. The boy groaned. The violet scar on his chest was throbbing, emitting small beats of light.

"It has been called the graft," Brighid said. "Not since the First Cycle... has anything like this been done. You don't know the cost. It eats... blood. Flesh. Riccardo, they won't stop with us."

Dominici glanced at the boy's chest. He didn't flinch. He looked... bored.

"Tragic," Dominici murmured, taking a sip of wine. "But... necessary overhead."

"Overhead?" Brighid stepped forward, her anger flaring. "It is the First Cycle returning! You know the stories. What it cost our people, all our peoples! If they take Alcia, there will be no taxes. No textiles to trade. And then, he will harvest your armies just as he harvested his own! You are next!"

Dominici laughed. It was a soft, musical sound. "You think we are here for *taxes*, little Queen? You think Xencid marched north for wool?" He stood up, walking slowly around the desk. "Alcia is a relic. A stagnant rock. But combined with Xencid? With our ships? Our banks and resources?" He spread his hands. "We are building an Empire that will span the continent. To save it."

"He is a butcher!"

"He is a partner," Dominici corrected. "And the contract is ironclad." He stopped in front of her, his cologne smelling of spices and wealth. "You speak of costs, *Regina*. But you do not know the price that was paid. The deal is not gold. It is blood."

Dominici gestured to the rear of the pavilion. A curtain parted.

A young woman stepped out. She was breathtaking. Olive skin, cascading dark hair, and eyes that held the same calculating intelligence as her father. She wore a gown of silver silk, outlining her frame that belonged on tapestries in the Castle.

"My daughter," Dominici said, pride swelling in his voice. "The Lady Isobel."

Isobel curtsied, her dark brown eyes never breaking contact with Brighid's. A mockery of respect. "Your Highness."

"She is betrothed," Dominici whispered, leaning close to Brighid's ear. "To King Alaric. The Union of the Highlands and the Iron Valley."

Brighid stumbled, her mind replaying the discussion with Ambassador Xarion. Pain poured out from her heart, the wound ripped open.

The blood drained from her face. "It's... it's true... how...?"

Dominici paused, his eyes examining her from head to toe. "*Bella Regina*... Lioness. Even in this squalor, you are more striking than I remembered. Your reputation never did you justice."

Brighid shook her head. She could barely hear the words. "Xar... Xarion..."

"Oh yes, that reminds me," Dominici said. "I will have to let the Ambassador know that I have found his missing... asset." Dominici clicked his tongue. "Yes, it is a shame. You did not give Alaric an heir. No future. But... we will build it correctly this time!" He placed a hand on his daughter's shoulder. "The wedding is in three days, in the Capital. And do you know what the seers have told us? The General... he whispers of the future. He has shown us the fruit of this union."

Brighid's chest tightened, she thought her heart would stop beating under the vice-like grip of grief.

"A son," Dominici said, his eyes gleaming. "A boy who is already written into the history of the world. Strong. Ruthless. Half Alcian, half Xencid. He is the Anchor Brighid. He is the reason that our peoples will survive long into the future."

Brighid stumbled back. It wasn't just a betrayal. It was a paradox. Alaric was using the magic to pull the future backward, to secure a legacy that hadn't happened yet.

"You are pulling a monster into this world," Brighid whispered. "The price is too—"

"We are pulling *tomorrow* into today," Dominici said, returning to his desk. "And I'm afraid, *Signora*... you are a part of yesterday." He waved a hand at the guards. "Take her. Put her in the carriage. Return her to Ambassador Xarion in Tarsis. Now that we have her again, the people will see our compassion."

CHAPTER 34

THE GREAT HALL OF the Inner Keep did not smell of a feast or ale on this day. It smelled of war. The copper tang of blood.

Neelin stood before the barricaded oak doors, his sword drawn, watching the wood splinter under the repeated strikes of their inescapable foes. The massive beams, reinforced with iron bands, were squealing and popping.

It wasn't just force. They were using magic, the cursed Gift.

Where the blows landed, the wood didn't just crack; it was graying, aging decades in seconds. Violet sap leaked from the fissures in the planks, dripping onto the stone floor with a hiss like acid.

It will not be long, Neelin thought, the sweat running cold on his neck. *Ruzzim...*

He looked around the Hall. He had sealed them in here together. A tomb in waiting. The wounded men of the First Battalion—those who had fought and been dragged in from the courtyard—lay propped against the pillars, walls and upon the long tables.

A young corporal, his leg bound in a bloody tourniquet, looked up at Neelin. He didn't ask to be saved. He gripped the hilt of his sword, his gauntlet creaking with strain, and nodded.

They know. They know that their Songs end here.

The guilt was a physical weight, heavier than his plate armor. He was the High Marshal. He was supposed to be the man who led from the front. But in this reality, he was just a failure. He had led his army into a hopeless fight. He had lost the Queen.

Betrayed by a king he once would have died for, a man he had once thought was his friend.

"Cedrik!" Neelin didn't look back. "Get the old man. Get to the eastern gate."

"I'm not leaving you," Cedrik growled from behind him. The Knight Commander was hoisting Pasin's unconscious body over his shoulder like a sack of grain. The old man muttered something unintelligible, his limbs limp.

"You are," Neelin snapped, his eyes fixed on the failing barriers. "Because if Pasin dies, we don't know what we are fighting. And if you die, there is no one strong enough to carry him. Find the Queen! GO!"

The wood groaned. A fist-sized chunk of oak flaked off and turned to dust before it hit the floor.

"Neelin—"

"That is an order, Commander!" Neelin roared.

He heard Cedrik curse, a low, guttural sound, followed by the heavy retreating footsteps toward the servant's passage.

Neelin was alone.

Alone as the only one left to fight. He stepped forward, placing himself between the rotting doors and his dying men.

Crack.

The central bar snapped, showering the room in splinters and shards of iron.

The doors swung inward.

They didn't rush in screaming. They flowed in. The Grey Army entered the Great Hall like rising water. A wall of dark gray steel.

And at their head, General Ruzzim.

He was huge, a hulking figure that dwarfed his own men. Neelin recognized the silver armor, the blood-red cloak, the wraps on the hands. And the eyes. The sand-colored eyes, burning with intensity and focus that belonged to a predator.

Those sandy eyes locked with Neelin's.

Ruzzim stopped. He raised a wrapped hand, no protective gauntlets. The gray tide halted instantly. The silence in the hall was deafening. He removed his helmet.

The deeply tanned face had lost some color, and the wrinkles were more numerous and cut deeper, as if he had aged years since their last meeting. Beneath the sweat on his brow, small streaks of violet energy flowed between his eyes.

"Marshal," Ruzzim said. His voice sounded like grinding stones. "The King sends his regards."

"The King," Neelin spat, stepping forward, "is a traitor who feeds his own people to the dogs." Rage emanated from deep within, surging through his body in anticipation.

"The King is a gardener," Ruzzim corrected, calmly. He drew his weapon; a massive crescent scimitar with a gruesome black tip, absorbing the torchlight. "And the weeds must be pulled so the harvest is plentiful."

Neelin didn't flinch. He smiled, a jagged, bloody expression that mirrored the one he had given Cedrik over their porridge.

"You've forgotten one thing about weeds, General. You can pull us. You can burn us. But we are the only thing that holds this mountain together. Try to pull me, and I'll bring the whole damn mountain down on your head."

"You are the past," Ruzzim said, stepping over the threshold. "You already had your chance, and you failed. This is our only chance."

Ruzzim charged.

He moved too fast for a man in plate. It was unnatural. Neelin didn't try to block; he knew the physics of it would shatter his arm. He threw himself to the left, rolling over a long banquet table.

The scimitar came down.

Shhhnk.

The stone floor where Neelin had been standing exploded. Fragments of granite shrapnel pinged off Neelin's plate.

Neelin scrambled up, using the table as a shield, as Ruzzim swung again. The scimitar cut through the heavy oak table like a knife through butter.

Neelin didn't retreat. He was the High Marshal of Alcia, had fought against countless men. He was a master of the blade. He used the momentum of Ruzzim's strike, stepping inside the General's guard.

Neelin thrust his ancient sword of the Alcian High Marshals through the debris. It was a perfect strike, aimed at the gap in Ruzzim's gorget. Precision against brute force.

His sword bit deep into the leather guard and his thick neck.

It felt like stabbing a tree trunk.

Neelin's eyes widened. There was no spray of arterial red. Instead, a deep red viscous liquid oozed from the wound.

The High Marshal didn't stop. He pivoted, using the hilt of his sword to hammer a strike into the General's unprotected temple. It was a blow that would have cracked a normal man's skull.

Ruzzim's head jerked, but he recovered quickly. It was like striking an anvil. The vibration traveled down Neelin's arm, numbing his fingers.

Violet streaked from his brow to his neck. Ruzzim didn't even flinch. He backhanded Neelin with his wrapped fist.

The impact lifted Neelin off his feet. A white-hot spike of pain shot through him as he crashed into a stone pillar. The air left his lungs. His vision swam in a haze of black and gold.

Neelin gasped, trying to force air into his crushed lungs. He used the pillar to haul himself up. His legs felt more like silk than iron.

Ruzzim turned. He touched the wound on his neck. The violet light pulsed, and the skin knitted itself back together in seconds.

"I always enjoyed reading about you, Marshal," Ruzzim said, walking slowly toward him. "But if you knew what was coming, you would come to the same conclusion that I did…"

Neelin ducked as the black-tipped scimitar cut through the stone pillar above his head. Dust rained down. Neelin snatched a dagger from his belt and drove it into the gap of Ruzzim's knee armor.

The blade snapped.

Ruzzim didn't bother to bring his blade back to ready. A forward kick caught Neelin square in the chest. The impact sent him across the room like a mule kick from a warhorse, his sword skittering away across the floor.

He tried to stand again, but this time his legs were water.

Ruzzim continued his course toward him. He didn't hurry. He sheathed his weapon, the violet sparks around his eyes glowing brighter.

"You fought well for your time, Neelin," Ruzzim said, looming over him. "But you cannot fight the future."

Neelin looked up. He saw a wrapped hand rising. The same wrapped hand from the Capital.

So, this is how it ends, he thought. *Cedrik... Brighid... I'm sorry...*

Then he caught movement in the shadows behind Ruzzim.

A body was dragging itself across the floor.

Kael.

The Lieutenant was a ruin of a man. His leg was twisted at a sickening angle, his face a mask of dried blood from the hammer blow in the courtyard. He was barely conscious. But he was moving.

He wasn't crawling toward Ruzzim. He was crawling toward the central support pillar; the massive wooden spine that held up the heavy stone ceiling of the Keep. Fractured from the siege.

An orange ball of fire began to form in Ruzzim's palm.

Neelin locked eyes with Kael.

The boy—no, the *man*—didn't cry or plead to Marshal. He looked at the base of the pillar. A keg of lamp oil, kicked over in the retreat, had pooled around the wood.

Kael's hand shook as he pulled a flint striker from his belt.

Honor Guide You, Neelin thought, forcing a grim smile through his pain.

Kael struck the flint.

The spark hit the oil. It didn't just burn; it exploded in a ferocious roar. The dry, exposed wood of the weakened pillar caught instantly.

Ruzzim paused. He sensed the heat. He turned.

It was too late.

The fire ate the unprotected wood. The pillar snapped with the sound of an ancient oak being felled by a storm.

"NO!" Ruzzim roared, turning back to Neelin.

The ceiling gave way.

Tons of limestone, slate, and heavy timber came crashing down. It fell directly between Neelin and the General.

Neelin threw his arms over his head as the world turned to dust and thunder. A shockwave of air and debris threw him backward, deeper into the alcove leading to the servant's passage.

When the dust settled, there was no Great Hall.

Silence.

It was a silence so heavy it felt like a physical weight pressing against his eardrums. There was no more pain. No fear. Only blackness.

Am I dead? Neelin wondered. The thought was strangely comforting. *It is over. The noise is gone.*

His mind hovered in the void for what felt like an eternity. He waited for the Gods to appear, for the judgement of his ancestors. He waited to see the faces of his brothers who had died under his command.

Then, the pain returned.

It started as a dull throb in his leg, then flared into a blinding, searing agony that tore a whimper from his lungs. The sound died instantly, swallowed by the dust choking his mouth.

He wasn't dead. He was buried.

Neelin opened his eyes. Darkness. Absolute, pitch-black darkness. The air was boiling, thick enough to drink, tasting of pulverized limestone and copper. He tried to move his arm but was pinned. Primal panic clenched his heart.

Trapped.

He thrashed, his armor scraping against stone. His gauntlet found purchase on loose rubble. He dug. He didn't dig like a Marshal; he dug like a badger. He scratched at the rocks, tearing his fingernails inside his gloves, shoving debris aside with desperate, wild breaths.

Not like this...

His hand broke through.

Cool air touched his fingertips. A faint, gray light filtered down through the shifting rock. He pushed harder, feeling the wreckage part above him, until his head broke the surface.

Neelin coughed, choking on the limestone dust... clawing his way out of the debris.

His ears rang with the sound of bells, fading in and out.

"Kael..." The name scratched his throat as he forced it out.

He crawled to the wall of fallen stone. There was no sound from the other side. No boom. No marching. Just the settling of rocks.

Alone. Only the bells reverberating in his skull had not abandoned him.

Kael was gone. The First Battalion was gone. Buried under the Keep they had sworn to defend.

Neelin fell back against the cold stone of the tunnel wall. He looked at his hands. They were shaking uncontrollably.

He was alive.

His insides twisted and turned, acid and bitterness building in his stomach. He should be under that rock. He should be dead with his lieutenant... his men... his kingdom.

"Marshal!"

A hand grabbed his pauldron.

Cedrik. The Knight Commander had come back. His face was white with dust, his dark eyes wide.

"The roof." Cedrik stammered, looking at the devastation. "Did you...?"

"No," Neelin whispered, his voice sounding broken and small in the dark tunnel. "I didn't."

Cedrik looked at the rubble, then at Neelin. He understood.

"We have to go," Cedrik said, his voice thick. He hauled Neelin to his feet. "The Xencid will be at the rear gate. We have to move. Now."

Neelin stumbled, leaning heavily on the Commander. He looked back one last time at the tomb of his army.

He had promised the boy he would remember them.

I will, Neelin vowed. *I will remember every second of this.*

"Move," Neelin said.

They turned and ran into the dark.

CHAPTER 35

THE HIDDEN SUPPLY TUNNELS beneath the Inner Keep were not built for troop moves, but they were wide enough for carts and horses. Barely.

No torches adorned the walls. The darkness was filled with the echoing clack of iron shoes on stone and the heavy, labored breathing of the animals.

"Easy, boy." Cedrik patted the muscular neck of his massive mahogany warhorse as he led with the bridle. The stallion tossed his head, eyes rolling white in the gloom, but he didn't bolt. He trusted Cedrik.

Behind them, a sturdy gray garrison mare snorted, pulling against her reins. Cedrik glanced back. Neelin sat slumped in the mare's saddle, barely conscious, as his armor scraped against the tunnel wall. Strapped behind him, lashed to the cantle with leather tethers, was Pasin. The old man was a dead weight, bouncing with each step.

Boom.

The sound vibrated through the tunnel, shaking dust from the rough ceilings. Cedrik's shoulders tightened. The tunnels dragged old memories from Tarsis to light, filling his mind. Running from the law. Running from the criminals. Running for himself.

Bastion reared, his hooves striking sparks against the stone path. Cedrik hauled the beast down, using his own weight to anchor the stallion.

"Move," Cedrik whispered, pulling hard on the reins. "We're almost out."

The Keep had been ruined. The First Battalion... Kael... they were gone. Buried.

The Second Battalion was cut off, fighting for their lives with nowhere to go.

The thoughts made Cedrik's stomach turn. He could feel the pressure, the bile reaching up into his throat. He wanted to stop and scream. But he looked at the High Marshal; slumped forward, gray-faced, holding onto the pommel like a lifeline. If Cedrik stopped, Neelin died.

And Brighid would be on her own.

Cedrik looked back at his leader, his eyes finding his hip. The scabbard was empty. The ancient Sword of the Alcian High Marshals—the blade Cedrik had seen lead countless charges—was gone. Lost in the chaos and devastation.

The tunnel sloped upward sharply. The air grew thinner, colder.

Finally, the blackness shifted, morphing into the dull gray of the mountain skies.

They burst out of a camouflaged fissure in the rock, spilling onto the high, snow-covered shelf of the Iarann Highway.

Cedrik shielded his eyes. Everything went white for what seemed like hours. The sun was fully up now, reflecting off the white peaks. The wind hit them like a hammer, freezing the sweat on Cedrik's face instantly.

His vision came back into focus and he looked down.

From this height, they were a thousand feet above the rear pass. The fortress of Dunvar was hidden behind the curve of the mountain, but the smoke... the smoke rose in a black pillar that stained the cloudy mountain sky.

And below them, on the winding road leading away from the Xencid camp, was movement.

"Marshal," Cedrik shouted over the wind.

Neelin lifted his head. The simple movement was sluggish, off balance. He squinted against the glare.

A carriage. Black lacquered wood, trimmed in gold with the Red Sun of Xencid painted on the side. It was moving fast, heading north. Away from the fortress. Away from the lines.

It was escorted by a dozen riders in black plate. They rode with relaxed posture, lances upright. Comfortable in their numbers.

"Xencid soldiers," Neelin muttered, his voice barely audible over the wind. "Leaving?"

"Transporting," Cedrik said. A flash of pale blue appeared through the small carriage window.

Brighid.

"It's the Queen!" Cedrik's thoughts immediately sharpened on the immediate task. "They have her."

Neelin straightened in the saddle. Cedrik watched the change come over him; the pain was shoved down, replaced by a cold, mechanical focus.

"We can't let them reach the valley floor," Neelin grumbled. "If they get to open ground, we lose her."

Cedrik studied the winding path below. "The road is two miles of switchbacks, we can't catch them."

"We don't chase." Neelin looked at the slope in front of them. "We cut them off."

"You can't be serious?" Cedrik surveyed the route to reach the hairpin turn where the carriage would pass in minutes. It was a suicide drop. A thousand-foot, sheer cliff face of loose shale, ice and scree.

Then he looked at Bastion. The warhorse's ears twitched, rotating toward the sound of the wind.

"He can't hold his footing on that," Cedrik continued. "It's loose rock."

Neelin reached down to the saddlebags of the gray mare. He pulled out a standard-issue cavalry saber. It looked wrong in his hands. Cedrik had never seen him without the ancient Marshal's Sword. Neelin tested the weight, his lips curling in frustration.

"He is a mountain horse, Cedrik." Neelin gripped the leather hilt of his saber, kicking the mare forward. "Trust him."

The horse screamed as her hooves slid on the ice, but she sat back on her haunches, sliding down the shale like a sled.

"Dammit," Cedrik cursed.

He vaulted into Bastion's saddle. The massive power of the animal surged beneath him.

Not just an animal. His best friend.

Trust him, Cedrik repeated in his mind. *Trust me, Bastion. We have to save her.*

"With me, boy. With me!"

He spurred Bastion over the edge.

They didn't run; they surfed.

The mountain seemed to dissolve under Cedrik. A landslide of rock and dust roared around them as the horse slid down the face of the cliff. Cedrik's stomach lurched into his throat from the speed of the descent. He leaned back, his thighs burning as he gripped the saddle, praying Bastion's legs wouldn't snap.

Below, the Xencid escort looked up as a storm of rock, dust, and snow rained down across the winding road.

"*Alto!*" a rider screamed, pointing up at the cloud of dust hurtling toward them. "*Valanga!*"

Neelin's mare hit the road first, stumbling but finding her footing on the mixture of dust, rock and snow. Neelin hauled her around, blocking the path, his sword held low.

But it was Cedrik who brought the thunder.

Bastion hit the road at a full gallop, momentum carrying him forward like a battering ram.

"FOR ALCIA!" Cedrik bellowed.

He didn't slow down. He drove Bastion straight into the lead pair of carriage horses.

CRASH.

The impact jarred Cedrik's teeth. Bastion, built of muscle and iron plate, plowed through the lighter draft horses. The carriage swerved violently, skidding on the ice mountain path, and slammed into the rock face of the cliff with the crunch of splintering wood.

Cedrik kept Bastion moving, wheeling the warhorse around, pulling his greatsword free from its leather bindings.

The lead rider didn't even have time to lower his lance. Cedrik's blade sheared through the man's shield and shoulder in one stroke.

"Ambush!"

Cedrik caught movement in his periphery. Neelin had slid off the mare, landing awkwardly on his bad leg, using the horse as cover. He slowed, vulnerable. A Xencid rider charged him. Cedrik tensed, but Neelin parried the lance expertly with his blade—the steel ringing flat and tinny—and thrust it up under the horse's ribs.

"Protect the asset!" the Xencid captain shouted, drawing his own sword.

Six riders turned toward Cedrik.

He did not back down. He was astride a monster. Bastion bit and kicked, a whirlwind of hooves and teeth, while Cedrik swung his greatsword like a scythe.

A lance struck Cedrik's pauldron, shattering on contact with the steel. The force spun him in the saddle, but he managed to keep his balance. He used the momentum, swinging backhanded, crashing the heavy pommel of his weapon against the attacker's helmet. The man fell from his horse and slammed into the road with a loud thud.

Cedrik parried a flurry of blows and thrusts from his remaining attackers as he glanced toward the carriage. Neelin was in trouble. He was on foot, fighting two men with an unfamiliar weapon. The Marshal parried a strike, the saber buckling under the impact, but he was too slow to dodge a shield bash. Neelin staggered back, blood bubbling on his lips.

One of the Xencid raised a mace over his head for the kill.

The carriage door burst open.

Taillte tumbled out into the snow, dragging Brighid with her. She saw the soldier raising the mace. She didn't scream. She acted. She grabbed a rock from the road and brought it down on the soldier's exposed wrist with a feral cry.

The man howled, dropping the mace.

Neelin didn't waste the opening. He drove the saber into the man's throat.

"Cedrik!" Brighid screamed.

"Get back!" Cedrik shouted, wheeling Bastion around to trample a soldier breaking off to grab the Queen.

The Xencid captain saw the battle turning. He checked his surroundings, stopping at the avalanche blocking the road behind them. His focus settled upon the man mounted on the giant mahogany horse dismantling his squad.

"Retreat!" the Captain ordered. "Regroup at the main camp!"

The six surviving riders didn't hesitate. They spurred their mounts, galloping back down the road toward the army.

Thank the Gods, she is safe...

Cedrik slid from the saddle. His legs gave out, and he hit the ground hard. Bastion stood over him, sides heaving, steam rising from his coat in the freezing mountain air.

Neelin leaned against the broken carriage wheel, dropping the bloody garrison saber into the dirt. He looked at his empty hand, then at the dead men. The color had left his skin. He looked gray.

Brighid ran to them. She didn't look like a Queen. She looked like a survivor. Her blue leather was scratched, her face wild.

"You're alive," she whispered, grabbing Cedrik's face, thumbs wiping away the blood and grit. "By the Gods, you're both alive..."

"Barely." Neelin wheezed.

Cedrik looked up at her. "Back to Tarsis?"

"Yes, to subdue the people," Brighid said, her eyes hard.

Taillte helped Mara and Fromme from the wreckage, breathing heavily after her outburst. "Marshal, it's worse than we could have thought."

Neelin closed his eyes. "What do you mean, Captain?"

"A wedding," Brighid said, softly.

"King Alaric," Taillte said, the name now a curse. "He is marrying the daughter of the Consul. He traded us..."

Cedrik placed a hand on Brighid's shoulder, but did not speak. He felt the trembling at the mention of her former husband. *Sadness or rage,* he wondered.

"Neelin." Brighid closed her eyes. "He will have a son.... He said something about bringing tomorrow into today..."

Neelin shook his head. "The man with the General, not a younger Alaric."

"During the First Cycle, there were stories. The Gift was not meant to do this," Taillte whispered, her voice hushed as if discussing a forbidden topic. "It's the graft... a twisted use of the Gift. An abomination."

"His son..." Neelin trailed off.

Cedrik looked at the dead Xencid soldiers. "He sacrificed a kingdom for what? A son that hasn't been born yet? I don't believe—"

"He didn't save him," Brighid said, her voice hollow. "They believe he is... The Consul called him an anchor."

The wind howled through the pass, carrying the smell of smoke from the ruins of Dunvar.

Anchor? Cedrik felt the cold bite deeper at the thought.

"We have to go," Brighid said, breaking the stillness. "They will be back with a hundred men within minutes."

"We can't go back to the Keep," Cedrik said. "It's gone."

"Up," Neelin said, pointing toward the high peaks of the Iarann. Toward the border of Regat. "We have horses now. We go up. Into the snow. Where their armor will freeze and numbers do not matter."

"Pasin," Cedrik remembered, rushing to the gray mare. The old man was still strapped to the saddle, unconscious but breathing.

"We're leaving everything," Taillte whispered, looking back at the smoke rising from Dunvar. "The Song truly is ending..."

"No," Neelin said, struggling to his feet with Brighid's help. He looked at the small, battered group. The Queen. The Knight. The Healer. The Boy. The Girl. The Scholar. And the Horses.

"We are Alcia now," Brighid said, raising her head.

Neelin grabbed the mare's reins. "Ride."

CHAPTER 36

THE CAVE WAS LESS of a sanctuary and more of a stone cage, shallow and open to the elements. It sat high in the jagged teeth of the Iarann peaks, a place where the air was thin enough to make lungs burn and the only sound was the wind howling through the scree.

Outside, the storm screamed. It was a relentless, mournful wail that scoured the mountain face, driving needles of frozen grit into the mouth of the cavern.

Brighid pulled her cloak tighter, tucking her chin into the collar, but the cold here didn't care about leather or wool. It was a mountain cold; a living thing that sought out the marrow. She couldn't stop shivering. The tremors started in her core and rattled her teeth, a constant reminder of how close they had come to the void.

She looked across the small, pitiful fire Cedrik had managed to kindle from dried moss and splintered crates. It offered more smoke than light, casting long, jerky shadows against the weeping stone walls of their cage.

Neelin sat like a statue carved from salt and ash.

He had removed his breastplate, revealing a tunic stiff with dried blood. His chest was bound in linen strips that were already spotting red. He hadn't spoken since they reached the ridge hours ago. He simply stared into the weak flames, his eyes unblinking, dark circles bruising the skin beneath them.

His hands rested on his knees. Every few minutes, his right hand would twitch, drifting toward his hip. Toward a sword that was not there.

The High Marshal of Alcia was gone. In his place sat a broken man, a man Brighid thought was staring at a ghost.

Near the back of the cave, where the shadows were deepest, the animals provided the only real warmth. Bastion, the massive mahogany warhorse, stood like a wall against the wind, his head low, shielding the smaller gray mare. They stood head to tail, their labored breathing creating a steady, rhythmic cloud of steam in the freezing air. The smaller Xencid steeds crowded deeper, seeking whatever shelter they could find.

Cedrik was with them. The Knight Commander leaned against Bastion's flank, his arms crossed, his eyes fixed on the cave entrance. He wasn't resting. He was watching.

"He's moving," Mara whispered.

The servant girl was crouched over Pasin, rubbing warmth into the old man's gnarled hands.

Brighid shifted, her muscles protesting at the movement, and crawled toward them. Pasin lay on a bed of dry moss and saddle blankets. His face was a map of gray, burst vessels, the skin translucent as parchment.

His eyes fluttered. The lids were crusty with salt and discharge. When they finally opened, Brighid recoiled.

They weren't the simple green eyes she had remembered. They were clouded, the whites stained a sickly yellow, the pupils vibrating with a faint, pulsing violet light. It looked as though something was swimming behind the iris, moving against the natural current of the world.

"Water." The old man coughed.

"Your eyes," she whispered, her heart hammering.

"Too much... the price," he struggled to say. "I had to, otherwise Vane would have..."

Brighid unhooked a skin from her belt and lifted his head. It felt frighteningly light, like a bundle of dry sticks. She pressed the skin to his lips. He drank greedily, coughing as the water hit his throat, some of it spilling into his matted beard.

"Vane is gone, not dead," Cedrik said, his voice low and gravelly.

"Dunvar?" Pasin wheezed. "Tell me... tell me the walls held."

Neelin didn't turn his head from the fire. "Nothing could hold against what we faced."

The High Marshal's voice was hollow. "The Battalions. The Keep. The Banner. Everything is under a mountain of rock, Pasin. We are all that's left."

"Then the bridge is open." Pasin closed his eyes. A long, shuddering breath racked his thin frame. "This isn't an invasion, Marshal. It's a colonization."

Neelin frowned, feeding a splintered branch to the flames working to keep the mountain chill at bay. "Colonizers want land, Pasin. This army... they want us."

"They don't want us, Marshal. They *are* us," Pasin corrected. "Ruzzim isn't a conqueror. He must have somehow shown Alaric a future... shown him he failed. A future where the Second Cycle ends in devastation. Where Alcia and Xencid bleed each other dry, bleed the whole continent dry. Leaving us all open to the Iron Fleets from across the Great Sea. They are refugees, running from their own extinction."

Cedrik shifted his grip on the reins, the leather cracking in the silence. "The equation. We paid the price so they could run from the ghosts of the future."

"This magic, it was thought to be destroyed during the First Cycle." The old man covered a wet cough. "Ruzzim must have given Alaric the key."

"The son," Brighid whispered. Her hand went to her stomach; a phantom sensation of the children she had failed to give Alaric. "The Consul told me... he said he was bringing tomorrow into today. Half Alcian... Half Xencid... An Anchor."

He is the Anchor, Brighid. He is the reason that our peoples will survive long into the future. Consul Dominici's smooth voice replayed in her head.

The words felt like a block of ice in her mouth. She remembered the state visits, the subtle glances Alaric had cast toward the Consul's youngest daughter, Isobel, during the peace summits three years ago. She had thought it was mere diplomacy; now she realized it was an audit. Alaric hadn't been mourning their lack of an heir. He had been preparing for his new lineage.

"Half Xencid," she repeated, hollow and low. "He didn't just choose a new army. He chose a new life. He sat in our bed, Neelin. He held my hand while we discussed the 'tragedy' of our barrenness. Consoled me when the Court was merciless. All while he was already looking across the border for the womb that would Anchor his godhead."

Small flecks of violet lightning crossed Pasin's eyes, the green starting to battle back into his pupils. The pity in his expression struck her harder than any steel. "Alaric is the Anchor in our time; his son is the Anchor to theirs. Bound by blood."

Brighid's throat tightened, as if his fingers were still tightening their grip; squeezing, crushing, owning.

"So, we send them back," Taillte said, stepping forward. "We find the Anchor—the son—and we break the bridge. We stop the wedding in Tarsis. He won't be born."

Pasin shook his head slowly. "You can't unburn a log, Taillte. The bridge has been crossed. Their blood is locked to our dirt now. Every Grey Soldier you see is now here, matter for matter. If you kill the son, if you stop the wedding... it changes nothing. They are real. They are here. And they have nowhere else to go."

"So, there is no undoing this?" Cedrik asked, his face pallid.

"Our Alcia is gone," Pasin whispered. "It wasn't conquered; it is being rewritten."

Cedrik's face darkened, blood rushing to his cheeks. He tightened his grip on Bastion's reins until the leather groaned. "So, we were just numbers? Our brothers and sisters... they died for a man who had already replaced them in his head?"

"More than that, Cedrik," Pasin said, his voice gaining a feverish edge. "To Alaric, you aren't just soldiers who lost. You are a daily reminder of the impending failure. Ruzzim showed him, proved that your tactics, your steel, your blood would fail against the Iron Fleets. He agreed to harvest his own people to make room for the 'survivors' he thinks are worthy of his rule."

Taillte stepped away from the cave mouth, her dagger quivering in her hand. "I've spent fifteen years guarding his door. I've taken scars meant for him. For our people. And I'm a weed?" Her voice broke, a rare crack in the Captain's iron exterior. "He didn't betray the Throne. He betrayed the *why*!"

Silence fell over the cave, heavier than the mountain above them.

Brighid stared into the fire. Every touch, every word Alaric had ever given her felt like a layer of skin being peeled away. She hadn't been his Queen; she had been a placeholder for a future he liked better.

She looked at her hands, reddened by the cold, calloused from the flight. They were the hands of a woman Alaric thought was a weed. But weeds were persistent. Weeds grew back through the cracks of even the heaviest stones.

"How do we stop it?" Neelin asked. His voice was quiet, but it had regained that iron resonance.

"I don't know," Pasin said. "The price has been paid; the consequences are left to play out."

"Think," Taillte cut in. "They didn't attack civilians. They were careful to preserve the farms, the hamlets and villages. They only wanted military targets."

One life emptied, one life returned, repeated in Brighid's head.

"They need our resources, food, water. They can't trade everyone. Maybe they don't have enough survivors to replace the common folk," Brighid said. "If the wedding happens, they unite with Xencid. Where would they go next?"

"Regat," Neelin said. "The single largest standing army left."

Bastion shook his great head and grunted, the sound echoing in the chamber.

Cedrik shifted, looking doubtful. "Regat is a citadel, Marshal. And their Imperator is a proud man. He won't open the gates to a handful of beggars and a story about time magic. He'll think we are deserters."

Brighid turned to the shadows where the servant girl was huddled. "Mara," she said, softly.

The girl scrambled forward, her hands trembling as she dug into the folds of her dress. She produced the small leather pouch Brighid had given her on the ridge.

Brighid took it. She undid the strings and tipped the contents into her palm. The heavy gold band caught the dying light of the fire, the Royal Signet of Alcia. The Lion on the Highlands. It was Alaric's ring, the one he used to stamp laws, official letters, and death warrants.

She didn't put it on her finger. It was too large. Instead, she slid it onto her thumb and made a fist, the gold pressing hard against her skin.

"They won't open the gates for beggars," Brighid said, her voice rising. "But they will open them for this."

She stood up. The cloak slipped from her shoulders. She stood in her tattered blue leathers, shivering, but her chin was high. The cold, the grief, none of that mattered anymore. It was her history.

Only the path ahead mattered. Her future.

"We go to Regat," Brighid said. All that remained was the burning fury coursing through her veins. "Alaric wanted a legacy that would last forever. He wanted to change the timeline. Fine. We're going to make sure the Lorindan line ends here. Not in the future. Not in a story. Here. In the mud."

Neelin looked at her. A grim smile touched his lips, but his eyes still held the cold distance of a man whose vision was still focused on the past. His hand twitched again, reaching to his hip.

"Rest," Neelin said, the familiar tone of command not quite reaching his voice.

He walked to their pile of supplies and picked up the sword he had taken from the dead Xencid rider. Neelin gripped the handle and began to run a whetstone over the edge.

Shhhk. Shhhk. Shhhk.

"The wind will die down by dawn," he said. "Then we move."

The world had been rewritten. So would she.

Epilogue: The Gardener's Harvest

The Great Hall of the Inner Keep was open to the sky, the vaulted stone having collapsed into a jagged graveyard of limestone and Alcian banners.

Alaric Lorindan stood upon the shattered dais, his Royal Cloak of Alcia, blue and gold, billowing in the wind. His hands, he noticed, had finally stopped trembling. The cost had been steep, in blood and in grief. But the garden was clean now.

Below him, the courtyard was packed. On one side stood the Grey Army; thousands of silent men and women who looked as if they had seen terrors found only in the worst nightmares. On the other side were the remains of the Alcian battalions: a few hundred infantry, disarmed and kneeling, their faces a mask of soot and terror.

Beside Alaric stood General Ruzzim and a man adorned in gold and white royal armor. He was a mirror of Alaric only twenty years younger, save for the hair, black and slicked back, and the olive skin that marked him unmistakably Xencid. He watched the prisoners with a clinical curiosity, his hand resting on the pommel of his brilliant sword: the Red Sun.

Alaric stepped to the edge of the dais. He didn't need to shout; the acoustics of the remaining walls carried his voice across the ruins like a cold wind.

"People of Alcia," Alaric began, his voice steady and resonant. "You look at these ruins, and you see an ending. You see the blood of your brothers on the stones, and you feel the weight of a defeat you do not understand." He paused, his gaze sweeping over the kneeling soldiers. "But I do not see defeat. I see a bountiful harvest.

"For years, you were led by a High Marshal who clung to the tactics of a dead age. Neelin was a man of stone in a world that moved on to iron. He led you into this slaughter because he lacked the vision to see the rot beneath his own feet. He was a shield that had grown brittle with pride."

A murmur of fear rippled through the prisoners, but the Grey Army remained motionless.

"And your Queen," Alaric continued, his voice softening into a feigned tragic regret. "Brighid was a woman of the old world; a queen of a barren lineage, symbol and symptom of a kingdom that had already begun to die. She could not even provide us with an heir to lead our great Kingdom into the future.

"They were the anchors of your failure, dragging you into the mud of a history that was already forgotten." He stepped down one tier of the dais, closer to the people. "I did not bring this war to destroy you. They did. But now, I am here to save you. To give you a future that cannot be broken. Today, the Lorindan line does not end; it evolves."

He gestured to a small group of riders entering the courtyard. At their center was a woman draped in Xencid silk, her face hidden behind a veil of gold thread. Isobel, the daughter of the Consul.

"My marriage to Isobel of Xencid is not a mere treaty," Alaric proclaimed. "It is the merging of the two strongest bloodlines in the world. It is the Anchor that secures our place in the cycles to come.

"With the Xencid at our back and the wisdom of the graft in our veins, Alcia will never again fear the dark. We will not just survive the future; we will own it." He looked at his son, who stepped forward to stand by his side. "The price has been paid. The weeds have been pulled," Alaric said, looking back at the survivors. "The soil is ready. You have a choice; cling to the ghosts of men who failed you or stand and join the harvest." He turned to Ruzzim. "See to the prisoners. Those who swear the oath are to be reintegrated into our forces. The rest... the rest will pay our price. Clear them."

Alaric didn't wait to hear the protests or screams. He turned his back on the ruins of the Alcian Battalions and began to walk toward the waiting carriages.

"The wedding will be in the Capital," Alaric whispered to his son as they walked. "We will marry in the ruins of the Temple of Songs. I want the people to see the new God sitting where the old ones died."

The man smiled; a cold, knowing expression that mirrored Alaric's own.

"The Anchors are set, Father," he said. "There is no changing course."

Alaric nodded, his heart at peace. He looked out over his new Kingdom, a gardener satisfied with a hard day's work.

The Blood of Tomorrow had flowed, and the world was finally, perfectly quiet.

ACKNOWLEDGEMENTS

Writing this story has been a dream decades in the making. I have been living in this world for years. Imaging, questioning, and challenging its people and its history until the characters and world felt as real to me as anything I have known.

This book would not be possible without the unwavering support of my amazing wife, Jessica. She has been my foundation throughout this process. Her belief in me gave me the confidence and space to finally bring this world to life. Without her encouragement and constant support, this story would have never reached the page.

To my wonderful daughter, Ali. Your enthusiasm of this world was contagious. Your curiosity, ideas, and excitement were a constant reminder why I wanted to tell this story in the first place. It is a gift to share this adventure with you.

To my collaborators, Steven and Julian—my editor and artist. You elevated the prose, structure and visual identity of this book well beyond anything I could have achieved alone. Your clarity, professionalism, and care for craft strengthened every part of this work.

And finally, to every reader who took a chance on this story—especially those that are still reading here. Thank you. Your time and imagination are extraordinary gifts, and I truly hope these characters stayed with you as deeply as they stayed with me.

ALSO BY ROBERT W. RILEY

THE SECOND CYCLE

The Iron Tithe: Prelude to Blood of Tomorrow
Blood of Tomorrow—Book 1
Blood of Yesterday—Book 2 (Coming 2026)
Blood of Today—Book 3 (Coming 2027)

Extract from The Second Cycle: Book 2

Blood of Yesterday

The bridge has been crossed. The price has been paid. But for those fleeing the end of the world, the sanctuary of Alcia is not a gift—it is a harvest.

A cheer exploded from the ranks of the Grey Army. It wasn't a cheer of victory. It was the desperate, weeping howl of the damned seeing an open door to a freedom promised by their Supreme Commander.

"General Ruzzim," the name passed through the ranks like a prayer. "The Architect has done it. The bridge is open."

Rufus rose to his feet. He looked at the Iron Fleets, looming closer, their shadows swallowing the ash fields. They wanted slaves. They wanted the last dregs of humanity to fuel their engines.

They would only find dust.

"Form up!" the officers screamed.

Rufus fell into line. He was part of the Tithe now. A weapon forged from the heart of his civilization. They had burned their women, their children, their history, fed them all into the graft to fight the Iron Fleets.

General Ruzzim had found a new way to feed the graft.

Survival requires surrender, the Supreme Commander had said. *But surrender has a cost.*

He looked at the portal. Beyond the swirling violet vortex, he caught a glimpse of something that made his breath hitch.

Green. Wet, living green. And stone that hadn't been disformed.

"Forward," the command pulsed in his mind. "To the sanctuary."

ABOUT THE AUTHOR

Robert W. Riley writes character-driven epic fantasy shaped of myth, memory, and consequence. He is the author of The Second Cycle, a series that explores the failures of those who ignore history and the struggle of those forced to bear the consequences of repeating the same mistakes.

When he isn't plotting the downfall of kingdoms or the corruption of "The Graft," Robert navigates the real-world complexities of the automotive industry as an executive of a Tier 2 with operations in Puebla Mexico.

When the work is done, he returns to his house in Indiana ruled by 4 dogs, 5 cats, and the incredible wife who is his world. It was his daughter, however, who inspired him to finally put pen to paper and launch this saga.

www.robertwriley.com
@robertwriley_author